Dolphin, she tho...
would become a fai...
carried to the surfac... ...y from the
evil that had tossed her in to drown.

But the creature drew close and it was no dolphin.

It was a man.

Jenny forgot she was dying. Everything faded, her life shrinking to nothing but a flash of strong white arms, silver drifting hair, and a face that was high-cheeked, masculine, and edged with faint white scars. She glimpsed a set mouth and pale blue eyes staring hard into her own. Fear thrilled through her, and awe.

You know those eyes, she told herself . . .

Resounding Praise for
MARJORIE M. LIU

"Liu is an amazing voice: ingenious, fresh, and utterly spellbinding."
Romantic Times BOOK*reviews*

"Readers of early Laurell K. Hamilton, Charlaine Harris, and the best thrillers out there should try Liu now."
Publishers Weekly (*Starred Review*)

"Anyone who loves my work should love hers."
New York Times bestselling author
Christine Feehan

By Marjorie M. Liu

Marjorie M. Liu

In The
Dark of
Dreams

A DIRK & STEELE NOVEL

AVON
An Imprint of HarperCollinsPublishers

AVON BOOKS
An Imprint of HarperCollins*Publishers*
10 East 53rd Street
New York, New York 10022–5299

Copyright © 2010 by Marjorie M. Liu
ISBN 978-0-06-202016-1
www.avonromance.com

First Avon Books paperback printing: December 2010

Avon Trademark Reg. U.S. Pat. Off. and in Other Countries, Marca Registrada, Hecho en U.S.A.
HarperCollins® is a registered trademark of HarperCollins Publishers.

Printed in the U.S.A.

10 9 8 7 6 5 4 3 2 1

To my Daddy

我爱你, 爸爸!

In The
Dark of
Dreams

My own songs awakened from that hour,
And with them the key, the word up from the waves,
The word of the sweetest song and all songs,
That strong and delicious word which,
    creeping to my feet,
(Or like some old crone rocking the cradle,
swathed in sweet garments, bending aside)
The sea whispered me.

"Sea Drift," *Leaves of Grass*,
WALT WHITMAN

There are sleeping dreams and waking dreams;
What seems is not always as it seems . . .

"A Ballad of Boding,"
CHRISTINA GEORGINA ROSSETTI

PROLOGUE

SHE found the boy at dawn, during her morning escape from the big house on the hill. Not running, not walking either—occasionally skipping down the narrow path to the rocky shore, dragging a beach towel behind her and a tote bag for her drawing pad and pencils. Dawnlight was the best; but it was always cool and windy, and she was bundled in so many layers of wool and cotton, she felt fat.

It was a relief to leave the house. Her grandparents were kind, but their business occupied them all the time, and the girl did not always care for their guests, or the fights those strangers brought with them. She also disliked the way some of them looked at her—with puzzlement—and sometimes, disdain.

Twelve, she had overheard one of the visitors say, the night before. *Twelve years old and ordinary.*

Better ordinary than rude and mean, thought the girl, listening to the gentle throbbing roar of the waves rushing the shore. She had better things to do with her time than listen to stupid men who wore stupid suits and smelled like ladies' perfume. That, and her grandfather had told her more than once that she was perfect the way she was. The girl knew that was a lie, but it was enough that he loved her.

The path curved. Gulls cried. The sun was just beginning to peer over the ocean horizon, a glint of gold carved in an endless wash of peach light. The girl inhaled deeply, throwing out her arms. Pretending she could fly toward the dawn and burn in that light.

A fantasy interrupted by a low moan.

She flinched, heart thudding, and spun around to search the beach for another person. Ready to run if she had to. But she saw nothing. Just rock and driftwood, and the water rushing in, dark with glints of silver that lengthened, and were lost in shadow, again and again, shimmering as the sea sometimes did, as though the foam were made of diamonds.

Nothing. The girl saw nothing, until she heard that moan again, soft and anguished. She took a step, staring. Sensing movement behind one of the pale, twisted logs that had drifted onto shore.

She almost fled. Her grandparents were always telling her to be careful, that bad people might try to take her, that she should trust no one but them, ever, because their business made enemies, and even though they had taken precautions, even though no one but a handful, mostly family, knew their faces. . .

The girl took another step, then another. Slow, halting, her lungs aching from holding her breath. She was going to run, she told herself. Fly in the opposite direction and go get help.

But that voice sounded so pained. What if someone was really hurt? What if there was no time to get help?

She had to see. Had to be certain.

It seemed to take forever to cross the distance. Just thirty feet, but it felt like a mile. The girl finally got close, though. She was short, and the driftwood was large. All she could see on the other side was a shimmer of light covered in tangled seaweed. And then that light shifted, and became . . . scales.

Her breath caught, again. But scales were less frightening than human legs. Emboldened, she walked quickly around the end of the log.

And saw the boy.

She did not expect him. Something else, maybe, but not him. Not a boy her age, with a gaunt white face covered in dried salt, or large eyes the pale blue of a sea glacier. His lips were cracked, and his hair was long, tangled, a white-blond halo glinting silver around his face. The sun was rising behind him. She felt blind for a moment, her knees weak.

He had no legs. Just a tail. A fish tail.

The girl staggered backward, and fell into the sand. She sat there, frozen, so terrified she could not breathe. She tried to cry out for help, for anyone who might be near, but her voice caught in her throat, and all she could do was wheeze. Tears pricked her eyes—and for a moment, just one, she imagined the same terror in the boy's face. He tried to push away from her, and she saw a bright splash of blood on his pale, skinny chest.

The blood woke her up. Snapped something free inside her chest. She could suddenly breathe, opening her mouth to scream—

—and stopped. Just stopped, staring into those pale blue eyes, which *were* glinting with tears, and fear. And the girl thought of her grandparents, whom she trusted, and those visitors whom she did not, and the choice flowed through her before she was hardly conscious of it.

She bunched her fingers into the cool damp sand and closed her mouth. Forced herself to breathe, then slowly, carefully, angled forward. She had seen strange things before, she reminded herself. Not as odd as this, but she could cope. She *would* cope.

The boy tried to slide away toward the water. His tail hampered him. It was like watching a seal flop, only more disturbing. He was human above the waist, though his white flesh merged at his hips with silver scales—the rest of him, long and muscular, glimmering in the early sun. The girl felt like she was losing her mind, but the cool air nipped her hot cheeks, and her heart beat so hard she knew that she was alive, conscious.

This was real.

The boy had a cut on his chest, still bleeding. He seemed weak, and kept wincing as he tried to get away. His low, muffled cry was dull, keening. The girl flung out her hand but did not chase him.

"Don't be afraid," she whispered.

Her voice made him stop, and he peered at her over his shoulder. He was breathing hard, his eyes narrowed with pain. The girl slowly, carefully, crawled toward him. She was afraid to stand, that it would scare him. He tensed when she got close. She froze, then moved again. Humming a song her grandmother liked to sing to her at bedtime. The boy's gaze flicked down to her mouth, then returned to her eyes.

A moment later, he began to hum the same melody.

His voice was unearthly. Chills swept over the girl, but she found herself smiling, and the corner of his mouth ticked upward, ever so faintly. She settled down in the sand, watching him—not too shy to let her gaze travel down the length of his body. He did the same to her, staring at her toes. She pushed her feet toward him, just a little, and wiggled each one into the sand. The boy stopped humming.

"You're hurt," she said softly, and pointed to his chest.

The boy touched the cut, very gingerly. It was a clean wound, as though a knife had been used. Blood still seeped from the wound. Red blood, like hers.

He gave her a mournful look, and the girl remembered the beach towel. She had dropped it only a few feet away. She found a corner still untouched by the sand. Watching him carefully, she mimed rubbing her chest with it. The boy hesitated, then nodded.

The girl crept close. So close she could feel the warmth of his skin, and the heat of his breath against her face. She dabbed at the wound, then flinched as the boy suddenly covered her hand with his and pressed the towel hard against the cut. For a moment her mind went blank—all she could think about was that he was touching her—and then she remembered the basic first aid she had learned in school and realized that he was trying to stop the bleeding—not clean the wound, as had been her first instinct. She felt like a fool.

And it was hard to breathe again. She tried to tug her hand free, but his grip tightened. He looked down, and so did she. His skin was white—not like snow, but white as the perfect marble statues that sat on wooden pedestals in her grandfather's library. A white stone that seemed to glow in sunlight. Much like the boy seemed to glow, perfect and unblemished.

The girl had always been fair and freckled compared to her tanned, rambunctious cousins, but against the boy she was a dark peach pink, rich with color. He reached out with his other hand and touched a loose strand of her red hair, which had come loose from her braids and was blowing in the wind toward his face. He held it—and suddenly brave, she reached out to touch his hair. He tensed, then relaxed— flashing her another tentative smile.

She loved that smile. She loved it with a fierceness that startled her. Never mind the impossibility of the moment— and him. His smile, shy and warm, was perfectly human— and better than human. The towel slipped down between them. The girl hardly noticed. She could not look away from his face. Memorizing every line. This was magic, she thought. This was what it meant to like a boy. To *really* like a boy and have her heart in her throat, and her head faint, and her skin rebelling with goose pimples. She understood now.

The boy made several clicking sounds, wincing as he reached down to pick up the towel and press it against his wound. The bleeding had slowed, but it still looked painful. The girl thought about the first-aid kit that was in the kitchen, but she was afraid to leave the boy. He might not be here when she got back. Or someone else could find him. She couldn't let that happen.

"You need help," she said despondently. "I don't know what to do."

He frowned, staring into her eyes, and uttered those clicking sounds again. Words, she realized. But nothing she could possibly understand.

"Help," she said, and pointed to his chest. "Ouch."

"Ouch," mouthed the boy, grazing his fingers across her brow, then trailing down, her thick red braid sliding against his palm. Her scalp tingled. Everything tingled. The tip of his tail twitched against the sand. She touched his hip, lightly. His scales were surprisingly soft. The boy shied away and made a strange gasping sound. She felt instantly terrible for touching him, until she saw his smile and warm eyes—a darker blue now, like the sky.

Laughter. That was laughter she had heard.

"Ticklish," she said, awed and delighted. "You're . . . *ticklish*."

He gave her a puzzled look, still smiling.

Until, quite suddenly, he froze. His smile lost its warmth. Color drained out of his eyes. He turned stiffly, staring at the sea. The girl tried to follow his gaze, but the sun had risen, and it was bright. She shaded her eyes.

A man emerged from the water. Rose from the waves like some story of Poseidon that she had read in school. His hair was long and silver, braided partially into thin, tangled rows. At first, she could only see him from the waist up, but as he came closer, she saw that he had legs. He was also very naked.

The boy drew in a sharp breath and shoved the girl back, away from the sea and himself. She stared at him, and the fear in his eyes hit her like a fist. Sharp clicking sounds tumbled from his throat. When she did not run, he grabbed a fistful of sand and flung it at her. Tears filled his eyes. Desperation.

The girl stared helplessly and looked at the man, who was striding free of the water. His gaze was thunderous when he stared at her, but she could not tell if it was anger or actual hate that made his jaw so tight and his eyes so black.

The boy screamed at her, and the piercing wail of his

voice shook her to the core. She stumbled back a step, and her heel hit a driftwood branch, long and crooked, small enough for her hands. She picked it up without thinking and ran at the man. She swung the branch like a baseball bat and smashed him on the arm.

It was like hitting a brick wall. The impact jarred her to the bone and hurt her hands. The branch broke against him.

For a moment, both the boy and the man stared at her in astonishment. And then, much to her horror, the man laughed. Not like the boy—not in broken gasps—but full-bodied human, male laughter. A cold sound. Nothing gentle or warm about it.

He picked up a piece of the branch and hefted it carefully, staring into her eyes. The girl knew he would hit her with it, but her feet refused to move. Rooted in one spot, frozen. The boy howled again and lunged across the sand. He sank his teeth into the man's calf.

The man jerked wildly, breaking eye contact. The girl staggered, able to move again—and this time she did not hesitate or fight. She turned and ran.

She flew across the sand, certain at any moment a rock would slam into her head—or that strong arms would crush her to death. She ran mindlessly, terrified, and did not stop until she reached the top of the dirt path, well off the beach. She turned, breathless, and saw the man hauling the boy into the sea. He held him by the tail, and the boy was dragging his fingers in the sand, struggling wildly, trying to catch himself and hold on to something, anything.

All the while, he stared up the hill at the girl.

She stared back, horrified and grieving. Too far away to help. Not strong enough to fight the man hauling him into the water. She wanted to call out to the boy, but her throat choked on the words, and all she could do was dig her clenched fists into her stomach and hold his gaze until he and the man disappeared into the sea.

The girl stood for a long time, watching. Not once did they reappear.

Finally, feeling faint, she made her way back down the trail to the sand and the driftwood log. She was scared to be there. The beach suddenly felt very big, and she was hot, sweating. Her knees were weak all over again, but she couldn't bring herself to sit. She saw large footprints in the sand. Human. As human as the imprint of the boy's tail was not.

Something small glinted where he had lain beside her. She bent, and found a single scale. Larger than her thumbnail, and the color of white pearl, with iridescent hints of silver. The girl held the scale very carefully, then, with reverence, slipped it into her pocket.

She gathered her things and walked slowly to the house on the hill. She hid the bloodstained towel, and threw it out the first chance she got. Not once did she breathe a word of what she had seen though her grandfather gave her a piercing look over dinner when he asked how her day had been.

THE GIRL RETURNED TO THAT SPOT EVERY MORNING, all that summer. She did the same, the following year—and every year after that. Until, one day, she told herself that the boy was never coming back. Not there.

But she kept looking.

CHAPTER ONE

I T is a truth universally acknowledged, thought Jenny, that a single girl in search of mysteries must occasionally be in want of a big damn knife.

Or a gun. But Maurice was in charge of those.

"You should have stayed on the boat," muttered the old man, wiping sweat from his brow. "Jesus, sweet pea."

Jenny flashed him a tense smile. Maurice was a grizzled sailor, probably in his eighties, though it was hard to remember that sometimes. Sun brown, covered in fading tattoos, and a bear in a fight. He was her grandfather's best friend and had taught her everything she knew about surviving on the sea—which had very little to do with handling a boat.

Boats are easy, Maurice liked to say. *And the sea doesn't care. It's the people you meet out there who're the monsters.*

All kinds of monsters. Jenny jammed a stick of chewing gum in her mouth, needing something to take the edge off the nauseating flutters in her stomach. She never got seasick, except for times like this. Too much pressure. She chewed hard, fixing her gaze onshore, where ten men waited for them—armed with machetes, fishing spears, and one AK–47. Simple fishermen, she had been told, but they looked ready for war.

And given the remote section of Malaysian beach they

were standing on, no one would be around to stop them if it was blood they were really after.

"You sure about this?" Maurice asked the third person with them—Ismail Osman, a slender brown-skinned man with narrow features and huge black-framed glasses that kept sliding down the greasy bridge of his nose. He was an employee of *A Priori,* a white-collar scout for the Singaporean arm of the company's bioresearch department. Jenny had been corresponding with him for only a week—which made her miss his predecessor even more; a goofy man obsessed with *Star Trek, Star Wars,* and the possibility of dinosaurs still living in the deep rain forests of the Congo.

He, though, had retired—and Ismail had gotten a promotion. Go-getter. No sense of humor. She wished he hadn't insisted on being here for the recovery operation. Not that she blamed him. Nor was it his fault that she trusted no one but Maurice to do this right.

Right being a relative term. In more ways than one.

"These people are not prone to exaggeration," Ismail insisted, pushing his glasses up his nose, then wiping his hands, rather fussily, on his pants. "And despite appearances, I assure you that . . . that they're all quite civilized. Poverty, you know—"

"No one's saying they're bad people," Maurice interrupted. "But they're fuckin' armed to the teeth."

Ismail gave the old man a disdainful look—not the first of the morning, either. The *A Priori* scout might not judge Malay fishermen by appearances, but he had not been so gracious with Jenny or her two-man crew.

"What you see on that beach is mere precaution," he said, very slowly, enunciating each word as though Maurice might not understand him otherwise. "If the . . . the thing . . . is stolen before they can receive payment—"

"Of course," Jenny interrupted smoothly, ignoring the grunt that came from the man seated behind Ismail. Les, the second member of her crew—a bronze god, the girls back home liked to call him. Buttery brown hair, golden-tanned skin, perfect body. A smile to die for. He glanced past the scout at Maurice and Jenny, shaking his head and mouthing, *"This is crazy."*

They were all crazy, Jenny thought, as Les cut the engine of the battered flat-bottom skiff that Ismail had met them in. He had bought the boat from a nearby village using company funds, and was going to donate it to the fishermen, along with a large cash payment from *A Priori. If* their claims proved true.

Several men waded into the ocean to help pull in the skiff. Up close, they were small, compact, and young. Early twenties, perhaps, dressed in shorts and faded T-shirts dotted with holes. No one spoke or smiled, but Jenny watched their faces carefully and found no malice. Just tension. And, perhaps, fear.

"Something's wrong," Maurice muttered, also watching their faces. He reached down, ostensibly to scratch his upper thigh, but Jenny knew he kept a small pistol holstered beneath his oversized cargo pants. His right pocket had a hole large enough for his hand to fit through, and he always carried a little something strapped to the small of his back and between his shoulder blades. Never would have dreamed it, just by looking at him.

Ismail spoke to the fishermen. Jenny didn't wait for him to finish before she jumped out of the skiff. Too late to run, even if things turned bad.

Maurice followed close behind, moving with only a little stiffness. Les, however, lingered in the skiff just a moment too long. Jenny glanced at him and looked away almost immediately. He had been tense all morning, but now his hands were clenched into fists, held tightly in his lap against his stomach. His face was white. He looked ill, but it was more than that. As though he were staring at a ghost.

Les could skydive from two miles up, or face a great white shark without the protection of a cage; but whatever he was seeing on this beach was giving him second thoughts about doing his job. It was an unexpected reaction. They had been in more uncomfortable situations than this.

Ismail finished, and the man who held the AK–47 stepped forward, waving his hand toward the south. He was older than the others, his voice sharp, biting—but not angry. Frustrated.

"He says that we'll call him a liar," Ismail translated slowly. "But he wants us to know that he's not. None of them are. It . . . changed . . . on them. They couldn't stop it."

Maurice scowled. "Is that his way of saying that we came all this way for nothing?"

"What a surprise," Les muttered, finally climbing out of the boat.

Jenny ignored them both, stepping past Ismail to face the armed man. "Tell me everything."

"Easier to show you," Ismail translated, moments later. "They locked the creature in a special place."

"Creature," she echoed, and spat out her chewing gum. "Show me the woman."

IT TOOK LESS THAN FIVE MINUTES TO REACH THE PLACE where they had hidden the woman. It was a short distance off the beach, down a narrow trail barely visible in the jungle growth. The heat was suffocating, and within moments of her leaving the stiff ocean breeze, Jenny's limbs turned leaden, her skin slick with sweat. Cotton stuck to her body. She'd had to cover her arms and legs. This area was predominantly Islamic.

Walking was difficult, too. Her body wanted to sway with the sea, but the world around her was solid and far too still. Everything felt alien; all those golden-tinged shadows, and the cries of birds—twisting knots of vines and thick tree trunks bruised with undergrowth so solid, so tangled with leaves, she felt caged.

Maurice strode in front, following Ismail and the man with the gun. Les walked behind her, several of the fishermen well in the rear. But not all of them. Keeping watch on the beach—or worse. Not that anyone could steal *The Calypso Star,* which was moored less than a quarter mile offshore. The security was state of the art—bulletproof glass, reinforced doors—and a biometric lock that secured the science yacht's interior. The worst any thieves could do would be to sun themselves on deck.

"I don't like this," Les muttered.

"You didn't need to come," she replied, watching the trail for anything that could trip her. "Maybe you shouldn't have."

"You're angry."

"Confused. You're scared."

Les tapped her shoulder. "That happens, Jenny. Even to you."

All the time, she wanted to tell him, so bottled up with the words, her throat hurt.

Ahead, she saw the tin roof of a shanty through the trees, and the glint of a machete held across the lap of a man sitting guard some distance from the crude door. He stood quickly when he saw them, swaying nervously on the balls of his feet like he wanted to run.

The man with the gun spoke quickly. Ismail glanced over his shoulder at Jenny. "He says that several days ago, some men attempted to steal . . . *it.* Word had gotten out. A group from another village came in the night, and there was a fight. Our . . . friend . . . had the larger gun."

"Not so large," Maurice muttered.

"It . . . the creature . . . was fine, at the time," Ismail replied. "Or so our guide says."

"Not it. *Her,*" she corrected, and the man shrugged, shoving his glasses up his nose while giving her a faintly condescending smile.

"You're a scientist. Perhaps you should . . . *observe* . . . the creature before speaking of it in . . . human terms."

"I know what I am," Jenny replied tightly, wishing she didn't have to speak at all. "I stand by what I said."

"As do I. I have a job here, Ms. Jameson. One based on complete accuracy."

Jenny exhaled through her teeth and tugged her soaked blouse sharply away from her back. "I hope you're not implying that our goals are different."

He said nothing, which was almost as insulting as what she was certain he was thinking.

Spoiled rich girl. Working for her grandparents because no one else would hire her. Only pretending to be a scientist while she traveled around the world in a multimillion-dollar motor yacht with a beach bum, a babysitter, and a closetful of cocaine and bikinis.

More or less. Jenny had heard it all before, in different variations. Trying to defend herself only made it worse. She couldn't stand whiners—least of all when she was doing the whining.

"Mr. Osman," Maurice said gruffly, and Ismail suddenly pitched forward, falling hard on his knees. His jaw hit the ground a second later, and she heard the painful sound of his teeth snapping together.

Maurice stood at least ten feet away from Ismail. And he continued standing there, carefully keeping his distance, until the injured man rolled over and looked at him. First, with accusation in his eyes—and then confusion.

"You pushed me," he said hoarsely, but he didn't sound convinced.

"How could I?" Maurice replied, holding up his hands— his tone utterly conciliatory, even sympathetic. He walked quickly to Ismail and helped him up. "Nothing broken," he added, moments later. "Can you walk?"

Ismail nodded, carefully not looking at Jenny. With measured steps, he hobbled down the trail after their armed guide, who had stopped and was giving him a disdainful look. Behind, Les made a small sound that she thought was laughter, but when she glanced at him, he was staring past her at the shanty, now clearly visible through the trees. His face was deathly pale.

"You okay?" Maurice asked, waiting for them to catch

up. Jenny thought he was speaking to Les, but when she looked at him, his gaze was focused entirely on her.

She managed a faint upward tick at the corner of her mouth. The old man nodded and clapped her on the shoulder. He stayed close as the trail emptied out into a small clearing barely large enough for the shanty. The man with the machete gave them all a questioning look, then used the tip of his blade to push open the door.

The smell hit Jenny from more than ten feet away.

"Fuck," Maurice growled, staggering to a stop. So did the fishermen, staring at that open doorway with mixed expressions of fear and loathing.

Jenny gritted her teeth and ran toward the shanty. The men got out of her way. She had her penlight out before she even reached the door, and breathed raggedly through her mouth as the stench of rotting flesh hit her again.

The woman had been left on the dirt floor. And she *was* a woman—not an it.

Had been, anyway. She was dead now. Hard to estimate just from looking, but given the state of decay, Jenny thought she had been gone for at least two days. She was skinny, long-limbed, her face nearly obscured by matted blond hair. Totally naked and covered in blood. Her body had been gouged with long, raking wounds that resembled claw marks. Jenny saw exposed bone—her ribs, and part of her hip. Savaged by an animal, maybe. She had died in agony, that much was clear. Died in the dirt, alone amongst strangers.

Something small and round glittered beside her blood-rusted knee, caught briefly in the penlight beam. Jenny swooped down and snatched it up, just as Maurice shadowed the doorway. He stopped, staring—and made the sign of the cross. Jenny hardly noticed. She was fighting not to shake, or drop to her knees, or stop breathing entirely.

Hold on, she told herself, clutching that small, hard object. *Hold on.*

"Poor girl," Maurice said, just as Ismail pushed through behind him.

The scout trembled, looking away and covering his mouth. His glasses almost fell off, and he grabbed them in his hand before sneaking another peek at the woman's corpse. "She has legs."

"Yes," Jenny whispered, crouching. "She seems quite human."

"So they lied." Ismail took a half step outside. "Hard to believe. They seemed very . . . certain."

The object she held so tightly bit into her palm. "Pay them anyway. And arrange to have this woman's body taken to the boat. We'll put her in the cold locker until we can turn her over to the authorities." Jenny pulled a single latex glove from her pocket and slid it on. Ever so gently, she pushed the woman's hair away from her face. It was difficult to tell what she had looked like while alive, but her cheekbones were sharp and high, almost inhumanly so. Pale skin, broken with small holes where the flesh had been chewed away, perhaps by rats.

Jenny covered her face again and stood. Too quickly, maybe. She felt faint, and swayed, shoving the heel of her palm against her forehead. Maurice started to hold her up, but she slipped away from him and staggered to the door—stripping off her one glove and shoving it into her pocket. Ismail was already outside, speaking with the fishermen. Les stood bent over, his hands pressed against his knees.

"You saw?" she asked him roughly.

"Smelled," he mumbled. "So what is it? Wild-goose chase? Another fake?"

Jenny dug into her pocket for chewing gum and held it out to him. He took several pieces, and stuffed them all in his mouth. As he closed his eyes, sighing, she turned away and glanced down at her other hand, fingers slowly, stiffly, uncurling.

A silver scale glinted on her palm.

"Yeah," she whispered. "A fake."

—

HOURS AFTER THE BODY WAS BROUGHT ABOARD *THE Calypso Star,* Jenny found herself underwater, pretending that she was drowning.

Or just holding her breath for so long, it was almost the same thing.

Records were always being made and broken, but the last time she had checked, the world record for holding one's breath underwater had been broken by a Frenchman, at eleven minutes and thirty-five seconds. Took the man six months to train and two months to recover.

Jenny could hold her breath for a little over four minutes. It wasn't hard. Especially when she had a lot on her mind. Some people took a shower when they needed to think. She always had to go deeper.

Right now, fifty feet.

A weighted cable hung beside her, a ten-pound anchor tied at the bottom to maintain a straight line. Lead bands were strapped to her ankles, as well. With one hand on the cable, it wasn't difficult to keep from sinking, and she could climb back up when it was time to breathe. She had been down here for half an hour already, rising like a porpoise every four minutes to take a breath.

Red hair, caught in pigtails, floated around her face; and in the ocean twilight, her fair, freckled skin looked ethereal, cast in silver and blue. Much the same as the scale she held in her hand, contained inside a small glass jar for safe-keeping.

She turned the jar around and up and down, unable to look away as the scale shifted colors: shades of pale green, lavender, and silver; iridescent as mother-of-pearl. It was thicker than a regular fish scale—almost like a very thin shell—but pliable, too. She had found two others over the years. A beach walk on Galapagos had yielded a find—and a shop of curiosities in Madrid the other. Random moments, like some higher power speaking to her. Or destiny, using Morse code.

You're the only one who knows the message, thought Jenny, tearing her gaze from the scale to stare into the darkness below. At least at night, when she gazed at the sky, there were stars. The ocean deserved stars. It felt as vast as the sky. Three-fourths of the earth was covered in water. Scientists knew more about Mars than about the deep ocean. More people had stood on the moon than had traveled five miles under. No light penetrated deeper than five hundred feet. Anything was possible. Anything could be hiding.

Mermaids. Mermen. People of the sea.

Her lungs began to ache a little, but she didn't pull herself up the cable. The next time she broke the surface, she would have to climb back onto the boat—and she wasn't ready. She did not want to face that corpse. According to the fishermen, the woman had been discovered a week earlier in the aftermath of a storm. Washed ashore, nearly dead. Attacked by some gang of men, Ismail was saying now. Tossed into the ocean, perhaps. Pirates were a problem in the area.

Jenny didn't know whether to be pleased or annoyed that Ismail was so ready to dismiss what the fishermen had first claimed—that the woman was not just a woman, but a monster. Part fish.

Never mind that she had legs now. Ismail didn't know as much as he thought he did. His specialty was bioprospecting—scouting for plants and animals that might prove medically beneficial to humans. It was big business—cutthroat, in the most literal sense of the word—and *A Priori* had one of the largest, most extensive research networks in the world. Even if no one realized it.

Part of that network had been built upon the backs of paid informants, most of them locals in third-world countries where remote areas still remained virtually unexplored. Nor was it just plants and traditional healing remedies that they reported on. Rumors of strange sightings, miracles—anything inexplicable—were investigated quickly and quietly by people with far more experience in the odd and arcane than Ismail Osman.

Less than a week ago, ten miles from here, a man who knew a man who paid for unusual stories had told of a monstrous woman. Ten minutes later, Ismail had received a call in Singapore, which he had then passed on to an office in London. Which had placed another call to Nova Scotia.

Until, finally, Jenny had been brought into the loop. There were other marine biologists in *A Priori,* but none were family, and few could be trusted with the possibility of anything so . . . sensitive . . . as a woman who might not be human.

A flicker of light caught Jenny's eye, but it was just a small school of narrow-barred mackerel, glinting silver as they darted through the water. She watched them for a moment, until she sensed movement on her left. When she looked, though, nothing was there.

Jenny's skin prickled—and her lungs were aching fiercely. She had waited too long. Tucking the jar into her swim pocket, she hauled upward on the cable with her other hand, kicking hard with her finned feet.

Halfway up, she sensed another streak of movement—a flash of light near her head. Bright, brief, and gone in a moment. Jenny strained to see, but again, there was nothing. Even the mackerel were gone.

Seconds later, something cool brushed against the back of her neck.

It felt like fingers, sliding into her hair to pinch the base of her skull. Jenny whirled around the rope, heart pounding, but she was alone. No signs of life, not even fish.

Jenny kicked hard, using both hands to pull herself toward the surface. Her heartbeat refused to slow, eating up even more oxygen. By the time she shot out of the water, gasping, her vision was full of all kinds of dancing lights.

"Shit!" shouted Maurice, leaning over the edge of the yacht. "What took you so long? I thought I was gonna have to jump in after you!"

Jenny was coughing too hard to speak. She yanked down her goggles and grabbed the ladder. Maurice held out a towel when she reached the top, and stood there with his arms folded over his massive chest, watching her with a frown as she took long, bracing breaths. When she could finally breathe normally, she buried her face in the soft terry cloth. It was hot out, humid, but she felt cold to the bone. The base of her skull ached.

"Jenny," Maurice growled.

"'M fine," she muttered. "Got distracted."

"For five minutes?" He gently tugged the towel away from her face. "That's how long you were down there. I timed it."

"Thought you were reading a book."

"My watch beeps every four minutes. I hear you come up for air, then I keep reading."

Jenny pulled the goggles over her head and dropped them in the bin by the ladder. Her fins were next, but the shorty wetsuit was going to have to wait until she reached her cabin. If she could make it that far. Everything suddenly seemed too tight. She tugged hard on the collar, strangled, ready to jump out of her skin.

"Hey," Maurice said, and caught her wrist. "If this is about the woman—"

"No," she interrupted; and then, softly, "Maybe."

The old man glanced longingly at the beer bottle sitting beside one of the lounge chairs. "Ismail tried to make a call to the Malaysian coast guard. I let him think it went through."

"How soon can we have him off the boat?"

"Tomorrow morning. I'm making him bunk with Les."

Jenny smiled grimly and patted his hand. "I'm not giving her body to my family, Maurice. You know that, right? I'll take blood and DNA samples, but she stays with the sea."

He tore his gaze from the beer and gave her a long, unflinching look. Too long, too thoughtful. Jenny tried to pull away, but his grip remained firm.

"I know you have your reasons," he said quietly. "But you can trust them."

Jenny finally yanked her hand free. "You have a short memory."

"It wasn't their fault. They didn't know."

Bitterness twisted her mouth. "*I* knew. When I was twelve years old, *I* knew something was wrong. And when I tried to tell them, *they didn't listen*. They didn't listen for ten years, until it was too late. And now look what's happened."

Maurice closed his eyes. "The Consortium will be stopped, Jenny."

The Consortium. Sins of the parents, straight out of hell. If *A Priori* was the good side of the family, then the Consortium was everything that had gone wrong—in the most terrible ways possible. All the contacts, all the connections, all that power—used not for research or knowledge, or even just to fill a bank account—but to control others. To shape the world in ways that none of them could yet predict.

"They won't be stopped," she whispered, compulsively touching her abdomen. Maurice's gaze dropped to her hand, and pain filled his gaze.

"I'm sorry," he whispered. "I—"

Jenny didn't let him finish. She couldn't stand it. She turned and walked away.

It was quiet belowdecks. Jenny had to pass the small science lab on the way to her quarters. The center of the door was made of glass, and she glanced inside out of habit. She was shocked to see Les slipping out of the cold locker.

Jenny froze, backed up a step, and opened the door. Les faltered, but only for a moment. He slid past her, out of the lab, into the hall. Not smiling, but not looking worried, either.

"I needed to see her," he said. "Because of my reaction today. I had to face up to it."

Jenny fought down the urge to go and check the body. *Trust,* Maurice was always telling her. *You need to trust.*

Right. Fine. She'd wait until after dinner to check.

"You feeling better?" she asked him, turning with difficulty away from the lab and continuing down the hall.

"A little," he said, following her. "Something large killed her, Jenny. Teeth marks wouldn't have made those injuries."

The cuts were too clean for claws, she added silently. *Unless they were razor-sharp and thin as a blade.*

"There are defensive wounds on her arms," Less said quietly, as she reached her door.

His voice sounded hollow, preoccupied, as though he was speaking mostly to himself. Jenny caught him staring at his hands, which he closed into fists. An odd gesture, pained, with a hint of violence. Les rubbed his knuckles against his thighs.

Jenny said, "You noticed."

"You keep me around for more than my good looks."

She tried to smile. "Sharp man. I know you flirted shamelessly with the Human Resources manager before she hired you."

"Nah." Les leaned against the wall beside her door, flashing her a rueful grin. "I'm just good at what I do."

"The Indiana Jones of marine archaeology," she replied. "How many shipwrecks have you found?"

"Enough." But there was an odd gleam in his eye when he said it. Bitterness, maybe. She realized it was the same look he'd had on his face right after he had come out of the cold locker. Before he saw her watching.

The base of her skull began to throb. Jenny didn't feel like talking anymore. She needed to lie down and think about that dead woman—and what could have killed her. She had been attacked first in the sea. Jenny was certain of that. No other way she would have allowed herself to be stranded onshore. She had been chased, driven on land. And yes, it was possible that the fishermen had added to her wounds. That was the logical explanation of those fine cuts.

But this situation was not logical, or rational. And Jenny had her own memories to draw from.

Her cabin was small but comfortable. She had been in earlier to change into her wetsuit, and had forgotten to turn off her battery-operated candles—which mimicked the flicker and glow of firelight and even gave off a vanilla scent. A bookcase covered one wall, a wooden lip built across every shelf to keep things from sliding off when they hit rough water.

Jenny had painted the walls pale lavender though it was difficult to see behind the tacked-up paintings and photographs she had collected on her journeys. Her bolted-down furniture was white and simple; and her desk was covered with her laptop and stacks of paper, including a handwritten unfinished article for *National Geographic* that was due in a week. A braided chenille rug covered the floor, and an old quilt had been laid upon the twin-sized bed. Two portholes revealed miles of sea.

She had her own bathroom—all of them did. She glanced to the right and saw Les reflected in the mirror. He was watching her. He hesitated in the doorway, then took that final step into her room, walking up behind her.

She turned before he could get close. "Stop."

"You always say that," he said, going still. "No preamble, no discussion."

"We've talked about this before."

"For years," he said. "And in all that time, you've been alone."

The base of her skull throbbed. "What do you want me to say? You're gorgeous, Les. You're smart, nice, everything a girl could want."

"Every girl but you."

"You're not . . . right . . . for me," she told him haltingly, wishing he would just leave her alone. Wishing, too, that she were the kind of woman who would ask him to stay. She wanted to be that woman. She wanted to want him. It would be so much easier.

A bitter smile touched his mouth. "You're looking for . . . magic."

"Just a feeling," she whispered. "I'll know it when I find it."

And if you don't? If you never feel that way again?

Jenny swallowed hard and turned from Les. She felt him watching her, silence thick between them. Maybe he was angry. He got that way, sometimes. Jenny didn't care. Some things couldn't be changed, no matter how much she wished otherwise.

Les walked to the door but paused at the last moment. "You ever think maybe you see everything except what really matters? What you're looking for could be right in front of you."

Jenny closed her eyes, and the strain of an old melody poured through her mind, followed by an embracing warmth that felt like sunlight on her face.

Blue eyes. Pale skin. Strong hand.

Followed by another, more recent, memory—and a harder, fiercer, heartache. One that would never leave her, that she could only chase away, in pieces.

"Jenny," Les said.

"No," she replied hoarsely. "I never think that."

CHAPTER TWO

THE dolphins knew something was wrong before Perrin did.

He was too busy getting punched in the face to notice. Down on his knees, trying to breathe as blood trickled down his chin from his mouth. He licked his lip, tasting the cut. The salt from his body was good as seawater, and he was so thirsty.

"Crazy fucker," whispered Dmitry. "Stay away from me."

Perrin licked his lip again and started laughing. All that got him was another slam behind the ear, but he was ready for it. Knuckles glanced off his skull. Perrin hardly felt the blow. He turned his head to the right and saw his reflection in the blue shadows of the viewing glass: a ghost, pale and sharp, half his face obscured by tangled blond hair coming loose from the knot at the back of his neck.

A dolphin made a pass near the glass, distracting him. Perrin was yanked away. He landed on his back, getting an eyeful of a muddy boot sole racing toward his face. He jerked sideways, missing the blow, and shot upward with his fist—catching the human nearly between the legs, against his inner thigh, just a whisper from the sweet spot.

An intentional miss. A fight was just a fight until some-one's genitals broke. After that, anything was possible—and

Perrin did *not* want to go back to jail. He could not. The first two times had almost killed him.

Dmitry staggered away, hands crossed over his crotch. Perrin pushed himself up on his elbows. "Come on. Don't stop."

"Crazy," said Dmitry again, voice breaking on the word. "I didn't touch her."

"You *thought* about it," he replied, not caring if he said too much; here, with this piece of shit, it didn't matter. "You're still thinking about it."

"I told you," whispered the other man, staring up at Perrin like he was a monster. "Stay away, or I'll fucking kill you."

"Stay away," Perrin echoed, nauseas now. "You wish *she* would say that to you. You want to see her fight. You want to feel her fighting beneath *you*."

Dmitry touched the tool belt slung around his waist, lingering on the paint scraper. Sharp angle. Good for stabbing. Perrin stood, unsteady. His mouth and head throbbed. He licked his lip again, but this time his blood tasted sour. Dmitry swayed on his own feet, still handling the paint scraper. Fight or flight. One or the other. Perrin steeled himself for the worst.

Dmitry whispered, "Boss likes me. And he thinks you're a fag."

Perrin forced a smile. "Maybe I am. Maybe I should fuck *you*."

The man's knuckles turned white around the paint scraper. "Cut your balls off first. Make you eat them."

Perrin said nothing. Just kept staring, the corner of his mouth tilted up in a smile that felt cold and ugly—that came from an ugly place inside him. Nothing beautiful, nothing serene, nothing left of what he had been. It was all ugly now, all the time.

He waited. Dmitry tried to stand firm, but his gaze flickered past Perrin's shoulder, and the color drained from his face. He took a step back, then another. Stopped himself, and pointed with the paint scraper. His hand shook.

"Later, we finish this," he whispered, his other hand drifting down to hold his crotch as though the blow still hurt him. He took another step back, but this time didn't stop, and walked quickly from the viewing room. So quick he might have been running. Almost.

Perrin watched Dmitry go, conscious of his own pounding heart and a throbbing sensation that crawled into his throat. A trembling weakness spread from his chest into his arms. Rage, despair, relief—he couldn't name what he felt—just that it made him feel weak instead of strong.

When he was certain the human man would not return, he glanced over his shoulder. Four dolphins drifted behind the glass, lined up and staring. Just staring. Nothing easy or gentle about their black eyes—and those singular grins that humans always loved were not in the least bit friendly.

Hurt, one of the dolphins whispered mournfully in his mind.

Perrin rolled his shoulders, ignoring the long searing ache in his muscles. His head pounded, as did his pulse, and when he wiped his split lip with the back of his palm, blood smeared his pale skin.

It's nothing, he told them, and knelt in front of the glass, beside the tools he had abandoned after Dmitry's first blow: a spray bottle, a sponge, and a paint scraper. He stared at those very human things, hit with a fierce sensation of alien unfamiliarity. Watched, as though from a great distance, as his fingers wrapped around the battered plastic handle of the paint scraper. It looked very small in his hand. He picked it up and set it hard against the viewing glass, beneath a piece of dried chewing gum. The dolphins gathered on the other side, watching. He was always watched when he worked.

No, whispered the dolphins.

Yes, replied Perrin, and forced his hand to move, scraping against the gum. He hurt, he was tired and thirsty, but this was work—human work he needed to survive—and he had learned years ago to compartmentalize violence, exhaustion, and move quickly from it. A punch was nothing. A threat was nothing. Dmitry was nothing.

Even if the human man's dreams were not.

It was early. Doors opened for the cleaning crew as soon as the sun rose. Only specialized personnel were allowed near the tanks after eight in the evening, which provided just a three-hour window after the Shedd Aquarium closed to clean the aftermath of eight thousand daily visitors—with their muddy feet, dirty fingerprints, and gum. Not much time to do a proper job, which meant that Perrin and others had arrived at six that morning—as they did, every morning—ready to do battle using paint scrapers and oversized toothbrushes. No chemicals of any kind were allowed near the animals. Just water, an occasional splash of vinegar, and patience mixed with brute strength.

The Boss was off that morning, though. Dmitry had found a corner near the shark tank to take a nap. And Perrin, in passing, had felt the fragment of a dream, a cold thread he could not help but follow. He knew better. But he still hadn't learned how to stop being a fool.

I hope you run, thought Perrin, wishing the young subject of Dmitry's fantasy could hear him. Just a girl, not quite a teenager. A stranger whose name and face he did not know, only that in Dmitry's dream she had pigtails and freckles, and a wide, white smile that was sweet—

—and reminded him too much of another young girl he had known briefly, in another life.

Run far, stay away, he thought again, jamming the paint scraper against the dried gum in a burst of violent strength. *Don't let him get close enough to touch you.*

The gum popped off. Perrin tossed it into the garbage sack, stifling the urge to sneeze as the chemical scent emanating from the plastic made his nostrils burn. He wore no gloves, unlike the human men and women of the cleaning crew. His skin was sensitive to rubber and latex, as were his lungs—a weakness that had grown worse over the years.

He plucked a small razor blade from his tool belt, beginning the more detailed work of removing the gum residue. Dolphins drifted even closer, jostling each other for space as they pressed near the glass. Perrin tried not to look at them.

You're distracting me, he said.

You are breaking, they whispered. *You are broken.*

Perrin stopped working. Staring at them. No one else was around. Just them, him. He tried to breathe but found his throat too tight. Like he was drowning in air.

He placed his palm, then his forehead, against the cool barrier. His eyes drifted shut, and a sigh filled his mind— soft and melancholy, tugging so sharply on his heart that he placed his other hand on his chest, clutching at his soft gray uniform.

You should not be here, whispered one of the dolphins. *Even we, who have never been free, know this. We know you, in our blood.*

But you have no time left to punish yourself. No time for regret.

Something is coming.

Perrin gave them a sharp look, but when they said nothing else, he gathered up his tools, prepared to move on. He had a men's bathroom to scrub and more displays to check for fingerprints and gum. Dolphins were far too fond of riddles.

It took him several moments to realize they had begun screaming.

He had never heard such a sound. It started first in his mind, like the swell of a wave: soft in the beginning, just a pulse from four directions. Enough to make him freeze in midstep, trembling as those spectral voices gained in strength. Haunted with terror.

Perrin tried to block them out—and pain exploded through the base of his skull.

He doubled over, choking, and reached back to touch the shallow hole hidden by his hair. His hand traced the lines of scar tissue radiating down his neck, feeling for blood. There was none. Instead, he suffered a spidery sensation across his thoughts, like the light scrape of nails. Premonition, burning. It made him want to rip off his head.

Perrin tried. He dug his fingers into the hole at the back of his skull—and those four voices hit him so hard, with such fear, he doubled over again, gasping.

He turned, tears of pain blurring his vision as he watched the dolphins twist inside their tank, writhing violently through the water. One of them came too near the glass and hit it so hard Perrin heard a crack from the other side. The dolphin went still, drifting to the bottom of the tank. The others took no notice, still lost in their seizures.

Perrin ran.

He heard human cries of distress and confusion as he careened through the aquarium—shouts from the direction of the beluga tanks, and the sharks—and he glimpsed a glittering school of silver fish flailing madly as he passed. He did not slow. Just ripped through the employee door and raced up the stairs toward the dolphin center.

People, everywhere. Shouting, bumping into each other. Frantically struggling with scuba gear while some were already in the water, clinging to the shallows. Perrin passed them all and dove straight into the tank, entering the cool dark water with such force he was almost halfway down to the dolphins before his mind—and body—registered where he was and what he had done.

Perrin almost shifted shape. He came so close. But he did not lose his legs or shed his skin for scales, nor did he shift his lungs. He held his breath and swam as hard and fast as he could, heart thundering, listening to the screams inside his mind. The water shook with the physical cries of the dolphins, their voices vibrating through his chest as they thrashed wildly, bending their spines so far backward he feared they might break.

He was nearly struck when he got close, but dodged awkwardly, abandoning himself to instincts gone unused for years: rusty, cold, buried too deep. Like a human trapped for a decade in a wheelchair, suddenly forced to run. Legs might work, but not easily. Mind over matter.

Human limbs and clothing hampered Perrin, but not enough to stop him as he twisted around the struggling dolphins, shooting up between them to lay his hands on their bodies. The contact burned his skin, then deeper, into bone, into his mind, shooting through his nerves and veins with a heat that was better than heroin—and more painful. He gritted his teeth, squeezing shut his eyes.

Let me in, he demanded of the dolphins, hoping they could hear him. *Let me see what is hurting you.*

And they did. Just a glimpse.

But that was more than enough.

What he saw felt like a punch inside his brain, a physical blow that echoed within the hole at the base of his skull, echoing on and on as though that hole traveled through him into an abyss: endless, shattering. He flung himself away, throat locked against his own scream. The base of his skull burned. Above him, he glimpsed divers in the water, finally swimming toward him—hampered by equipment that made them look alien, deadly.

Perrin stared at them, numb and cold.

He was still feeling numb when he dove deeper, toward the bottom of the pool and the dolphin resting so still on the bottom. Nothing in his mind, just darkness and a sick cold nick in his heart. And that feeling of endlessness inside the base of his skull.

The injured dolphin was alive, but unconscious. Drowning. Perrin gathered her in his arms, and pushed off the bottom of the pool with one powerful kick of his feet. The others had finally stopped seizing, blissfully silent. Drifting, turning slowly, lost and confused.

Perrin opened his mind to them, calling for their help as he struggled to swim to the surface with the injured dolphin. The human divers seemed miles away, but he could see their eyes behind those thick goggles—watching him, watching only him—and he realized that their movements were also hampered by their uncertainty of *him*. He had acted outside the parameters of what was acceptable. He had defied assumptions. He had torn away part of the mask and become . . . other.

Too late. No alternative. Especially not when the dolphins finally shook off their shock and dove toward him, just out of reach of the humans who finally reached the spot where they had been drifting.

Two dolphins slid beneath their injured podmate, bearing her weight and pushing her to the surface—while the smallest, another female, moved hard against Perrin's side. He grabbed her dorsal fin and allowed himself to be pulled to the surface. His lungs were burning, but he hardly noticed. He opened his mouth at the last moment and swallowed salt water—choking on it, and savoring the taste. It was not as good as the real thing—nothing could be that good—but it was enough.

You know what you have to do, whispered the dolphin beside him, her thoughts weary and sick, and frightened. *You must. Even for us, you must.*

But Perrin said nothing to her. They broke the surface, and he gasped for breath, kicking hard to stay afloat as he twisted around to search for the injured dolphin. He saw her a short distance away, still held by the others. Human shouts rebounded off the walls—so loud he wanted to clap his hands over his ears and descend back into the deep water. Instead, he swam hard toward the hurt dolphin. Behind him, more shouts, loud splashing sounds.

The dolphin was not breathing. She had not been breathing for several minutes. It was impossible for any dolphin to breathe while unconscious. Perrin staggered into the shallows where she had been brought, reaching her only moments before the aquarium staff. He breathed hard into the dolphin's blowhole, again and again, before hands grabbed his waist and arms, pulling him away. He fought—or tried to—until he saw someone else take his place.

Perrin was dragged, pushed from the water—not gently, but not with anger, either. Just fear, uncertainty—and a few wild looks.

"That was stupid," one man said to him, but he sounded unsure. "You could have gotten hurt."

Perrin hardly heard him. Too busy looking over his shoulder at the dolphins. The young female had not yet been revived. Out in the ocean, in the old days, he might have been able to do something. But not here. Not as he was now.

" . . . did you do that?" Perrin heard dimly, and glanced down to find one of the shark experts standing beside him, her gaze sharp, intense. Her clothes were soaked, and she wore no shoes.

"Excuse me?" he asked, angling for the door.

She planted herself in front of him. "How did you do that? With the dolphins? Why did they respond to you and ignore their handlers?"

Other people were watching them. The last time he had felt such hot scrutiny was in a prison yard before a fight: a breathless, ruthless energy, as if those were the first and last times anyone would see a man driven to his knees.

Perrin did not flinch or blink. "Did they?"

Her eyes narrowed. "Who are you?"

"No one," he said flatly, and pushed past her. He was much larger than anyone else in the room, and though her hand flew up to grab his arm, her fingers closed around air. Her choice. She had time to catch him. So did everyone else, men and women who stared and let him pass, just before moving toward the edge of the pool where the injured dolphin had begun to move weakly.

Perrin glanced back and met the gaze of the dolphin who had pulled him to the surface, her one eye above water, staring across the humans at him.

Hurry, she whispered.

BUT HE DID NOT.

He forced himself to walk through the employee corridors of the Shedd Aquarium, standing aside for staff who hurried past him while speaking urgently into walkie-talkies. He remained calm and in control, carefully distant from his own thoughts as he stepped outdoors into the crisp autumn air.

It was sunny outside. It hurt his eyes. When he had first ventured on land, the sun had almost blinded him. So much intolerable light. He had never accustomed himself to the sun—not since boyhood. Artificial lights were little better, but the blue glow of the water and the womb of shadows surrounding the viewing chambers inside the aquarium had been an illusion of home.

You'll be fired now, he told himself, suffering a moment of terrible, aching regret. It was the first emotion he had felt since leaving the dolphins, and it stayed with him as he unzipped his soaked gray uniform and left it in a puddle on the sidewalk, along with his tools. He wore jeans beneath, and a white T-shirt, both plastered to his skin. His skull ached, but he did not touch the hole hidden by his wet hair. Not at first.

He had his palm buried against the spot an hour later, when he finally reached his apartment building. A quiet brick walk-up in an even quieter working-class neighborhood where no one asked too many questions—or even spoke languages that Perrin could understand. He smelled hot spices as he climbed the rickety stairs and listened to the cadence of some unintelligible Spanish rap burn into his bones, beating time with his thudding heart. His head hurt so badly he could barely see straight. Sharp, stabbing, traveling upward from the base of his skull into his brow. Some of the children playing in the hall stared at him with big eyes and scurried out of his way as he passed. He did not want to imagine what he looked like to them—a monster, maybe, the strange albino.

He fumbled with his keys, almost dropping them, and pushed inside his home. It was very dark and cold inside, air conditioner running on high with his window blinds pulled down, taped along the edges to keep even more light out. He had tried fitting cardboard over the glass, but the landlord had complained and looked at him like he was a murderer or pervert.

His place was small and cheap. Just a studio. No furniture, but a sleeping bag lay in the corner, alongside a cardboard box where he kept his clothes folded. The room was clean, and the bathroom had a tub. That was all he needed.

But he stood in the doorway, savoring the damp of salt water still clinging to his skin, and remembered what it felt like to descend into the pool.

A hard memory. The world seemed to shift around him, and what had been familiar—what he had *trained* himself to find familiar—was suddenly alien again. This was not his world—and though the tank at the aquarium was just an illusion of the ocean, a bubble, a fake, and prison—he suddenly wished he could be one of the prisoners, even just for a moment. He was already in a prison, one he should not have survived in as long as he had.

The base of his skull throbbed: deep inside, deeper than should be possible, as if his brain were trying to claw free. It had been eight years since he had felt such pain. Eight long years.

He reached around, but all he touched was bone—and with that contact roared a sense of emptiness so vast he leaned over, choking, suffocating with loneliness.

Stop, he told himself, but it was too late. He needed to run. He needed to tear his skin from his bones. He needed to finally die.

He tore the collar of his T-shirt in his haste to pull it over his head. His jeans were next, left behind as he stumbled toward the bathroom. Pain worsened, throbbing in time to his pulse. He was almost blind from it when he reached the tub—already filled with salt water.

Scales erupted over his skin as he tumbled sideways into the water—sloshing a great deal over the side. He was too long for the tub, almost too broad, but he squeezed himself to the bottom as best he could, limp and hurting, savoring the flimsy cocoon that covered some of his burning, rippling skin. His legs fused together, the bones of his human feet stretching and flattening with cracks and joint-jerking jolts even as ribbons of silver scales flowed down his hips and across his torso. The skin between his fingers flexed outward into pale webs, and, when he opened his eyes, he gazed through a translucent second lid that sharpened the darkness into flecks of shadows.

Bubbles chased free of his throat. Perrin drew in a slow breath through gills that slit down the sides of his neck. The water tasted heavy and stale, even dirty, too much like rusty Chicago, with its train tracks and clogged roads. Perrin dug his knuckles into his brow. The pain in his head eased, but not the roaring emptiness.

He heard a scream. Not from a dolphin. This was human. Female.

Just a premonition, he told himself, filled with dread. *Not real.*

Not real here. But real somewhere, now or in the future.

Perrin squeezed shut his eyes as another scream filled the bathtub water—not his, though he would have preferred that to the strangled gasp of a woman's terror. The water seemed to echo with that voice, driving straight through him with unrelenting precision.

No, he thought, twisting in agony. He had not suffered visions, or magic—not once in eight years. But today, with the dolphins, he had shared in a terrible vision.

This vision. Part of it, anyway.

Perrin dug his nails into his scalp, crying out as the woman's voice broke into a furious sob. Desperate, he pushed himself off the bottom of the tub. He had been a fool to think water would be a respite from the pain.

Just before he broke the surface, his vision darkened—pricked with flickers of light, like stars. Perrin steeled himself, but instead of blood and death, the only sight that confronted him was a pair of green eyes. Staring right through him, without tears or pain—filled with nothing but terrible, furious, rage.

And then those eyes disappeared, blown apart as though made of sand—each grain floating through the water toward his face, slow and glittering. Perrin watched, breathless. No longer hearing anything but the sound of his pounding heart.

Until, suddenly, he saw something else.

And everything changed, again.

Perrin pulled himself out of the tub and fell hard on the cold wet floor. He lay for a long time with parts of him crammed between the wall and toilet, though his head was mostly outside the bathroom, one cheek pressed against old rough carpet: beached, exhausted. He stared at the ghostly pale skin of his hands and arms; and strands of his white-blond hair, plastered to the floor.

Time to return to the darkness, he told himself.

Perrin rolled over on his back. Green eyes flashed through his mind, and an ache pulsed briefly through the base of his skull. He thought the headache would begin again, but after a moment spent holding his breath, nothing happened.

The long pale fins of his tail receded, bones shifting and popping as his toes re-formed into human feet. Scales reabsorbed, flashing silver, and the flesh binding his legs split with a soft whisper. Perrin reached down with trembling hands to rub his legs. The skin felt tender. So did his heart.

He crawled, slowly, to the small box beside his sleeping bag. His knees were weak, heart beating too quickly, lungs aching as he readjusted to breathing through his nostrils and mouth. There was a thermos in the box, and he drank from it—a couple careful sips of seawater, or a close approximation—bought from a local store that specialized in obscenely expensive fish. He had tried to find ways to sneak water home from the Shedd, but even after three months, that had proven impossible.

He picked up a small CD player and slipped the head-

phones on. Nat King Cole crooned gently in his ears. Just
one song, played over and over. Perrin focused on the music,
rummaging through his few belongings. He had tossed
something inside just the other day—disposed of quickly,
because he had imagined a burning sensation in his fingers.

He found it quickly. A postcard. Not mailed to him, but
used as scrap paper during a surprise encounter with an old
friend who he had thought was dead. Someone like him—or
close enough, that the differences did not matter.

M'cal. Son of a human mother and a *Krackeni* male.
Soul singer, warrior, and soon-to-be father—whose wife
was a famed musician. And, perhaps, a witch.

Perrin had not told M'cal of his exile, but somehow the
Krackeni half-breed had guessed. Not difficult, he supposed. What Perrin had once been was nothing that any of
their kind would voluntarily reject. Even if they wanted to.

You don't have to be alone, M'cal had told him. *There
are others. Shape-shifters, gargoyles, those who make
magic with their minds. You are not alone, Perrin O'doro.
And if you ever need help, ever. . .*

"All you have to do is ask," Perrin murmured out
loud. He began to toss the postcard back into the box, but
stopped—burning with misgivings. Still seeing those green
eyes, hearing that scream.

Filled, again, with that last terrible premonition he had
shared with the dolphins. The one thing he had never imagined. The only thing that could send him back to the sea.

Perrin picked up the phone, and dialed the number on
the card.

HE ARRIVED IN SAN FRANCISCO THAT NIGHT. HIS TICKET,
paid for by strangers. He had been on a plane only twice
before, many years in the past, and he would not have flown
now given another choice. Airplanes made him ill. Closed
walls, no way out. Nor could he travel with large bottles of
seawater. Reduced, instead, to buying several three-ounce

containers and filling each one with the precious liquid—carrying them in a single quart-sized plastic bag, which he dipped into several times during the flight. Perrin felt like a junkie getting a hit each time he took a sip.

He started shuddering before the plane finished its descent into San Francisco. Even a thousand feet up, he smelled the sea. He could feel it in his bones like a hard chill, sinking from flesh to marrow in throbbing waves. His gait was occasionally drunken as he rushed through the terminal. People stared. He ignored them, unsure whether it was his walk—or his height and albino coloring—that drew the eye. Or worse: something about him that was inherently alien, that gave him away.

His reaction to being near the ocean was worse in the cab. Perrin rolled down the window, and cool sea air whipped at his long hair, bound loosely at his neck with a leather cord. Each breath made him ill—but not because he found the salt scent disgusting. Instead, it was too much pleasure, too much that he had forgotten. Eight years living inland, forcing his body to acclimate, trying to pretend that he was not lost.

All that effort, gone in an instant.

"You can never go home," he murmured to himself, ignoring the flicker of the cab driver's eyes in the rearview mirror. It was a Saturday night, and the streets were crowded with bodies and light. Perrin tried to focus on that; but between the buildings of downtown, beyond the canyons of those tremendous city hills, he continued to catch glimpses of the dark sea.

His legs started itching. The base of his skull ached. His vision flickered. He wanted to jump out of his skin, and run screaming—toward the water or away, he could not say. Just that it hurt. It hurt so badly he could not breathe. He forced himself to drink from one of the vials, and his hand shook so much he almost dropped it.

"We're here," said the cab driver, swerving to the curb.

Perrin paid him and slipped out onto the sidewalk. He did not have a suitcase, just a backpack. No need for anything else where he was going. Not even the clothes he wore.

He stood still as crowds parted around him—searching for a building number, anything at all that fit the brief instructions he had been given over the phone. Just an address, really. A simple reassurance that someone would be there to meet him. Even in dark jeans and a T-shirt, Perrin didn't think he was hard to miss. All he saw, though, was a Starbucks and a small Italian pizzeria. He smelled chocolate, too. No sign of an office.

Until, from within an alcove so narrow his gaze nearly passed over it, Perrin glimpsed movement. A door made of copper and leaded glass, which pushed open slowly. A young man stepped out: tall, slender, dressed in black jeans and a white T-shirt frayed with burn marks. He looked at Perrin without hesitation, as though he had been watching him for some time already.

"Mr. O'doro?" he asked quietly.

Perrin hesitated. The young man quirked the corner of his mouth into a faint smile but said nothing else. Simply waited in the alcove, like he had all the time in the world. Perrin also waited, studying those eyes—finding them dark and old, and unflinching.

He forced himself to take a step, then another, until he stood in front of the young man and that open door, feeling like it was ready to swallow him into darkness. Which was true, more or less.

"My name is Eddie," said the young man, breaking the silence. He held out his hand. Perrin found his grip strong, and very warm—almost hot.

"Perrin," he replied, and walked through the door into an empty lobby, where the rubber soles of his shoes squeaked on the granite floor. Eddie pointed to the single elevator.

"The Dirk & Steele agency owns the building," he explained, voice echoing faintly in the cavernous room. "The elevator will only go to the top."

Perrin did not feel like small talk. He remained silent as he stepped in, feeling the skin on the back of his neck crawl as Eddie walked in behind him and hit the topmost button, for the eighth floor. Without pausing, he also flipped the stop switch—preventing the doors from closing.

Perrin frowned. "You better have a good reason for doing that."

A faint flush touched the young man's cheeks, but his gaze remained steady. "You came at a bad time, sir. I apologize for anything . . . anything you might hear upstairs."

"Should I come back?"

"No." Eddie released the button, and the doors closed. "I wanted to warn you, that's all."

Warnings already. Perrin swayed as the elevator groaned upward. "I was told things about you people. That you're . . . different."

"Different enough. But we try to do good." Eddie smiled, but it was tense, and his knuckles were white as he gripped the handrail. He glanced at the ceiling, then the floors and walls. Perrin took a wild guess that it was not being around him that made the young man nervous. It was the small space.

Indeed, it suddenly felt very warm inside the elevator. Hot, even, as though he stood in front of an open oven. Perrin shifted on his feet, uncomfortable—and smelled something burning. A whisper of smoke drifted upward from behind the young man. Eddie's face drained of color.

"Um," Perrin said.

"Almost there," Eddie replied tightly, staring at his feet like he was going to be sick. "Sorry."

Perrin wasn't certain he wanted to know what Eddie was apologizing for. He was more relieved than he wanted to admit when the doors finally opened and the young man rushed out, cold air pouring into the elevator in his wake. Eddie leaned against the nearest wall, breathing hard. No more smoke, but on the back of his shirt there was a new hole, singed black around the edges. Perrin had trouble looking away from it.

He forced his gaze past the young man, taking in the un-
decorated hall—and beyond that, immense floor-to-ceiling
windows. The lights of downtown glittered on the other side
of the glass, only slightly obscured by the golden reflection
of a lamp burning on a low table. He also heard shouting,
but the words blurred together. Too many voices.

Wary, he stopped beside Eddie. Surprised, again, by the
heat radiating off his body. "You all right?"

The young man nodded though his shoulders remained
hunched. "I was sick for a while. Getting better."

He sounded embarrassed. Perrin considered pretending
that nothing had happened—no smoke, no heat—but he had
leaned on his own share of walls, ill and alone, and frightened. Some suffering was universal.

"It'll pass," he said. "Whatever it is."

Eddie peered over his shoulder, his gaze weary, old.
At the end of the hall, a hulking figure stepped into view.
Perrin felt again that sense of ugly premonition, just a tickle
in his mind, followed by a short throb within the hole at the
base of his skull.

Eddie followed Perrin's gaze and pushed himself off the
wall. "Roland. Mr. O'doro is here to see you."

"You okay?" asked the man, ignoring Perrin.

Eddie shrugged, still tense. And, too, there was something else in his eyes when he looked at the man who stood
at the end of the hall.

Anger, thought Perrin, his fingers curling against his
palm, a loose fist, which he hid against his thigh. He had
rarely fought with his hands before coming on land, never
fought much at all. As a child, defiance had been discour-
aged in numerous, painful ways. As an adult, no one had
dared confront him.

But all that had changed, in the end—and he had learned
hard lessons over the past eight years.

"Go rest," said the man to Eddie. "I'll take care of this."

Eddie shook his head and gave Perrin a measuring

look—or a silent warning. Made him uneasy, either way. He strode past Eddie, footsteps light, ready for anything.

"M'cal contacted me," said the other man gruffly, as Perrin approached. "Months ago. Said there might be a time—"

"—when I need someone like you," Perrin interrupted coolly. "Yes, I know."

The man—*Roland*—made a small, dissatisfied sound. He was tall by human standards, though several inches shorter than Perrin. Broad like a bear, grizzled. His brown hair needed a cut, and though he didn't sport a beard, the bristles around his neck would be long enough for one in a day or two. His dark eyes were bloodshot, and his checked flannel shirt and sweatpants were wrinkled. He smelled like beer.

Not impressive in the slightest.

Roland looked him up and down, his gaze flat, as though he found Perrin just as lacking. "Come on. We'll try not to scare you away."

Perrin held his tongue and followed the man. Eddie remained a short distance behind, a silent, warm shadow. They passed through a large room filled with antiques, couches, and books—newspapers scattered on tables, most of them printed in different languages. Perrin smelled something sweet, like hot pie, and heard pots clanging beneath an exasperated tangle of voices. The argument, which had faded, seemed to be starting again. It got louder when Roland turned to walk down a narrow flight of stairs.

"It's ridiculous, and you know it," snapped a woman, but whatever else she was going to say choked into silence when Perrin reached the bottom of the stairs.

He found a kitchen. Quite possibly the largest he had ever seen, dominated by those immense·floor-to-ceiling windows. The entire floor felt as though it were floating in the heart of the city—a sensation enhanced by the shadows enveloping almost everything except the kitchen core: long counters, numerous glass-fronted refrigerators, gleaming golden tile set in the wall, and other copper accents. Nearby, a pit of deep couches surrounded a gas fireplace. And on his right, a cream-colored curtain covered the entire wall. A gap in the center revealed more glass and darkness on the other side. Not the city. A separate room.

Fleeting impressions. And, for a moment, the only things his mind could handle. Because, despite what he was—what he had been—it was too hard, too impossible, to accept the presence of the two people before him.

One of whom was not human.

Perrin saw the gargoyle first. Impossible not to. Perched on an iron stool, he was huge, his leathery wings hanging loose down his back and trailing against the stone floor. Silver skin, red, glinting eyes; a glimpse of horns from within the long thick hair bound away from his craggy face. He wore human clothes, which was an incongruous sight— straining T-shirt, jeans—and he held a stainless-steel thermos in his clawed hand.

He gave Perrin a look that was wary but unafraid, and quietly assessing—his reaction as much of a surprise as his presence. Perrin would not have been so calm if strangers found him in his sea form. Even now, he struggled.

A woman sat on the counter beside the gargoyle, her bare feet balanced on his thigh. She was muscular and round, with smooth brown skin and a mane of tight dark curls that brushed past her shoulders. She gave Perrin a sharp look and glanced at the gargoyle.

"Told you," she said; and then, to Roland: "Don't even think about using this as a distraction."

He rubbed the back of his neck. "We're done talking."

"I think not," said the gargoyle. "You know what the Consortium has done, again and again, to others. Experiments, kidnappings—and this latest incident in Africa —"

"Breeding programs," snapped the woman, pressing her fists hard into the counter. "We have to go after them, Roland. I don't know why we haven't already."

"It won't stop, otherwise," rumbled the gargoyle. "And if they continue to recruit the people I think they are, it's only going to get worse. If they involve witches—"

"Enough," snapped Roland. "We have a guest."

"Don't," Perrin muttered, giving him a cold look.

The grizzled man raised his brow. "Excuse me?"

Perrin swept his gaze over the room, trying to make sense of its inhabitants, deciding it didn't matter. Air breathers, all of them. "I don't know what is going on here, but the woman is right. Don't make me your distraction. Don't make me part of this."

Roland laughed, but it was a bitter sound. "You sought us out. You're not human. That makes you a member of the club, whether you like it or not."

"Leave him alone," said Eddie.

Perrin released the breath he had been holding. "I've come to the wrong place."

"Just the wrong time," replied the gargoyle, with unexpected gentleness. He scooted off the stool and helped the woman from the counter by wrapping his arm around her waist and lifting her carefully down. She remained pressed against his side, which surprised Perrin. And made his heart ache, just a little.

There was a woman who had once fitted against his side, just so even if she had existed only in his dreams. Every night, growing with him inside his head, from childhood to adulthood—becoming a woman who had saved his life in more ways than he could name.

Until eight years ago, when he had stopped dreaming of her.

Stop, he told himself; and then: *Nothing about this place should surprise you.*

He, who was not human, who had come from a world no human—or gargoyle—could survive, should not have found anything at all shocking about this place, or these people.

The woman, however, suddenly winced—reaching back to rub the base of her skull. Much as he caught himself doing, at that exact moment. The similarity made him uneasy. Especially when she fixed him with a hard look that softened, after a disquieting moment, into compassion.

And worse, pity.

"I'm sorry," she said softly. "You should brace yourself."

"No time," murmured Roland, also studying him. "Never enough time."

Perrin's head ached. He stared into the faces of strangers and felt so utterly alone he could hardly breathe. Being here was too much. Too much, too soon. He needed air.

"I need to go," he croaked to Eddie, and without another word, turned and began to climb the stairs.

Or tried to. Someone was standing on the landing above him.

Another young man, tall, with golden skin, golden eyes, and thick black hair cut with streaks of silver and ocean blue. He held pizza boxes, but they started to slip out of his hands when he saw Perrin.

"No," he whispered, shaking his head. "Not you."

Perrin felt like saying the same thing. He sagged against the rail and dug the heel of his palm into his throbbing skull. Lights flickered in his vision, followed by waves of darkness. He fumbled for the vial of seawater shoved into his front pocket.

He felt very old. Bone tired. This was not what he had expected—or needed. Destiny, he thought, was cruel.

"Rik," Perrin murmured, unable to bear the sight of the shape-shifter's familiar face. "We both should have run farther."

Eddie ran up the stairs to the young man, who turned away from him with an expression of pure agony. Perrin sympathized. He heard movement at his back, then a hush. Everyone, staring at him.

Green eyes. A voice, screaming.

Darkness rising.

"What," rumbled the gargoyle, "is going on here?"

Perrin drank the last of his seawater. It burned his throat

going down. Wiping his mouth with the back of his hand, he glanced over his shoulder and studied the strangers watching him. They would have to be enough. There was no one else.

"Millions of people are going to die," he whispered. "And I need your help to stop it."

CHAPTER THREE

H ER headache wouldn't go away.

Jenny was on her fourth ibuprofen and was considering downing another two. Chased with vodka, maybe. Reading was no distraction, either, no matter how much she loved Jane Austen. *Pride and Prejudice* usually took her mind off all her problems, including aches and pains, but even Mr. Darcy could do nothing for the incessant throb at the base of her skull. It was beginning to feel like someone was drilling into her brain.

It was late, or very early—almost four in the morning—though time had ceased to mean much to Jenny. Sun rose, sun set, and in between she studied mysteries. Searching for truths, history, that had been relegated to myth and superstition. Just last week they had been in Vietnam, exploring Ha Long Bay for evidence of a sea monster rumored to terrorize fishermen. Two months before that, *The Calypso Star* had anchored in the Aegean Sea, helping another team from *A Priori* recover a two-thousand-year-old wreck filled with enough artifacts to keep the researchers in the company's archaeology department busy for years.

Never about the money, her grandfather would say. *We don't do this for the money. Just knowledge. Preservation.*

Liar, thought Jenny, touching the worn leather pouch

resting on her chest. She turned it over, shaking, and a single scale tumbled free.

His scale. Smaller than the other three she had found, but that made sense. He had been young, a child. His scale, however, was the same as the others in its thickness—hard as shell, silken surface shimmering, glowing, in the dim lights of her cabin. She stroked it with the tip of her finger and closed her eyes, filled with an ache that had burned inside her since that day on the beach. More than sixteen years suffering some delusional, inexplicable need that would never be satisfied.

It was stupid.

But here she was.

You're using this as an excuse to run away, she told herself. *You bury yourself in something you'll never have, because that's safer, right?*

If Jenny could have flipped herself the finger, she would have. Instead, she slipped the scale into the pouch, sat up, and dropped the whole thing into her desk drawer. Her laptop screensaver winked at her. She had that article to finish writing on Ha Long Bay. No mention of sea monsters, thank-you-very-much.

Jenny frowned. The locals also told tales of underwater people. Several had seen pale human faces in the sea, usually in the evening, there and gone like ghosts. The fishermen called them ghosts—souls of the drowned trapped between human and . . . something else. Dragon, some said. Serpent. Cursed by the spirit of Lac Long Quang, Dragon King of the Sea—a shape-shifter—whose union with the faery, Au Co, had produced mortal and immortal descendants still said to live amongst humans.

Jenny knew just a little too much about the world to dismiss all of that as complete myth. The shape-shifter part, anyway. And immortals. Maybe faeries, too.

Right. She needed a drink.

But one thing first.

Jenny prowled from her cabin to the lab. It was very quiet.

She doubted that Maurice was asleep, or Les—but Ismail had disappeared early in the evening, claiming fatigue.

The sleeping pills that Maurice had dropped into his wine might have contributed to that. No offense to the man, but Jenny couldn't risk his getting nosy. Ismail might be good at procuring rare plants and animals, but world-altering secrets were something else entirely. No confidentiality agreement could guarantee that level of trust. If the woman's body had been more obviously nonhuman, different precautions would have been put into place. Namely, the complete and utter ruination of Ismail Osman's career—but only if he talked. The family had *some* morals. Just not many.

Nothing was out of place in the lab, which on another ship would have been the stateroom. Jenny shrugged on the hooded gray sweatshirt hanging on a wall hook and keyed in the code to the cold locker.

It was a glorified walk-in refrigerator, built to hold all the biological samples they collected while at sea. Larger than average, because *A Priori* liked to be prepared for any contingency. Including bodies.

The body bag had been strapped to a stainless-steel table that unfolded from an alcove in the wall. Jenny stood at the door, staring—chilled by more than the cold air. She had to force herself to take the first step, but after that it was easier. She even managed to unzip the bag without hesitating.

The woman's hair had been cleared from her face, which was turned slightly to the side. Under the bright light, her skin was waxy, ghost white, and covered in a thin rime of salt and frost. Her eyes were closed. Just looking at her, it was hard to imagine anything more than a dead human woman. No magic. No impossibilities.

You could tell yourself she isn't a mermaid, that this isn't the closest you've come to one in almost sixteen years.

She could do that. She could pretend that the firsthand accounts of the fishermen and the scale she had found meant nothing. She could pretend that this woman's coloring and bone structure did not resemble the most treasured memory of her childhood. She could lie to herself, like some people already thought she did—and live the safe, comfortable, illusion of a normal life. As much as her family allowed her.

No one forces you to take their money or use their resources. You stay within their reach because you need them.

Needed them because she could do some good with that long *A Priori* reach. Use all those connections and power to make a positive difference.

And search for mysteries. One mystery, in particular.

"I wish I knew your name," Jenny murmured to the dead woman—and thought again about that boy from so many years ago. He might as well have been Peter Pan: always a boy to her, forever young. She hoped he was still alive, somewhere. That the man who had dragged him back into the sea hadn't killed him.

Is that what happened to you? Jenny wondered at the woman. *Your kind hurt each other the same way humans do?*

She unzipped the bag even farther, and pulled the edges apart. Little of the woman's body had been left untouched, but down, to the left of her stomach, she noticed something odd. Puncture wounds, one of them half-hidden by the deep cuts that had exposed her hipbone.

Jenny pulled the overhead light close and unfolded the massive magnifying glass attached to the stem. There were four puncture marks, perfectly round and small. Like she had been shot with tiny arrows. Or darts. Three of them had gone straight through.

Deep inside the fourth, a metallic gleam.

Jenny went looking for latex gloves and forceps. Bending close, holding her breath against her headache, she managed to get a grip on the lodged object, and pulled it slowly out.

Took forever. The object was almost one and a half inches long, with a smooth bottleneck case at the base and the main body tapering into a semisharp point that resembled the end of a knitting needle. Not much wider than one, either. A serial number had been etched into the side.

"Shit," she muttered. Her first thought was the fishermen, but this was a high-quality piece of ammunition, distinct enough that she recognized it almost immediately. These bullets were made for only one type of gun—an SPP–1M underwater pistol, which was still used by the Russian Navy Special Forces. It was a relatively easy weapon to handle, very effective underwater. They had two such guns on board. Last time she had checked, a person could buy them online.

Someone had fired on this woman. Someone—presumably human—had gotten close enough to shoot her in the stomach.

And then what? Slice her up, Freddy Krueger style?

Not the fishermen. None of them had carried a gun like that, and she was pretty damn sure one of them would have been showing it off, given the reception on the beach.

No. This gun had been fired in the water, close, controlled shots, by someone who knew what they were doing.

The throbbing at the back of her head grew worse, more terrible than the spike of any migraine. Jenny briefly closed her eyes, nauseous.

You need a doctor. This isn't normal.

No shit. None of this was normal. Jenny needed to find Maurice, show him these bullets. If humans had been involved with the death of a nonhuman. . .

It would have taken more than luck to kill this woman.

Jenny dropped the bullet onto a metal tray and put away the forceps. When she began to zip up the body bag, she noticed something else odd. A thumbprint along the edge of the dead woman's jaw.

It was incredibly faint. Less a print than a disturbance in the fine sheen of salt and frost that covered her skin. Jenny only noticed because of the way the light fell upon her face. Someone had touched her in the hours since she had been brought on board.

Les, she thought instantly. *Not Maurice*. He might have access to the cold locker, but the old man had not been near the lab today. He had spent the afternoon fishing and baby-sitting Ismail. Les was the one she had seen coming out of the cold locker.

Les had touched the body.

It wasn't a crime, and it shouldn't have bothered Jenny. But it did. She attempted to arrange her hand as Les might have, trying to understand what he had been doing. It wasn't a simple touch—like some kid poking a dead bird to see if it moved. The angle was wrong for that. It was as though he had been trying to turn her head.

Jenny began to do just that—and heard a scratching sound behind her. She flinched, heart in her throat, and whirled around.

It was Maurice, peering at her through the glass in the locker door. Brow furrowed, eyes narrow with concern. A moment later she heard a beep, and the lock opened.

"I was looking for you," he said, walking in and shutting the door behind him. "When you weren't in your room, I got worried."

"Worried."

"I had a bad dream," Maurice said vaguely, but Jenny straightened, giving him a questioning look. He made a dis-gusted sound and waved his hand through the air. "No, I don't know what it meant. Made no sense. Just . . . water. And you, drowning."

"Not a premonition, then."

"Didn't say that." He gave her a hard look. "I've had an uneasy sense of things for days now, sweet pea. Got worse today after you came back from that long dive of yours."

Jenny tried to smile, but both the headache and the dead woman conspired against her. She swallowed hard, and mut-tered, "I found something that won't make you feel better. Look what I pulled out of the woman."

She handed him the plastic bag, and the old man held it beneath the light, staring hard at the bullet. He said nothing for a long time.

"SPP–1M," he finally muttered.

"Four shots to the left of her stomach."

"She was murdered, then." Maurice drew in a ragged breath. "The fishermen—"

"Makes no sense. You'll agree if you think about it."

He went quiet again, but after several minutes—during which time Jenny leaned against the cold wall, trying not to pass out from her headache—he nodded slowly. "Theories?"

Jenny forced her jaw to relax. "There's a reason why these creatures are considered myth. They're impossible to find. So what would it take to get close enough to *shoot* one? Let alone cut one up?"

"The Consortium is the only group I know of that hunts nonhumans. But they usually want their targets alive." Maurice fingered the bullet through the plastic bag. "I need to check our guns."

The same thought had crossed her mind. "Les was in here earlier. Unless you've got a thing for corpses now, I think he was handling the body." She felt dirty saying the words, like she was a kid tattling tales.

Maurice gazed down at the woman's face. His hand, again, traced the sign of the cross over his chest. "That doesn't sit well with you."

"No. I don't know why. I trust him."

"As much as you trust anyone." Maurice smiled humorlessly. "He told me you rejected him. Again."

Jenny blew out her breath. "Les needs to keep his mouth shut."

"Won't argue with that." The old man flashed her a crooked, far more genuine, smile—though it faded quickly. "He was in my dream, too."

"Yeah?" Jenny closed her eyes, bowing her head to rub her neck. She felt something warm and slippery. When she drew back her hand, there was blood on her fingers.

She swayed. Maurice hissed between his teeth, and spun her around.

"Fuck," he said.

"W-what?" Jenny asked, dazed.

"There's blood running down your neck. I can't see . . ." His fingers pushed roughly into her hair at the base of her skull. And froze.

"Oh, my God," he whispered.

"Maurice," she rasped, and then winced as the pain suddenly changed—feeling more like teeth digging into her skull rather than some vague vascular ache.

"There's something attached to you," he said, and dragged her toward the door. In moments he had her out in the lab. Drawers began sliding open before he even approached the workstation, and a tweezers and scalpel floated upward, jerkily—as though caught on invisible fishing lines. Maurice snatched them out of the air, muttering to himself.

"Uh, no," Jenny said, pointing to the blade.

"You didn't see what I just did."

"Then give me a mirror." When he didn't move fast enough, Jenny blew past him out of the lab, racing down the hall toward her cabin. She slammed into her bathroom, nearly yanking the drawer entirely out of the cabinet as she pawed through Band-Aids, lotions, tampons—down to the bottom, where she kept the makeup she sometimes wore when she went ashore. She snapped open a compact and twisted around, trying to make out the back of her head reflected in the larger wall mirror.

Hard, at first. Her hair was thick, tangled. All she could see was blood, trickling down her neck. But then Maurice loomed over her, and reached around to part her hair in the back. His hands were rough, trembling, and his breath smelled like beer.

She saw the color green, first—and thought it must be her imagination. Not just any green, but a pale sea-green turquoise that reminded her of the clear waters in some island lagoon. She reached around, fumbling, and touched the thing. It was the size of her thumbnail, flat, hard as shell—smooth, even slick—and hot to the touch.

Jenny swayed and took a deep breath. "It looks . . . it looks like an echinoderm. A sand dollar. It has . . . it has a similar rigid external skeleton."

"Looks like it's sucking your blood," Maurice muttered, and turned her around. "Makes it a parasite to me."

Jenny normally resisted classifying anything without a detailed analysis, but in this case she was willing to make an exception—of the *oh-shit* variety. She could *really* feel its teeth now—digging deeper into her.

"When I was in the water . . . I thought something touched the back of my neck. I told myself it was my imagination. I didn't feel a bite, or anything. Just . . . a headache. I've had a headache ever since."

Maurice didn't say a word. He tilted the back of her head toward the light. He did not need to tell her to hold still.

He tried the tweezers first. Jenny felt him trying to angle them under the organism, but she could tell without looking that there was no space between the edges and her flesh.

"You're going to have to cut it out," she snapped, knuckles white as she gripped the edge of the counter. But all he did was mutter angrily, forcing her head down. She felt the moment he finally managed to pierce her skin and get a grip on the thing—but the pain that hit her seconds later felt like an explosion consuming the entire length of her spine. She seized, breath stolen, unable to scream, her vision wiped out in a cloud of white light.

When Jenny could finally see again, the world was twisted, upside down. Wrong angles.

She was on the floor, her cheek pressed to the tile. Maurice crouched beside her, holding something soft against the back of her neck. There was a ringing sound in her ears, and her entire spine—and skull—throbbed in time with her heartbeat.

She exhaled slowly. Wiggled her toes and fingers. Swallowed, and opened and closed her eyes. Not paralyzed, then. But it felt as though she should be.

"Maurice," she breathed.

"You need a hospital," he murmured raggedly. "I thought . . . I thought it would come right off like a tick, but when I yanked I saw . . . tendrils of *something* . . . linking it to your body. Your reaction—"

"Still attached?" interrupted Jenny hoarsely.

"Yeah. I even tried using this old thing"—he tapped his brow—"but it's embedded too deep. I could feel it, sweet pea. Burrowed all the way down to your spinal cord. And I think it's still . . . growing."

She managed to roll over enough to look into his eyes. "You're fucking kidding me."

Maurice's face looked terrible, as though ten minutes had aged him ten years. He didn't have a decade to spare. Jenny tried to sit up, and he helped, still compressing the back of her neck. He guided her hand until she touched a towel.

"Hold that," he growled, raking her over with his blood-shot gaze. "I'm gonna get Les to sit with you, then I'm steering us for the nearest port. The office should be able to send a helicopter from Singapore for a medevac."

Jenny wanted to protest but forced herself to stay quiet and nod. She had never seen anything like this creature. Never mind the poisons it could be pumping into her bloodstream—the fact that trying to remove it had felt rather close to *killing her* was enough to scare Jenny shitless.

Maurice left at a run, shouting for Les. She didn't hear a response, and the boat wasn't so large that voices wouldn't travel. He kept calling for the other man, until suddenly, abruptly, he went silent. She waited, listening hard. Heard nothing else.

Jenny managed to stand, swaying as her vision briefly blurred. After several steps everything cleared. She could walk.

She left her quarters. The door to Les's room was open, but he wasn't there. Neither was Ismail. She pushed onward, heading for the stairs that led to the bridge. She had to pass the main deck, at the back of which was the only access point to the interior of the ship. Given their proximity to the

Strait of Malacca and other known pirate territory, that door was kept locked at night. Always.

It was standing wide open.

"Maurice?" Jenny called up the stairs, but the old man didn't answer from the bridge. Unease prickled through her. She walked through the galley and salon, stopping briefly to crouch by one of the love seats. She tossed the bloody towel to the floor and fumbled behind the chair until her fingers hit a loose panel. She removed it, one-handed. Found a pistol.

Fully loaded, ready to fire. Weapons were hidden all over the ship. It was illegal to carry firearms into the ocean territories of most countries, but random searches from customs agents had never found their caches.

Holding the gun in a solid two-handed grip, Jenny ignored the open door and made her way to the stairs leading up to the bridge. There was another door on that level that could be locked from the inside as a secondary barrier in case of an emergency. She, Maurice, and Les had run through the plan a hundred times, in about as many different variations. Control of the ship and radio had to be maintained at all costs. Even a hint of trouble—that was where they would meet.

Her head hurt like hell, but she kept her breathing steady and clicked the safety off the gun. A freighter had been hijacked a week ago, less than one hundred miles from here—crew thrown overboard and cargo stolen. The same had happened to a pleasure cruise near Indonesia, but the couple who had arranged the tour was less fortunate. Held for ransom, she'd heard. Same group of pirates, or different—it didn't matter. Theft, kidnapping, and death had become big business, and the larger the haul, the more powerful the criminal organization behind it.

The Calypso Star was worth millions. And so were Jenny and her crew.

Opportunists, she told herself, edging up the stairs. *Nothing more than that. No one knows who you are. If the ship was boarded, then it's by men with guns and a motorboat, thinking you're easy pickings. No conspiracy. No betrayal. Just bad luck.*

Bad luck that the outer door was open, and Maurice hadn't answered her call. Bad luck that Les and Ismail weren't in their cabin. Bad luck there was a parasite of unknown species attached to her neck, and a murdered mermaid in the cold locker.

Right. Jenny was fucked.

She reached the top of the stairs. All she could hear was the sound of her own breathing. Her palms were sweaty as she tightened her grip on the gun.

Go, she told herself. *Go, go, go.*

So she did, keeping low as she spun around the top of the stairs, searching for Maurice, Les—anyone.

All she saw was a fist driving toward her face.

Then, darkness.

SHE WAS ON THE BEACH AGAIN. DOWN BY THE BIG HOUSE in Maine. She could see it in the distance, a hulking gray shadow on the golden sand, embedded beside the water instead of on the hill. Waves pulsed around the porch, breaking against the eastern wall. The windows were broken and dark, and there was blood on the porch. She could see that even from where she stood, which felt miles away and too close. The blood was wet. She smelled it on the wind. Like poison.

Someone stood beside her. She could not see him, but she had a sense of his size, and he was quite tall. Tall and warm. His hand was huge, gentle, as it scooped up hers in a loose grip. She knew him before he spoke, and began to tremble, weak in the knees with relief.

"Dreams are odd," he said quietly, in a voice so familiar she wanted to weep. "I never know what's real. Except for what I feel. I tell myself that can't be a lie."

"You were always an optimist," she whispered.

"Only with you." His lips brushed against the top of her head, and she closed her eyes, sagging against that hard, strong shoulder.

"It's been a long time," she said, wondering why it mattered. This was just a dream. He was only a dream.

Such a long time since she had dreamed of *him*.

"Eight years," he murmured, with a hint of wonderment. "I went eight years without you in my sleep. And now . . ."

He stopped. She heard a roaring sound and turned to face the ocean. A wave was bearing down on them, so large it threatened to block the sun.

And then it did.

It was too close to escape. No chance in hell. But the man grabbed her tight, spinning them around in a stumbling run. His arm was strong around her waist, and he was yelling something she couldn't understand. She felt a breath of cold damp air against her neck, and the man slammed her in front of him, dropping into a crouch over her body. His mouth pressed hard against the back of her neck.

"Breathe," he whispered, just as the tsunami hit them.

The impact was immense. No pain, just an all-encompassing, dizzying pressure that was so intense she felt as though she were being squeezed to death inside a giant shaking fist. A scream jerked loose, and her mouth filled with water. She struggled, fighting to salvage what breath was left in her lungs, but the sea poured in and in and in, and there was no end to the hole that her body formed. She could not breathe. She was drowning.

And those arms around her were gone.

She heard shouts in the water. A man, screaming in rage. Not her dream man—the dream boy who had become her dream man—but someone else, whose voice she knew but could not name. Just that it was close.

So close, she woke up.

No delay, no grogginess. Jenny snapped to consciousness riding a rush of adrenaline that left her gasping for air, tears leaking from the corners of her eyes. The pressure on her body wasn't gone, though—just displaced. Someone was sitting on her back, tying her hands.

Jenny pushed her forehead into the ground and twisted

with all her strength, dragging up her leg to give herself enough leverage to turn over and knock aside the person holding her down. In theory, anyway. She managed to surprise her assailant enough that he loosened his grip on her hands and slid partially off her. Jenny tried to roll away, but the man grabbed her waist and shoulder, slamming her down so hard the side of her face bounced with bruising force against the deck. The impact stunned her into a moment's stillness—long enough for him to finish tying her hands.

She was outside. It was still night. That was all she could tell. Something covered her eyes. Her sweatshirt—she had never taken it off, and at some point the oversized hood had flopped over her head. Sweat trickled, and a solid throbbing ache traveled from the base of her skull down her spine in nauseating waves.

The man tying her did not make a sound. When he finally stepped away, she tried to roll over. This time no one stopped her. She tilted her head, peering from beneath the hood.

Ismail stood over her.

His glasses were gone, but he was wearing his paperpusher clothes from earlier: slacks, loose white dress shirt; unbuttoned and untucked, revealing a rock-hard body that looked as though it should belong to a soldier instead of a pseudo-desk jockey. He was barefoot. Blood spattered his clothes and chest. His eyes were . . . so cold. So cold she wanted to look away and scream though she kept her gaze locked on his and bore the fear.

"I knew about the sleeping pills," he said quietly. "Maurice was not careful enough."

Jenny said nothing. Ismail crouched, graceful and silent, and rapped the deck in front of her face with his knuckles. Sharp, loud, staccato. She saw a gun holstered beneath his shirt. She remembered that he had come on board with a duffel bag. *Extra clothes,* he had said. *Money for the fishermen.*

Do you know who I work for?" he asked. "Answer me. I want to hear you say it."

Go to hell, thought Jenny, afraid of what her voice would sound like if she unclenched her jaw.

Ismail's eyes narrowed. He touched her face, brushing his fingers over her split lip. He smelled like blood. Jenny wrenched her head away, and he grabbed a fistful of her hair, pinning her down with all his weight. He wasn't much larger than her, but he was all muscle—and untied. Her ear felt crushed against the salt-encrusted deck.

"Where's the man?" asked Ismail in a deadly quiet voice. "Your lover?"

Les. But if he wanted to know where Les was, that meant the blood had come from. . .

"Maurice," she croaked.

"Telekinetic. Not a strong one, but he had to go first." Ismail said the words in a matter-of-fact tone, dry and cold. It was something he should not have known about Maurice. No one knew that much, except the family and a few trusted individuals. He leaned sideways, and pointed.

It took Jenny a moment to see. Shadows everywhere. But one shadow was darker than the others, shaped like a body. Maurice. Sprawled on the deck. She couldn't see his face, but she saw his white hair. He was so still.

Jenny closed her eyes, fighting to keep her breathing steady. Her heart was beating too quickly. Pressure, building inside her skull. She was going to burst, die, lose her mind. Her throat swelled with grief, but she sucked down a deep breath and ground her teeth. No tears. Not yet.

"Make this easy on yourself," Ismail whispered close to her ear. "You don't want me to think you're capable of anything."

"I'm capable of killing you," she breathed, finally able to speak. "You stupid son of a bitch."

Ismail leaned back, giving her a cold look. "You lied about the creature being human. But even if you hadn't, this would still be happening. You're a loose end, Ms. Jameson. But the Consortium finally has a need for you."

Behind him, something moved in the shadows near Maurice's body. Jenny didn't dare look. Ismail was still talking, but she could hardly hear him past the roar of blood in her ears. All she could do was stare at his face, and shift her legs, ready to kick, fight, roll—anything. Anything it would take.

She was ready when Les lunged out of the shadows. He was completely naked and dripping with seawater. He held a knife in his hand, and swung it down with perfect accuracy toward Ismail's back. The man must have felt him coming—he glanced over his shoulder at the last moment, and rolled sideways with incredible speed. His fists were a blur. He caught the other man in the gut and face, but Les hardly seemed to notice. He had a longer reach, and was just as fast. He feinted—Ismail backed too close to Jenny—and she kicked up and out with all her strength, catching him in the back of his knee.

Ismail staggered. Les plunged the dagger in his chest, and held on—held on as the smaller man dropped to his knees, screaming in pain. There was an expression on Les's face that Jenny had never seen before—wild and determined, and utterly ruthless.

He twisted the knife as Ismail reached up to grab it. Twisted, and pushed, until the man lay on the deck of the yacht, and died.

Jenny shuddered, afraid to breathe. Les stared at the dead man for one long moment, then looked at her.

"You okay?" he asked hoarsely, and all she could do was nod.

Les hesitated, then looked down at his hands and wiped them slowly on his damp thighs—leaving streaks of blood against his skin. Jenny expected him to untie her, but instead he walked across the deck toward Maurice. He stared at the old man, too—a long time. And then bent down and scooped him into his arms.

Jenny stared, unsure what she was seeing. Maurice had

to weigh at least two hundred pounds, but Les acted like it was nothing. Instead of carrying him toward Jenny, he started walking to the edge of the yacht.

"Les," she croaked. "Les, what are you doing?"

He ignored her, and in his arms, Maurice stirred. She was certain of it, despite the darkness on deck. His eyelids fluttered, and his mouth opened, just a little. She heard a groan.

"Les," she shouted, more urgently. "Les, stop. Look at me."

Les kept walking. Faster now. Maurice began to open his eyes.

"He's still alive!" she screamed. "Les—"

He tossed the old man overboard.

Jenny barely heard the splash, choking on her own voice—too horrified to do more than stare at Les's back, watching that scene replay in her head again and again.

Les stared over the edge, then turned around to walk back to her. She tried scooting away from him, but he grabbed her ankles and pulled her close with ruthless efficiency. His mouth was set in a grim line, though his eyes . . . his eyes were no longer cold. Just weary.

"I'm sorry," Les whispered, and Jenny wanted to kick him in the teeth.

"You're working with them," she whispered. "The Consortium."

"No." He shook his head, and drew in a long, ragged, breath. "This is . . . something else. Ismail was . . . a complication I didn't expect."

Jenny tested her bonds. Her wrists and shoulders ached, and tears finally leaked from her eyes. She couldn't stop them. This hurt too much. "Why?"

He didn't answer. Just stood, and grabbed Ismail's arms. He dragged the man across the deck, leaving behind a trail of blood, and threw him overboard as well.

"*Why?*" Jenny screamed at him, though her voice was muffled with grief.

Les still said nothing. He walked back to her, and she said brokenly, "You'll be caught. You know that. It doesn't matter who's protecting you now. When the others find out—"

"I'm not scared of the old women," Les interrupted, but his voice hitched on the last word, and his hands trembled. "Not scared of the family, or any . . . any of those maniacs they employ. I'm done with that."

"Bullshit," she said.

Les shook his head. "No one's going to find you, Jenny. They won't even know you're in trouble. And if they do figure it out, it'll still be too late."

"Les—"

"I'm sorry," he said again, his voice cracking. "I'm so sorry. You don't understand. You don't have a fucking clue. You never did."

He walked away and left her on the deck in Ismail's blood.

CHAPTER FOUR

SOMEONE was shaking him.

Perrin drifted on the edge of sleep. He needed to dream. Whatever it took. If he had been in possession of pills, he would have popped a handful, just to fall unconscious and open himself to possibilities.

Like seeing *her* again.

Even now, she was just an impression—a voice, a small warm hand—but those two parts of her were as familiar as his own voice, his own hand, and he could still feel the press of her fingers entwining with his own, as though she was here, sitting beside him now.

I miss you, he thought. *Come back.*

No damn luck. That dream, the first in eight years, had been fleeting and terrifying—and ever since waking from it two days ago, screaming, he had been unable to go back to that place—or her. Cut off, again. Made him crazy. Made him want to use his fists. Again. He was still picking splinters out of his knuckles from an unfortunate encounter with a palm tree.

He opened his eyes, tapping his sunglasses to make certain they were there. It was still uncomfortably bright.

Eddie stood over him, frowning. Sun high in the sky, blazing through scattered clouds. Gulls swooped overhead, crying out their hearts. The sea glittered like a razor blade and smelled sharp, sweet. He could taste it beneath the stink of Singapore's polluted air. Unsettled him, made his skin chill, and his stomach hurt. He wanted to be sick when he thought too hard about slipping under the water. Of what he would find there.

He stared at Eddie, saw his mouth moving, and realized he hadn't caught a single word. "What?"

Eddie's frown deepened. "Everything's been arranged. We're ready."

Perrin stayed seated. "You shouldn't come with me. You *or* him. Like I told Roland, all I needed was for someone to get me here."

"I know what you told Roland." Eddie glanced over his shoulder at Rik, who sat a short distance away on manicured grass, sipping some fruity drink through a straw. "He doesn't want to be with us. But he got on the plane. I guess he made his choice."

Perrin also looked at the shape-shifter, studying the sharp angles of his face and that golden gaze, focused on some faraway spot on the ocean horizon. He held a paper napkin in his left hand, which he kept squeezing.

Eight years changes everything, Perrin thought. Rik had been hardly more than a boy the last time he had seen his human face. Eight years had aged him. Just not enough to make the young man unrecognizable.

"How did Rik find you?" he asked, unable to stifle the shock he felt at being near the shape-shifter. It was not a good sensation; he would have been happy—happily ignorant—if they had never crossed paths again.

"*We* found *him.*" Eddie gave Perrin a sharp look. "And we're going to lose our boat if we don't go now."

Perrin pushed himself off the bench. Rik also stood, ducking his head before their eyes could meet. Only when Eddie walked past and murmured in his ear did his spine straighten. He still didn't look at Perrin, though.

Eddie hefted a duffel bag over his shoulder, the air shimmering around his body, a heat wave. He seemed very young, no older than twenty or so—but that glint in his eye, especially as he stared at Perrin and Rik, never stopped being old, and slightly worn.

"I don't know what history there is between you," he said carefully. "I'm not certain I *want* to know. But if we're going to be stuck on a boat together—"

"He walks in front of me. I don't want him where I can't see him," Rik blurted out, clenching the plastic cup so hard it crushed, spurting fruit juice all over his hand. He swore, and tossed the cup on the ground.

Perrin, very calmly, bent down and picked up the trash. "If I wanted to kill you, I would have on the plane. Or in San Francisco." He walked to a garbage can that had been placed alongside the pedestrian walkway to the dock. "You are not important to me, *Rik'agoa*. You're not even a threat."

Rik took a step toward him, golden light flickering in his eyes. "Don't call me that name."

"Stop." Eddie stepped between them. "Just . . . stop."

Rik gave him a hard look, but the other young man didn't back down. Perrin watched, assessing them both, and after several seconds that dragged on far too long, he wiped sticky, juice-stained fingers on his jeans and walked away toward the dock. Rik wasn't going to stab him in the back— not yet, not with Eddie around.

Still, his neck prickled. Scars itched. Or maybe those were his new rashes. The pollution in Singapore was worse than he remembered; and the hot air made it hard to breathe. He had started coughing last night and hadn't been able to stop until he dunked himself in the tub. His chest ached every time he inhaled.

"The next boat on your left," Eddie called out from behind. Perrin did not acknowledge him—too focused on the sea beneath the dock. He had not tasted the waters, not even dunked a toe into the dark waves, though he ached to. He glanced down and saw filth, oily scum. Might well poison himself if he tried now. Nor did he dare risk revealing his presence before he was in deeper waters. Timing was the only way he would stay alive. Time enough, hopefully, to explain his return to the others who would come hunt him.

He stopped in front of a battered fishing vessel, perhaps a decade old, and quite small. Not much room belowdecks for a man of Perrin's size, but he wasn't planning on remaining on board for long. All he needed was an engine strong enough to take him out to deep sea.

Perrin glanced over his shoulder, watching Eddie and Rik approach. He felt strange again—out of body. Eight years ago, in another life, this moment would have been inconceivable. As would the idea of using human technology to travel the . . . the *surface* . . . of the sea. Seemed so wrong. Alien. Weak.

Such weakness will not be tolerated, a low voice echoed in his mind; just a memory, though it chilled him. *You will be strong, or die. You will be strong, or they will die.*

It had been a long time since Perrin had heard his father's voice inside his head. Months since he had let himself think about him with that kind of bitter self-indulgence. He didn't need any more sleepless nights, or holes punched in walls. No good ever came from letting memories of his father creep into his thoughts. Just waves of resentment, rage, hurt—and a weariness that ran soul deep.

But his father, Perrin realized, had been skirting the edges of his thoughts ever since he had made his decision to return to the sea.

If he saw him again, he had no idea what to do.

"You," said a loud voice behind him. Perrin turned and found a man crouched on the edge of the boat. Black eyes glittered, set in a bony face that was sweat-slick and brown. A tattoo of a dragon covered his shaved head, and a gold hoop dangled from his right ear.

Perrin said nothing, waiting. The man grinned, revealing a row of broken yellow teeth, and pointed at the boat. "Come, giant man. Come for a ride."

He had heard similar invitations in prison. His feet remained rooted to the dock. Eddie drew near and passed his duffel to the sailor. "This is Sajeev. He's been . . . highly recommended."

"By who?" Rik muttered, eyeing the smaller man. "The Pirate Association of Singapore?"

Eddie sighed. "He's good with secrets. *Our* kinds of secrets."

Perrin grunted and stepped aboard the vessel. Sajeev hopped gracefully out of his way, giving him that same toothy grin—not quite friendly but filled with a delighted sort of avarice that made Perrin's skin crawl. He didn't want to imagine how much this man was being paid, but he hoped it was enough to keep their throats from being cut.

Sajeev untied the lines, tossing them hard at Rik, who staggered back under the weight. Eddie smiled faintly and followed the sailor into the bridge. Perrin joined them, unwilling to leave anything with these strangers to chance—but found nothing suspicious. Just the young man, standing aside with his arms folded over his chest, watching Sajeev start the engine.

The controls were old, flecked with salt and fish scales, but duct taped to the wall was a portable stereo and an MP3 player. Sajeev tapped the device and "Highway to Hell" blared, loud enough to make Perrin flinch.

The old sailor shuffled from one foot to another, swinging his skinny hips, and began singing with the song at the top of his lungs. When he saw Perrin watching, he grinned and gave him a thumbs-up sign—that turned suddenly into a slicing motion across his throat.

"Nice," Rik said, standing in the cabin doorway. "I feel so much better."

SIX HOURS LATER, SINGAPORE WAS GONE.

Perrin stood at the rail and watched the glittering city disappear into the horizon. His memories of the place were bittersweet. He had been naked when he'd last arrived there—against his will, alone, unable to speak a single human language. A man had found him on the beach, bleeding from the back of his neck, disoriented and sobbing.

And now you're going home.

Nausea made him hold the rail and bend his face toward the sea. Salt spray touched his bare arms, and he stared down at the water, the soft waves. *The mirror,* he had been taught to call the surface. *Two worlds, separated by light and dark, skies above and skies below. And never the two shall meet.*

Bile rose up his throat. He imagined cool slick water rushing over his skin and turned away. This was so much harder than he had thought it would be, after all the years fantasizing how he might return to the ocean. Peace, he had always told himself. He would feel peace. Peace at the chance to live as himself for however long it took until others of his kind found and killed him.

But living as human was already a slow death. He couldn't even reside in freshwater lakes, of which there were many that could have accommodated one *Krackeni* male, in secret. Other *Krackeni* tolerated freshwater, but his father had taken even that from him.

He, and the old sea witch, thought Perrin. *I hate magic.*

He turned. Eddie sat behind him on a plastic lawn chair that had been bolted to the deck. His head was tilted back, eyes closed. Perrin didn't think he was asleep. Rik certainly wasn't. He stared at the sea, shoulders hunched, head hanging.

How did we end up in the same place? Perrin wondered, wishing he could ask Rik that question. But after the initial shock of seeing each other, communication had shut down. Not that it should matter. The shape-shifter was the least of his concerns.

Green eyes. A scream.

Darkness.

Perrin kept trying to think about the darkness, but those green eyes refused to be ignored. He had a feeling he should know those eyes.

You know them, whispered a small voice in his head. *You're simply afraid to admit it.*

"No," murmured Perrin, and winced as the base of his skull throbbed, just once. Like a ghost, fleeting. He held his breath, hoping it would simply go away, but the pain returned and did not stop—pulsing to his heartbeat. Perrin gritted his teeth, reached back, and traced the edge of the hole. The ache went deeper than his skull. Deeper, into his heart.

He sensed movement on his right. Rik, watching him. He looked away when Perrin turned, but then straightened and settled his gaze on him again, swallowing hard. Flinching, only a little, when Perrin set his jaw.

"Say it," Perrin said.

"I don't need to," Rik replied, searching his face. "You were on land, which means they exiled you. If they exiled you, they gutted you of everything that made you powerful."

"Not everything." Perrin forced himself to stop touching the hole in his head. The idea of showing any weakness to Rik was utterly distasteful. Unfortunately, the pain worsened: a radiating stabbing sensation. He half expected to find someone standing behind him, driving a nail into his skull. The sun seemed suddenly too bright, even with his sunglasses, a dizzying light. He heard a woman's voice break on a sob and squeezed shut his eyes.

"Hey," Rik said, sounding very far away.

Perrin gritted his teeth, trying to focus past the pain. "Go away."

"You look sick."

He sucked in a deep breath and tried to open his eyes. All he managed was a squint that left him nearly blind. He hoped his sunglasses were dark enough to hide that fact, though given Rik's wary expression, he doubted it. Perrin turned back to the rail and bent over, breathing hard. Saliva dribbled from his bottom lip.

"Shit," Rik muttered. "They did more than gut you."

"Shut up," Perrin whispered, finding the strength to wipe his mouth.

Rik drew closer. "They broke you."

Perrin's fist shot out. He was too weak to use his full strength, but he was bigger than Rik, and his aim was good, even half-blind with pain. He caught the shape-shifter across the face, knocking him against the rail so hard he almost tumbled over. Someone shouted—Eddie—but Rik turned a blazing golden eye on Perrin.

"Stole a part of your soul," he whispered, blood trickling from his cut lip. "You must have killed someone to deserve that."

Perrin snarled, and punched Rik again, pummeling through his attempt to block the blow. Each movement was agony, but he didn't stop. Every blow made him angrier, more bitter, until he was blind and deaf and dumb; until Rik—curled into a ball, covering his head—hardly seemed to exist. He was just a thing. A punching bag. Perrin hated him for it, and he didn't know why.

He reached down and hauled Rik over the rail into the sea. He splashed out of sight.

Eddie rushed forward. Smoke rose from his clothing, between his fingers. Perrin hardly noticed. Moments after Rik disappeared, a dolphin shot free of the water, graceful and powerful. Golden light shimmered against his slick body.

All Perrin felt was jealousy. Sick, brutal, heartache.

And shame.

He spun away, holding his head. Eddie said his name, but his voice was lost to the roar in his ears. He needed to lie down, fall apart. He was going to anyway. His legs were so weak.

Perrin stumbled toward the main cabin, clipping his head on the door with such force he slammed against the wall and slid to his hands and knees. He couldn't stand again, so he crawled down the short flight of stairs to the lower deck, seeking darkness, a place to hide like some wounded animal. He half expected to find blood running from his nose and ears.

He crawled until he hit another wall, and stopped, drawing his knees up to his chest. Focused on breathing, on staying alive.

You will be strong, or die.

Strong. Strong. Perrin chanted the word to himself, digging his fingers into the scars at the back of his head. This was not the worst, he told himself. He had lived the worst. He had lived.

Footsteps echoed, but he could not see who was coming. Perrin did not care. He heard shouts, voices filled with dismay, and anger—and then something sharp jabbed into his throat. He hardly noticed.

The pain faded. He fell unconscious.

PERRIN LAY ON THE BEACH AGAIN. WAVES CRASHED behind him. Bright morning, with the sun shedding a white light that was cool and clear, and did not burn his eyes. Instead, it was the rippling shimmer of the sea that hurt his vision, and he had to look away.

He felt weak. When he tried to move his legs, he found them gone, fused into a silver tail that pressed heavily into the damp sand.

A woman was beside him, her breathing soft and familiar. Perrin grappled for her hand, wishing just once he could see her face. Or her eyes. For a moment he glimpsed red hair glinting in the sun, and peace stole over him, and sorrow.

"I never thought I would find you again," said the woman. "I stopped depending on dreams."

"I stopped depending on a great many things," he murmured.

The woman made a small sound, tilting her head away from him to stare down the beach. Perrin looked, as well, and saw a battered house looming from the sand, so old it was gray and stained with mold; and a sagging porch, and broken windows that looked empty and black as shark eyes. Dread filled him when he gazed too long at the house, as though it might sprout legs and slouch across the sand to crush them both.

"That house," he said slowly, to the woman. "What is it?"

"A bad place," she whispered. "I lost someone there."

Perrin tried to see her face, but no matter how hard he tried, some terrible force compelled his gaze down, down, no higher than her white throat. He had never seen her face. "I'm sorry."

Her hand tightened in his. "It's happening again."

His pulse quickened, and he heard the echo of that sobbing scream. The woman did not seem to notice, but those green eyes flashed in his mind, and this time, they were not from his vision—but from an old memory.

Green eyes, staring at him on a beach just like this one. Green eyes, set in the face of a girl who had tried to save his life.

A human girl. Who had been kind, and unafraid. A girl who had fought for him. Fought, and come so close to losing her own life. Not a day went by when Perrin didn't think of her—the same girl who, after almost two decades, had grown into the woman with him now.

He had always known who she was. He had met her in his dreams only a day after meeting her on land. He had no idea how it had happened, but dreams never lied—and the connection between them, forged by accident, had been real to him as blood, and light, and the water in his lungs. Perrin had grown to manhood with her at his side, knowing she was alive in another world, always wondering if she thought of him in waking as much as he did of her. Torturing himself with the knowledge they could never be together.

And then, his exile. Followed by eight years of silence, without her in his dreams. Harder to bear than he could have imagined. Exile had been agony, but losing her presence in his dreams had almost killed him.

Now he had her again. He didn't want to know what that meant, or how it was possible. It shouldn't have been, after what the others had stolen from him.

It was difficult to breathe. Fear felt the same here as it did when he was awake. "Are you in danger? Where are you, outside this dream?"

"Doesn't matter," she murmured, though the quiet of her voice was tense, strained, as if she could barely bring herself to speak. "I think he's going to kill me. I really think he is."

"Don't say that. Tell me where you are."

"A boat. But I don't want to talk about it. If I remember where I am, I might wake up. I'm not ready for that."

"Tell me," he insisted, again. "Please."

"This is just a dream," she said wearily, pushing her face against his shoulder. "Nothing dreams can do."

"You didn't used to believe that." Perrin squeezed her hand—or tried to—but her fingers slipped through his. Made of air and not flesh. He twisted violently, trying to hold on to her body—or even see her face—but the beach fell out from under him, and he dropped into darkness, screaming.

He did not wake, though. Something cool flowed through the base of his skull, and the sensation sank down his spine, spreading into his bones. He floated, but could not be at ease. The woman filled him.

Green eyes.

Certainty crept slowly, starting first in his heart, threading down into his stomach until it took a roundabout path to his brain. Perrin could still recall the glitter of the sand on those pale knees and the unearthly gleam of red hair, which had seemed so alien and lovely to his color-deprived vision. He had thought, as a boy, that she must be magic.

That girl with the green eyes.

Her eyes, staring with rage. Her voice, screaming.

It was her all along. In your premonition. She's part of it. She's in trouble.

Impossible. Insane. Made no sense, no matter how loudly his intuition screamed.

Wake up, he told himself. *Wake up now. You have no time.*

Panic suffocated him. The cold air traveling through the

base of his skull faded into heat, becoming a throbbing sensation that was not pain but something worse, as though a small heart beat there.

Stole a part of your soul, Rik's voice echoed.

And Perrin thought, *Yes.*

WHEN HE WOKE, IT WAS FAST—JUST A SNAP FROM DARKness, straight into the harsh light burning from a table lamp that had no shade, only the bare bulb. He was in a very tiny room. No window, no furniture except the bed he sprawled on uncomfortably. His legs dangled so far off the thin mattress, his right foot was planted on the cool floor.

Eddie sat beside the bed, his back against the wall. Shadows darkened his eyes, and he did not smile when he looked at Perrin.

"How do you feel?" he asked, quietly.

Perrin touched the side of his neck. "Like someone gave me drugs."

"Sajeev. He took matters into his own hands."

"I was in pain, that was all."

Eddie rubbed his face, grim exhaustion making lines around his mouth that he was too young to have. "Really."

Perrin heard the condemnation in that one word—made worse, because the young man's judgment felt unsurprised, quietly disappointed. As though he was accustomed to dealing with the kind of man that Perrin had suddenly become.

Violent. Abusive.

Shame filled him, but he didn't know what to do about it. Apologies would be useless. "How is . . . Rik?"

Eddie flashed him a hard look. "Bruised. But he'll be fine."

Perrin looked down at his split knuckles. "I don't . . . I don't know why I hit him. I was just . . . so angry."

The young man stared down at his own hands, which appeared riddled with pale round scars. "That's no excuse."

"I'm not making one." Which was a lie, he realized. There was so much else he wanted to tell him. Exile. Homelessness. Prison. But blame couldn't be reassigned. Not when his knuckles ached so badly.

He began to sit up. Eddie watched him, and said, "If you had tried to kill Rik, I would have stopped you."

Perrin looked him dead in the eyes. "I would hope so."

Eddie's jaw tightened. Perrin continued to stand, but the young man stopped him again, holding out his hand. "Something happened while you were unconscious. Rik found a body while he was in the water."

Perrin froze. "A woman?"

"An old man. He's alive, barely." Eddie gave him a strange look. "Why did you think it would be a woman?"

Perrin did not answer. He stood and nearly banged his head on the ceiling. Head turned sideways, spine aching, he shuffled to the door and had to bend double to enter the hall.

"Where is he?" Perrin asked.

Eddie shadowed the doorway behind him. "Still on deck. You had the bed."

He grunted, refusing to feel guilty about that, and made his way topside. It was night. Air had cooled, and tasted sweet as the sea. Stars glittered. Thirst crowded his throat. But none of that mattered. He kept thinking about the woman.

"Here," Eddie said. Blankets had been put down, and on them lay a wrinkled, shivering wreck of a man: ashen skin, blood staining a soaked T-shirt and shorts; white hair pressed against his skull. He looked almost eighty, but it was hard to judge human ages.

Rik held a flashlight while Sajeev cut open the man's shirt. An empty water bottle stood nearby. Perrin crouched on the other side of the wounded man but looked first at the shape-shifter. The right side of his face was swollen and purple, one golden eye rimmed with blood.

"Happy?" Rik mumbled, wincing when he tried to speak.

"No," Perrin said, reminded of his own reflection after his first night in prison. No glass mirrors, just stainless steel. Distorted, twisted images.

He focused on the old man, who seemed conscious—if the white knuckles of his clenched fists were any indication. Not one sound passed through his tight cracked lips.

"Bullet hole," Sajeev announced, pointing to the puckered wound in the old man's chest. "Should have hit his heart, lungs. Don't know if it exited."

"Did," muttered the old man, suddenly.

Sajeev grinned. "Good, good. But you should be dead."

"Suck shit." He cracked open one bloodshot eye, teeth beginning to chatter. "I need a . . . phone . . . radio. S-something."

"We're getting you help." Eddie dragged a blanket over his lower legs. "Coast Guard is coming."

"N-not good enough." He tried to sit up, and screamed. Perrin placed a hand on his shoulder and held him down. Incredibly, he tried again to move, but this time swallowed his pain with a strangled whimper.

"This should be bleeding," Sajeev announced, almost to himself. "*Should* have bled out."

"Forget it," whispered the old man. "Got to . . . get Jenny."

Jenny. The name hit something in Perrin. Premonition burned. He struggled against it, but green eyes flashed, and he heard her voice. That voice, from his dreams.

A boat, she had said. *A boat.*

You're insane, he told himself. *This is impossible.*

More than impossible. But Perrin leaned in close, utterly focused on the old man's face. He squeezed his shoulder, ignoring sharp looks from the others—and squeezed again until the old man opened his eyes and met his gaze.

"This . . . Jenny," he said roughly. "Does she have red hair and green eyes?"

The old man stared. "Who the f-fuck are you?"

His fingers dug in harder. "Tell me."

Fury filled those bloodshot eyes, and fear. Perrin was flung suddenly backward, against the rail—as if swatted by a giant, invisible hand. The old man cried out at the same time, writhing. Sajeev shouted.

"Crap, he's bleeding," Rik said, reaching for a blanket. He pushed it hard against the bullet wound and gave Perrin a hateful look.

Perrin didn't bother standing. He crawled on all fours to the old man, who watched him like he was a shark coming in for the kill. Eddie stepped between them. Smoke curled from his back. Perrin didn't care.

"I'll kill you," whispered the old man. "I'll fucking snap *all* your necks if you t-touch her."

"No," Perrin said, voice strained to breaking. "If she's the woman I think she is, I will help her. I will do anything to keep her safe. You have my word."

"Bullshit." Tears of frustration gathered in his eyes. "God help me, but I won't l-let you hurt her."

"Perrin," Rik snapped. "Perrin, stop this."

Perrin searched the old man's eyes. "There was a house where bad things happened. A house near a beach. And it's happening again, those bad things."

Eddie, who had been reaching for him, hesitated. The old man's eyes narrowed, but the sharpness was fading into fatigue, and pain. "That wouldn't be a s-secret if you're C-Consortium."

Rik froze. Eddie made a small sound of disbelief. "How," he began, then stopped himself for one long, thoughtful moment.

"Sir," he continued, very deliberately. "We're not . . . them. We're part of an agency called . . . Dirk & Steele."

The old man twitched, staring—then closed his eyes. "Oh, hell."

Perrin didn't think he sounded particularly relieved. Sajeev pulled the blanket away and peered at the bullet wound. "His bleeding is slowing."

Eddie crouched. "Sir? Who hurt you?"

"Never mind that," Perrin muttered, leaning past the young man. "The woman. Where is she?"

The old man's eyes snapped open, and he focused on Perrin with new, raw intensity, a searching gaze, relentless and cold. Perrin stayed still, letting him take his fill, hiding nothing.

"Red hair, g-green eyes," he whispered finally. "That's my Jenny. She's on a boat. Been drifting a long t-time, so I don't know where. She might even be d-dead by now."

"She's not," Perrin said, thinking of his dream. "Where were you when you were attacked?"

The old man rattled off coordinates that made no sense, but Sajeev nodded as if he understood and looked at Eddie. "Many islands near that place, but the waters are deep. Good fishing. Not far, either."

"We have to go there," Perrin told him. "Right now."

Eddie grabbed his arm, fingers burning against his skin. "We need to talk."

Perrin opened his mouth to argue, but the look in the young man's eyes stopped him. He nodded once, began to stand—and a cold, grizzled hand grabbed his wrist with surprising strength. Bloodshot eyes burned into his own.

"I still need that radio," whispered the old man, but even as he said the words, his grip loosened, that crazed gaze becoming glassy, dim. Perrin caught his hand as it slipped away. The old man struggled to stay conscious, his eyes rolling around in his head, mouth moving. A visceral fight. Perrin could not look away, and a hot streak of admiration filled him. The old man was strong.

But he finally closed his eyes, and his grip went totally slack. Sajeev pressed fingers against his neck.

"Still alive," he announced. "Bleeding again."

"Telekinetic," Eddie murmured raggedly, and gave Perrin a hard look. "What is going on? I thought we were here because of a problem *in* the ocean."

"We were. We still are. But this"—Perrin steadied himself, seeing those green eyes again—"is something else. Something I didn't expect."

"Right," Rik said sarcastically. "You expect us to believe that?"

Perrin didn't answer. No good protesting. But Eddie

searched his face, shadows gathering in that old hard gaze. "Yes. I believe him."

"I need to find her," Perrin said, surprised at how his voice broke.

"And this man needs medical attention," Eddie replied. "Malaysian Coast Guard is coming. We're going to meet them. But if we go off course—"

"I know." Perrin took a deep breath and stared at the ocean. He could feel it beneath him, all around him, cold and immense and sleeping with endless power. Entering the sea would be a death sentence, but he had known that. Death now, death later.

But if the others of his kind discovered his presence, and he died too soon . . . so many would suffer. Might suffer anyway. He wasn't certain he could stop what had begun.

"I'll go alone," he said quietly, making his decision. "Just point me in the right direction."

"No." Rik stood, golden light burning in his gaze. "I don't know what the hell you think you're doing, but we came here for one thing only. You won't abandon that for some—some—"

"Woman," Perrin finished for him. *A friend,* he almost added.

Rik made a rough sound. "A woman. You going to kill this one, too?"

Perrin flinched. All he could hear for a moment was his heartbeat, the rasp of his breathing, all the essential parts of him scuttling into the dark corners of his soul. Hiding. Small. Afraid of remembering too much.

He knew which woman Rik was referring to.

But there was no way he knew about the second woman whose life Perrin had taken.

"You will never understand," he said to Rik. "I don't expect you to. I told you then I was sorry."

Rik snarled, swaying on his feet. He looked ready to kill. Under other circumstances, given the history between them, Perrin might have given him the chance. But there was a girl with green eyes on a boat who needed him, and for the first time in eight years, Perrin had a purpose beyond mere survival. His hand twitched into a loose fist.

Eddie stepped in front of him, giving them both a disgusted, weary look. "Go, Perrin. You said yourself, from the beginning, that you only needed us to get you out here. I hope this is close enough." He focused on Rik. "You going with him?"

Rik set his jaw and said nothing. Perrin smiled, grim. "Sajeev. What direction are those coordinates?"

"West," he said, holding a new bottle of water against the old man's slack mouth. "Follow the stars west, and when you hit your first island, head south."

"Might as well look for Never-Never Land," Rik muttered, which was a reference Perrin did not understand though he comprehended the meaning. These were terrible directions. A needle, as humans might say, in a haystack. But if that was all he had, then it would have to be enough.

Perrin stripped off his clothes. Sajeev began laughing quietly, which he ignored as he walked naked to the rail. Both Rik and Eddie stared as well, which bothered him only slightly more.

So few had ever seen his scars.

But that was nothing to the sea. His heart thudded, with fear and anticipation; but every step he took, every breath, cemented his resolve. Dreams had kept him alive as a child.

That dream. *That* girl.

If you're wrong? If it's not her? What are you sacrificing, for nothing but a possibility?

Perrin almost laughed out loud. Eight years, surviving on land. Eight years, living broken, trying to rebuild his heart. Utterly, unrelentingly, alone. All that had kept him going was defiance, and a small shred of hope. Hope, that one day he might find a good reason to keep on breathing, and fighting.

This was it. Even if it was a mistake or the wrong woman. Even so. He had to take that chance. Fate had conspired to create a possibility that he could not abandon.

He gripped the rail, and a dull ache settled in the base of his skull. Eddie joined him. Rik stood back, radiating tension.

"You sure about this?" asked the young man quietly. "From what you told us in San Francisco, there's a lot at stake."

Perrin glanced at him. "I was exiled from the sea for following my convictions. Not just exiled. What was done to me was . . . worse, even. But I've never been sorry for what I did. Never. I would do it again."

"This is another one of those moments, for you."

Perrin smiled bitterly. "It won't end well. But it'll be worth it."

Eddie's gaze remained steady. "Go, then. Hurry."

He nodded and sucked down a deep breath, staring at the waiting sea. Home. Death. His hands tightened, and he pulled himself over the rail. No time to second-guess.

He dove into the ocean.

CHAPTER FIVE

JENNY attacked Les the first time he untied her hands.

It was in the bathroom. She tried stabbing him in the throat with her toothbrush. He knocked her into the wall, and that was it. Les was strong. And her head was killing her. Maybe literally. Her skin prickled like she was developing a fever though the sensation soon faded.

That was the first night, only hours after Maurice's death.

The next morning, while Les fed her oatmeal, Jenny pretended to choke. This was harder to do than she had anticipated, and the result was that she very nearly did get food lodged in her throat. Enough to be convincing, anyway.

Whether or not Les believed she was actually dying, he nonetheless stood from the table—at which point Jenny leaned back in her chair and kicked him hard in the crotch. That worked long enough for her to run for the pistol he had placed on the galley counter, tantalizingly in sight.

That probably should have been her first clue. When she tried to shoot him, hands still tied behind her back, the pistol merely clicked.

"No bullets," Les said, wincing. Jenny did not have time to find a knife.

That afternoon, she finally tried talking. Les had led her out on deck, where it was sunny and warm, and placed her in a lawn chair. He also set a soft drink on the table beside her, complete with a straw, so that she could drink something if she got thirsty. She watched him open the can, so she knew it wasn't drugged—but she hated taking anything from him.

He stood at the bow, watching the sea. Islands touched the horizon, far away, but none looked familiar. Not that Jenny would recognize any.

"We have to be careful," Les said, suddenly. "I don't know if Ismail managed to radio anyone before I . . . killed him."

"You were gone," she replied. "In the water. Your skin was wet."

"I took a swim," he said shortly, but it sounded like a lie. She wanted to kick him again in the nuts, but this time with scalpels tied to her toes.

She had to settle for staring holes into the back of his head. "If you're not Consortium, then why are you doing this? I thought we were friends."

"We *are* still friends," Les replied, glancing over his shoulder at her. "That's why you're alive."

"But Maurice," she began, choking on his name—unable to finish what she wanted to say, which was fuzzy in her mind anyway. Every time she thought about the old man, coherence left her, until all that remained was sorrow and rage, and disbelief.

"I don't want to talk about him," Les whispered.

"That's not your fucking choice," Jenny replied, throat thick with grief. "He was alive and you . . . you tossed him overboard like a piece of *shark bait*."

"He drowned." Les's voice was flat. "Painless, Jenny. Better than bleeding out slowly from a gunshot wound."

"Bullshit," she whispered. "Bull. Shit. You're a fucking animal, Les. I would have preferred to stick with Ismail."

He finally turned to look at her, and his gaze was cold and weary, and hard. "Think about what they took from you, and say that again."

Jenny went still. "You don't know anything about that."

"Sure I don't." His gaze dropped to her stomach. "Not like people talk, or anything."

She almost jumped right off that chair, hands tied and everything, but forced her backside to stay glued to the wood. "Tell me why, Les. Why are you doing this?"

Les smiled grimly. "How long have you been hunting monsters, Jenny? All your life? I always wondered what put that burn in you. Never mind your family . . . that drive you've got, it's more than just some tradition. You hunger. You stay on this boat, and sail the world, because you *need* to. You need to so badly that nothing else matters." His smiled dimmed. "I need something that badly, too, Jenny."

"Something worth killing for."

"Or just finishing the job someone else started." Les walked to the equipment bin and pulled out a fanny pack that he belted around his waist. He dropped in a set of keys that had been clenched tight in his fist. "I'm going for a swim. I disabled the biometric locks for the old-fashioned kind, so don't bother with the door. Sit tight, Jenny."

Fuck you, she thought, but clamped her mouth around the straw and took a long swallow of soda. Les gave her one last glance, his expression unreadable, and climbed down the ladder into the ocean. The minute he was gone, she jumped to her feet and tried the doors to the interior. None opened, and it was no good trying to break the glass. If bullets couldn't make a dent, then neither would her elbow—or skull.

No weapons around, and the air tanks had been cleared from the equipment bin. So had the emergency ax, the flares. The only things Les had left behind were some nylon rope and a little AM/FM radio.

If only MacGyver were here, she thought dryly.

She took the radio anyway, nearly bending backward to reach into the bin for it. Hit the on switch—listened to static—and carried the thing back to the chair. Her skin was prickling again, feverish. The dull ache in her skull, which had faded but never really left, began throbbing. Not as bad as before, but even the promise of worsening pain made Jenny break into a sweat.

Reception was bad. She found only two stations that worked, even a little. One of them, luckily, was for English-speaking listeners. Like a zombie, she sat through a jaunty melody sung by a girl with sunshine in her voice, about boys and love and shit like that—but it didn't do much to distract Jenny from her problems. She didn't *want* to be distracted.

Les had betrayed her and Maurice. Not just them, but *A Priori*. And she didn't know why.

Someone killed that mermaid. Someone used a gun like the kind we have on board. He could have gone out like he did last night, in secret, while everyone slept.

But that was ridiculous. How could Les even find one of those creatures?

Maybe he's a treasure hunter, then. Black market, illegal, on the side. That is what he did before he joined the company. Old habits die hard.

Along with people he had called friends.

Jenny's throat itched. She sipped more soda. The prickling sensation worsened, and for the first time, she noticed an ache in her legs.

Fever. Muscle ache. The beginning of a sore throat.

And a parasite attached to her head. The two had to be related.

Tell him. Tell him as soon as he gets back.

And, what? What did she expect Les to do? Rip it off her head? Maurice had tried, and—no thanks—she wasn't going to attempt *that* again outside of a hospital. Jenny wasn't even certain she trusted Les to keep her alive if he knew she was sick. Might be too much trouble.

Grin and bear it, she told herself. Not much choice, anyway. She lay back on the lawn chair, trying to ignore the worsening ache in her body and head—as well as the unrelenting sun on her face, which didn't help the heat rising in her skin. She closed her eyes. The radio played. She focused on music and Maurice, mermaids and Les, trying to wrap all the pieces together. She slept, too, but did not dream.

When she woke, her neck was stiff, and her throat dry as dust. Almost took too much effort to drink the warm soda, but she managed—and settled back in the chair with a groan. Maybe she *should* talk to Les. That had to be better than leaving this parasite attached to her head. It was an unknown species, after all, and people died from less.

The radio crackled, and the news hour binged. Jenny hardly noticed the broadcaster speaking until she heard, suddenly, *Malaysia*.

"An earthquake measuring 7.6 on the Richter scale has struck deep in the ocean less than a hundred miles off Malaysia's coast," said the man on the radio. "A tsunami alert has been issued for that country, and surrounding nations."

Jenny heard a choked cough behind her. Les. He had lost his swim trunks somewhere in the water, and stood naked except for the fanny pack belted to his waist. Dripping wet, staring at her. His gaze was terrible, intense. Frightening. All the hairs rose on her neck, and she scrabbled off the chair when he rushed toward her. Except, it was the radio he grabbed.

"Dammit," he muttered, and looked at Jenny. "What was that he said, about the earthquake?"

She stared at him, aching and feverish, head pounding. "What?"

"The earthquake." Les reached out and grabbed her shoulder. "When did that happen?"

"I don't know," she snapped, trying to break free. "Recently, I think."

Les let go, though it felt more like a push. Jenny staggered back, breathing hard. Her head felt woozy. "What is it?"

"Nothing." Les set the radio on the table by the soda, and his hand shook. "You seem unwell."

"I'm fine."

"Your skin is hot."

"Been sitting in the sun. I'd like to go inside now if you don't mind."

Les studied her, and after a moment, stepped sideways to the door and unlocked it. He gestured for her to precede him, which was fine. She didn't particularly want to see his naked ass.

Jenny walked in silence until they passed the lab. The steel door was ajar, and when she looked through the glass, she saw that the cold-locker door had also not been properly shut.

She teetered to a stop. "What did you think you would learn from her body?"

Les went still. "I don't know what you're talking about."

"You examined her body. That first night we had her. And you've done it again." Jenny leaned against the wall, aching and dizzy. "Does all . . . this . . . have anything to do with finding her?"

His eyes were so dark. "Come on, Jenny. Let's get you in bed. I have work to do."

"Don't patronize me," she whispered.

Les gave her a bitter smile and slammed open her cabin door—so hard she flinched. "No kicking. No biting. Promise that, and I'll even let you use the toilet."

Jenny pushed herself off the wall, using all her strength to walk in a straight line. She stopped in front of Les and forced her own smile. "I'd rather piss my pants than promise that."

Les said nothing. He grabbed the front of her shorts and yanked her close. His fingers slid against her lower stomach. Jenny's smile froze—and his dimmed. He undid the button and slid the fly halfway down. Slow. Deliberate. Never blinked, not once. Neither did Jenny.

"There," Les whispered, some terrible emotion sweeping through his gaze. "You should be able to manage now, even with your hands tied."

Jenny didn't dare speak. Les shoved her into the cabin, and she fell hard across the bed. He slammed the door shut.

None of them had ever had any use for locks, and doors on the yacht opened outward into the hall. She heard him shove a board beneath the knob—no doubt bracing it against the opposing wall.

Jenny listened to him walk away. Tried to sit up, but her head swam. All she could do was lie on the bed, hands tied behind her back. Every time she shifted, even a little, she felt the rub of that unzipped fly on her stomach; and the memory of Les's fingers on her skin made her eyes fill with tears. Jenny buried her face in the pillow, but it was too difficult to breathe. The cabin air was hot—or maybe that was her.

Fever, she thought dimly, as the base of her skull ached. *I'm burning up.*

She managed to roll off the bed and stumbled to the bathroom. Everything that could be a weapon had been taken away, but there was ibuprofen in the top drawer. Fumbling behind her back, she managed to pop three pills from the bottle to the counter; then turned, bending to lick them up. She swallowed the medicine dry, gagging when the pills got lodged in her throat. But they finally went down.

Jenny looked at herself in the mirror. Flushed face, bloodshot eyes. Mouth sagging on one side, as though misery was etching new lines in her face. White hairs would probably be next. After that, the grave.

"Not yet," she whispered, staring into her haunted eyes. "Not like this."

Jenny managed to use the toilet—awkwardly—and tottered back to bed. Her desk looked so empty: computer gone, along with the satellite phone and wireless uplink. No way to contact anyone.

Les has been planning this a long time.

Practically had gone through a checklist. Jenny just didn't get it. Memories filled her; laughter and music, and dancing; and all those days and months living together on this ship, traveling the world and hunting for the unknown. What had she missed? Where were the signs? She couldn't think of even one.

Jenny lay down, shifting restlessly. Her wrists and shoulders hurt. Still hard to breathe. But finally she managed to sleep. And dream.

It was such a relief to be back on the beach, to find *his* body, pressed warm against hers; and hear *his* voice, insistent and calm. All of him, so real. She had never seen his face, but he had been younger, once upon a time. Younger, smaller, like her. As Jenny had grown, so had he. Her imaginary friend.

Her boy from the beach.

The house was there, too, but that was nothing she wanted to dwell on. Those dreams—those special dreams that had disappeared from her life for a full eight years—had always been a place of peace.

As well as heartache for something she could never have.

But this time the dream ended early—that warm hand slipping through hers—and Jenny found herself drifting in another place that felt just as real, but full of contorted shadows that rippled in her vision. Like water. Deep water, lost to light.

She was not alone. No sign of life, but she felt something huge in the darkness, surrounding her in a coil of heat. She was afraid to breathe, or speak, and the longer she remained still, and silent, the more terrified she felt. Her heart thudded in her chest, and she suffered an echo of her pulse in the back of her head, as though a tiny heart beat there, too.

Wake, whispered a melodic voice. *Open your eyes.*

They're open, Jenny tried to answer, but water rushed into her mouth with crushing force, ramming down her throat. She thrashed wildly, her foot kicking something hard—and in front of her, large as a mountain, something moved. A strange rise and fall of golden light, cut with a slit.

An eye.

JENNY WOKE, GASPING. DRENCHED IN SWEAT, CONFUSED, head pounding. Took her a long time to remember where she was. It was dark, and the cabin walls and ceiling kept merging with deeper shadows that moved in her vision. A golden eye hovered on the edges, but every time she looked, it slipped away. She could feel it, though: massive, and wild, and pitiless.

It was hard to move, so Jenny didn't. Everything was tender, even her throat. Looked like night outside the porthole. Or early morning, according to the clock on the desk. Around 4:00 A.M. She had slept a long time.

Jenny dozed a little more, and the next time she was fully conscious, the sun had risen, and it was well into morning. She felt better. Less achy. Footsteps sounded outside in the hall and she slowly, carefully, sat up. Her shorts had slid halfway down her hips in the night, but she managed to tug them up before her door opened. Les entered, carrying a tall glass of ice tea and a muffin. Shadows clung to his face, and his cheeks seemed more hollow. No sleep, maybe. Guilty conscience, she hoped.

"Oh, look," Jenny said. "You've come to kill me with kindness."

Les arched his brow and took a very deliberate bite out of the muffin. "Sorry," he said, mouth full. "This is *my* breakfast."

Jenny shook her head. "Your pettiness used to be endearing."

"It still could be." Les held out the ice tea. "Drink."

She didn't feel like arguing. Her throat was too dry. He pressed the glass to her lips, tilting slowly, and she drank and drank, spilling some down the sides of her mouth, until there was nothing left.

"You look less . . . feverish." Les brushed his fingers against her brow, and Jenny flinched away from him.

"Don't touch me," she said. "Really, just don't."

His gaze darkened. "I should have been honest with you from the beginning. About . . . everything."

"Everything." Jenny pushed past him, heading for the door. "In this case, I really can't imagine how honesty would have solved anything. What . . . you would have told me how you were going to hijack the ship, murder Maurice, and keep me tied up? Don't think so. At least now I know who you really are."

Les grabbed her arm. "You have *no* idea who I am. If you did . . ."

Jenny straightened, staring dead in his eyes. "So tell me. Make me understand."

For a moment she thought he would try, but uncertainty burned in his gaze, and he let go. "Later, maybe. I'll need to . . . show you."

No time like the present, she almost said, but kept her mouth shut. Not entirely certain she was ready for the truth that he seemed so afraid of telling her.

He shuffled her to the galley. Fed her oatmeal. And then took her up on deck where the sun was warm and deliciously bright after a night of hard dreams.

"My wrists are raw," she said to Les. "Will you untie me?"

"Not a chance." He disappeared inside the main cabin, closing and locking the door behind him. Five minutes later he came out with a first-aid kit, a soda with a straw, and a bottle of whiskey.

"This is going to be a long morning," she muttered, looking at the alcohol. Les's haggard expression softened, but only as long as it took for him to take a long swallow directly from the bottle. The whiskey seemed to go straight to his eyes, turning them a hard golden brown.

"Wrists," he commanded, and Jenny obeyed, turning to face the bow. As he rubbed antibiotic gel into the raw welts, she noticed a tarp-covered lump on the deck. It was about the same size as a body.

"Les," she said slowly. "What's that?"

His fingers stilled, and then kept rubbing. "Nothing you need to worry about."

She pulled away, glaring. "If that's a dead person, I sure as hell am going to worry."

"It's not . . . not a person." Les gave the tarp a haunted look, rubbing his hands together. "Not like that."

Not like that. Jenny ran from him, ignoring his shout. Before he could stop her she kicked aside the tarp.

A dolphin lay underneath. Dead at least several hours, given the dried look of its skin. Its eyes were rimmed with milky clouds, and its mouth gaped open. A jagged hole had ripped open its side. Spear-gun wound, maybe.

"You're psycho," Jenny said, as Les drew near. "What? This dolphin look at you wrong?"

"Yes, actually," he replied tersely, and yanked her from the dead animal. "Leave it alone."

Jenny gritted her teeth and slammed into Les. He staggered back, and she kicked out his knee, sending him down hard. But when she tried to smash her heel into his face, he caught her ankle, twisting. Jenny crashed into the deck, but rocked sideways, fighting for some kind of momentum that would let her stand. Les got to her before she could. He grabbed her hair, placed his knee between her shoulders, and yanked her head so far back she thought her neck would break.

"Make no mistake," Les said raggedly, "about how much I care about you. Because I do care, Jenny. But you seem to be under the false impression that you have power here. And you don't. You really, really, don't. So it seems to me that I'm going to have to prove that to you. Because if you keep interfering with my work, I'll take permanent measures to get you out of the way. And I don't want to do that."

"You talk too much," Jenny whispered. "Asshole."

His mouth twisted, and so did the anger in his eyes. She wished she had kept her mouth shut—but it was too late. He dragged her to the side of the boat, and hauled her up into his arms.

"No," she gasped. "Les."

"You're good at holding your breath," he replied coldly. "Don't worry. I'll come get you before you drown."

He dumped her overboard. Jenny didn't have time to take a deep breath, and she hit the water with jarring force, which expelled additional air from her nostrils. She sank like a stone, and kicked with all her strength to reach the surface. She managed to, just for a moment, and swallowed air. Glimpsed Les standing on the boat, watching. And then she sank, again.

I had a bad dream. You, drowning. Maurice's voice echoed through her head. Jenny kicked hard, straining to break free of the ocean, but the surface remained tantalizingly out of reach. It shouldn't have. She was a strong swimmer. But the fever had taken more out of her than she realized. She was weak.

The more you fight, the harder it'll be to hold your breath.

But if she stopped kicking and sank, Les might never find her. If he even meant to. Screwed, either way. So screwed.

Jenny kept kicking, but not as hard. Just enough to keep her from descending too far into the deep. Her lungs burned. Stars danced on the edge of her vision. She wasn't going to last four minutes. Maybe not even two.

Warmth spread against the base of her skull. With it, a throbbing pulse, a little heartbeat, slow and steady. Jenny closed her eyes, focusing on the sensation, on staying calm.

But it was too little, too late. All her thrashing, every kick, ate up the oxygen in her blood—and her lungs screamed and screamed, those stars fighting behind her closed eyelids—and no one came, no hands grabbed her arms, no magic from the deep to save her.

Jenny opened her mouth, and water rushed in—a terrible crushing force, just like in her dream. She had always imagined that drowning would be a painless way to die, but it wasn't. Terror made her eyes bulge, and she writhed uselessly, screaming in her mind.

Until, suddenly, heat exploded against her skull. A violent rush of fire. And all that water in her lungs suddenly didn't hurt quite as badly.

It took her a moment to understand. Even when she realized what was happening, her mind still couldn't comprehend it.

She could breathe. Not well, or easily, but even as the

water choked, her lungs filled with air—a strange, heavy air that felt wrong and tasted bad.

But it was air. Jenny was so shocked she stopped kicking. *You're dying, and this is a delusion,* she told herself, sinking fast. But she clenched her hands together and dragged in another terrible breath—and still lived.

It didn't last. Each breath became more difficult and crushing than the last, and panic again supplanted wonder. Jenny's lungs burned like hell.

The parasite shifted against her skull. Some instinct made Jenny open her eyes. She was surprised at how sharp her vision was in the darkness, each particle that drifted past her face distinct and bright, as though lit from within— like stars. Below, far below, something moved toward her. It was impossibly large and fast, a silver streak.

Dolphin, she thought weakly, wondering if this would become a fairy tale. Girl rescued by dolphin, carried to the surface, drawn far and away from the evil that had tossed her in to drown.

But the creature drew close, and it was no dolphin.

It was a man.

Jenny forgot she was dying. Everything faded, her life shrinking to nothing but a flash of strong white arms, silver drifting hair, and a face that was high-cheeked, masculine, and edged with faint white scars. She glimpsed a set mouth, and pale blue eyes staring hard into her own. Nothing comforting about that gaze—just that it was frighteningly intense. Fear thrilled through her, and awe.

You know those eyes, she told herself, even though it was impossible. She was dying. This *was* a delusion. No one was there.

But that same *no one* placed his hands on her arms and gathered her close against a hard warm body, and those same hands touched her face, and those imaginary eyes gave her a look of such ferocious wonder that her heart ached with a different kind of dying, and if this was death and insanity, then she welcomed it. Jenny was ready.

He pulled her toward the surface, fast as a bullet. She looked down and saw a long silver tail propelling him, and then their heads broke free of the ocean. She tried to breathe and vomited water. Coughs wracked her, so violent she half expected to taste blood in her mouth. But those arms never let go, and held her close, strong fingers smoothing back her hair. She tried looking into the merman's face, but he was too close. All she caught were glimpses: puzzle pieces, riddles.

Jenny heard a shout. She twisted, and found the boat some distance away. Les stood at the rail, staring. The merman holding her stiffened, and when she pulled back far enough to see his face, all she saw were his eyes, staring back at Les.

Staring as though he knew him.

Les dove into the water. The merman muttered, "Shit."

Jenny blinked. "What?"

He never answered. Just spun her around, fumbling for the restraints holding her wrists. It was a plastic cord, the kind that needed a knife to cut. He made a low frustrated sound.

"Kick," he ordered hoarsely. "Try to stay afl—"

He was slammed away from her, caught in a torrent of foam and thrashing limbs. Jenny kicked hard, gasping for air—staring as Les reared briefly out of the water. Time slowed down as he threw back his head, silver water flying from his hair, waves crashing against his chest and shoulders as his arms moved steadily through the water. He stared at the merman without fear. Just grim, unhappy acceptance.

The merman's expression was far more terrifying. Calculating, thoughtful, filled with a fury that hit Jenny as primal and cold. His skin was white as marble, as new snow in sunlight, glimmering with water and salt crystals. Long hair clung to his hard muscles. Scars crisscrossed his arms and upper shoulders.

Memories slammed. The beach. That boy.

Jenny sank below the surface, lungs full of air. Eyes open, staring. She saw two bodies twisting through the water, and expected to witness one human confronting a merman—bizarre, insane, as that might be.

But what she saw was even stranger.

Both men had tails.

CHAPTER SIX

THERE was a homeless shelter in New York City that played old movies in the evenings—classics, some of the guys had told Perrin, though he had little use for such definitions, or for film. Westerns, however, were occasionally enjoyable; if nothing else but for their historical value, which he knew was minimal at best. It awed him, however, that humans could live and thrive in deserts. Fascinated him to see what deserts looked like, even on grainy film: golden rock and sand, and sharp-needled plants; and skies that never ended.

Gunfights also intrigued Perrin. Standoffs between men who refused to relent, who knew they were going to die but continued on, carried by nothing but conviction. Everywhere, he saw this, and not only in film. Humans valued the individual moral fingerprint—as long as it was just and good.

As did he. Much to his misfortune.

Wyatt Earp. Magnificent Seven. Pale Rider. Movie titles rolled through Perrin's head like some secret chant, which he hated. He wanted quiet inside his mind, a place to think, but the sun was high, spreading a glitter of light against the waves, and if this had been the desert with a gun strapped to his side, he would have felt more at home than he did now.

He had expected many things, in coming to the woman's aid.

But not this. Not . . . him.

"A'lesander," he said, more calmly than he felt—trying to keep his eyes open against the glitter of sunlight on the water—bright, too bright. "Thought you were dead."

A'lesander's answering smile was bitter, cold—but that wasn't mask enough to hide the hint of uncertainty in his eyes. His skin was darker than Perrin remembered, hair a lighter shade of golden brown. Sun rich. His grandmother had been human.

"Same to you," he said.

Three words. Just three. But Perrin was astonished at the emotions that filled him, simply by hearing the sound of that voice—like a hot poker searing an unhealed wound. Hurt like hell. Cut the breath right out of his lungs in ways that simply seeing A'lesander did not.

All he could do was harden his heart. He had no time for anything less.

Perrin drifted carefully to his right, just out of arm's reach, and saw the woman on the periphery of his vision—head above water. "You thought I was dead," he said, forcing himself to focus on A'lesander: every word, every nuance. "Why would you think that?"

A'lesander's expression hardened. "I might have been exiled before you, but I was finally allowed back into the sea, within my clan territories. I suppose you never had that . . . luxury. What you did, I heard, was beyond forgiveness."

Perrin said nothing: still circling, assessing. Burying all the emotions riding hard in his heart. Might be the sea, but this was still a prison yard: only one person could leave free.

A'lesander watched him, eyes narrowing. "Imagine. Perrin O'doro, getting exactly what he always wanted. A life on land."

"Yes, imagine," Perrin replied. "But you're still denied what you want most. Nothing can change that. And," he added slowly, "these territories don't belong to your clan."

"But what do you think the others might give me if I dragged you home?" A'lesander cut the water with his hands, finally baring his teeth. "You shouldn't have come here, Perrin. They won't just take your life. You know that."

"I know," he replied—and lunged for the other's throat.

Just a feint. When A'lesander raised his fists, Perrin dropped his right hand and shoved two fingers hard into his side, a trick he had learned in prison. Humans and *Krackeni* might be two different species, but the physiology was close enough to cripple. A'lesander cried out, twisting away—his expression not just pained, but shocked.

"Yes," Perrin muttered. "Things have changed."

A'lesander panted, clutching his side. "You won't stop me."

"I'm not here for you." Perrin sensed the woman behind him, and watched the other *Krackeni's* gaze flicker past his shoulder. His mouth tightened into a hard white line.

"No—" A'lesander began, still looking at her—but Perrin slammed a fist into his head before he could finish. He followed with another punishing blow, and another, and another. He gave him no chance to recover. Long ago, he might have. Long ago, he would never have raised his fists. But those days were gone.

Blood spurted from A'lesander's nose. Part of his cheek looked dented. He fumbled in the water, trying to dive, but Perrin grabbed his hair and finished him off with one last blow. Suffering, for a brief moment, A'lesander's dazed gaze, which was hateful and stunned, and brought back too many memories.

The *Krackeni* went limp in the water. Perrin didn't let go. He stared, breathing hard, taking in that familiar, broken face. Wondering how the fight could be over so quickly. It didn't seem right.

Nor was it right to see him again. Now. Here.

He looked for the woman, but she was gone. Panicked, he released A'lesander and dove beneath the surface. He found her only a foot or so down, kicking hard, staring in his direction with those clear green eyes. His pounding heart stopped, again.

He had found her. This was no dream. He could see her face. She was here, flesh and blood. Looking at her for the first time in sixteen years had left him so stunned, it was a wonder he had managed to bring her to the surface.

Now was no different. She was so beautiful.

He was suddenly afraid to touch her. She was much smaller than him, more delicate than he had imagined. His memories of her, as a child, were larger than life.

He held her carefully, hands curling around her bare arms. She was hot to the touch, feverish, and the light from above cast a white glow across her skin. Her gaze sought his, and he searched it for any sign of fear. Found none. Just a stunned sort of wonder, and awe.

Like time travel, as though Perrin was stranded on the beach again, little more than a boy. He could still see that girl in this woman's face—in the curve of her cheeks, in her mouth—and those eyes. He wondered what she saw when she looked at him, if she even remembered that day the same way he did; or whether the dreams meant as much. Assuming she had ever understood their significance.

You don't know her, whispered a small mean voice. *Eight years of silence. She's changed. You have, too. Be careful.*

Careful. If he had been careful, he would never have been exiled in the first place. Or come back.

Perrin pulled the woman to the surface, holding her head high. She sucked down a deep breath that ended in a raw, hacking cough.

"Are you hurt?" he asked roughly, rubbing his aching eyes with the back of his hand.

"No," she replied, hoarse. "Y-you?"

He was surprised she asked. All he could do was shake his head, feeling dumb, throat too tight for words. His mind couldn't wrap around what was happening: seeing her, seeing A'lesander. All this, and the darkness stirring below them all. It was too much.

Perrin twisted around until he floated on his back. The sky was so blue. He held the woman close, one arm wrapped around her upper waist. She had no way of holding on to him with her hands, but he was nonetheless startled by the sensation of her leg sliding across his lower torso and tail. He flinched, and she froze.

"I'm sorry," she whispered. "But I need —"

"Yes, I know," he replied tersely. "It's . . . fine."

More than fine. He savored the sensation of her body pressed against his own. Not a dream. This was real. She was here. Same voice, that glint of red hair. He had found the girl.

And it made him feel as though he were losing his mind.

Perrin swam them toward A'lesander and grabbed a fistful of his hair. The woman exhaled sharply, her breath warm against his shoulder. All of her was warm, so much so that he feared she was ill. Her gaze, too bright, traveled down the *Krackeni's* bobbing body.

"He's not dead," Perrin said, but that elicited no response. He wanted to hear her voice. He wanted to ask who had tied her hands and put her in the water, but he knew the answer. He couldn't imagine how this woman had gotten mixed up with A'lesander. His presence here, now, was a very bad sign.

Perrin pulled them back to the boat. Only when they were close to the ladder did he let go of A'lesander, and grab the bottom rung. His tail shifted, bones cracking; skin rippling in silver streaks as his legs re-formed. The woman stared down through the water, first in astonishment, then with a thoughtfulness that made Perrin feel ill at ease, exposed. Like he was a guinea pig. He tightened his hold around her waist.

"This may be uncomfortable," he said.

She gave him a questioning look, which ended in a grunt as he tossed her over his shoulder. She made no other sound as he climbed the ladder, taking care not to let her slide away from him. She almost did, and he was forced to dump her, rather awkwardly, onto the deck.

Perrin followed. "I promise to free your hands, but I need rope, quick. For *him*."

"Equipment bin," she said, without hesitation. Perrin scanned the deck—but stopped when he saw the body near the bow. Dolphin. He thought of Rik, and shook that thought from his head.

The woman followed his gaze. "I think he did that last night."

Perrin said nothing. He knelt beside the corpse. His hand hovered over the cold cracked skin, and that black glazed eye could have been a fragment of polished stone. The wound was vicious.

He heard a shuffling sound. Found the woman staggering toward the equipment box. He beat her to it, placing a steadying hand on the small of her back. She froze when he touched her, and he snatched his hand away.

"I'll take care of this," he said, glancing back at the dolphin. Anger filled him, a primitive rage that started in his chest and rose high into his throat until he wanted to scream in frustration.

"Do you know why?" asked the woman, gesturing with her chin toward the corpse.

"Dolphins talk," Perrin replied, and sensed her frown before he saw it.

He grabbed the rope and strode quickly to the ladder. A'lesander continued to drift, but his fingers were twitching. Perrin jumped into the ocean, and hauled the *Krackeni* close, tying his hands behind his back with one end of the rope. He carried the other half up the ladder—braced his feet into the deck—and began hauling A'lesander into the boat.

The woman peered over the rail. "I suppose you know that you're pulling his arms out of their joints."

Perrin grunted. "You care?"

The woman gave him a long look. "Not in the slightest."

A'lesander slipped onto the boat, his arms twisted in odd directions. His dorsal fin flopped, and silver scales rippled from his torso down the muscular length of his tail. Perrin looped the rope around the *Krackeni's* neck—once, twice—

and tied the end around his bound hands. No good restraining the rest of him until he shifted shape.

"Do you have a place to secure him?" he asked the woman.

She had been staring, and blinked hard. "Yes. Follow . . . follow me."

Perrin grabbed A'lesander's hair and dragged him off deck through the door that the woman passed through. Bits of scalp tore away. He didn't shift his grip except to tighten his fingers, and refused to let go until she led him to a room that had to be hers.

"It's already been emptied of anything that could be a weapon," she explained, voice breaking on that last word.

Perrin tossed A'lesander on the floor and rubbed his hand against his thigh.

"Your knuckles are bleeding," said the woman.

"So is he." Perrin backed out of the room and closed the door. A thick board was in the hall. He laid it lengthwise across the floor—bracing it against the wall and door—and found that it fit perfectly as a rough lock. He suspected it had already been used as such.

The hall was small. Perrin had to bend over to keep from brushing his head against the ceiling. His shoulders touched the walls. The woman stood before him, a good deal smaller, though her gaze was bold—if not a little wild. A tic in her right cheek betrayed a hint of nerves. Perrin didn't know what to say to her, how to explain anything—or even how much he *could* say. He had no time.

"My hands," she said.

"Yes," he replied. "Knives."

Her bottom lip trembled, and she backed away from him, slow and careful. He followed, holding his breath, afraid he was losing his mind.

She led him to a kitchenette. He found a knife in a drawer. Her shoulders tensed when he picked it up. He wanted to smile for her but could not. Reassurance had never been his strength.

"Turn around," he said roughly. "Hold still."

She did not move. "Are you real? Did I imagine all this?"

Perrin slid around her, studying the plastic strip binding her hands. "Your wrists are raw. Are you imagining the pain?"

He received no answer and set the blade against the restraint. Her skin was so warm. *Definitely a fever,* he thought.

"You're sick," he said.

"Later," she replied, voice strained. "I need to be free."

He cut the plastic carefully but caught her hands in one of his before she could pull them apart.

"Slowly," Perrin said, swallowing hard as her scent filled his nose. Fresh as the sea, and clean. He set down the knife and drew her back against his chest, wrapping his free arm across her upper shoulders. Her feverish warmth flowed into his body. "How long have you been bound?"

"Days," she said, stiff inside his embrace.

He wanted to kill A'lesander. "This is going to hurt."

She nodded, and he loosened his grip on her hands, just a little. Her breath hissed, and he held her tighter, bracing her shoulders against his chest as she spread her hands farther apart. Another small sound of pain escaped her.

"Easy," he murmured.

"You act . . ." she swallowed hard, breathless, " . . . like you've done this before."

Perrin smiled, knowing she couldn't see him. "You'll be sore for days, but it'll pass."

She was silent a moment. "I know your voice."

He stopped breathing and closed his eyes. When he did that, when all he could count on was touch and sound, it felt like the dream again, on the beach in the cold sunlight.

"How do I know your voice?" she whispered, trembling beneath his arm.

He didn't know how to answer her. Except, after a moment of dead quiet, a melody coursed through his head, and he hummed it. Just a few bars.

That was enough. The woman sucked in her breath, leaning hard against him—and then, with a hiss of pain, pushed away. She staggered across the room, arms hanging limp at her sides. Tangled red hair covered half her face, but he could see her eyes—wild, haunted, as though he had cut her with that song.

"You," she whispered.

"Me," he said, just as quietly.

She shuddered, backing away. He did not follow. His feet were frozen to the floor, just like his heart. All he could see were her eyes, the eyes he remembered from childhood and his vision—wide with wonder, then wide with rage, and now stormy with emotions he could not name, but feared. He was so afraid of her, of what it meant to find her. Now, of all times.

"I don't . . ." she began, and touched her head, swaying. She tried to speak again, looking at him with an urgency that made him step toward her. She held up her hand as though to stop him but didn't. Her eyes were turning glassy, blood draining from her face—which was hardly enough warning when her legs buckled. He dove to his knees and caught her. The base of his skull throbbed.

He cradled her close, breathing hard, pressing his hand against her brow. Her skin burned him, and she wouldn't open her eyes. The pain worsened in his head. So did panic.

"Come on," Perrin whispered, pulling her tight against his chest as he found his feet, awkward and unsteady. He didn't know where to take her, and the helplessness that hit him was almost too much to bear.

He finally remembered seeing a bed in some room he had passed while dragging A'lesander. He made his way down the corridor, and the bed was where he remembered it: unmade, rumpled, thick with the *Krackeni's* scent. Turned Perrin's stomach to lay the woman on those sheets, but he did, and rushed to the nearby bathroom to wet a rag. He placed it on her brow. She never stirred.

Fevers killed. He knew that about humans. About himself, too. He had suffered terrible illnesses for his first several years on land. No immune system. Common colds were devastating. The seasonal flu, before he had learned about vaccinations, had nearly killed him.

Perrin rummaged through the bathroom drawers but found nothing useful for bringing down a fever. Nothing in the main cabin, either. The drawers were full of clothes and maps—cash in one, books, a passport with A'lesander's picture in it—all the trappings of a normal human life, one that had been lived with ease and safety. Put a bitter taste in Perrin's mouth.

He checked the woman, flipping the rag to the cool side, and left the cabin. He needed to find aspirin, ibuprofen— even antibiotics. After that, radios. She needed a doctor.

Perrin passed a metal door with a glass insert. Inside, he saw lab equipment. He entered, scanning the room, opening drawers. No first-aid kit, no medicine. He didn't give much thought to anything else he saw, though it seemed to him that this must be some kind of science vessel.

There was another door at the end of the room. He pulled it open, got hit with a blast of cold air—and stopped in his tracks.

A dead woman lay on a stainless-steel table. Not just a woman. A *Krackeni*.

He knew without getting close. Blood knew blood. She was long and white, and her hair was silver. He stared, breathless, leaning hard against the doorway. He could see her face where he stood. Not well, but enough.

Bile pushed up his throat, and he bent over, gagging. He couldn't stop. He vomited nothing but air and spit, so long, so hard, his throat and chest felt like they were going to crack open. Tears burned his eyes.

By the time Perrin stopped retching, he was on his hands and knees. He nearly had to crawl to reach the corpse. Reached up, tentatively, to touch a cold, still hand. He glimpsed her face—closer now, familiar—and looked away. He pressed his brow against the rim of the icy steel table. Scented death and rot.

"Pelena," he whispered, shaking. "Pelena, Pelena."

He finally managed to stand, his gaze falling upon gaping wounds, bruised flesh. A white sheet lay on the floor beside the table, as though someone had torn it off her body and not had enough respect to replace it.

I'm sorry, Perrin thought, suffering a trembling grief that he didn't know how to express. Gone eight years, and now this. He forced himself to touch that cold face, heart breaking as he traced a line against her familiar cheekbone.

And then, swallowing hard, he used both hands to turn her head—and felt the base of her skull.

He found a hole. But nothing else.

Perrin hadn't even realized he was holding his breath, but it left him in a rush. He picked up the sheet and very carefully pulled it over her body. He stood for a moment, staring at that long white lump—exhaustion bleeding into his bones.

He went to find A'lesander.

STILL UNCONSCIOUS. OR JUST PRETENDING. PERRIN stood in the doorway, watching his old friend. He didn't have time for this, but he couldn't move. Too tired, in body and mind. It had taken him all night to get here. He was not as strong as he had once been, but being in the ocean was a better high than heroin, and the adrenaline that surged through his body was power enough to keep him going. Bittersweet though it might be.

He had been seen, of course. Sharks, small schools of fish—and from a distance, a pod of dolphins. He couldn't be certain any of them recognized him, but word would get around. Only a matter of time before one of his kind learned he had returned. No such things as secrets in the sea. Eyes everywhere. It pained him that he couldn't trust those eyes. Hurt more than he thought possible. Being home, in the sea, did not fill his heart with comfort as he had fantasized it would. It just made him feel emptier—and, perversely enough, homesick for land.

Perrin went to the bathroom and found plastic cups. He filled one with water, which he splashed on A'lesander's face. When that elicited little more than a twitch, he grabbed the *Krackeni's* broken nose and twisted. The *Krackeni* jerked awake with a scream.

"Fuck," he gasped, tilting his swelling face to peer at Perrin. "Gonna torture me now?"

"Maybe," Perrin replied evenly. "I just saw my cousin's body."

A'lesander's gaze darkened. He had legs again, and lay on his stomach, arched backward to accommodate the rope around his neck and hands. No good way to hide his face, which he tried to do—jerking sideways, pushing his cheek into the floor. Perrin swayed closer, following him. Rage pulsed in his throat, but he swallowed it down. If he let go now, he wouldn't stop until A'lesander was dead. He couldn't afford that. Too many questions needed answering.

After that, anything was possible.

"Pelena," he said, voice breaking on her name. "She was always kind to you."

A'lesander's jaw tightened. "I don't know why you think I hurt her."

"Didn't you?" Perrin grabbed his shirt, hauling him close. "She was murdered. Any fool can see that from her injuries. Murdered, A'lesander. She was the only Guardian for this region, and her *kra'a* is gone." He jammed his fingers through the *Krackeni's* hair, feeling around the base of his skull. All he found was solid bone. No warm lump, no second heartbeat.

"I don't have it," A'lesander snapped, but there was a strangled note in his voice, like grief.

Perrin shoved him away. "But you tried. I know you did. What did you possibly think would happen if you harvested her *kra'a*? Did you think it would bond with you, simply because you willed it? You were rejected from the process for a reason. It takes —"

"I know what it takes!" A'lesander snarled, wrenching

sideways. Not far, and the effort made him pant—but the hate and grief in his eyes was strong and too real. Perrin stared, and then leaned backward until his shoulders hit the wall with a hard thud.

"You killed her for nothing," he whispered. "You must have known that. And you know, too, what happens next. What's happening even now. If someone—anyone—could find her *kra'a,* there might be time to bond another Guardian—"

"Like you?" A'lesander interrupted bitterly.

"No," Perrin breathed, head aching. "But there are always candidates. Even one of the children would be better than the alternative."

That earned him only silence. He stood, slowly, dragged down by despair. "I had a vision, A'lesander. I saw the darkness, and the awakening, and the end of things. I came here to deliver a warning—just in case. It was too important to risk doing nothing. And now I'm here, and the only person who could have prevented all those deaths is gone. Her *kra'a* is gone. Unless you *do* have it? Please . . . please say you do."

"I told you," A'lesander whispered, closing his eyes. "No."

Perrin wanted to kill him. Just looking at his face made him want to step on his throat until he stopped breathing. But he blinked, and looked again, and A'lesander was suddenly pathetic, broken. Not worth the effort, or stain, of becoming a murderer. Again.

"The woman is sick," he said. "I need to bring her fever down."

"Jenny?" A'lesander twisted around, finally meeting his gaze. "What's your interest in her?"

Perrin stared. "Is there medicine on this boat?"

He almost didn't answer. He took so long, Perrin began to back out of the room. At the last moment, though, he cleared his throat. "Her bathroom drawer, I think. Try that. And there's a first-aid kit near the radios. But those . . . I destroyed those."

"Of course you did," Perrin replied, ready to rethink his resolve not to crush his throat. "Anything else I should know?"

A'lesander wet his cracked lips. "The earthquakes have begun."

Perrin went still. "More than one?"

"I don't think so, but I can't be certain."

"Maybe this was what you wanted all along." He forced himself to walk to the bathroom and watched A'lesander's restrained body in the mirror. "But I never would have imagined it. You were spiteful, but not insane."

"Still not crazy," he muttered, hoarse. "But some things just have to be done."

Perrin gritted his teeth and closed his hand around a bottle of ibuprofen. It had already been opened, some of the pills spilled on the counter. He scooped them back inside, replaced the cap, and walked out—refusing to glance at A'lesander. As he closed the door, the bound *Krackeni* said, "Why Jenny? How do you know her?"

Perrin finished shutting the door and reached for the wood bar. On the other side, A'lesander shouted, "You don't know who she is. Men will be coming for her. She's marked, Perrin. Hunted."

"Won't matter in a week," he mumbled, uncaring if A'lesander heard him. She might be safer out here than any-where else.

He walked back down the hall to the room where he had left her. She curled on her side now, and the wet rag had slid off. She was still too warm. He cooled down the cloth and dabbed it against her brow as a nurse had done for him, long ago when he was still living in Sweden.

"Jenny," whispered Perrin, her name strange in his mouth.

He found water, shook three ibuprofen into his hand, and tried to wake the woman. She remained deep in sleep, and he gave up—moving a safe distance away, near the door. It was difficult being close to her. Difficult, in so many ways he hadn't anticipated.

Fate, he thought. All those twisted knots, binding him so tight he couldn't breathe. Grief made it impossible.

Pelena was dead, and her *kra'a* gone. The others must have realized by now that something was wrong, and perhaps—perhaps, by some miracle—the *kra'a* had been found. If that was the case, then Perrin needed to do nothing at all. And if that was *not* the case . . . then *nothing* he did would matter.

Guardians soothed the dreams of the beast. And the beast was waking.

CHAPTER SEVEN

HER skull burned. Dreams, hot with fire. Jenny rolled through a vast darkness cut by rivers of lava. Fissures cracked open, split apart by a heaving body so massive, even a fragment of its scaled flesh loomed in the night like a mountain. When it breathed, the earth groaned; and when it twisted in its sleep, earth shattered and broke her bones.

"Come on," said a man, in her dream. "Hurry."

Jenny knew his voice and reached blindly for his hand. Nothing reached back. Her fingers slipped through air.

"Hurry," he said again, louder; and somewhere beyond his voice, thunder rumbled into a growl.

Jenny woke. Pushed from darkness to shadows. She glimpsed hair so pale it was almost silver, and stared, and stared. Confused, thirsty, sweat soaking her skin and clothes. She was afraid to move, watching as all that hair shifted, revealing a man with ice blue eyes—eyes that were impossible to look away from, though small details stood out on the periphery of her vision: high cheekbones, a firm mouth; his size, immense and rawboned. Faint white scars covered the edge of his face and chest. One looked like a bullet wound.

She remembered a melody, hummed softly.

She remembered everything else, too.

"Your fever broke," said the man, and picked up a plastic

cup that looked ridiculously tiny in his hand. "You need to drink something. And take these."

He showed her the ibuprofen tablets. Jenny stared, struggling to focus—but all she could think of was the beach and a silver boy with a silver tail, and those blue eyes—eyes like the ones looking at her now. That alone would have been difficult enough, but his voice, the deep familiarity of it . . . as though she had listened to him speak for more nights than she could remember . . .

It's him, she thought, and then: *No, impossible.*

Despite everything she had seen in her life, despite the fantasies that had driven her from childhood onward, this was the one thing she couldn't believe was real. No matter how much she wanted it to be. Maybe the parasite was messing with her brain. Maybe she had finally cracked. Maybe, maybe.

"Hurry," he said.

Jenny sat up. Her shoulders hurt, but the weakness was everywhere, in her bones. She took the cup—uneasy when their fingers brushed. That felt real enough.

The water tasted bitter, metallic. She almost spat it out, but thirst raged, and she couldn't help but wet her tongue again. It was better on the second try. She drank the whole cup and swallowed the pills. The man watched her with frightening intensity, and she felt unaccountably small and fragile beside him—more so in her heart than her body.

"The radios have been destroyed," he said.

Jenny froze, about to ask for more water. "Les?"

His gaze hardened. "Les. Yes. Yes, it was him."

"How . . ." she began, and shut her mouth, shaking her head. How this man knew Les wasn't important. Not yet, anyway. "Did he damage the rest of the boat?"

The man pried the plastic cup from her fingers. Jenny let go, surprised she had crushed it. He tossed the cup into the trash bin beneath her desk and stood, pacing to the porthole window. "I don't know. There are other things we need to discuss."

"I can't imagine what," she muttered, dazed.

The man didn't seem to hear. He prowled across the room to the door, peering up and down the corridor. Incredibly graceful, but too contained, as though all the energy bottled beneath his skin was ready to explode. Watching him made her feel claustrophobic.

He finally glanced at her, long hair shrouding much of his gaze: thoughtful, unreadable; alien in his utter remoteness, as though part of him was a million miles away. Jenny wished she could say the same about her own emotions. "I set us on a northerly course, toward a nearby chain of islands. I'm sure there are other places you would prefer to go, but we're being pursued."

Jenny stared. "Pursued?"

"Three vessels. That's why I woke you. We're now dead in the water."

She held up her hand, desperate for a moment to think—without passing out—and tried to get off the bed. She managed to move a full inch before the man crossed the room and held her still. It was like hitting a wall. He wore shorts, she noticed belatedly; swim trunks that belonged to Les.

"I'm sorry," he said. "I wasn't trying to scare you."

"The only thing that scares me," she replied, hoarse, "is the possibility I'm losing my mind. Now let me up."

He removed his hand. Jenny stood. Or tried to. Her knees buckled, and the man caught her against him. Her face pressed against a rock-solid chest that smelled like salt and minerals, and kelp.

"You're not crazy," he rumbled. "But I understand the feeling."

Jenny swallowed hard. She could hear his heartbeat, as well as her own. And, for a moment, a third pulse, in the base of her skull. All three, beating together at the same time. The sensation frightened her.

She shuddered, and tried to push him away. His arms tightened. "Easy. You're still weak."

"Doesn't matter. I need . . . space."

"No time," he replied. "Our pursuers appeared less than ten minutes ago, circled, got close. The boat had been having trouble before that, and when I pushed the engines, they stalled out. Someone had begun the process of breaking down the wiring."

"Les," she muttered, though that didn't make sense, despite everything he had done. He seemed to need the boat. Ismail, on the other hand. . .

"The outer door," she added, and the man shook his head.

"Locked. But I don't trust that. This is a cage now." His voice dropped so low when he said the word *cage,* she almost didn't hear him. "The men have made no attempt to board. It's as though they're waiting for something."

Jenny pushed against the man with all her strength. Which wasn't much. She was incredibly weak. "Get out of my way. I need to see them."

He gave her a look so grim, Jenny felt afraid. But he surprised her by bending down and scooping her into his arms. His strength was effortless, and she swallowed her gasp, barely. "I can *walk.*"

"I'd rather not scrape you off the floor," he said, with surprising dryness. "The first time was hard enough."

She stared. "You're a smart-ass."

The man grunted, but it might have been with laughter. "I've been told that, in less polite terms."

There was barely enough room in the corridor for him to carry her, and the lab door stood ajar. He kicked it closed. Jenny glimpsed the cold locker on the other side of the glass. *That* door was open so wide she could see the mermaid's sheet-covered body.

She gave the man a sharp look. He was staring inside, faint scars even more pronounced against his face—battle scars, marks of war, violence. Bad things had been done to him. Maybe he had done bad things to others. The look in his eyes—unforgiving, distant—suggested yes.

He had been in that cold locker. Jenny knew it. But the way he stared at the body was heavy with more than just memory. He had known that dead woman, and the idea was horrifying. Not *just* because it meant he had lost someone. In all Jenny's dealings, in every part of the world, the right perception—how strangers viewed each other—meant the difference between life and death. Here, now, especially.

"We found the woman several days ago," she said, afraid of what he would do. In all her fantasies, finding *him* again was not supposed to feel dangerous, like walking on a mine-field. "She had washed up onshore, alive. I believe she died soon after she was found."

He seemed to think about that. "You were looking for her?"

"Not her, specifically," she replied carefully. "We received word of something . . . strange . . . about her body. That's what we . . . *I* . . . do. Search for . . . odd things in the sea."

I didn't kill her, she wanted to add, but couldn't speak those words. She was afraid it would sound like begging. But he looked at her as though he could read her mind, and said, "Breathe. I don't blame you for her death."

Relief made her voice embarrassingly ragged. "Why wouldn't you? You don't know me."

He stared dead into her eyes. "Not even a little?"

Jenny's breath caught, and after a moment of her continued silence, his mouth twisted into a bitter grimace that was too mysterious and unhappy for Jenny's comfort. He started moving down the corridor, hunched over to keep his head from hitting the ceiling. His long hair was soft on her face.

The man managed to squeeze them up to the bridge. The radios had been smashed. Wires and plastic covered the floor. He put her down but kept an arm slung around her waist like some supporting brace. Which, unfortunately, she needed in order to stay upright.

"Right there," rumbled the man, gazing out the window. Jenny looked, and saw a boat circling them almost one hundred feet out. It crossed paths with two other small vessels, going in the opposite direction: both little better than cheap tin cans, though their twin-engine propellers appeared new.

The men on board were armed with machine guns and machetes, weapons strapped over flimsy T-shirts and shorts. They had already donned black ski masks.

The first boat was different. Newer. Sleek. Driven by only one man. He wore little except black slacks, a sleeveless black muscle shirt, and two guns holstered in a shoulder rig. No mask. Stone-cold face. He stared at *The Calypso Star* with dark eyes.

Looking at him sent chills through Jenny. She had never seen that man before, but she knew his type. The others might be local fishermen turned pirates. But *he* was a mercenary.

A mercenary . . . or something else. With the Consortium, you could never tell if what you were dealing with was fully and boringly human. Not until it was too late.

Sweat broke out. Feverish, but this time it was from fear. It was starting all over again. She had avoided her family for six long years, taken herself from the fight and all the bad memories she still couldn't shake—but the old war had come to her anyway.

What had Ismail said? The Consortium *needed* her.

Well. Fuck *that*. Fuck *them*.

If she could just stop shaking and untwist her guts from her throat.

"You're right," she said, sounding calmer than she felt. "They should have boarded by now. They're waiting for something."

"Or testing you to see if you'll attack and make yourself vulnerable. If that's the case, they won't wait much longer."

She hoped the mercenary was not psychic. "The windows are tinted to prevent anyone from seeing inside, *and* the glass is bulletproof. They can be opened, just enough. I have guns."

He was quiet a moment. "Do you want to kill them?"

The question took her off guard. Made her think about what it would mean to point a gun at someone and pull the trigger.

Again.

She still had nightmares. All these years, she hadn't let herself consider what it would feel like to live through that again. Not in the heat of the moment, unthinking—but deliberate. Intent. Picking up a gun to take the offensive.

Good. Bad. Maybe she would feel nothing at all. Perhaps some part of her would shut off, dead to taking another life—those lives, those Consortium lives.

"I want to live," she said, feeling ill again. "But no, I don't *want* to kill them. Most are probably just locals, hired to do a job. Pirates. Bad guys. But not . . ." Jenny stopped, unable to finish, unsure what she was trying to say. *Stupid pawns? Poor, ignorant men trying to make a living?* Whatever. Even if that was the case, it didn't make it better. Most of them probably had blood on their hands. They wouldn't hesitate to hurt her if that was what they had been paid to do.

Truth was, she just didn't want to take a life. Not again. Not unless she had to. Killing a stranger wouldn't be any easier than killing a family member. She didn't want it to be easy.

"Do *you* want to kill them?" she asked, tripping over the words.

"No," he said, after a moment that lasted just a little too long. "This isn't the O.K. Corral," he added, surprising her with the reference. "And men who are shot at shoot back."

She glanced at the old bullet wound in his chest and felt relieved by his answer—though she didn't know why. It shouldn't have mattered.

Always matters, her grandfather would have said, as memories flashed, memories of that bad day. Jenny's nausea kicked up another notch. She wished she had chewing gum, and barely noticed when the man pointed to the unmasked mercenary. "That one is no simple pirate."

"No," she admitted, touching her throat, trying to think very hard about bunnies and daisies, and—and blood—*all that blood from the bullets, and oh, oh God, the pain in her stomach—*

Jenny bent over, gagging. Covering her mouth, tears streaming from her eyes. The man's strong arm stayed around her waist. She tried to wriggle free, or at least turn away from him—tried to make herself as small as she could without actually curling up on the floor—but he moved with her, holding her, until finally she gave up trying to maintain even one ounce of her pride.

"Sorry," she mumbled, wiping her mouth.

"Don't be," he said, with surprising gentleness. "You'll feel better now, I think."

Jenny wanted to disagree with him, but the truth was, her nausea was gone. Even if her mouth tasted like shit, and the base of her skull throbbed.

She straightened slowly, still wiping her mouth and eyes, and stared blearily through the window at those speedboats and the men inside them. Her heart thudded. It was hard to breathe.

"I hate them," she heard herself say, and stared at the mercenary in his nice boat, trying not to flinch or back away when his gaze settled on the bridge—and, seemingly, her. "I hate them so much."

The man drew her from the window. "A'lesander warned me you were being hunted."

It took her a moment. "Les?"

"Who wants to hurt you? Besides him?"

Jenny fumbled for words, still grappling with the idea that Les wasn't human. "I don't know how to explain. We were double-crossed by a person who works for a . . . a rival organization. He tried to kidnap me."

"That was more than two days ago. If he was supposed to contact someone—"

"Wait," Jenny interrupted, frowning. Hit, again, with how little she knew about this man. He wasn't human, he was frighteningly familiar—*he had sung the song, the song she had sung to the boy, the boy on the beach, oh my God, oh my God*—but that was all.

And she—who was usually so careful—had let him assume a peculiar command over this situation. She had even accepted medication from him, drinks that could have been drugged. Based on nothing more than instincts that were so insidiously rooted in her unconscious, she hadn't even given it a thought until now.

You know him, whispered a tiny voice. *Don't fight it. He won't hurt you. He could never hurt you.*

Jenny shook her head in denial. "How do you know how long it's been since the attack? Why are you even here?"

He hesitated. "I was in the region on . . . other business. We found an old man in the sea. He said there was a woman in trouble, and I had . . . strong reason to believe it might be you. So I came."

There was a great deal in those words that needed questioning, but Jenny could focus on only one thing. "Old man?"

"With a bullet wound. Alive when I left."

Jenny felt feverish again. "Let go of me."

"I don't think—"

"Let. Go." Her voice was so cold, so hard, she didn't recognize it.

The man's jaw tensed, his gaze utterly unreadable. Jenny suspected she should be afraid, but right then, she was too numb for fear—so close to losing it, she couldn't even feel her own body anymore.

The man's arm slid from her waist. "He was very concerned about you."

Jenny shoved him. He didn't have to move, but he did, and she staggered past him to the control station, leaning hard against it. Staring at him with new eyes, unsure what she was looking at anymore. Merman one minute, man the next, something else . . . something else now.

"His name is Maurice," she said, hoarse. "I watched Les throw him overboard. We were . . . attacked. Someone shot him, but Les . . . finished the job. Are you sure he was okay?"

"Not okay, but alive. Fighting to stay that way with . . . friends of mine. The Malaysian Coast Guard was coming for him when I left."

Friends. Malaysian Coast Guard. Business in the region. Words that registered, and skipped like stones through her mind.

Oh, God, she thought. *Oh, my God. Maurice.*

"I need to get to him, and contact . . . contact our . . ." Her voice trailed away, and she peered at the man, blinking hard as light trickled briefly through the clouds, from the sun behind his head. His hair resembled a silver halo, and she could see, finally, the boy he had been—in those cheeks, in that mouth. A hard, terrible loss settled in her heart, and it wasn't because of betrayal or attempted murder.

"You," whispered Jenny, and the moment she spoke, she had to escape. *Runner,* she accused herself, but she didn't care. She'd finally found the impossible, and it hurt too much to be near him.

She pushed away from the control station, heading for the stairs. Not thinking. Acting only on instinct. He caught her before she went two steps.

Jenny elbowed him in the gut. He grunted, loosening his grip—which nearly sent her toppling over. She managed to catch her balance and staggered backward, fighting for distance.

"Stay away," she warned, breathless, light-headed. "Stay the fuck back."

But there was nothing Jenny could do when he grabbed her arms with his big rough hands and leaned in, breath hot. She had to crane her neck to meet those glittering blue eyes, and it made her dizzy, nauseous.

But what was worse was the eerie resolve in his face. Not fury. Nothing cruel. Just a cold determination that sank through her like a knife.

"Maybe I don't know you," he whispered impatiently. "Maybe you don't know me. But there *is* something between us. You feel it. I know you must. So trust that. Please."

Jenny swallowed hard. "And if I don't?"

Disappointment flickered. "Too bad."

He let go of her, far too abruptly. Jenny sagged backward against the smashed console. Outside, men shouted, but she hardly heard them. Her heart pounded too loudly, and there was a roar in her ears when she stared at the man. He wasn't looking at her now—away, out the window—but she felt his eyes on her all the same, burning ice in her veins. She suffered a gnawing, grinding hunger, pushing and pushing until she thought she would explode with the sensation, the terrible *knowing* of it.

"There was a beach," she heard herself whisper.

His shoulders sagged. "And I was a boy who had never seen red hair."

Her legs couldn't hold her weight. Jenny sank to the floor, trembling. Wondering, dimly, what was wrong with her. She had waited a lifetime to hear those words. She had never stopped looking. Never stopped hoping.

But this was not the fantasy she had built in her mind. This was not the sweet boy of her memories. Not the frightened boy who had looked at her with wonder and fear, and tentative friendship.

A very large part of her, she realized, had never expected to find him—not the boy, and certainly not this rawboned, scarred, giant of a man he had become. She wasn't ready. She didn't know what to do, or how to react. She didn't even know if she could trust him.

Her mouth tasted like a bitter pill. "Why are you here? Why . . . after all these years?"

He finally looked at her, and for the first time she realized that constant cold expression was nothing but a mask—a mask that slipped, briefly, to reveal raw heartbreak. "Because I found you."

Because I found you. If there had been a gun to her head, she still wouldn't have found words to answer that. All Jenny could do was drink him in, listening to his voice, blind to everything but his eyes. Those eyes.

She tried to stand when he crossed to her side, but her aching legs wouldn't work. He reached down and picked her up in his arms. His touch was uncannily familiar. His skin, hot.

"You were expecting something else," he said, quietly. "Not . . . this."

"I'll settle for your name," she replied, allowing her head to rest against his chest, too sick and weary to fight. She felt reduced to taking life in moments, one at a time. Too much had happened for anything else.

He hesitated. "Perrin."

"Perrin," she repeated, unable to help the grim smile that ghosted over her lips. "I'm Jenny."

"Jenny," he said. "We're leaving this boat."

LES HAD DUMPED THE SCUBA EQUIPMENT IN MAURICE'S room. The old man's scent was everywhere when Perrin opened the door. Cherry tobacco and beer, and the sea. His bed was rumpled, sheets limp. His desk, cluttered with fossils and shells, and old books he collected in every port. No computer. Maurice didn't like them. If he had, Jenny suspected it would be gone. Les had left nothing that could be used to call out.

Air tanks, suits, masks—everything had been dumped on the floor. Perrin stood just inside the room, holding Jenny in his arms. Staring at the mess.

He made a small sound of frustration. "You'll have to tell me what you need."

She blamed exhaustion for the tears that burned her eyes—certainly not being near Maurice's things, or the man holding her. Certainly not.

Either way, she didn't want him to see her cry. "Put me down. You're making me dizzy."

Perrin loosened his arm and set her gently on her feet. "Sorry."

Jenny really did feel dizzy. "Don't be. Just . . ."

"Calm down," he finished.

"You seem perfectly calm." She craned her neck to see his eyes. "If you're screaming, I can't hear you."

"Good," he rumbled. "I'd sound like a girl."

Jenny coughed, staring. Tears slipped over her eyes, and she wiped hurriedly at them. His strong fingers slid around her hand. "Sit down on the bed."

She couldn't stop looking at him, and felt like a fool. "You don't have to help me."

His hand tightened, though his expression remained unreadable. Such a familiar touch, even if the face didn't match the warmth of his skin. Such a familiar voice, even if its low rumble didn't fit the cold glitter of his eyes. Never mind any of that. Every time he spoke, or touched her—she felt herself sliding from reality, and it was all she could do to snap herself out of it and wall up those memories. Not now. Not here. Not the time.

But he said, "Pretend this is the beach," and all her resolve shattered, making her feel uneasy and fragile.

"Pretend," he said again. "Pretend, and stop telling me I don't have to help you. Don't wonder why. Just accept it."

"You wouldn't accept it," she whispered, frozen under his touch and stare. "You don't get that many scars and accept just anything."

Perrin blinked and stepped away from her. Not much room—his back hit the wall. Jenny couldn't move. Wondering where those words had come from and how they had hit their mark so hard.

He circled her. Just a couple steps, until he stopped, turning slightly. Not looking at her. She was glad. Afraid he would see her trembling. Or staring at his scars. There were so many of them—all over his back and sides, his arms, even his legs. The same scars, as though he had been cut open with the same knife, the same hand. She thought of the boy on the beach, whose skin had been unblemished except for the wound on his chest, and wondered what the hell had happened. Had he received the other wounds then? Later? Why would anyone hurt him?

She stumbled to the bed and sat. "Where are we going?"

He hesitated. "There's someone I need to find."

Someone. Another mystery. She had so many questions. Les, that murdered woman . . . was that his business in this region? And what kind of business did a merman have? How was it possible that he spoke English, or made references to the O.K. Corral, or—

Stop, she told herself sternly. *Stop it. Focus. Prioritize.*

You need a doctor.

You need to stay out of Consortium hands.

You need to make sure he stays free from the Consortium.

The rest could wait. The rest didn't matter until they were safe.

"You mentioned friends," she said. "Calling the coast guard. You must have a radio."

"It's too far for us to reach. I assume, though, the old man—"

"Maurice," she corrected him.

"Maurice," he said, still turned away her, "probably already contacted someone. Assuming he was conscious enough to do so. My . . . friends would have."

He stumbled over the word *friends*. Not an easy word for him. Maybe those people weren't his friends. Maybe he was lying about helping Maurice.

Maybe, maybe.

But if he was telling the truth, it also meant she could wait this out. Help would come. Pathetic how much she relied on her family for help when she didn't even want to see them anymore.

You want to be a sitting duck? You think you can trust them to come in time? Is that so much easier than fighting your own fight? When did you become a coward?

Six years ago on a bloody day, that was when.

But she had been a sitting duck then, too, for different, important reasons. And Jenny never wanted to feel that helpless again.

Perrin bent and hefted up an air tank, already clamped into the black harness. "What about the suits?"

Jenny didn't move. "I want answers."

"Answers with no questions." Perrin stared at her, dangerous, inscrutable—until the corner of his mouth twitched. "I want those answers, too."

She swallowed hard, unable to understand her reaction to that ever-faint, barely there, smile. He put the tank on the bed and pulled a wetsuit from the pile. "Do you need this?"

"Yes," she whispered.

He shook it out, knelt in front of her, and held open the legs. She had to tell herself to move. Had to concentrate in order to push through the moment. It was all too strange.

Jenny shoved her feet into the wetsuit, and studied his bowed head as he pushed and pulled her into the skintight gear. Being so near him, just a breath away, sent a roar of heat through her, matched by an equally cold tingle that rushed over her skin and made every hair rise on her arms. She wanted to touch him, desperately, just to tell herself that he was real.

Just to touch him, for the sake of a touch.

When it was time to stand, he said, gruffly, "Put your arms around my neck."

"I can do it alone," she lied.

Perrin took her hands and placed them around his neck. His touch was gentle, firm, his skin warm and dry. Her palms brushed the rough ridges of his scars, and it felt too intimate, touching them. She suffered the sudden, striking feeling that no one else ever had.

He also stilled, and did not look at her face.

"Hold on," he whispered, and stood. Jenny rose with him, until her feet nearly dangled off the floor. Pressed together so tight she could feel every hard line, warm, intimate in a wholly different way. His presence, larger than the world. She refused to look at his face, afraid of what he would see in her eyes. Too deeply affected. Frighteningly so. Her heart, raw and naked.

Perrin pulled the suit over her clothes. The material felt hot, stuffy. Jenny regretted saying she needed it even though it wasn't safe to enter the sea without protection for her skin.

"What about Les?" she asked, watching his jaw tighten.

"What about him?"

"If you leave him, and others discover what he is, there'll be trouble. Not just for him, but all your kind. Same with the . . . the woman."

"No time for trouble," he muttered cryptically, and picked up an air tank. "Come on."

"I'm serious."

"So am I," he snapped, but with an unmistakable tremor in his voice that made Jenny close her mouth. "Anything else you need?"

Jenny hesitated, then grabbed one of the waterproof packs. "Something from my room."

"I'll get it for you."

"No."

"Yes." Perrin held her gaze. "I don't want you near him. Tell me what you want."

"A pouch," she whispered. "In my top desk drawer."

He frowned and left her.

The moment he was gone, she went to Maurice's dresser and scrabbled around until she found a sheathed blade in his underwear drawer. She dropped it in the waterproof pack, along with a bottle of ibuprofen and a container of matches. On an afterthought, she included a small signal mirror.

Shouts echoed down the hall. She froze, heart pounding, and tried to listen to what they were saying. She caught a few words—*no, you don't understand*—but then everything switched over into a tangled mess of clicks and snarls. Wood crashed. She jumped, frightened—then took one step down the hall, afraid not to look. If Les had gotten free . . .

She heard Perrin's voice. He sounded calm, unhurt.

"Don't tell me why," he said. "Doesn't matter anymore. But you won't hurt her again."

"Would never," Les said, his voice ragged, pained. "Not Jenny."

She flinched again, hearing her name—then twitched one more time as she listened to another crash, a meaty thud, a long groan. She tried to move, but her feet were frozen.

"Not Jenny?" Perrin echoed, and the quiet fury in his voice stunned her. "You kept her tied up for two days. She had a fever. You tried to drown her. And I saw her shorts. If you touched her—"

Jenny started and touched her waist. Her shorts were buttoned. She hadn't done that. Had Perrin fastened them while she lay unconscious?

She couldn't listen anymore. Couldn't think about it. Finally, her feet moved, and she wrenched herself around. Fleeing down the hall, another headache brewing at the base of her skull.

Near the engine room, she dropped to her knees and pulled up a loose flap of carpet, revealing a small panel that slid open with one gentle push.

The Russian SPP–1M was inside. Along with a box of bullets that had been torn open. She stared, thinking hard, and picked up the weapon. Checked the ammo.

Four shots had been fired. The same number that had pierced that woman's body.

"What is that?" Perrin asked, behind her.

Jenny flinched, startled. "You're so quiet."

"Sorry." He crouched, pointing. "Tell me."

She thought of the conversation she had overheard, the rage in his voice as he had accused Les of hurting her.

"Your knuckles are bleeding again," she said.

His face revealed nothing, nothing but cold and shadows, and a quiet menace that should have terrified her.

But she crouched there, holding his gaze—bold, unflinching—and felt no fear. She tried, she looked for it, she told herself to be uneasy—because that was smart, anyone should be uneasy of him—but her stomach didn't hurt, and she wasn't afraid.

Just tired. Head hurting. Feeling used.

I will never trust anyone ever again, she told herself, thinking of Les.

Except for Maurice, she added.

And this man, an insidious little voice whispered. *Trust him.*

"My knuckles," he said, slightly hoarse, "had to make a point."

She made a small sound. "Does that happen often?"

He looked down, but not quick enough to hide the shame that flickered in his eyes. She also looked away and held up a bullet. Her hand shook.

"This is ammunition for an underwater gun. I found . . . similar wounds . . . on the woman."

She tamped down the desire to explain modern weaponry. He seemed to know more than enough about humans already.

Perrin took the bullet from her. "This is what killed her?"

"It wounded her. I think it took her several days to die." There was no good way to say that, but he needed the truth. She tried to gentle her voice.

His jaw tightened. He still refused to look at her. If he did, Jenny suspected there would be grief in his eyes.

Maybe he loved that dead woman. Maybe he had someone else. Children, even. She didn't know how it worked amongst his kind or what his life was like.

Just violent. Bitter. That much was written all over him.

"Why would Les try to kill her? He did, didn't he?"

Perrin rubbed the back of his neck. "Later. Too much story."

"No. I've worked with him for years. I thought we were friends. I never guessed. And if he . . . if he used me—"

"Were you close?" he interrupted sharply.

"Don't ask it like that."

"Did he . . . did he hurt you?" His tone wasn't any gentler, but his voice roughened, and broke. She knew what he meant, though—and that question was almost worse. Jenny could still feel Les's hands on her, unbuttoning her shorts. She settled back on her heels, staring at him. Staring, until he finally had the good sense to look down at the bullet in his hand.

"No," she said.

He put down the bullet, very carefully. With equal care and silence, he opened up his other hand. The scale lay on his palm, on top of the pouch. It glimmered like a pearl from white to silver, to pale ice blue.

"This was mine," he said quietly.

Jenny held out her hand. Perrin stared at the scale; and then, gently, gave it to her.

"Thank you," she whispered, finding that it hurt to look at him. She tucked the scale back into the pouch, which she placed into the waist pack. She stood, awkwardly. Perrin rose, too, watching her. Jenny could barely meet his gaze.

"You look feverish again," he said.

"No," she said. "I'm ready to go."

He placed his palm against her brow, but his hand trailed down to her cheek and stayed there. Made it hard to breathe. His eyes were so cold, but there was something else there, too. Hunger. Regret.

"No secondary doors," she whispered, trying to stay in control. "Have to go on deck if you're planning on taking us into the water. We'll be exposed. They all have weapons."

Perrin removed his hand. "We'll move fast."

He had left the air tank at the end of the hall. Jenny checked the regulator to make certain it was mounted properly, and slowly opened the valve to check for air. She examined the pressure gauge, too. Quick, throat tight. Perrin helped her slide on the harness, and she tried not to stagger under the weight of the tank. She hated feeling so weak. He handed her a mask. "Let me do all the work. Just hang on."

Perrin hooked his fingers beneath the waist of his swim trunks and began to pull them down. Jenny tensed—he hesitated—and for the first time since encountering him, he seemed embarrassed.

"I'm sorry," he muttered. "I can't shift—"

"Yes, I know," she said quickly, then added, "I have some experience with shape-shifters."

Perrin tilted his head, but Jenny didn't want to answer the question in his eyes. She waved her hand at him, heat crawling into her cheeks. "Go, strip."

His mouth twitched. "Now I feel awkward."

Jenny stared at the ceiling, listening to cloth rustle. "You weren't earlier."

"I didn't have time to think about it." His face appeared in her line of vision. She couldn't look away from him, not even when he tugged the pack around her waist. She heard the seal suck open, listened as he pushed the shorts inside. He didn't look away from her, either. Not once.

Jenny stepped back, needing room to breathe. Rattled. Even when he finally dropped his gaze and turned from her to face the outer door, she suffered a jolt.

His every little move made her heart feel heavy and strange, as though she had awakened never knowing another living creature, except him. Every gesture new. Every breath. Those eyes, and the way he looked at her.

As though she was just as new to him.

They made their way down the narrow corridor, and up a short set of stairs to the main salon and the outer door that led to the aft deck. Her fingers trailed against the walls. Her home, another home she was running from.

Perrin reached the door first and peered through the window. Jenny joined him. One of the boats had stopped circling and drifted in plain view. Men watched *The Calypso Star*, guns at the ready. Some watched the sky. Gulls winged overhead, hundreds of them. An eerie sight. Unexpected.

Not so unexpected was the man who stood on deck.

The mercenary. Alone, a gun held in his right hand, his eyes dark and narrowed as he stared at the door. He wasn't tall, but he was whipcord lean, and looked fast. Jenny went very still on the inside when she saw him. Still and afraid.

"Hello," he called out, his surprisingly elegant voice carrying through the steel door and tinted bulletproof glass. "I know you're there, Ms. Jameson. I can practically feel you breathing."

He turned in a slow circle, his gaze falling on the dead dolphin. "This doesn't have to hurt."

Jenny whispered, "We'll need a gun, after all."

"Fastest draw in the West?" Perrin rested his large hand on her back. "Wait."

She looked up at him. He was staring out the window at the mercenary, expression cold, hard, his gaze so level and intense she wondered if mermen could kill with a stare. Because if they could, she suspected that mercenary was about to drop dead.

Instead, she heard a scream.

Not human. Jenny looked up. Found that entire winged mass of seagulls crashing from the sky like one giant fist—plunging toward the speedboats. And the mercenary. He turned, eyes widening, raising his gun.

Perrin yanked open the door and grabbed her around the waist. "Hold on."

There was nothing to hold except air. Perrin held her tight against him, lifting her feet off the ground as he slipped out the door and made a sharp left to the rail. She felt like a rag doll, legs swinging wildly, arms flopping. She couldn't see anything but his chest and a glimpse of wings. She heard gunfire, men shouting.

Perrin threw her over the rail into the sea.

The impact stole her breath. Jenny sank, grappling for the mouthpiece. She shoved it into her mouth, reached back to start the flow of oxygen, and forced herself to take shallow breaths.

Again, she felt a pulse in the base of her skull, terrible aching pressure—and for one desperate moment she wanted to swallow salt water.

You breathed, she told herself, remembering the sensation of drowning without choking. *You breathed.*

No. She had been delirious. Mermen might be one kind

of impossible, but her developing the ability to breathe water like a fish was a whole other kind of crazy. Jenny was human—the most human person in her occasionally not-so-human family.

Perrin plunged into the water beside her—a clean pale spike of man cutting the sea like a knife. Jenny forgot about breathing, forgot to swim, staring at the white shimmer of his skin, and the lines of his muscles as he sank through the shadows, impossibly graceful.

He met her gaze through his mask of swirling hair, eyes glowing as though lit with blue fire, fire and hunger, and power. Skin rippled from his torso down his legs, creating its own dappled light as flecks of scales rose from his flesh, swallowing his legs and pouring through his feet. His toes lengthened, disappeared; and what unfurled was a dorsal fin that glimmered like moonlit silver. All of him glittered. Stars were buried in his skin.

You're beautiful, she wanted to tell him, suffering a peculiar madness, the trauma of a new obsession. *My God, you're beautiful.*

Perrin swam toward her. Jenny felt absurdly mortal beside him, and a scene from a movie flashed through her mind: Lois Lane meeting Superman for the first time, awkward and haunted with nerves. Her heart swelled, blood burning—every inch of her tingling with such sensitivity, she wondered how she had survived so many years without feeling so alive.

He didn't smile when he looked at her. She glimpsed the scars on his chest and shoulders, even more pronounced in the watery light; and when his hair drifted upward, she saw other old wounds against the back of his neck, as though someone had tried to skin him with a chain saw.

Jenny felt so strange looking at those particular scars. Terrible pressure gathered at the base of her skull, and when the parasite twitched, the root of its body brushed bone. Visions of paralysis and brain damage filled her head: feeding tubes, wheelchairs, drool.

She fought down a silent scream. No hospitals, no way to pull the parasite out. Perrin might know what to do, assuming he had seen such creatures before—but this was certainly not the time to ask.

He dragged her arms around his neck, turning until she lay against his back. Jenny pressed her cheek to his ear, analyzing and savoring every sensation, every tickle of his hair on her face. She could not believe this was real. Not even when his tail moved against her legs, a long, pulsing stroke of muscle that knifed them through the water like a bullet.

It didn't feel as though they went far before Perrin pulled them to the surface, but when he spun them around to look at *The Calypso Star*, it was quite some distance away. The gulls had dispersed, and there were men on deck, small as ants. Jenny stared, numb, feeling as though she was watching her home burn down.

Perrin squeezed her hand. "Listen."

All Jenny could hear was her heart, and the whisper of the waves against their bodies. She removed the mouthpiece and held her breath, listening.

And heard a helicopter.

Perrin shielded his eyes. "In the east. Coming fast."

Jenny didn't want to look, but forced herself to. The helicopter flew low to the horizon, a massive Sea Knight, capable of landing in the ocean. She refused to consider that one of her own family had sent it to rescue her. Possible, but nothing she wanted to risk her life on. Better to assume it was from the Consortium, with its links to almost every major criminal organization in the world—and, by extension, all the minor organizations, as well.

Ismail was supposed to check in. When he didn't, the Consortium sent hounds to go sniffing.

"They'll torture Les," she couldn't help but say. "Not the men on the boat, but those who are coming."

"Like they would have tortured you?"

"Yes."

Perrin stared at the boat, then the helicopter, and covered her hand with his. His touch was gentle, but when he finally looked at her over his shoulder, his eyes were dead, so empty they seemed made of glass. "They won't hurt you, Jenny. Not again."

"What do you mean, not again?"

"The dark house on the beach."

She stared, stricken. "But that was . . . that was a *dream.*"

"Yes," he said, holding her gaze. "It was."

Jenny felt numb, and very small. Thrown back, thrown down, run over by feelings she couldn't even name. Perrin squeezed her hand and pushed the mouthpiece into her hand.

"Breathe," he whispered.

CHAPTER EIGHT

BREATHE, Perrin told himself.

Easier said than done.

The woman—*Jenny*—was warm against his back, and so very alive. Her arms were clasped around his neck, held in place by his hand. Strange, familiar weight. She had held him like this, long ago, in their dreams. On the beach, watching a dream sunset. Laughing in his ear as she leaned against his back.

Reality. Fantasy. He did not know where one began and the other ended. He wasn't even certain it mattered anymore. Just this moment. Now. Teetering on the cusp, at the end of the world.

Perrin swam fast, keeping them close to the surface—straining to listen for dolphins. Dolphins could not be trusted. Talkers, all of them.

And they would remember what had happened with Rik. Dolphins had long memories, passed on in blood, song. If one of them saw him, word would spread to his kind. He wasn't ready for that.

But I wouldn't kill one of them, he thought.

And he would never have murdered his cousin for her *kra'a*.

Poor Pelena. Sweet as starlight, best of the candidates—and utterly unprepared to be a Guardian. She had always hated being alone. Solitude frightened her. Made her feel empty, lost—as she'd told Perrin, while visiting him in the darkness of the deep. Where he spent all his time alone. Except for his very secret dreams.

You have no heart, she would tease him. *No heart, if you're satisfied with only the company of a monster.*

And then she would tease him even more for refusing the females who were sent to him, for companionship and breeding.

My only comfort, he could still hear her say, *is the certain knowledge that I will never bear the burden of the* kra'a. *Because, dear cousin, by the time you die, I will be little more than a wrinkled wisp in the waves, and there will be a whole army of youngsters bursting their tails at the chance to bond with your odd little friend.*

And he'd said, *I would hardly call my* kra'a *odd.*

That must be you, then. Punctuated with a silver laugh, and a sharp tap on his head with her fist.

Sweet, sweet Pelena. For her to have died, *alone*, onshore. . .

I should have killed A'lesander, thought Perrin.

He almost had. Some lines he still couldn't cross. And it was hard to forget A'lesander, the child: who had been his friend.

Those pirates, and whoever had been in the helicopter, would have found him already. If Jenny was right, then he faced torture, experimentation, eventual death.

I should have killed him, he thought again.

Jenny's arms tightened, her legs bumping against his tail. Perrin squeezed her clenched hands, holding them closer to his chest. Warmth spread through him, and a terrible pain in his heart. Pain, and determination.

You are going to live, he told her silently. *You are going to live, and nothing else matters.*

His dream woman, his dream friend, in the flesh.

Alive. So alive.

Would A'lesander have killed her, too? Like Pelena, who also trusted him? Lonely Pelena, who would have been intrigued by his presence, despite A'lesander's exile? Who would have remembered only her childhood friend—and not thought about the man he had become?

Perrin pushed himself harder, ignoring the strain in his muscles, the fatigue. Pelena, dead. Her *kra'a* gone. He had never imagined that. Not even a little. There were myriads of reasons for the beast to wake, but the murder of a Guardian? That had never happened, not in ten thousand years.

And if Perrin had not thought of it, then likely no one else would, either. Guardians spent so much time alone, there was no way to know for certain whether the rest of his people were yet aware that Pelena and her *kra'a* were no longer bonded.

Though if the earthquakes have started, then they must realize something is wrong. They'll be looking for her.

Just as Perrin would be looking for her *kra'a*.

Unfortunately, there was only one person who could help him locate it. And she might be just as happy to see him dead.

Jenny's hands loosened beneath his. He turned his head, and glimpsed her checking the gauge on her tank. He could not see the device, but her eyes narrowed behind her mask.

She tapped his chest and pointed up.

Perrin took her to the surface, breaking into the light with a wince. Even an overcast sky felt bright after being underwater. He closed his aching eyes and stretched his tail, trying to ease the ache in his lower body. Away from the sea too long, and his adrenaline rush had faded. Even the pleasure of being in the sea was losing its power. The base of his skull ached.

"Sorry," Jenny said, breathless. "Ran out."

He rubbed his eyes. "I needed to rest anyway."

She was silent a moment, her body warm against his. "Where are we going?"

"To find someone who has answers that I need."

"I need a radio."

"I know." Perrin tried opening his eyes, but the sky was so bright all he could do was squint at the water. "I know, and I'm sorry. If this wasn't important, I would take you first to . . . to . . ."

He stopped, unsure what to tell her. Where would he take her? He had no idea where Eddie and the fishing vessel were, and even if he did find some other ship in the area, he couldn't simply toss her on it without making certain she found her own people, safe. Assuming he could stomach letting her out of his sight in the first place. He wasn't sure he was that strong.

A swell glided them up, then down, a rolling motion that happened again, and again. Perrin had been on a roller coaster, just once—a little one—and this reminded him of that. Before his exile, he had never thought much about the surface of the sea, except as a boundary, but now it felt as alive as the back of a twisting eel, or a dancing whale. Perrin pulled Jenny closer, kicking his tail to keep them afloat as the surface grew choppy. Bright spots of red appeared in her pale cheeks. He hoped it wasn't the fever.

"You need a doctor," he said, and felt sick himself, and torn. She needed a doctor, human medicine, and they were hundreds of miles away from help. Help that would be on land, which might as well be a death sentence if he couldn't set things right.

Jenny clung to his shoulders, blinking away the salt spray in her eyes. Her clear green gaze settled on him with a steadiness that made him forget himself, the world, everything but her. "You said you had business in this region."

He hardly remembered telling her that, and didn't know how much to say. Words filled him, awkward and uneasy, and frightening. But he couldn't lie. Not to her.

"Something bad is happening in these waters," he finally said. "I came to stop it if I can."

"Bad," she echoed. "What's that supposed to mean?"

"Many people will die."

"Your people?"

Enough would die, too many, trying to stop the beast. "Humans, mostly."

Another wave tossed them, this one more violent, twisting them sideways and underwater, briefly. Jenny also twisted, right out of his grip. He followed, afraid of losing her.

Close, but not touching. Her red hair glimmered, coming loose from her braids in wispy strands. She watched him with those unnerving green eyes, so thoughtful. He considered how alien he must seem, and that made him feel lonely.

Perrin reached for her. She kicked just enough to slide away from his hand. He reached out again, just beneath the surface. Caught her wrist and pulled her near. She did not fight, but every inch of her was rigid, tense.

"Get rid of the gear," he said, hating his voice for sounding so rough. When she didn't move fast enough, he fumbled around her waist for the harness clip. Jenny pushed his hand away. He didn't apologize. He was not good with words. Not human, or otherwise. Not when it mattered. Like now.

"Don't be afraid of me," Perrin said, and wanted to punch himself in the head, both for the statement *and* his tone. Like he was back in prison, where talking gentle got you killed, or worse.

But Jenny stared at him with those steady eyes, not looking particularly afraid. Just confused. Slowly, carefully, she shrugged out of the scuba gear and let it sink. She almost went down with it, and he caught her around the waist, holding her up. His tail bumped against her legs. He wondered suddenly if that disgusted her. Or worse, his scars. His scars were ugly, and everywhere.

"Why?" she asked him. "Why will people die?"

Again, it was so hard for him to speak. "The woman . . . the woman of my kind who you found dead . . . is, *was*, special. She had a . . . a job to do. And without her now . . ."

"Bad things," Jenny filled in, after an awkward moment of silence. "Bad, deadly things. But you think you can stop it."

"I don't know," he said, heart aching, drowning. "But I have to try."

Eight years, lost. Eight years without purpose, except to survive. And now he had a good reason to live. The perfect reason. Right in front of him, in his arms.

Except he was going to lose his life, anyway. He was going to die, and it didn't matter, because if he didn't try with all his will to change things, then Jenny would die. Quick, or slow. But lost, all the same.

Jenny kept staring at him. Her eyes, those eyes. As though she could see right through him. He had never felt so naked in all his life, stripped down, and small.

"I used to trust my instincts," she whispered. "But I trusted Les."

"I'm not him."

"Not yet."

"Never." Perrin's voice felt raw in his throat. "I was never like him."

Grief flickered in her eyes. He could only imagine the burden, the insanity, the fear she had to be suffering. Her world, upended.

His world, too. Crushing them both.

"That doesn't mean anything," she said. "I don't know you. I didn't know him, either, I suppose."

Cutting words. Perrin struggled to show nothing on his face, but it was a losing battle. What he felt for her was too strong. For eight years she had shared his dreams, his soul—and for eight years after that, during his exile, she had still inhabited his thoughts.

Now, she was with him in the flesh.

You're my missing heart, he wanted to tell her—and felt like a fool. All he'd ever known of her was in a dream. This . . . what he felt . . . this need to draw her close, as though she was the only thing keeping him alive . . . was ridiculous. So ridiculous he couldn't help but touch her braid, and then the edge of her jaw, afraid to look into her eyes. Feeling like a boy again, afraid of the sky because it was too large for his small life.

"Jenny," he whispered, tasting her name. "Some things cannot be explained."

Like us. Like this moment. Finding each other again, when we should never have met that first time.

Don't throw me away, he wanted to tell her. *Please.*

The grief in her eyes did not fade as she searched his face. Perrin held as still as the sea allowed, holding her, his breath, his life.

"I have so many questions," she murmured, finally. "Is this real?"

Perrin felt so helpless. "I don't know."

She gave him a long look, and slowly, all that sadness and confusion in her eyes disappeared, replaced by grim resolve.

"Okay," she said.

"Okay," he echoed, barely able to speak. "What does that mean?"

Her jaw tightened. "I'm not done with you yet."

She said it like a threat, but Perrin didn't care. He wasn't done with her, either. He wouldn't ever be done with Jenny.

"Can you hold your breath?" Perrin asked. His voice sounded like sandpaper.

"Yes," she said unevenly. Before he could muster the courage to look into her eyes, she slid around him to press against his back. She wrapped her arms over his shoulders, and her small hands touched his chest. He couldn't help but reach up, and hold them. He wanted to hold them there forever.

It was just dreams. You don't know her.

He closed his eyes, glad she couldn't see his face. "Tell me when you need air."

Jenny didn't say a word. Just pressed her forehead against his shoulder. Her drifting legs bumped against his tail.

He wanted to tell her to wrap them around his waist but couldn't say that. So he reached back, placed his hand under her thigh, and guided her around him. She tensed, but followed his unspoken direction, wrapped herself tight and close against his back.

It was almost more than he could take. Better than dreams.

"Okay?" he whispered, still holding her clutched hands. Jenny nodded, and he took them below the water.

It was different, this time. Perrin didn't know why, but he felt her vulnerability, and his—their fragility against the world around them. It made his heart swell, aching with life. He had not felt so alive in years.

But it frightened him. He had come back to the sea, feeling as though he had nothing to lose.

He had something to lose now.

Near shore, it occurred to Perrin that they had been underwater a long time. For a human. He glanced over his shoulder, and found Jenny staring down at the seafloor, her braids flying behind her, his own silver hair tangled around her throat and face. Small bubbles trickled from her nose, but she didn't seem to be in any discomfort. Just caught up in the moment. A hint of wonder in her eyes.

He could not look away. Not until her gaze flicked to his—locked—and that same hot frisson of fear and longing slammed into his heart. He faltered in the water, forgetting where he was, who he was, just that those eyes were staring at him. Her eyes.

Perrin broke the surface with too much power. Jenny clung to him, nearly falling off, dragging down deep breaths. His breathing was also ragged. He found himself squeezing her hands too hard and relaxed his grip.

Again, the overcast sky was bright. He closed his eyes.

Jenny said, "Are you okay?"

No, he wanted to tell her. *Yes.*

"I have trouble with bright light," he said instead. "It'll pass."

Jenny was silent again, then: "I see an island."

Surprise touched him. Perrin twisted, and saw an island behind him: a lush green mountain rising from the sea. It had been many years, but he recognized the knot of stone that jutted from the western ridge—like the edge of sharp knuckles. A faint haze clung to the edge of the beach, and the peak. No other island in this region bore such mist, which shimmered silver, and delicate.

He'd followed his instincts, and they had not led him astray. But then, all it had ever taken was a strong will, and an even stronger need, to find the home of the old sea witch, last of the siren crones.

"It's odd you can see the island," he said to Jenny. "Not many humans can."

She gave him a look, as though *she* wasn't surprised, and oh, by the way, get-on-with-it. The corner of his mouth twitched.

"Stay here a moment," he told Jenny. "I need to listen to something."

Perrin dove underwater, cutting only a few feet below the surface. He focused on his heartbeat, on the hushed whispers of the sea. Falling into the moment. Just one moment, quiet.

Far away, he heard a woman singing. Unearthly, sorrowful, a voice soft as crushed pearls. A voice to lure, and charm, and kill—though Perrin knew it had been many long years since the crone had murdered with a melody.

That had not stopped her from helping his father, though. An act he had never understood. The sea witch rarely involved herself in any affair that did not concern her, and his crime should not have warranted her attention—or her curse. It hadn't been enough to exile him from the sea, but fresh bodies of water, as well. Denying him even that little mark of freedom.

And you are still not sorry for what you did. Not truly.

Anger swelled. He pushed it down.

When he opened his eyes, ready to surface, he was sur-

prised again. Jenny was underwater with him, her face
closed and still. As though she was also listening. Light
from above the surface cast a spectral glow upon her pale
skin. Her red hair, a cold flame.

Perrin stopped breathing. *Rose of the sea,* he wanted to
call her. *Rose of dawn,* just before first light, when the sky
was caught in a transcendent glow—that promise of life, a
new beginning. For eight years he might have pretended to
be human, but he had never needed to pretend to love the
dawn.

Her eyes opened. Jenny looked straight at him. He
flinched. So did she. Perrin recovered first, grabbed her
hand, and hauled her to the surface.

She was breathless and tried to pull away from him. He
let her go.

"I heard singing," she said.

"The sea witch." Perrin wanted to duck beneath the
waves and listen, again. "She is the last of her kind."

"So she's not . . . like you."

"She shares our blood. And the blood of . . . other things.
She is very powerful."

"That doesn't sound safe."

"She won't hurt you. She has always had a soft heart
for humans." When her eyes narrowed, he added, "I didn't
mean to scare you."

"Oh, no," she murmured dangerously. "Why would I be
scared?"

I'm sorry, he wanted to say. *I'm sorry.*

Instead, Perrin held out his hand and waited for her to
take it. She hesitated too long, and he rasped, "I won't bite."

"It's not that," she said. "I know your hand."

"Yes," he replied. "Just like I know yours."

*Your touch. Your touch, for sixteen years of my life.
Holding me in my dreams, keeping me sane in the darkness.*

It frightened him now. Frightened him that he felt so
much.

Jenny winced, touching her head. "God," she said, then gasped, arching backward in the water with her mouth twisted open, contorted with pain. She grabbed at him as she began to sink below the waves, and he pulled Jenny into his arms, frightened for her. She trembled violently as they bobbed and tilted, and he kissed the top of her head and whispered her name, unsure if she heard him, but needing to say it. Needing to say the name he had never known, like a prayer.

"I'm better," Jenny whispered, but she sounded as though she was trying to convince herself. Nor did she pull away.

Gulls wheeled overhead, and he settled his mind behind their eyes, glimpsing a wide expanse of blue sea, a thick green canopy shrouded in that silver mist—and nothing else. Flashes so brief they were almost meaningless.

He let the waves carry them in, swimming easily, careful not to look at Jenny. She was so quiet against him, small and light, and warm. Her fingers were tight around his. Every now and then, a tremor shook her.

Close to shore, she disentangled herself. Her hands were the last to leave him, sliding from his, slow and careful. Perrin felt light, and disturbingly empty, when she stopped touching him.

Jenny tried to stand. Almost fell. Crouched, finally, with one hand buried in wet sand, buffeted forward by the waves that crashed against her. Perrin watched as she crawled out of the water and collapsed on the beach—first on her face, then rolling on her side to look at him as he beached himself near her feet. She was pale, shadows under eyes.

Exhausted, he thought. Of course, she would be.

Perrin lay still, letting her take him in, from his face down to the silver sheen of his tail. Even he wanted to look at himself. He needed the reminder that yes, this was real. He was real. After eight years of exile, he had entered the sea, and now lay on a beach with the girl who had haunted his dreams. A girl who had first met him just like this, on another beach, sixteen years ago.

He had been cleaning toilets on Friday. Scraping gum from glass cages. Living in a bathtub.

Now Perrin tasted salt in his mouth. His skin was wet and warm. Sand ground into his skin, against his scales, and the waves that crashed over his tail lifted him, pushed him, soothed and lulled him. Each sensation rich and heavy.

He felt Jenny's gaze, heaviest of all. Another kind of heat, a tingle of awareness that spread over him, through him, into his bones. He had felt it before, as a boy, with her. Before he even understood what it meant.

"We were both so young," he found himself saying.

Jenny looked away, her face crumpling with grief. It lasted only a moment. He would have missed it if he hadn't been watching her.

But the sight, the memory, hit him low in the gut and hard in the heart. He couldn't breathe. All he could do was watch as she pushed her fists into the sand, trying to stand. She managed to sway into an upright position, teetering there. Perrin suffered the insane desire to put her arms around his neck, just so he could hold her up.

Idiot, he told himself, forcing his focus to his lower body, which resisted his desire to transform. One taste of the sea, and his unconscious refused to leave.

But Perrin managed finally to tap that native, primal instinct, and shifted shape. Bones cracked, joints popping.

Jenny's gaze slid toward him as his tail receded, those silver scales rippling and dividing into pale human flesh. She watched every moment of his transformation, unblinking and intense, until he lay in front of her. Human. Naked.

She didn't stop staring.

Perrin rolled over and sat up. Too quickly. His head spun. He pressed his palm against his forehead, steadying himself.

Swim trunks flew into his lap. He glanced over his shoulder, and found Jenny struggling from her wetsuit. When she shimmied it down, her soaked shorts went with it. He glimpsed the edge of her hip, the smooth pale curve of her backside, and was hit with another jolt. Hot, aching.

She hitched up her shorts. His gaze ticked upward, meeting hers. Her cheeks were red, but this time he didn't think it had to do with her fever.

Perrin cleared his throat and stood. Slipped on the swim trunks.

Behind him, Jenny said, "I dreamed."

He closed his eyes.

"From the first night I found that boy," she went on, softly. "Until eight years ago. And now . . . now it seems . . . you were really there, inside my head. It wasn't just . . ."

"No," he finished. "It was real."

She was silent too long. He opened his eyes and turned. Found her staring at him with a terrible vulnerability that the grim line of her mouth did nothing to hide.

"This is too much," she whispered.

Perrin could not move, except to look away, at the sea.

"I didn't expect to find you here. Or to ever find you, at all."

"You remembered me."

He glanced back at her, sharply. "You changed my life. You were with me, always."

He might as well have hit her. The look she gave him was so stricken, so devastated, he wanted to drop down on his knees and crawl to her. The strength of his reaction frightened him. He had *never* felt this way. Even those dreams felt pale in comparison.

Perrin couldn't face it. Eight years, burying himself. Eight years, forcing himself to feel nothing.

Bleeding now, on the inside.

He turned and walked away.

Not far, before Jenny caught up with him. He heard her feet digging into the sand, and her soft labored breathing. Still weak from the fever.

Or from being tied up, kidnapped, terrified, nearly drowned. Stolen away into the sea by a virtual stranger who refused to return her to her people. Take your pick.

As if one of those things alone wasn't bad enough. He could have lost her.

Because of A'lesander, he thought, and something ugly unfolded inside his chest. He might still lose her. Chances were good he would, one way or another.

Perrin slowed his pace. She didn't match his stride but lingered behind. His skin prickled, every nerve strung tight, knowing she was there, so close. He stopped, and turned. Jenny had already quit walking. Her cheeks were flushed, and there was a look in her eyes that he didn't like. She fumbled with the pack belted to her waist and dropped down on her knees in the sand. Hard, quick, exhausted.

Perrin crouched, and nudged her hands aside. He wasn't certain what she had inside the pack, but when he found the ibuprofen, she reached for the bottle.

"I'll do it," he said, flipping open the cap. "Two or three?"

"Two for now." Jenny swallowed the pills dry with a grimace and gagging cough.

Perrin rubbed his thigh, uneasy. "You need a doctor."

"I need an ER," she muttered, which frightened him. "Before all hell broke loose on the boat, something happened in the water. I didn't know it at the time. Not until later. It's making me sick."

Dread touched him. "There are many poisons in the sea."

"This isn't poison. Not like that." Jenny swallowed hard, her gaze pained, frightened. "I don't even know what to call it."

Her hand twitched, and moved haltingly to her neck. Perrin suffered the urge to mirror her movements. A jolt hit him, followed by an even deeper unease. It was the placement of her hand. Just coincidence. It *had* to be coincidence. And yet, he wanted to touch the hole just above his neck, in the base of his skull. To see if he felt the impossible presence of something that had been ripped away from him, eight years ago.

His head throbbed. He imagined a voice whisper through him, incomprehensible but familiar.

Jenny stilled, closing her eyes. "I'm losing my mind."

Her voice was tight, restrained. Everything about her, tense. Perrin stopped rubbing his thigh and dug in his fingers instead, hard enough to feel pain. "No. You're not."

"I'm hearing things," she said, then shook her head, small jerky movements, her right hand gingerly touching the back of her head. "A woman singing."

Perrin stilled, and glanced around them. The mist had faded, but it always did upon reaching shore. The island was just an island—beautiful, but very much of the world. The old crone had never cared for illusions, except the ones that left her safely anonymous.

But he did not hear her song. Not here, on land.

"Jenny," he said, but she shook her head.

"I heard her before in the water, just like you did. If this is just my imagination . . ." Jenny looked away. "Help me stand."

Perrin drew her up, and she looked down the beach. Her hair was coming loose from her braids, tangled around her clear green eyes; and there was a wildness in her face that wasn't fear but something darker—and vulnerable. "I hear her, that way."

"I believe you," he said, and watched her shoulders relax.

They walked. Slow, careful. Neither of them wore shoes, but the sand was soft. Perrin studied the shadows of the forest, listening to birds caw and trill. He saw no other animals but sensed eyes watching him. Animals, or something else. He made Jenny walk ocean side, just in case, and picked up a long piece of driftwood to hold in his hand.

Jenny glanced at it. "Not dangerous, you said?"

Perrin grunted. "Maybe I shouldn't have brought you here."

"Was there ever a choice?"

"There's always a choice," he muttered. "But the other options were worse. No other boats nearby, no settlements."

Jenny looked down at her feet, stumbling a little. "I don't understand any of this, and I've seen some . . . strange things. I was just never one of those strange things."

"It won't get easier," he said. "Dealing with the strange and unfamiliar. Even when you think it has, that you've finally acclimated, something will happen, and you'll realize that all you were was numb."

"That's depressing."

Perrin had never thought of it as depressing. "It's survival. You shut down your fear to focus only on what is necessary, until you see nothing else. Until nothing else can affect you."

"The strange can be beautiful," she said quietly. "Even if it frightens you. Even if it confuses."

"And when it's too much?" Perrin gave her a sharp look. "If you're alone, and it's too much?"

Jenny stared at him. He looked away, ashamed and irritated.

"You were on land," she said. "You spent a lot of time there."

"I don't want to talk about it."

"You've already said plenty."

Perrin rubbed the back of his neck. "Fine. I lived on land for eight years. I had no choice in the matter. It was difficult."

"No choice?" He could hear in her voice, *But you told me there's always a choice*, and he thought, *It's easier to lie to myself than to you.*

"I was exiled," he told her. "On pain of death."

Jenny stopped walking. "But you came back."

"I told you. It was important."

Her gaze was so full. "Why were you exiled?"

"I won't discuss that."

Jenny wanted to argue with him. He knew it, felt it, braced himself—wondering how long it would be before he broke, and told her the truth, and saw real fear in her eyes.

But she surprised him. In a quiet voice she said, "Was it always horrible, living like a human?"

Perrin marveled that one simple question could reach into his heart and make it stop beating. Or maybe that was her voice, the thoughtfulness of it, and the compassion he heard in each word.

It had been a long time since anyone had even pretended to care.

"No," he told her. "It wasn't always bad."

"And you would have lived your whole life as human?"

"For as long as I could. Which might not have been long. My health was worsening. Household chemicals, smog, the common flu . . ." Perrin hesitated, glancing down at his arm, with its fading rash. "I planned to return to the sea if it became too bad. I didn't want to die on land, even if it meant my own kind would execute me on sight." He forced himself to look at her. "My soul belongs to the sea."

And to her, whispered a dry, familiar voice inside his mind. *You belong to each other first.*

Perrin stopped walking. Jenny said, "What?"

What, he thought. *What was that?*

Something impossible. A voice he should never have heard again.

The whisper of his *kra'a.*

"Maybe *I'm* losing my mind," he murmured, and Jenny grabbed his hand.

"Tell me," she said, and her alarm brought him back.

"I heard something," he told her, and closed his eyes as he heard something else, then.

A woman singing.

"Perrin," Jenny whispered.

"Come on," he said, still shaken.

She didn't move. "Wait."

"Jenny," he said, but she squeezed his hand, and he realized she was staring behind him, at the forest. Jaw tight, every inch of her tense, straining, like she was fighting the urge to run.

Perrin turned. And saw that the forest had loosened its many shadows, the eyes he had felt watching them.

Not animals.

Children.

CHAPTER NINE

JENNY had never been a big fan of all those Mad Max movies. Postapocalyptic wastelands rife with brutality, bad teeth, and men in assless chaps were not her idea of entertainment. She preferred historical romances, light with banter and stolen looks; classic black-and-white films where women were dames and the comedy screwball; or those old Westerns where the men moved slow and easy—except on the draw—and talked with sparse tongues.

The children who walked out of the woods were straight from the proverbial wasteland, fitting into another world: where laws did not exist; where adults were myth; and over the next hill might stand a place where it was common to fight to the death.

Small, lean. None was older than ten. Few shared the same ethnicity. She saw an Asian girl with straight black hair, a lean blond boy covered in freckles, and another with ebony skin and no hair at all. A Hispanic-looking girl with haunted eyes stood in the shadows, and there were smaller children near her, very young, with round faces and sturdy little bodies that should have been tumbling over soft rugs dragging teddy bears and sucking their thumbs instead of standing barefoot on the border of a rain forest, on an island in the middle of nowhere.

All wore loincloths made of soft pale leather, and nothing else. Jenny counted twelve children, but she was afraid there might be more, out of sight. Their youth didn't make her feel safe. She had heard of kids going feral—mostly to describe schools where bullies were getting rougher, more violent. That was nothing compared to this. This was old-school feral. Raised-by-wolves feral. Hunger in their eyes, and distrust, and just enough curiosity to make it all very dangerous.

"This is new," Perrin said, mildly.

Jenny didn't dare look at him. "Is that good or bad?"

"She's old," he replied. "I'm not sure."

She decided to err on the side of bad. "I'm not going to hit a kid."

"That would probably be for the best," he replied, still with that soft voice. And just like that, something snapped inside her: a peculiarly rich vein of anger, throbbing in her gut. Anger, combined with a streak of wild protectiveness.

Jenny's hands curled into fists. "Who is this woman, and why are these children here?"

Perrin tensed. "I don't know. She's not human. Her reasons—"

"I know plenty of nonhumans," she snapped. "Some are shit, but if any of them messed with kids? No mercy. A bullet in the brain."

And you remember what that looks like, she thought, with disgust, and nausea. *What it feels like to pull the trigger.*

Jenny's knees weakened, but she took a step toward the children, and then another. All of them swayed sideways with shambling grace—like little zombies—watching her with silent, feral hunger. She was afraid of them, but her concern was stronger.

Perrin loomed, warm and solid, close enough that their arms brushed. Jenny felt ashamed of her relief. Ashamed, and uneasy that his presence was so familiar, so comfortable, that instead of feeling like a stranger, he felt more like a constant, a touchstone, some piece of home.

He made her feel safe.

It wasn't right. It was too easy. Her heart was going to find itself broken into pieces. Because he *was* a stranger, he wasn't even human, and those dreams—those dreams, now that they were flesh and blood, and *real*—

Coward, she told herself. *Brave until you get what you want most.*

But she'd had what she wanted most, not so long ago. And lost it.

Perrin gripped her shoulder. "Careful."

Yes, she thought, and swallowed hard, meeting the flat, assessing gazes of all those staring children, before settling on the Asian girl.

"Hey," she said, trying to smile. "What's your name?"

"Stranger," whispered the girl. But the word had power, as though saying it released some strange current that raced against Jenny's skin. The base of her skull throbbed.

She heard the woman singing again: delicate, haunting, each note shimmering in her mind like a storm of falling light. Warm air rushed over her face. Smelled like rain. She felt sticky with sweat, weak, and suffered the overwhelming urge to throw herself naked into the sea, as though that would solve all her problems.

"And why wouldn't it?" asked a woman, suddenly.

Yes, said another voice inside Jenny's mind, echoing oddly, as though it wasn't quite part of her. *Yes, heal.*

Jenny flinched, turning. Perrin moved with her. Around them, the world spun with a sickening jolt, sky melting into sand, the sea roaring over the thunder of her heart. The parasite pulsed, trembled, fluttered like it was growing wings—

—and everything stopped.

Jenny found herself staring at sand. On her knees, in the sand. Her body tingled, and her head swam. She sucked in a deep breath, and slowly, carefully, looked up. Perrin stood beside her. Large, rawboned, his alabaster white skin carved with scars. *Fresh from the fight*, like the line from an old song. Frightening, intimidating.

Until he glanced at her, and she witnessed a heartbreaking vulnerability in his eyes that stole the breath right out of her. He was a boy again, that little boy, afraid and alone.

There and gone. She blinked, and found herself looking at a cold hard mask, his eyes empty, unreadable. He reached down and helped her stand. Her knees shook.

"Perrin O'doro," murmured a low, feminine voice. "Guardian."

Jenny stopped breathing, again. Slowly, as slowly as if her life depended on it, she turned her head.

A woman stood in the sea. Naked in the foam, her skin ice white. Even her nipples were white, her breasts heavy and round, shrouded in tumbling waves of blond hair that lifted in the breeze like strokes of floating sunlight. Her face was not clearly visible, but Jenny glimpsed a flash of terrible beauty, and a pale light that shone in her eyes, in her mouth. Jenny felt afraid all over again. Afraid and small, and infinitely vulnerable.

The sea was a pitiless place. Maurice called it spiteful, a jealous lover, but those were human emotions. If the sea had a spirit, nothing of it was jealous, because jealousy needed love, or hunger, or need, and the sea was a god without a heart. Too powerful for mercy. Too powerful for right and wrong. A force of nature, old as the world, beyond the tethers of a soul.

Jenny was reminded of that when she studied the woman—and it sent her past terror into cold, numb horror.

Focus only on what is necessary, until you see nothing else, she suddenly remembered Perrin saying. *Until nothing else can affect you.*

"Lady Atargatis," said Perrin coldly. "Or have you become Aphrodite?"

"My names slip away," she whispered, and Jenny steadied herself, trying not to sway as she listened to that melodic voice. "My names always leave me, and I have tired of wearing new ones. Call me crone, or witch, or lonely, for those are the words that will follow me into death."

Then her eyes narrowed. "You believe that I will kill you."

Jenny believed it, in that instant. Death would be easy for this creature, whatever she was. Death was nothing to the sea.

For a moment she was a child again, watching a man rise from the waves. Breathless, frozen with fear. Then that passed, and Jenny heard screams and the shots of guns, and a phantom pain in her stomach made her touch herself. She had been near the ocean that day, too. Listening to the waves crash as she lay bleeding in the grass.

I would have run that day, too, if I could have.

Hot shame filled her. Shame, and the absolute certainty that it was the truth. Jenny would have run away. If she could redo that day, she would still run. For one good reason.

But that was the past, and this was now.

No, she told herself. *Not again. You will not run.*

Jenny gritted her teeth and stepped into the ocean toward the woman. No plan. No idea what to do. Just that if she was going to die, it would be *there,* defiant, in death's face—

Perrin made a low rough sound, and grabbed her arms. With pure raw strength, he lifted her off her feet and placed her in the sand behind him. She glimpsed the forest, and the beach, but it looked different from where they had just been, and the children were gone.

"Kill me," she heard Perrin say roughly. "But keep her out of it, and keep her safe."

"She does not want safe," murmured the woman. "Her heart is wild."

Perrin growled. "You know why I'm here."

"I know," whispered the woman. "But do you?"

Jenny turned to face them, feeling as though she were moving through molasses. Heavy, sticky, the taste of the air suddenly too sweet.

"I'm here to find the *kra'a*," Perrin said, his voice hoarse. All Jenny could see was his broad, scarred back, and his long silver hair. Beyond him, the woman—crone, witch, whatever she was—continued to stand in the sea with perfect, inhuman, stillness. Waves broke around her as though she were made of rock, rooted to rock, and the water did not cling. Her hair remained untouched, and her skin glowed dry and heavy with light.

The woman looked at her. It was just a look, but Jenny felt as though scales slithered against the inside of her skull. She knew what it meant, even though the sensation was colder, and more powerful, than any human's mental touch. None of her grandfather's training against telepaths kept the woman out. She slipped past those walls as though they did not exist, and Jenny fought to stay calm, and strong.

I'm me, she kept thinking. *You can't take that away. I'm me, I'm me, I'm—*

More than you were, said the woman inside her head, her voice carrying a hiss that her speaking voice did not—which Jenny heard, moments later, when she said, "You speak of the *kra'a* that was taken from you."

"Pelena was murdered. Her *kra'a* is gone, and the beast wakes. It must be found." Perrin stepped sideways to block Jenny from the woman's sight—anger in his voice, in every line of his body—cold, restrained hurt and fury.

"And so you come here, thinking I will help you? You *are* desperate." Somehow the woman moved without moving, so that suddenly she was in Jenny's line of sight again, staring at her with breathtaking intensity. "But are you desperate for yourself, or others? If you find your *kra'a,* will you kill for it? If it has bonded to another, will you steal it away as it was stolen from you?"

"No," Perrin said, with such sharp pain it stopped mattering to Jenny that she was afraid. She heard the words and felt the story behind them, and the grief. Puzzle pieces. *Beast. Wakes. Kra'a. Stolen.*

The woman's gaze left Jenny and settled on Perrin. "Liar."

That word was the same as a hammer strike, a physical

blow. Perrin slammed down on his knees into the sand—
with such force he bounced. He made a strangled sound,
twisting and guttural, and Jenny watched in horror as his
scars split open and bled. She reached for him, and found
herself frozen, her feet rooted in the sand as though she had
become part of the beach.

Helpless. Unable to do anything but watch.

Memories flashed again. She saw another beach, and
a boy being pulled from her—and in her memories she
also heard whispers, whispers from adults who meant her
family harm—only no one would listen to her. And in her
memories she heard a gunshot, and her own screams, and
saw blood that would not stop. She saw Maurice thrown
overboard. Les with his hands on her. And all she could do
then—for her entire life, it seemed—was watch, helpless.

*I will not run. I will not stand idle. I will not be helpless.
I will not, I will not—*

"Stop this," she whispered, hating herself—hating the
woman—watching as Perrin's eyes squeezed shut, and his
breath rattled in his throat. "Stop."

The woman did not move from the sea, or look at Jenny.
"Perrin O'doro, tell me the truth. Tell me what you would do
if you found your *kra'a*."

"I would not kill."

"Liar," she said again. "You killed once to survive, and
you did so without mercy or regret. Even after eight years,
no regret. You would kill again. Again, and again, in rage
and in calm. You are stained with blood."

Perrin's expression turned savage, agonized, every
muscle straining. His scars bled more freely, mixing with
his sweat, dripping into the sand around him. Jenny fought
the compulsion holding her, fought with all her strength,
and in the base of her skull, the parasite pulsed, once.

"You would kill all but one," murmured the woman,
almost to herself. "And for that one, you would let the world
die."

Jenny staggered, suddenly able to move again. Perrin fell

forward, bracing himself on his hands, dragging in deep, heaving breaths that sounded as though his lungs were shredding. Jenny flew past him, grabbing a rock. She didn't throw it, but stood in front of him, staring at the woman.

"Stop," she whispered.

"Stop," echoed the woman, and the light died from her eyes, and her hair stopped moving; and even the waves pushed her forward, just a little. "Some things cannot be stopped."

Perrin touched Jenny's ankle, then let go to slowly stand. Hunched over, blood dripping down his chest and arms. He nudged her aside, staring at the woman in the sea.

"Kill me, or don't," he said quietly. "But you know my reason for coming here is important."

"Everyone's reasons are important. I wish, sometimes, that it was not always so. I am tired of being used." The woman tilted her head, regarding him and Jenny with new thoughtfulness. "But then, I suspect the both of you will soon feel the same."

Jenny frowned, wondering what *that* meant. Perrin said, "Explain."

The woman replied, "You, both. Come to me."

He shook his head, grim. "No, this is all wrong. Never mind how you helped my father. You've changed. I want your promise the woman will be unharmed."

"The children," Jenny corrected him. "They matter more than me."

Again, he hesitated. But when she looked at him, ready to argue, all she found was his steady regard, and somewhere deep, deep in his hard gaze, a flicker of admiration and concern that was there and gone in a heartbeat.

"The children," he rumbled, looking again at the woman in the sea. "The children are a puzzle."

"Come to me," replied the woman. "No one has, or will be, harmed."

Perrin's jaw worked. "Harmed in body or mind."

The corner of her mouth coiled into a sad smile. "Once, you would have taken me at my word."

He said nothing. Just stared, his silence gathering its own power. Pressure gathered in the base of Jenny's skull, followed by a chill.

The woman sighed. "It was for the best, Perrin O'doro. There was much you needed to learn, though you are too close to see that—and so many other things."

He drew in a deep breath. "Jenny, stay here."

She wanted to. She was afraid. But she was certain that if Perrin went out there alone, he would not come back.

Losing him was not an option. Jenny might not be ready to confront, or even understand, her feelings, but she'd spent sixteen years of her life looking for him. Sixteen years searching for answers to one moment on a beach.

Like hell she was going to let that go.

She grabbed his hand. He looked down at her with surprise. "Jenny."

"Go on," she muttered. "You're stuck with me."

Only because Jenny was looking at his eyes did she see them shift with grief. Grief or loneliness, or something born from pain. Whatever it was, she felt her heart answer. Her hand tightened.

"Jenny," he said again, but this time his voice was low, quiet, almost a caress. Utterly at odds with the hard, brittle mask he wore too well. *Bent or broken,* she thought. Raw with more scars on the inside than out.

Perrin walked into the sea, pulling her close against his side as the waves buffeted their bodies. He was big as a mountain against her, and moved with unwavering strength. Jenny tried to do the same. She held her rock in her free hand. The woman watched them, her eyes mere glints of light behind her tangled hair. Up close she seemed even more unreal. A little too perfect. A little too human. As though she were trying too hard to be something she wasn't.

"We learn to pretend in order to survive," said the woman, as if she'd read her mind—and if Jenny hadn't seen her mouth move, she would have thought those words were inside her head. "Perrin O'doro knows this. As do you,

Jennifer Jameson, whose blood flows from the daughters of the Magi—who was born from the blood of the fae and twisted that magic into death."

Jenny went very still. The woman whispered, "You are not so ordinary."

Perrin tensed. Jenny could not look at him. All she could do was listen to the rumble of his voice as he said, "My lady. The *kra'a*."

"It is with you," she said shortly, still watching Jenny with unnerving intensity. "And you must go now. Your father is coming. He brings hunters."

He stiffened, fingers flexing painfully around her arm. "What do you mean, the *kra'a* is with me?"

The woman ignored him, and to Jenny said, "We are not so far apart, in blood. You know this, in your heart. You know what your family is."

"I know enough to be wary," she replied, unnerved. "But you seem to know more than I do."

"The *kra'a*," interrupted Perrin impatiently, and the woman hissed at him: a rattling sound that rose from deep inside her throat. All that pale white skin wavered, revealing rough scales against her torso, shimmering from green to brown in one strong, muscular ripple—while beneath all that long blond hair, a tangle of glinting golden eyes and dripping fangs.

Jenny stumbled, swearing. Perrin caught her.

"Blind fool," said the woman, her golden eyes glowing. "Look between the two of you for the answers you seek. And do not return here until you have found them."

She backed more deeply into the sea, her human illusion falling apart: she did not have legs but balanced on a massive tail that coiled and flopped through the shallows like the body of a giant snake. Her breasts sagged brown and heavy, and her fingers were little better than claws.

Jenny's mouth went dry, but she stepped forward, pulling against Perrin's hand. "The children. Are they illusions, too?"

The woman slowed, stilled. "Human. Real. Mine."

"Yours," echoed Jenny, terrible fury making it hard to speak even that word. "Now who's the liar?"

Perrin's fingers tightened again. Jenny shrugged him off, and this time he let go. She took another step, swaying as the waves crashed against her legs, and gritted her teeth as she stared unflinchingly into the woman's golden, inhuman gaze.

This is nothing, she told herself. *You've dealt with worse since you were five years old.*

She'd learned to walk in the shadow of men and women who could kill with a thought. But those had been good people. Good hearts. First to be murdered on that bad day, years ago. She could still smell the blood and see it on her hands. Her stomach suffered a ghost ache, and the parasite pulsed, shuddered. Fever stoked Jenny's skin in one prickly wave.

The woman tilted her head, and the human mask faded completely, leaving a creature of primal, alien beauty, purely serpentine in every way but her features: nose, mouth, eyes, ears. Black hair fell around her high-boned face, tangled and cut with green strands. She touched her face with surprising tentativeness, as though she had only just realized that others, too, could see her true form. Her clawed hands trembled.

"The past and future do not lie," whispered the woman, closing her eyes. "The world is changing, and there will come a time when all that is known now will be torn, and the old days will rise again. Magic, and chaos, and war. It can be delayed, but not stopped. And if humans are to survive . . ."

The woman paused. All Jenny could do was stare, wavering between horror and fascination. *Words,* much like the ones spoken by her uncles, aunts, and cousins, who had broken away to form the Consortium. Jenny had listened to the debates for years before the break and family war—and since then. All those precog warnings of the future, and the terrible arguments concerning what to do, if anything.

"We must all do something," said the woman, looking away at the sea. "Those children were unwanted, abused, tossed aside. So I took them. Not to hurt, but to save, to train. I will protect as many as I can, teach them what I can, and when the time is right, they will know what to do. They will know how to live in the world to come."

Jenny tried to speak, but her voice stuck. Perrin brushed close, something terrible in his eyes. "If the beast wakes, what you've seen—"

The woman turned away, interrupting him. "Go. You have what you need."

Perrin snarled. "I have *nothing*."

She glanced over her shoulder—gave him a look of pure, shriveling disdain—and her tail lashed out of the water and smashed against his chest, knocking him backward. Jenny tried to grab his arm. She was taken down with him, and the sea closed over both their heads. They couldn't have been more than a hand below the surface, but the pressure was immense, crushing, and when she clawed at the water, she could not break the waves. Perrin was not beside her. She had no air.

You will understand before he does, murmured the woman inside Jenny's mind, her voice slithering, rubbing, crawling cold. *When you are away from here, and those bonds begin to stir. Listen to the voice that comes, the voice that is waking.*

Time is running out.

CHAPTER TEN

I N darkness, Perrin fought. He had no weapons, no fists, no bones. He was a ghost, and all he had was rage.

His father was there.

"*You killed her,*" said the old *Krackeni.* "*There are witnesses. You destroyed her mind, then broke her neck.*"

"No, listen to me," Perrin tried to say, but he had no voice.

Listen to me, he thought, rage melting into desperation. *Listen, please listen. What she did, what she was going to do—*

"*I trusted you,*" whispered his father, floating above him, pale eyes blazing with grief as each word bore its own spectral light inside his throat. "*We all trusted you.*"

You can trust me. Please, don't say that. Please.

"*But I can taste it now, inside you. I can taste the . . . the contamination . . . in your mind. It goes . . . so deep. Into your dreams. Oh, Gods, it truly is in your dreams. How could you? How could you do this?*"

No, Perrin raged. *No, you do not understand. She did not understand. Just listen, please—*

Please, do not—

Do not—

DO NOT—

—

PERRIN WOKE UP, GASPING, CLAWING INEFFECTUALLY AT the air. He could hear his father's voice, echoing so raw inside him.

But that presence died when he opened his eyes and found himself sprawled in grass. He stared, numb, taking it in: trimmed, neat, with an edge of color nearby. Roses.

I'm on a lawn, he thought, knowing that must be wrong.

As wrong as the scent of smoke, and the strange rat-a-tat-tatting sound that filled the air.

Gunfire. Then, screams.

Jenny's screams.

Perrin rolled to his feet, but couldn't stand. No strength. His muscles were made of water. He continued to fight, though, as he had in the darkness—but even wilder, more desperate. He screamed Jenny's name. He could not see her. He could not see anything but grass. She was sobbing. She was choking on sobs.

"Oh, God," she cried. "Oh, God, no. No, no. *No, please.*"

Her despair killed him. Her despair was the most horrific thing he had ever heard in his life. It shredded his soul and spat it out, and there was nothing he could do. Nothing. He was useless.

I'm useless, whispered Jenny inside his head. *I'm useless. It doesn't matter how hard I fight, there's nothing I can do. Nothing.*

"No!" Perrin shouted at her, digging his fingers into the grass. "Jenny!"

He thought she said his name. Maybe. From far away. He strained for it, hands buried in grass—

—grass that was suddenly flesh.

Perrin's vision wavered, as did the lawn. He saw sand, rock, driftwood—the crashing roar of waves replacing screams—but not the gasp of the woman he was holding down.

He threw himself away, horrified. Jenny stared back at him, cheeks flushed. Deep red handprints on both arms.

"You were dreaming," he whispered, his voice breaking on every word. He should have known.

But it was so real.

Jenny trembled. "Is that how you wake someone?"

Perrin shook his head, suffering shock, revulsion. "I didn't know it was you. I was . . ." He stopped, unsure what to tell her, how to explain without making her feel violated. *He* felt violated. He could still hear her screams.

"I was inside your dream," he finally said, unable to quell the tremor that raced through him.

Jenny didn't move or speak. Her eyes were huge, and he wanted to kill himself when he saw the marks on her arms. She was so much smaller than he, and he had been crushing grass in the dream, crushing it in his fingers—

"Your arms," he choked out, and made a small movement toward her. Jenny flinched, and he froze, cold to the bone.

"How," she began, then stopped, wetting her lips. "You can enter dreams."

"Yes," he said. "But this was an accident. Jenny—"

"What was I dreaming?" Jenny rubbed her right arm and winced. "I don't remember."

Perrin winced, too. He tore his gaze from her injuries and swallowed hard until he could find his voice. "All I could see was grass. I heard gunshots. Your voice."

Jenny stared at him. "What was . . . what was I saying?"

"You were screaming," he whispered, hating himself for not lying. "Begging."

Jenny shuddered and looked down at her arms. Perrin hugged his knees to his chest, his hands clenched in fists. His palms felt dirty. His fingers were numb. He wished his heart felt the same.

"What were you doing?" she asked him, so softly. "When you grabbed me?"

"I couldn't move," he told her, barely able to hear himself. "I was fighting to move."

Jenny closed her eyes and nodded to herself. After a breathless moment of agonized doubt, Perrin said, "Let me see. Please."

She said nothing, but at least it wasn't a no. Perrin shifted close, never feeling more like a giant oversized brute than he did then. Her eyes stayed closed.

"I'm going to touch your arm," he told her, and waited several seconds before doing that—as carefully as he could.

He had large hands. Jenny was a waif in comparison. The angry red stain of his touch covered well over half her forearm, and the flesh was slightly swollen. Bruises would set in soon. But nothing appeared broken. She could squeeze her hands into fists and move her arms.

Perrin released his breath, sweating. "I'm sorry. I can never make you understand how sorry."

Jenny finally looked at him, and those clear green eyes knocked his heart sideways.

"Thank you," she said.

Perrin could not tear his gaze away. "Don't."

She studied him. Made him feel small, naked. Lost. Just when he wondered if he was ever going to breathe again, she nodded, almost to herself. Her look of grim understanding almost did him in, again.

"Where are we?" she asked.

It took longer than it should have for her question to travel from his ears to his brain, and he turned, slowly, taking in the beach, the forest, the ocean. He was going to tell her that they were in the same place, but those words faded away when he saw an unfamiliar stone outcropping to the east— and just beyond that, another island, small and lush.

"I don't know," he said, trying to focus past the guilt and shame eating his insides. "The crone has a way about her. Magic. Just like she brought those children to her, she must have . . . pushed us away. Somewhere else."

"She frightened me." Jenny rubbed her arm again, then the other. Perrin looked away quick, eyes burning. He had hurt her. Didn't matter that it was an accident. He should have known it was a dream. He should have been aware of what was real and in the mind. Even broken, living as a human, he hadn't lost that ability.

"Stop it," Jenny said, and he flinched, surprised to find

her right beside him. Her eyes still held that stern, grim light.

"Stop," she said again, taking his hand.

He tried to pull free. "You're the one person who should be safe from me. And now you're not."

"I'm safe with you," she said, and kissed the back of his hand, rubbing it hard and fast. It was the kiss that made him freeze, and her cheeks turned pink. But she met his gaze, clear and unwavering, and didn't stop rubbing his battered knuckles.

"Let it go," she said.

"I can't," he replied. "I've put men in hospitals with these hands. I've . . . killed . . . with them."

She didn't flinch. "I've killed with mine. I killed someone I thought I loved."

And then she did flinch, and let go of him, and stood. Perrin stared at her slumped shoulders and found his feet, towering over her. He felt his height, suddenly, and his strength in comparison to hers; but that was only physical, and he wasn't entirely convinced that he was as strong as she, on the inside.

He stared at the back of her head, at her tangled, matted hair coming loose from her braids. Felt a pulse in the hole in his skull, but ignored it—as well as his inexplicable urge to touch her hair and bury his fingers against her scalp, above her neck.

"Do you want to talk about it?" Perrin asked her, wondering where that question came from—hearing gunshots and screams the moment he spoke the words.

Jenny shook her head, hugging herself, staring at the sea. "Where do we go now?"

"I don't know," he said, despair creeping on him. He had been stupid to think the witch would help him find the *kra'a*.

It is with you.

Look between the two of you for the answers you seek.

What did that mean?

"What did she mean?" Jenny asked, as though reading

his thoughts. "About us? What is this . . . beast, and the . . . *kra'a* . . . you kept talking about? I need to understand."

"I told you that the woman you found was important."

"Pelena. You and she were . . . close."

He didn't miss the odd note in her voice when she said that. "My cousin."

Jenny blinked. "I'm sorry."

Perrin rubbed his face. "She was kind. She liked . . . A'lesander."

"He's good at that. Making people like him."

Rage clawed up his throat. "Pelena possessed the *kra'a*. It is an . . . organism . . . that bonds to the skulls of my kind and gives them special abilities. Specifically those related to calming the—" Perrin stopped, reaching for Jenny as she swayed, pale.

"Bonds," she echoed, her lips barely moving.

"Jenny," he said, touching her brow, finding it hot.

A strange ache swept through him. His scalp tingled. A deep vibrato hiss vibrated his eardrums, but the sound shifted, rising into a screaming, crackling crescendo that made him shut his eyes in pain.

The world rocked sideways. His bones turned liquid, and so did the sand beneath him. He didn't realize he was swaying until he toppled sideways, slamming his fist into the moving beach to keep from going down completely. The rocking sensation didn't stop. It got worse.

Earthquake.

He had never been in an earthquake on land. Panic hit him. Stomach-dropping nausea. Land had always felt strange—hard, heavy, all sharp edges. No safe place to rest, no place *ever* to rest, not with gravity bearing him always down. In the sea, he had been weightless, capable of flight, cocooned in that ever-present embrace of water. Land offered only cages, and unexpected pain.

Jenny made a small sound of distress. Perrin dragged her into his arms. Little on the beach could hurt them—they were too far from the forest to fear falling trees—but the shaking worsened, tearing rocks free of the sand, knocking his teeth together—jolting him and Jenny with a growing, gathering violence that made him feel as though he sat on top of some imminent explosion.

His fear disappeared. Burned up in rage. Useless, impotent. Just like him.

You caused this, he imagined his father saying. *You did this with your thoughtless, vile actions—and there will never be a place for you, never a home, never rest—*

Jenny's fingers dug into his shoulder. Perrin held her tighter, burying his face in her hair. She was talking to him, but he didn't hear her at first—too distracted, caught up in the terrible knowledge of what was causing this quake.

He closed his eyes and felt the thrust of energy from the quake pushing through the ocean like a fist, displacing water in a massive ring that surged outward with punishing force.

And behind that, deeper, not so far away–

—coiled, buried in heat—

—a stirring, the tremble of a terrible eye—

Perrin froze, unable to move or breathe as that vision, the encompassing fullness of it, sank from his head into the base of his skull, down his spine into his chest. His heart hammered. Overwhelmed.

He was too late to save anyone. No matter what he did, it wouldn't be enough.

Jenny made another small sound. Perrin came back to himself, gathering her closer. The earthquake was finally subsiding, but her eyes were squeezed shut, face pale, so pained her lips were white and pressed together in a hard line. Focused, fighting to hold herself together.

"Jenny," he said.

"There's something in my mind," she whispered.

Chills rode through him. "Tell me."

She shook her head, scrunching even deeper into his arms. Perrin didn't know how to comfort her. He didn't even know how to comfort himself. He was afraid to know what she was feeling, afraid that it was the same thing that had just been inside him.

Visions of the sleeping beast. The monster rising from dreams.

Impossible, he told himself. For her *and* him. He shouldn't have been able to see anything. His mind had been dead to the sea for eight years.

You share dreams. You might share other things. But the thought made him feel grim and helpless.

Perrin hummed to Jenny—for her, and himself. His rumbling voice was rusty, ill-used, but the memory of the song she had sung to him, sixteen years ago, bled bright in his mind. Centering his focus, as it always did.

There was a boy, a very strange enchanted boy . . . they say he wandered very far, over land and sea. . .

Human music was full of prophets. Magic. Nat King Cole.

Jenny relaxed in his arms. Perrin studied the ocean, music dying in his throat. The tide seemed unchanged.

But that wouldn't last.

"We need to leave the beach," he said. Jenny nodded, drawing in a deep breath as though to steady herself. Perrin slid his hand beneath her jaw. Her skin was soft against his scarred, callused palm.

He tried to speak, failed—and then managed to put words in his mouth that felt rough, even angry. He wasn't certain anymore that he knew how to speak without sounding like he wanted to fight.

"I won't let anything happen to you," he said.

She stared at him with such uncertainty. Perrin brushed his thumb over her mouth, filled with aching, terrible loss—and some nameless need that was stronger than fear, stronger than anger.

A need to just . . . *be* . . . with her. Didn't matter how or in what way, just that *this,* here, now . . . he had to protect her. Forget the rest of the world. Forget shame, forget pride.

This woman had only been a dream before—not flesh and blood. Losing her presence in his mind, in his darkest hour, had been almost more than he could bear.

Losing her again . . . was unthinkable.

"Your eyes," she said.

Perrin didn't know what she saw in his eyes, but he couldn't look away to hide. He couldn't speak. He felt huge compared to her. A scarred, broken monster.

But he tried, he tried very hard, to be gentle as he leaned down and brushed his lips over her brow. She tasted warm, sweet. Her fingers dug even more deeply into his shoulders, and he pulled her as close as he dared. He was afraid to wonder what her silence meant.

"I won't let anything happen," he whispered again, against her hair.

Liar, part of him said.

No, he told it. *No.*

Perrin tried to stand. The tremors were fading, but he felt dizzy, off-balance. Jenny staggered to her feet, gripping his arms as she stared from him to the sea. "You think we're in danger from a tsunami."

"A minor wave, but it will happen quick. We're near the quake zone."

"We need higher ground."

"And we don't have much time to find it." Perrin led Jenny toward the trees. Anything soft in her eyes was gone, her jaw set, hard with determination. *Tough,* he thought. But not tough enough to hide the hollows of exhaustion in her face. She didn't try freeing her hand from his. Not that he would have let her.

Find purpose where you can, he told himself. *Maybe the* kra'a *is lost, but you still have a reason to keep fighting.*

Sand gave way to rock, hard earth. Hurt his feet. Jenny wasn't wearing shoes, either. Perrin swung her up into his arms. She weighed nothing.

"I can keep up," she protested.

"One of us has to be able to walk after this is over."

Her expression hardened even more. "Put me down. Right now. Your feet—"

"I don't need my feet after this," Perrin interrupted sharply. "Don't squirm so much."

She hadn't been squirming, even a little, but he wanted her to stop telling him to put her down. Wasn't going to happen. He tried not to look at the bruises forming on her arms.

He pushed hard into the forest, angling for open areas that were few and far between, especially for a man his size, carrying a woman. Vines twisted, gnarly and thick, winding like ropes from the tall trees that shaded the ground in a canopy so thick the shadows were blissfully soft and dark. Eased the burden on his eyes, but not his body. Trapped air, no breeze. Hot air slammed his lungs, coating him in sweat. He had never done well in hot weather.

Birds screamed overhead, and small, furred animals rustled through the leaves. Once, he heard hissing. Perrin hardly noticed. He focused only on taking each hard step. Thorns raked his legs and arms, and the edges of leaves sliced open his skin. His feet tore, and bled. He lost track of time. Fifteen, twenty minutes. Enough time for the wave to hit. It might be hours yet for other coastlines, but they were near the epicenter, and he felt the pulse, the displacement of water. Energy released from undersea earthquakes moved as fast as human aircraft.

Perrin pushed himself harder, struggling up a rocky incline that strained his muscles to the breaking point. Jenny was very still and small in his arms, but he felt her watching him—her gaze burning through him—and he finally couldn't help but glance down at her. He had to stop when he did. Dizzy.

"Put me down," Jenny said, quiet. "You've taken us far enough. You're hurting yourself."

Perrin hesitated. She placed her hand on his chest, exerting a gentle pressure that was less a push than reassurance. The contact, and the compassion behind it, seared him to the bone. He looked away, quick, afraid she would see something frightening in his eyes.

He set her down. Jenny swayed, holding his arm for balance—so much smaller than him, but strong. When she stepped away, she winced—a rock, maybe, so many sharp things on the forest floor. She glanced down at her feet—then his—and swore.

"Stop," he said sharply. "I haven't crippled myself."

"Congratulations." Jenny gave him an angry look. "And when you do?"

"I'll keep moving. I'll keep surviving," he told her, sounding so cold—feeling cold. "This is nothing."

She stood still, studying him. Her gaze dropped to his shoulders, tracking the scars that covered his chest and arms. Most had been caused in the ugliness that had begun his exile, but there were old wounds from knives, home-made weapons. A bullet. Whatever could kill. Etched into his skin.

All of which was nothing compared to the scars that couldn't be seen.

Jenny stilled, glancing away from him. Searching the forest. Perrin also quieted himself, listening hard, trying to feel the world as he once had. He noticed instantly the hush in the trees—birdsong, gone—and suffered a powerful longing for the sea that slipped through him like a searing blade.

She closed her eyes. "It's coming."

Perrin didn't bother asking how she knew. The sea witch had indicated she was part of a special bloodline—and regardless of his personal feelings, he knew better than to question a statement like that.

He pulled Jenny up another incline, skirting rotten logs, and other debris hidden by the tangled, knee-deep undergrowth. She stumbled, her breathing labored. He led her to a tree that looked easy to climb, and sturdy. Strangling vines bristling with leaves covered the trunk, and wispy blooming plants that looked like orchids.

He crouched and cupped his hands. Jenny stepped onto his palms, and he propelled her toward a low-lying branch that was thick as his thigh. She grabbed on with both arms and hauled herself over with a grunt.

Perrin did not climb after her. He wasn't even sure he could. Learning how to walk and run, all those years ago, had been difficult enough.

Jenny wrapped her legs around the branch and reached down. "Come on."

"No," he said. "I'll be fine."

She gave him a hard look and began to swing herself down. Perrin reached up with one long arm and pushed his palm against her dangling foot. "What are you doing?"

"Shut up," she muttered. "You're not safe down there, either. You won't drown, but if a wave reaches this far inland, it could still break your bones. I was off the coast of Sumatra during that tsunami, years ago. I saw what it did to people, afterward."

Perrin had heard about that disaster. He had wondered, then, if it was a portent of things to come—though the earth often moved, and shifted, on its own.

What they had just felt was not nearly as strong. The waves would not be as high.

But he wasn't taking any risks with Jenny.

"Stay up there," he told her.

"Make me," she shot back. "Or get up here, too."

"I can't climb."

She drew back, thoughtful. "I guess not."

Having her agree didn't make Perrin feel any better. Worse, maybe. Far away, through the trees, he heard a hissing roar, followed by cracks, snapping pops—like bones breaking. Birds exploded from the canopy, screaming.

Jenny reached for him again. "Please."

Perrin set his jaw and hooked fingers and toes into the hard thick knots of the vines wrapped around the tree. He slipped—then tried again, making it a short distance off the ground. He felt as though he were trying to wrestle a whale—which, if memory served, was one of those fruitless idiotic things that only the young and very stupid ever tried to do.

Like him. And A'lesander. Pelena, too.

Perrin ground his teeth—listening to that hissing roar grow louder, in his ears and inside his head—a rough rumble of water rushing through the forest, breaking and pushing. Made him feel dizzy—but no, that was the earth shaking again. Aftershock.

"Come on!" Jenny shouted at him, pale.

Perrin ignored her, watching the bottom of the hill as muddy water swelled through the trees like a swollen river, smashing the rocky incline, flowing around it, searching out flat land and covering leaves, tearing vines, snapping branches. The hungry lips of the wave pressed and pressed higher against the slope of the hill.

Two feet, three feet—four—until finally, finally, it seemed to stop.

Perrin leaned away from the tree, and all it took was three steps to reach the water. He swept his hand through it, suffering a tingle in his skin—not from the sea, but from the lingering effects of the energy pulse released from the earthquake. He could feel it—still hot.

Jenny slid down out of the tree, gripping the trunk as though she needed it to stay upright. "That was no minor wave."

Perrin grunted. "Depends on your point of view. Stay there."

He slipped into the water before she could protest, sliding completely under the surface. He did not shift his lower body, but his translucent second lids dropped over his eyes. Gills tore open with a brief stab of pain.

All around him were shadows made of silt and kicked-up leaves. He saw the forest, dark, like massive prison bars—and between them, darts of silver. Fish, carried in by the wave. Slender, glittering in the muddy half-light. He did not have much time before the water would recede and carry them away—though a second wave might crash soon enough.

Perrin hummed a low, sonorous, *Krackeni* melody, warm and soft.

The fish drew near, attracted by his voice. Close, closer, until their movements turned sluggish. When they were directly in front of Perrin, he reached up—grabbed their thick bodies, and tossed them to land. A blind throw, over his shoulder. His hand was the only part of him that broke the surface. He imagined a yelp, muffled through the water.

Perrin captured five more fish, throwing them to dry land. He would have followed, except for the sudden wavering squeals he heard in the water. The distant sounds chilled him.

Dolphins. Signal cries of recognition, and alarm.

Some pod had just sighted something that did not belong.

Shark, he told himself, but he didn't believe it. Sharks didn't rouse that kind of agitation, but only because they were so easy for dolphins to drive away, or kill.

No. This was something else. Him, maybe. Didn't matter that he was here on land, and those dolphins were some distance away. He'd learned to appreciate the benefits of a little paranoia. Perhaps the sea witch had told where to find him—though his instincts said no. She had sent Jenny and him away from her island, when she most certainly could have kept them. And he *knew* this was not her island. No tsunami would have touched her shores.

Perrin dragged himself from the water. Jenny crouched at the edge of it, her toes digging into the rocks. Her mouth tightened when she saw him.

"You're funny," she said, her tone implying that he was anything but. "I survive kidnapping, drowning, earthquake, a crazy witch-woman, *and* a tsunami, only to get bashed in the brains by flying fish."

Perrin frowned. "Little fish. Where are they?"

Jenny jerked her head sideways. "I didn't throw them back if that's what you're worried about."

"I'm worried about hunger," he muttered. "I'm sorry if I . . ."

Hit you, he almost said. But that sounded more awful than he could bear, given the darkening bruises on her pale arms.

"Like you said, little fish." Jenny grabbed his wrist and pulled. She had a strong, sure grip, and his stomach did a dizzy flip at the contact. He let her help him out of the water—pretending he needed help, even though he was a good foot taller and more than twice as broad. Her touch was nothing he took for granted.

The fish still flopped, gasping. Perrin picked up a rock and smashed their heads, one good blow each to kill them. No remorse. No hesitation. He searched for it but felt nothing. Like that part of him was dead.

They broke you. Rik's voice, echoing in his head.

You would kill again. The sea witch, this time. *You are stained with blood.*

Perrin rolled his shoulders, ignoring the ache in the base of his skull. Broken. Yes. His soul, stained.

But still alive. Alive, and look what had happened. He had found something good. A reason to have kept breathing all these years.

A miracle, set to break his heart all over again. Jenny stared at that rock in his hands like it was a gun. "That's not what I expected to see."

"Because I'm from the sea?" Perrin couldn't look at her. "Humans eat cows. My kind eat fish. Some call it inhumane, but hunger usually trumps ideals."

She sat down beside him. "I didn't mean to offend you."

"You didn't." He flung the rock away. "I used to avoid eating meat. I couldn't stand the idea of hurting something for food."

Jenny didn't say anything. Perrin glanced sideways and found her eyeing the dead fish.

"Really," he said.

"I believe you," she replied. "But something changed."

Perrin hesitated, feeling naked and lost. Her gaze slid over his scars, then away.

"I'm hungry," she said. "I have waterproof matches in the pack."

Jenny began to stand. He caught her wrist.

"I'm not the boy you knew on the beach," Perrin said quietly, staring at her hand, those bruises, and not her face. "I'm not . . . good . . . like he was."

She stood very still. Silent. Watching him with those eyes he was afraid to look at. Those eyes that Perrin had spent a lifetime dreaming desperately to see.

He let her go and turned his back—skin crawling with shame and soul-searing loneliness. He could still feel things, all right.

And there would be more blood—on land, this time—if he did nothing to stop the events unfolding on the seafloor, amongst his kind. If he even could. What had the witch meant? Where was the *kra'a*? Was it truly so close?

If you leave Jenny and you fail, she will die.

You could protect her, though. If you manage to live long enough, evade your kind, you could keep her alive when the beast wakes and the waves destroy land.

You could save her life, if no one else's.

One woman, against millions.

We're all fucked, he thought.

CHAPTER ELEVEN

I *CANNOT fix on the hour,* Jenny recited silently, clinging to lines from *Pride and Prejudice,* which steadied her, brought her down into the world in ways that the rocks beneath her did not.

I cannot fix on the hour, or the look, or the words, which laid the foundation. It is too long ago.

Too long ago, when she had laid the foundation of what was happening now. And yet she *could* fix on the hour. She could fix on the look.

Twelve years old. A morning on a beach.

Jenny lay curled on her side, in leaves and dirt, her knees drawn up to her chest. She wanted to sleep, but was afraid to. Not that she was going to have much choice soon. Everything hurt, and her eyelids were heavy.

"How is your fever?" Perrin asked. His voice was low, rough enough to be unfriendly, even menacing. Jenny wasn't intimidated. Nor was she bothered by the bruises on her arms. Not anymore.

"Fine," she replied, which was a lie. She was not fine. She was exhausted, heartsick—and there was a parasite attached to the base of her skull, drinking her blood, burying itself to the bone.

Kra'a, she named it. The very thing Perrin was searching for. She was absolutely certain of that.

And every time she tried to tell him, some mysterious compulsion kept her mouth shut tight. The impulse frightened her more than the parasite. It made her angry, too.

Be angry. Anger is good, whispered a dry, almost masculine, voice inside her mind.

Jenny shivered with fear. *Shut up, I don't want you. You're not real. I'm losing my mind.*

You are losing nothing.

Jenny shut her eyes, trying to block out that voice. She had heard it for the first time right before the earthquake. No words. Just an incomprehensible murmur. Not part of her. Something else, a presence inside her head.

That sea witch, crone, shape-shifter—whatever she was—had a terrible sense of humor. What would it have taken for her to point one claw at Jenny's head, and say, "Look there?"

That would be too easy. Think of Grandma and Grandpa.

Always showing, never telling. *A lesson given,* they liked to say, *was never learned.*

A philosophy they had stuck to every time something new and strange needed to be introduced into Jenny's life. She'd learned about shape-shifters that way. Eight years old, at the circus. Her grandparents had taken her to see a special performance—a small, elite troupe of actors and performers, who had danced and sung, and done magic that seemed like real magic, and cast illusions so fantastical, so rich and bleeding with life, that Jenny had found her imagination—and heart—bursting with the strength of possibilities.

Not all the performers, of course, had been human.

Jenny hadn't known that, at the time. Her grandparents had planned her introduction to that side of their lives so carefully—arranging the performance as a way to open her eyes. Not with fear. But with love.

Even so, one performer had stood out above all the others. Serena McGillis. A tall, lithe, red-haired woman with golden eyes—those golden eyes that were so important, Jenny had later discovered. Serena's act—or genius—

had been with big cats. Lions. Tigers. Panthers and leopards. Gorgeous, sleek predators. Prowling and dangerous.

No jumping through hoops of fire. No standing on hind legs like trained pets. Jenny had seen those kinds of performances on television and despised them. She had been ready to despise Serena, too. No animals like *them* should be kept in cages, pacing bars or walls, hungry to run. Nothing meant to be so free should ever be locked up, simply for the amusement of people who thought they had power.

But in the end, she hadn't despised Serena. Because Serena had understood freedom.

And Jenny, in her own way, had dedicated herself to making certain that those like Serena remained free, and secret, and safe. Just as her grandparents had known she would. Jenny just wished they had been as clever about the rest of the family.

She shivered again. Perrin looked down at her. "You're cold."

"No," Jenny said, still trembling. *The* kra'a *is attached to my head,* she wanted to tell him. *Hey, look there. Remember what the witch said? It's with you. I'm with you. Take a closer look.*

He sighed and turned away to the fire he had been trying to start. Jenny wanted to howl with frustration, but her mouth wouldn't open. Not in any way, and she felt that presence at the back of her mind, tied to her thoughts. Knowing her thoughts, her intentions.

Stop it. Get out of my head. You don't want me. I'm human. Perrin will know what to do with you.

We chose you, it said simply, with chilling calm. *And it is not time.*

Not time for what?

But it did not answer, and Jenny remembered what the sea witch had said, inside her mind: *Time is running out.*

Time. Running out.

For a moment she found herself six years younger, sixteen years younger, knowing something was wrong, unable to make anyone listen. No proof. Just instincts that no one paid attention to because there was no flash behind them, no psychic fire. Just ordinary Jenny, with her obsession with the sea and her silly little notions that *something wasn't right*.

Something wasn't right, now. In so many different ways.

Except for Perrin. Her touchstone in the chaos, and she couldn't even explain why. Those instincts, again. Her heart and gut, moving in together.

"Safe," was the word she thought, watching him fuss with the fire.

And then, shockingly, another word filled her.

Mine.

Jenny had never felt possessive about a man. Never. But the need to make him hers, to keep him, rose up and overwhelmed.

He is yours, whispered that dry voice. *You are his. Your hearts have rested too long on the edge of dreams.*

Jenny closed her eyes. *Who are you?*

But the parasite did not answer.

She opened her eyes and found Perrin watching her. Stole her breath. There was nothing kind about his face, not one thing soft. His scars, the slant of his mouth, those sharp bones. He wore his face like a mask, but she suspected that he had seen enough to warrant all the hard lines. She hurt for him.

I know what it is to be alone, she wanted to tell him. *I know heartache.*

"How did you learn English?" she asked him, needing a distraction. "You don't have an accent."

Perrin hesitated. "I couldn't speak English when I came to land, but I understood the language when I heard others use it. I credited our . . . dreams. Perhaps I absorbed something from you. I don't know. Just that in under six months I could speak and read. But that was the only language I learned with any real fluency."

Jenny had other questions—so many—but Perrin frowned at the smoky patch of wood he was trying light, and she said, "Tinder. Dry leaves, grass. Something small and easy to burn. Place small twigs over that."

Perrin followed her instructions, and she watched him work, unable to look away. His scars were silver against his pale skin. So many scars. His long hair shimmered in the half-light, skimming muscles that were hard and lean, and powerful. He had carried her easily, and she was no lightweight.

Her gaze dropped to his hands, rawboned and large, his fingers moving with surprising delicacy as he plucked small vines, leaves, anything that would be easy to burn. Her bruises ached, shaped like his hands.

Nightmare. Screaming. Begging. Gunshots.

Jenny didn't remember what Perrin had seen inside her head, but knew that dream, or one variation of it.

The bruises seemed like a sign. She'd been frightened when she'd opened her eyes and found Perrin holding her down—desperate wildness in his eyes. Once she had calmed down, though, a small part of her had begun to take strange comfort in those bruises he'd left behind. As though they were proof she had not been alone in that dream.

Fucking twisted, she told herself. And maybe it was, but so what? All of this was nuts. Her own life, not just what was happening now.

Perrin finally started a fire. Small. Not much heat, which was fine. The air was oppressively hot. Hard to breathe. Sweat made her thighs stick together, and her clothing was soaked through. Not that it stopped her from shivering.

Perrin gave her a long, grim look. "This is my fault."

"I don't know how," she told him, but all he did was sit near her, not quite touching. He dragged the fish close and began cleaning them with a gentleness he hadn't shown earlier. Jenny could smell their bodies. Made her nauseous. She didn't say a word about it, though. Just closed her eyes and shifted closer to Perrin until her arm brushed his bare leg. It was stupid, but she needed to touch him.

Needed to. Had to.

What you're looking for could be right in front of you,
Les had said, just days and a lifetime ago. And she understood now, the double meaning in that statement. She had
been looking for mermen. Someone like Les.

But not him.

Just this man. Perrin.

He stiffened when she touched him, then relaxed. "Rest,
Jenny. I'll watch out for you."

He still sounded angry. No pleasantries. Nothing soft
about him.

But Jenny believed him. She believed him in that deep
place inside her heart that believed in magic, and mysteries,
and boys on beaches who were born from the sea.

Perrin. His name is Perrin.

She closed her eyes and fell asleep.

JENNY DREAMED, AND WHEN SHE OPENED HER EYES
inside the dream, she was on the beach, sitting in the sand,
watching the waves crash from far away. The old house
was on her left, windows dark, slumping on its foundation.
Blood trickled down the sagging porch steps. It was just as
far away as the waves, but she could see the blood as though
it was right beside her.

And it was. On her hands. On her legs.

"Don't look," said a deep voice, and strong pale fingers
slid around her jaw, guiding her until she stared at a broad,
scarred chest and strong throat. "It hurts you, so don't look."

"You don't know," she murmured.

"I know blood," he said. "I know trouble. I was in your
other dream."

Jenny wished she could see his eyes. She had never in
the dreams been able to see the face of the boy—and later,
the man. It would have helped now, though she couldn't say
how. She felt free to say things here that she couldn't while
awake; but there was new uncertainty in the air around her,
a sense of things falling apart.

"We never spoke of our troubles before," she said, feeling lost. "It was always safe here. The only place in my life where I had peace. Where I belonged."

"You belonged with me," he said, and there was no mistaking that rough voice, or the possessiveness of his hands sliding over her shoulders. "I belonged to you. I always did, from the first time I saw you."

"It was fifteen minutes. I barely touched you. And here in these dreams . . . all we did was hold hands. Watch the sea. Talk."

She had loved talking with him. She had loved holding his hand. Feeling that presence beside her, solid and strong. She had loved it so much. In her dream, she had loved him.

She still did.

His silence was long and heavy. "You're frightened now. Of me. Even here."

Was she frightened? And if she was, should it matter? She had a right to be uneasy, even of him. But only because of the way he made her feel.

Nothing was safe anymore. And this was no longer a dream, where a girl could love without consequences.

She backed away. Just two steps, but in the dream that might as well have been a quarter mile. Her legs bumped against the porch of that old dying house, and the blood on the boards burned her skin where it touched.

She hissed, and he pulled her close again, but there was a roar in the air and the sand shook beneath her, and the sun disappeared behind a wall of water that was big as the sky.

The man roared at the wave, pushing her behind him. Too late. Water slammed against them, crushing all the air from her lungs, tumbling her over and over in a blind spin. She heard nothing but the thunder of her heart, and no hands clasped hers. She was alone and dying, already dead.

Until, suddenly, she was not.

She floated, in darkness, insubstantial as a ghost. Water flooded her lungs, but it tasted good, and she could breathe.

In front of her, bodies shimmered. One, larger than the

others, broad and masculine. His lower half shone with scales and a silver fin. She could not see his face, but in the dream she knew him as well as she knew herself.

He was caught. Trapped.

Massive barbed hooks dug into his skin, attached to braided cords wrapped around the wrists of those who surrounded him. He fought, writhing and twisting, dragging his assailants—but the hooks were too deep, and there were too many. Blood drifted from his body through the water.

Jenny tried to go to him, screaming as he screamed, but not one inch of her body obeyed her. Frozen. Floating in place like she was just as trapped.

The base of her skull throbbed, and burned.

For you, whispered that dry voice. *For you he suffered.*

She woke up. Just like that. No lingering in the dream. She opened her eyes from the sea to a dark forest, and lay there, trying to remember who she was and why she kept thinking, *No.*

Jenny, she told herself, a moment later. *My name is Jenny.*

She heard movement and turned her head. Perrin was rubbing his eyes, half-sitting up from a spot so close to her she could have stretched out one finger to touch him. His long hair covered much of his face, and he moved as though his muscles were stiff, or just too tired to function.

"You slept," she said, her voice raw, hoarse.

"Didn't mean to. Closed my eyes for just a minute." He sounded little better, and hesitated, peering at her through the curtain of his hair. "You were there."

"The beach." Jenny rolled over on her back, closing her eyes.

"The house. The wave." Leaves crunched beneath him, and she thought for a moment he would touch her. She swore she felt the heat of his hand above her arm.

But the heat faded, and she listened to him stand. "Bad dream."

She opened her eyes and looked at his scars. Wondering

if hooks had caused those deep silver marks. "What else do you remember? After the wave?"

"I woke up," he said, not looking at her. Jenny couldn't tell if he was lying. It didn't matter. Real or not, what she had seen in that dream was nothing she would ever forget.

She heard a crackling sound. Fish cooked over the fire, impaled on sticks. He must have started them before nodding off. She looked at Perrin again, but he seemed uncomfortable. So was she, Jenny realized. It had been different when she didn't know the dreams were real. Just some figment of her obsessed imagination.

Dreams were intimate. Dreams were part of the soul. She felt a little like she'd just woken up from having sex, and this was the awkward morning after.

Perrin crouched in front of the fire, removing one of cooked fish. Steam rose from the cracked dark skin.

Not quite looking at her, he extended his arm and waited for her to take the fish from him. She hesitated, and he finally met her gaze. Pale eyes. Piercing. Jenny stopped breathing, maybe with a twitch.

"Don't be afraid of me," he said quietly. "Please."

Jenny held his gaze. "Why do you think I'm afraid of you?"

Frustration filled his eyes, maybe a little helplessness. She couldn't be sure. He turned his head before she could look too hard.

"Take the fish," he muttered in a cold voice. "You need to eat."

Jenny took the stick from him. The impaled fish looked at her with shriveled eyes.

"Did it ever occur to you," she said slowly, "that I might not be hungry?"

"Earlier, you said you were hungry." Perrin glanced at her. "When was the last time you ate?"

Jenny opened her mouth to answer him but had to stop. Les had fed her something, maybe, but that had been a lifetime ago. Her stomach felt queasy at the thought of eating.

"Eat," Perrin said. "I don't know where we'll find our next meal."

Good point. The fish was hot beneath her fingers, but she managed to tear off a piece of flaky white flesh and pop it into her mouth. It tasted good, and her nausea subsided.

Perrin removed another fish from the fire. He ate it with a little less care than she had. Jenny watched him openly, but except for a tightening of the muscles in his shoulders, he said nothing.

Judging from what little sky she could see beyond the canopy, it was early evening or very late in the afternoon—though it might as well have been full night in the forest where she sat. It was dark amongst the trees, and the small fire's light was welcome.

Jenny drew in a breath to tell Perrin about the parasite, but her throat closed, and the words only came out as a hiss. An attempt to point at the back of her head failed when her arm refused to move. And when it occurred to her to just flop down and plant her face in the ground—so that hopefully he might catch a glimpse of the damn thing beneath her hair—she managed to twitch a full inch before her body shut down. Frozen as a statue.

And thirsty. For salt water.

Desperately thirsty.

Hey, she called out in her mind, willing Perrin to turn around and look at her. *Hey!*

But Perrin threw away the remains of his fish and stood. Still not looking at her. Silent, tense, every movement fraught with suppressed violence. Should have scared her, but she wasn't afraid that he would hurt her. Her uneasiness was more intimate than that.

The parasite frightened her more. The parasite baffled her. It was clearly intelligent—unless she was hallucinating that voice in her mind. And it was important, the key to whatever the hell was going on with Perrin. So why was it lodged in the back of her head?

And what were the odds that it would have brought her

and Perrin together again? Why, now, had all the broken shit of her life become tangled with *him*?

What does all this mean? What happened to that scared little boy on the beach? Why did I dream about you, all these years?

And how, *how was it possible*, he had shared her dreams? Shared them, until eight years ago—with her always naïve enough to think it was simply her imagination? Her desperate, sorry-ass, pathetic heart—aching for something it could never have?

Jenny still remembered that first dream, that first night after she had found *him*. Falling asleep, only to find herself on the beach, with the sand beneath her feet and the waves lapping the shore, and the wind, the bright sun.

And a presence. The boy.

A flash of silver, pale skin. His hand warm on hers. A soothing touch. Sitting together, in the sand, watching the waves. Taking comfort in nothing but each other. Warm ghosts, with warm hearts.

You searched for him. Searched so long and hard. And he was with you, all along. Inside.

Perrin paced the edges of the small clearing. Studying the trees as though they were the bars of a cage. It wasn't overt. Anyone else might have called it restlessness, burning off excess energy.

Jenny knew better. She recognized that behavior. All the signs were there. And that upset her, more than she wanted to admit.

"Have you ever been locked up?" she asked him.

Full stop. Every part of him, rippling with unease. His skin was golden in the firelight. Silver hair fell over one eye and hung loose and tangled down his scarred chest. She could not see his eyes, but the rest of him was so beautiful, it almost hurt to look.

"Why," he said slowly, "would you ask that?"

Jenny set down her fish, a little too carefully. "Maybe you're claustrophobic. I could imagine that, if you've grown up in the sea, without walls. But there's something more, in the way you move. Like you've been in too many closed spaces. Helpless."

Perrin was so still. "Helpless."

Jenny refused to back away from that word. "You've spent time on land. The way you speak and act. I don't think it was pleasant. And then there's the way you keep telling me not to be frightened of you."

He stood there, silent. Outwardly calm, though she could feel, washing over her, that inexplicable hum of ready violence coiled inside him, along with that same ruthless determination that had let him beat Les until he was unconscious: the same resolve that had saved her life, cared for her while she was ill; carried her through the forest to protect her feet, while his tore and bled.

Innumerable little gestures so at odds with the rough anger in his voice and the remote coldness of all his other actions.

I'm not scared of you, she thought, waiting for him to say something, anything, her stomach tight, heart aching. Of all the impossible things she had learned to believe in . . .

Believe in yourself, she thought, leaning harder against the tree behind her. *Believe in what you see. Believe in what you know, in your heart.*

Easier said than done.

Perrin swayed toward her, his eyes still hidden in shadow, though the reflection of the firelight on the sharp angles of his face made him look even harder, more dangerous. "How would you know such a thing?"

"I've seen it. I lived it." Jenny tried to stand, but had to clutch the tree as a wave of dizziness made her sway.

Strong hands gripped her arms, then her waist. Those familiar hands. That familiar voice, deep and quiet, that she had only ever heard in dreams.

Those dreams.

"Jenny," he said, and hearing him say her name made her feel so strange. Words welled up in her throat, hard and pulsing, burning through her like fire. If she closed her eyes, she could pretend this was one of those old dreams.

But this wasn't the beach. This was real. She had chased mysteries all her life, for just one reason.

"Jenny," he said again. "You should sit."

"I feel small when I sit," she told him, eyes still closed. He sighed and pulled her close, his arms sliding around her with heavy, comforting strength. He shouldn't have felt so comforting. He was a stranger. No matter their history, tenuous and mysterious as it was.

"What did you mean?" His voice was rough, coarse, though his touch remained so gentle. "What have you seen, and lived?"

Her hand slid down between them, touching her stomach. A different kind of ache filled her. "The Consortium. The people who came for me on the yacht. The ones who were in that bad dream you saw."

"They hurt you, before."

Jenny tried pushing free, but he held on, and she found herself pressed against the tree. Not because of him. She had put herself there, backing away—but he followed, and now loomed above her, unmovable and warm. His hair touched her face, and Jenny shuddered.

"Forget I said anything," she said.

Perrin didn't budge. "You started it."

She shoved at him, uselessly. "Get off me."

He pushed her tighter against the tree—against him— one massive arm still around her. His other hand slid up her throat, stilling her, making every inch of her body tingle as his big warm palm pressed against her cheek. She had thought he would be extra careful after bruising her—and he was, so careful—but there was a determination in his touch, too. A thrill rolled through her body, followed by a hungry ache that she hadn't felt in years.

"Open your eyes," he whispered. "Look at me."

He hadn't been so eager before to stare into her eyes, but something in his voice cut her heart. Jenny looked up.

There, his eyes. Pale as ice, glittering. But not cold. His eyes were soft with pain, and a loneliness that seared her, down to the soul.

His loneliness. Her loneliness. Both the same. She hadn't realized how lonely she had been, until this moment. Faced with it, in his eyes. Hit her in a rush, a great, heaving heartache that she didn't know how to handle. Except not handle it at all.

"Eight years," Perrin said, his voice little more than a broken rasp. "Eight years on land. Some of that time in prison."

Jenny stared. "Prison."

His jaw hardened. "I didn't understand certain things. I committed crimes. Added up to a year of my life."

She tried to speak but couldn't. Her silence seemed to hurt him. Bitterness filled his gaze, and he pushed away from her. Jenny caught him, holding tight. He hesitated— then gently, carefully, pried her fingers off his wrist.

Perrin walked away. Not far, just out of arm's reach. He stared at the fire. Jenny had to lean against the tree again, steadying herself as she studied more scar tissue, old and rough, embedded in the muscles of his back and arms. The firelight softened the scars, but not the sense of barely contained violence—inside him, against him.

Hooks, she thought, pressing her fist over her heart.

"Tell me about the Consortium," he said quietly.

Tell me why you didn't go back to the sea for eight years, she wanted to ask, but a terrible dread rose in her throat before she could voice that question.

"They're family," she said.

"Family," Perrin echoed, and she waited for something more. But all he did was nod to himself. Cool, calm. Not the reaction she felt whenever she thought about the mess her relatives had created. Vomiting while screaming was more like it. Combined with insane rage.

"That's it?" she asked him.

"Family can be cruel," Perrin replied, as if that was all the explanation he needed to give. And it was. In a way.

Jenny pushed away from the tree. "I work for a corporation called *A Priori*. My grandmother and her three sisters founded it during World War II. Finding lost objects and people was their specialty, although that's changed in the last sixty years. Investments, bioresearch, oil, manufacturing."

"And things less mundane."

She wondered how much he already knew. "Yes. But that . . . was always on the side. My family has never been . . . normal."

"You said you knew about shape-shifters. You've been remarkably calm about what I am. You were brave in front of the sea witch."

Scared shitless, she thought. "I grew up around unusual things. People with unusual gifts. But the family split, decades ago. One of the sisters, when she saw the business changing into something increasingly commercial, broke away to continue her work as it had been originally intended: as a means of helping people. My grandmother and her other sisters, like I said, didn't follow that path. And some of their children took it even further."

She joined him at the fire. Staring at the flames, unable to look at his face. Her throat felt tight, and her stomach hurt. She hated thinking about the past. Even though she was so good at it.

"I have uncles, aunts, cousins . . . all of them with too much power. Up here." She tapped her forehead. "They can do things with their minds. Make other people do things. That was the line they crossed, but by the time my grandparents and everyone else realized just how far they had gone, it was too late to stop them."

"Those relatives betrayed all of you?"

"Only after we tried to stop them. Turned into a war, briefly." Jenny pressed her hand over her stomach. "When I thought you'd been . . . locked up . . . I assumed it was by them. They hunt, or try to recruit, humans who are born different, along with shape-shifters, and . . . other beings. I'm not sure how much you know."

"Gargoyles," Perrin said, surprising her. "Witches, who are fey in the blood. Your Consortium hunts my kind, too, I assume. Though I imagine we've been even more difficult to find. The sea is . . . vast. And we take precautions."

There was something faintly ominous in the way he said that. "Do your people have a name?"

He hesitated. "*Krackeni.*"

"*Krackeni,*" Jenny echoed. "I always called you merman."

"It works," he said, with a faint tilt of his shoulder. "What does the Consortium do with those they capture or recruit?"

"Experiments. Breeding programs. Brainwashing. Like your sea witch, they seem to think the end of the world is coming and want to be at the top of the food chain when it does. I won't rule out the possibility"—not after what the sea witch had said—"but I think it's just some excuse to hurt people. Lets them sleep at night, when they're not busy taking over almost every major criminal organization in the world. Drugs, human trafficking, weapons . . . follow the trails, and in the past ten years it's become difficult *not* to find a link back to the family, and the bigger they get, the harder it is to fight them."

Jenny finally looked at him. While she hadn't been certain what to expect in his reaction, she was surprised to see the deep-etched lines of strain in his brow, around his eyes. His gaze was distant, thoughtful. Unhappy.

"What?" she asked, alarmed.

His frown deepened. "Did A'lesander work for them?"

Jenny frowned, rubbing her arms. "He said no. He killed their agent who attacked me."

"Coincidence, then," Perrin murmured, and another chill raced through her.

"What are you talking about?"

He rubbed his face, but she thought it was less a gesture of weariness and more like another way to stall. Jenny waited, not entirely patient, moving so that she could see his face more clearly. Close enough to crane her neck and feel the heat rising from his body.

She wanted to touch his arms again and feel his strength beneath her hands. She wanted him wrapped around her.

Don't be afraid of me, he had said.

When I stop wanting you, she thought, and stifled the urge to flinch at herself.

You don't know him, one side of her protested, while another part of her, just as strong, whispered, *You do. You've known him since you were twelve years old. Dreaming every night of his hands holding yours.*

"Perrin," Jenny said.

He drew in a hard breath, like he was steeling himself for a blow. "I told you I was exiled. I returned because I had a vision. Something terrible. The earthquake we felt is only the beginning."

"Beginning of what?"

Perrin met her gaze, and his eyes were empty, cold. "Destruction. The earth's axis will shift. The shapes of continents will change. Millions will die."

Jenny grimaced. "No."

"Yes. Human mythology still remembers a great expanse of water that covered every land in the world. A flood. The last time was to stop a war. There have been breaks in the intervening millennia, but not many. This will be different. The waters will surge inland—"

He stopped himself. Jenny stared.

"You don't believe me," Perrin said.

"I don't know," she told him. Les had lied his ass off for years, and she'd bought it. Except Perrin looked like each word he spoke made him die a little.

You need this kra'a *to stop what's coming,* she wanted to say. *That was clear when you spoke with the sea witch. You need this thing inside me. I would give it to you. I would give it to you if I could.*

Let go of me, she thought. *Let go.*

But the parasite did not respond.

Perrin bowed his head, and this time when he rubbed his face, she knew it was weariness, bone deep. "By murdering Pelena, this event was caused deliberately. I don't know if it can be stopped. It's possible, even, that A'lesander had help. He might have wanted the *kra'a*, but others would be just as pleased with human deaths."

A sharp pain stabbed through the base of her skull. "Are we so terrible?"

"No," he said, almost growling the word. "But there are many of you, and just as many who aren't careful with the sea. And there are many of my kind who have never been overly fond of humans, and who believe that when we mix with your kind, we dirty our blood."

"So it's a mess."

"Few *Krackeni* have lived amongst humans as I have. If more did, perhaps they would understand that we are all one kind of people, no matter what we breathe."

"Idealist."

"No," he said, with particular bitterness. "Just tired."

She sat back, studying him. Seeing hooks in each of those scars. Ropes, binding him. Trapped. Helpless.

"Perrin," she began. "What do you want?"

He shot her a strange look. "What do you mean?"

"What's kept you going all these years?"

Something vulnerable entered his eyes, and he looked away from her. "I don't know. I was still alive. That was a miracle in itself though it wore on me. Being human was so difficult in some ways, but I kept going. Maybe for no reason. But sometimes, sometimes I suppose I hoped . . ."

Perrin stopped, and rubbed his mouth. "You? What were your . . . aspirations?"

To find you, she wanted to say, but that was only part of it.

"To do good," she said truthfully. "I had no lofty dreams. Nothing grandiose. I just . . . wanted to find a way to make the world a better place, in some small way. In my own way."

"Did you?"

She smiled sadly. "I'm not sure. I worked with children for a time, teaching them about the ocean. It was wonderful. Kids are born with passion, and it makes you feel bigger inside when you're the one shining the focus on something that captures their imaginations. But after . . . after what happened in my family, I couldn't go back to that. I focused on . . . other things."

"Searching for oddities," he said, grim. "Like me."

"You're not odd," she said gently, and smiled. "Not even a little."

He stilled, giving her that vulnerable look again, so at odds with the scarred, hard lines of his face and body.

"You're my other miracle," he said, but before Jenny could respond to that stunning statement, he added, "Why do your relatives want to hurt you?"

It took Jenny a moment to collect herself. "I don't understand the timing, or reasons. I'm just the granddaughter. I'm nobody. I like it that way. I keep to myself. Do my work. I never go home."

"Why?"

"Why were you exiled?"

Perrin stared at her. Maybe he would have told her—maybe—but leaves crackled loudly, beyond their small ring of light.

Jenny flinched. Perrin turned, searching the shadows, and glided away from the fire. He signaled her to stay behind. Jenny ignored him, but kept her distance: watching, and listening.

And then, not even that.

Dizziness struck her. She almost sat down. A hollow ache sank from the base of her skull, down her spine, into her chest. Her lungs hurt. Her heart hammered harder, then slowed. For a moment, all Jenny wanted to do was lurch on unsteady legs to the sea.

Several steps later, she realized she was doing just that.

Parasite, Jenny thought, chilled to the bone.

It wouldn't have been the first time that parasites had been found influencing host behavior, but never so extreme. Of course, nothing like the parasite latched to her spine had ever been documented.

She was so screwed.

Behind her, Perrin made a small sound of surprise. Jenny turned, ready for guns, knives—anything.

But nothing was there. Just Perrin, crouched low to the ground, one of his hands pressed into the leaves as he leaned forward and reached for a dark shape hunched in front of him.

Jenny narrowed her eyes. "Is that—"

"Shhh. Move slowly."

She sank to her knees and crawled on all fours. Close, closer, until she saw a pair of glittering eyes, a wet nose, and a tiny shivering body that ended in a wagging tail.

"Oh, man," she murmured. "Where did he come from?"

Perrin didn't answer. Slowly, carefully, he reached out— humming an achingly familiar melody under his breath. Jenny bowed her head, fingers digging into the ground. Heart in her throat. Maybe it would stay there, for the rest of her life, and she would never be able to swallow again without feeling like she was going to cry.

Enough with the melodrama, she told herself. *Enough.*

She heard a brief whine, a whimper, and rubbed her eyes as Perrin dragged a squirming little bundle of fur into his arms.

Dog. Skinny, black, with a short body and thin, curved tail. Alert eyes. Almost young enough to be a puppy, but not quite. Perrin held him awkwardly, frowning as the little dog licked his hand and snuggled deeper into his lap. She heard a sigh, from the man or animal, she couldn't tell—but it made her heart flop. Just a little. Not that she had a weakness for that sort of thing.

"You make a sight," she said, and reached for one of the cooked fish. The dog watched her, ears perked, and tumbled from Perrin's lap as soon as she began picking meat off the bones. He ate frantically, straight from her fingers, whining when she took longer than a few seconds to debone more fish.

Perrin watched her with an unreadable expression on his face. Made her cheeks flush. Something in his gaze. Warmth, maybe.

"He's scared," he said.

"He's lost. The dog is one of those village breeds. I see them all the time when I'm on land." Jenny stroked that sleek warm head. "Makes me wonder if there are people on this island. If there are, they might have a transceiver. I could get us help. Warn someone about what's happening. If the coasts are in danger . . ."

People needed to be evacuated. But even with her connections no one was going to leave their homes, businesses, entire cities on the say-so of some woman who—what? Had been told by a *merman* that bad things were coming? Apocalyptic tsunamis and floods? Ridiculous. Overwhelming. Even she had trouble accepting it.

Which meant it was her family, all over again. Danger and death, and no way to stop it. Except scream and scream while no one listened.

I'll make them listen, she promised, touching her stomach as it ached in sympathy to her heart. *This time, someone will listen.*

But even if someone did, if some explanation could be concocted that the public would understand, one that *didn't* involve the supernatural, what then? Panic? Chaos? People were still going to die.

Perrin looked uneasy. Jenny said, "I won't tell anyone what you are."

"It's not that." He ducked his head, and stood. "Let's go look. We shouldn't waste any time."

The dog whined, wagging its tail at him. Jenny felt a little whine at the back of her throat, too. Surprised her, how suddenly reluctant she was to find other people—even though it was logical, necessary. She needed medical help. The Consortium was after her. End of the world was coming. Maybe.

But there was another little world here, between her and Perrin, that she didn't want to end. Fragile, desperate world. Just the two of them, and so many questions left unanswered. So much she needed to say even though she didn't know how.

"It's dark," she said. "We could wait."

"I can see." Perrin reached down. Jenny grabbed his hand. He pulled her up, but she didn't let go.

" 'Nature Boy,' " she said, staring into his pale eyes, heart aching, unsure what was going to come out next from her mouth. "That's the name of the song I sang to you, all those years ago. The one you've been humming."

The corner of his mouth tilted into a faint, sad smile. "I know. Nat King Cole."

She wanted to ask how he knew—because the boy she'd met hadn't even been able to speak English—but he bent, swinging her up into his arms. His strength was effortless, and so was his rare smile, which deepened just a fraction.

"Good song," he said, as the dog whined.

"The best," she replied, with difficulty. "What about your feet?"

He held her closer. "Just rest, Jenny."

"Take your own advice."

"None for the wicked." Perrin started walking. "An old human man I knew was fond of saying that. He was homeless, but he taught me how to get work. No rest for the wicked, he always told me. I never heard truer words."

"What happened to him?"

"He died." Perrin's smile faded, and he looked down, past her. "The dog is following us."

Jenny barely heard him. "How many times has your heart been broken, Perrin?"

She hadn't meant to say that out loud. She couldn't take it back, either. He faltered, arms tightening.

But he didn't answer her.

CHAPTER TWELVE

I T was common knowledge amongst Perrin's people that to invite a lie was to invite trouble, but as subterfuge was rather difficult anyway, given the number of eyes in the sea, telling outright untruths had become a significant rarity.

Omissions, on the other hand, were something else entirely. Omissions were polite. If you hated the *Krackeni* in front of you with a red-hot passion, and wished nothing more than to break his bones and scatter them for the bottom dwellers, you omitted that from the conversation. Just as you omitted any other potentially damaging emotions, thoughts, and inclinations. Humans were not much different. Except for the lying. And assholes who never omitted anything.

But that didn't keep Perrin from feeling rather awkward about the fact that he had known, before the dog appeared, that there were people on the island. And omitted that from the conversation.

He had heard their dreams. Echoes, drifting into his mind in whispers and threads, dissolving the moment he tried to see anything beyond those hints of shadows.

He hadn't told Jenny. For the simple reason that she had done exactly what he was afraid she would the moment the dog had discovered them.

Asked to go look. For help.

You are a selfish one. She needs a doctor.

That, however, would mean going on land. Real land. Not this island. And he didn't know where it would be safe. He wasn't even certain how much time was left.

And she seemed better.

"Son of a bitch. Look at that," Jenny said, hunched down in the leaves, holding the panting, squirming dog against her side. "Bastards. I wish I had a gun to blow all their heads off."

A lot better.

Perrin sat beside Jenny on a rocky hill, overlooking a lush cove that curled into the island in the shape of a fist. The tsunami had struck here, but the curve of the hill below them had formed a natural seawall: high, wide, and protection enough that the rough camp that had been built not one hundred yards from the beach was still—mostly— standing. Some buildings had collapsed, torn up into strips of wood that looked like toothpicks from this distance. Several small boats, tossed on land like discarded toys, appeared the same.

None of it, though, was enough to have anyone running scared. Cookfires pierced the night, high in the forest above the ruined village. Perrin heard laughter. Dogs barked. Pop music blared.

A motor yacht was moored offshore, in the lee of the sea- wall. Not Jenny's vessel. This one was much smaller but still expensive. A pleasure cruiser.

Bullet holes marked its hull. Several windows were broken. A man's body lay on deck, but Perrin couldn't see much of him except that he wore white shorts and had fat legs. He didn't observe a guard on board, but three much smaller speedboats were anchored nearby, also empty. The vessels appeared remarkably similar to the ones that had surrounded Jenny's yacht.

The sea witch, Perrin thought, was devious.

A woman started screaming, sobbing—out of sight, lost inside the forest. He had been listening to her, off and on, for the past thirty minutes, and wanted very much to stick his fingers in his ears to block out the horrifying sounds she was making.

Instead, he let it sink in. Compartmentalized. All his disgust and anger placed in a box that he would open, later, if given the chance. Perrin couldn't tell just how many men were camped above the village, but he caught glimpses of them. This was not a small operation.

Jenny cursed, digging her fingers into the leaves. She wasn't looking at the camp, but the yacht. "See the name on the hull? *Templesmith?* That vessel disappeared less than a week ago. Pirates blamed. The owner is Indonesian, but he rented out his yacht to tourists. A French couple."

"You want to go down there," he said.

"Can you listen to that woman and walk away? Even if we can't reach her, we need to find some way to call for help."

Perrin wanted to survive. He wanted Jenny to survive more than he cared about his own life. But there was living, then there was *living,* and he still knew the difference, even after all these years.

"Stay here," he told her.

"Like hell," she muttered, rising with him. The dog barked, and Perrin tapped it sharply on the nose.

"Quiet," he snapped, and the dog sank to its belly, tail dragging between its legs.

Perrin frowned, patted it more gently on the head, and said, "You could get hurt."

"And what do *you* know about fighting?"

He gave her a long look. Jenny settled back on her heels, holding his gaze. Watching him with that measuring thoughtfulness that made him feel so naked.

"Sorry," she said quietly. "I guess you probably know enough."

"I guess I do," he said tersely. "Stop looking at me like that."

"Like what?"

He rolled his shoulders, trying to loosen his muscles.

"Like I'm not . . ." *Human,* he almost said. Which was ridiculous, because he *wasn't* human. He had never thought of
himself as such. Always *other.* Always *outsider.*

He didn't want to be an outsider to her.

"Like my humanity is in question," he found himself
saying, instead. Which wasn't much better. The air was
too hot, hard to breathe. It was getting to him. So was she.
Losing his mind, after eight years of learning how to hold
it together.

Jenny was frowning. "I would never question your heart."

His heart. Perrin found his feet but didn't stand. Just
crouched, tense. "You look at my scars all the time. I understand that. I would look, too. But each one of them was
a lesson learned. How to move faster, see things sharper, hit
harder." He stopped, biting his tongue, and slid away from
her through the undergrowth. Needing distance.

The dog followed. Perrin tore his feet a little more, slipping down the hill, but he pushed the pain aside, listening
to Jenny catch up, her breath hissing, voice muffled as she
swore at him. He had not expected her to follow, and he
remembered suddenly how dark it would seem to her. How
dangerous that darkness would be. She couldn't see as well
as he could at night. Not that it was holding her back.

He slowed. Her fingers scraped against his hip, then
managed to catch his arm.

"Stop," she said. "*Stop.*"

Perrin leaned hard against a tree. His heart thundered
until it was all he could hear, all he could feel—except for
her touch, her fingers, tightening warm against his skin. She
was so warm.

And when she drew even closer, and pressed her forehead against his arm—resting there, quiet, her breathing
ragged—he died a little.

"I don't know how to talk to you," she whispered. "I'm
always offending you. I know how I feel, in my gut, but the
words come out wrong."

"No, they don't," he told her. "You just have the misfortune of talking to someone who is irredeemably dysfunctional."

A rough laugh escaped her, but it lasted for all of a second. He wanted to hear her laugh again. Her silence was deep, heavy. The dog whined. Pop music played on. The woman had stopped screaming.

Jenny didn't move. Her hand tightened around his arm. Perrin closed his eyes, still dying, and bent to kiss the top of her head. He needed to, more than he needed to breathe.

The need spread, and deepened, flowing through his veins with a heat that made him dizzy, lost. He leaned down again and brushed his lips against her brow. She did not pull away or act afraid, and he took that to heart, sliding his hand up her throat, rubbing the corner of her mouth with his thumb until she leaned harder against him, rising on her toes. Her eyes were closed. With anticipation, maybe.

But it felt deeper than that. Anticipation was cheap. This was survival. This was a moment on a beach, and dreams, and sacrifice. This was a lifetime of needing to be close to someone who had never been real except in his dreams, so heart-hungry for that dream he had never lasted with any other. Never mind he had been called a fool for that—and worse.

"I missed you so much," Perrin whispered, and, as her eyes flew open, he kissed her.

Just a brush of his lips against hers. So light, but he felt that touch down to the root of his soul. Heat poured into the hole at the base of his skull, and for one moment—just one—it was as though his *kra'a* had returned and he was complete again. Heart humming. Aching with all the terrible beauty of life, stretching his skin.

Jenny sighed, loosening her hold on his arm, but not her touch. She pressed her hands against his chest, featherlight on his ribs. Seared him, burned him, pushed him near an edge he hadn't known existed. He deepened his kiss, groaning as her mouth widened, and her tongue grazed his.

The dog barked. They broke apart. Jenny swayed, and

Perrin crushed her to his chest. Both of them were breathing hard. He couldn't swallow. Too much heart in his throat.

"I'm losing my mind," she whispered, breath hot against his skin.

"I'm losing mine," he muttered, voice torn, ragged. Suffering, again, the pulse of heat at the base of his skull. Not pain, not emptiness . . . but life. Purpose. He wasn't sure what good he could do anymore, but if keeping her alive was all that was left to him, then so be it. She was all that mattered.

Jenny pushed away from him. Not far, but it was enough to steal away all that rich warmth. Perrin wanted to grab her back but forced himself to remain still and harden his heart. Just enough.

"Stay here," he said. "Let me go."

"No," she whispered, staring at him with haunted eyes. "I won't do that. Not again."

Not again. Perrin felt punched in the gut, and suddenly he couldn't stand the idea of letting her out of his sight. "Stay close, then. You want to free hostages, I assume. And find a radio?"

"Radio first. We'll help the woman if we're able, but we're not equipped to stage a full rescue. Not without possibly making things worse. I know people who can help."

Pragmatic. Perrin liked that. It occurred to him that it wasn't just childhood memory and the bond of dreams that made him want her, but the woman herself. Guts and intelligence, and fire. She hadn't lied to him yet, either—though he was an expert with omissions. Perrin studied her face, unmoving. "You're not saying everything."

Her mouth opened with a strangled cough, and her eyes focused inward, conflicted. He had the distinct, uncomfortable sense that she was trying to tell him something and couldn't. He held her face in his hands, wishing he could read her mind. Marveling at the miracle of being able to touch her at all.

The sea witch's face wavered in his memories. All he could recall, with clarity, were her golden eyes.

Look between the two of you for the answers you seek.

Perrin wasn't certain anymore that he knew the questions. Find the *kra'a*? Learn how to survive and make a life for them both? Assuming she even wanted him for life?

"Jenny," he said. "What's wrong?"

Defeat flickered in her eyes, and she closed her mouth, jaw tight. Stared openly at him, so much in her eyes he leaned in, closer. He heard her sobs in his mind, and before he could push those memories away, his gut clenched so tight and hard with pain and fury, he felt sick.

"Jenny," he said again, his voice hard and brittle.

"Don't get hurt," she said. "Please."

He stared. Jenny looked away, as though ashamed. "If I didn't think someone was down there who needed help more than we do, I would just turn around. No matter what I said earlier. But I can't do that now. So please. Please. Just . . ."

Her voice trailed off. The dog whined at her feet.

But he heard the words. *Stay alive. Just stay alive.*

"You, too," he said.

THE VILLAGE WAS IN WORSE SHAPE UP CLOSE. BROKEN, reeking of human waste. The wave had definitely hit, stirring up the latrines, scattering material belongings. He could see where someone had tried to clean away debris, but it was an exercise in failure without a way to maintain basic sanitation. Cleaning up human filth was something he had become intimately acquainted with.

He and Jenny huddled in the undergrowth, at the edge of where the wave had crested. Less than fifty yards away, a man sat on a fallen tree, hacking at the trunk with a machete. He looked bored, but his head was bobbing to the pop music blaring through the forest. Not exactly subtle. No one was worried about being found.

Other men sat nearby, talking loudly, cleaning guns and knives. Bottles clinked. Perrin smelled meat roasting, and smoke—which curled upward and sideways, toward their hiding place. His eyes watered, and he stifled a cough.

"You see the woman?" Jenny asked.

"No," Perrin murmured, just as the earth swayed. He grabbed her arm, holding on until the shaking stopped. Aftershock. All the laughter died for several long seconds, then started again with a roar, and several guns fired. The woman's voice broke into a startled, hysterical sob that did not quiet but only gained strength.

"Shut up," Jenny muttered. "Come on, lady."

Just what Perrin had been thinking. He'd known a man in prison—a boy, really—who on his first night had sobbed in his cell. Loud, endless sobs. Perrin had wanted to gag him. Tears and misery were weaknesses, prey markers. You were prey until you proved otherwise. Everyone was. Something he had never understood until his exile.

Size and strength had given him enough time to learn the ropes. The boy was not so lucky. Perrin hadn't been close enough to stop the abuse that followed after that first night.

Jenny slithered away from him, crawling on her belly through the undergrowth. Perrin hissed at her, but she ignored him. The dog pawed at his thigh, whining, and he pushed the animal gently aside with a frustrated sigh.

He got down on his stomach and tried to follow Jenny. A whale pretending to be a goldfish. The dog licked the side of his face, then disappeared through the undergrowth after her.

Perrin watched its wagging tail—and her feet—and stopped worrying about being heard. The blasting music, combined with the woman's sobs, were both loud enough to drown out anything less than a bomb going off. He also suspected that the men were more than a little drunk.

Perrin found Jenny pressed flat to the ground between two trees, less than thirty yards from the encampment. He squeezed in close, so tight and hard he was practically on top of her—one leg hooked over hers, his arms resting on her back so that his hand clasped her shoulder. Better to keep her in one place, he thought—though having her pressed so close had other advantages.

Jenny didn't look at him. Her gaze was locked on the woman.

He saw her through the undergrowth. Fully clothed, which he found oddly comforting. Her long blond hair hung tangled around her face, which was bruised and smeared with mud. All of her was muddy, cut. She sat against a tree, unrestrained, hugging her knees to her chest and weeping.

Perrin looked past her at the men. He counted ten, but knew there were more, perhaps twice that number scattered around several fires, and deeper, in the woods. Some of them had to be sleeping. He could hear and see their dreams: cars and airplanes and children; glimpses of women who rolled naked in sand and sea, the singing sea, which buoyed silver fish that transformed into silent gods, buried in stars. . .

He shook himself, disturbed. Not all those dreams were human. Threads tugged on him from the sea. For some reason that made him want to look at Jenny. Her eyes were closed, brow furrowed in discomfort.

"What?" he breathed in her ear.

Jenny shook her head. "I don't know. I heard something. I saw . . ."

She stopped. He said, "You saw the sea, but it was twisted, like a dream."

Her eyes flew open. "How did you know?"

Perrin shook his head. They needed to talk. Soon. He had a feeling about what was between them, but it was not something he could explain here, now. It wasn't even anything that should exist. Although, as some humans would say, *Whatever.*

She was still waiting for an answer, staring at him with those piercing green eyes. He squeezed her shoulder and pointed with his chin toward the woman. Her sobs were quieting, but Jenny tensed beneath him as a man stood and stumbled drunkenly toward her.

He said something in slurred Indonesian. The woman squeezed shut her eyes, shaking her head. The other men laughed harder and shouted at their friend. He grinned at them, teetered to the woman, and grabbed her hair. She screamed. Jenny flinched. The man slapped her so hard, her head rocked to the side, slamming against the tree trunk.

The woman choked down a sob with a muffled whimper.

"Fucker," Jenny muttered. Perrin said nothing. He'd noticed another man, sitting deeper in the shadows, away from the others. Bronze skin, long hair. Tattoos covered his arms like claws. He wasn't laughing or smiling, but he was watching. His eyes were very dark, almost black.

Yes. Definitely these were the same men who had attacked the yacht. Of all the islands the sea witch could have dumped them on. . .

She does nothing without a reason.

An electronic hiss filled the air. A crackle. Perrin almost didn't hear it beneath the raging music, but all the men flinched—even the one who stood above the Frenchwoman. Someone turned the music off. Silence fell over Perrin like a hammer.

The tattooed man set aside his beer, reached down beside his legs, and seemed to fiddle with something. Perrin couldn't see what it was, but that electronic hiss filled the air again, broken by a man's voice.

Rough, coarse, gruff. Vaguely familiar. Jenny stiffened.

"You were supposed to contact me," said the man. *"Did you get the woman?"*

The tone was angry. The mercenary did not seem bothered. He held the receiver to his mouth with preternatural calm, his dark eyes seeming to catch the firelight instead of reflect it. "No. She escaped. There was a helicopter. Armed men, led by the red-haired woman you warned me about, the one with only one eye. We had to leave, or die."

Jenny bowed her head, muttering something under her breath. Perrin wanted to do the same. He had been certain that helicopter meant danger. He had taken her away from her people instead. Stupid. So stupid.

The tattooed mercenary's English was slightly accented,

but far more cultured than that of the man in the radio, who growled. *"Did she go with the fuckers?"*

"She was gone before then, into the water with a man. She never surfaced."

"What man?"

"Unknown. Big. Naked. Long silver hair. There was nothing on him in the files you sent."

Silence. Long silence. *"Stay close to the radio. We'll be in contact."*

The mercenary began to reply, but the woman lurched forward, scrabbling in the leaves. Terrible hope in her eyes. She screamed something in French, a long stream of words that were desperate, raw.

"What's this?" asked the man on the radio. *"Who the hell is that?"*

For the first time, the tattooed man looked uncomfortable. "She was here when I arrived. The men commandeered a yacht earlier this week. I needed to keep them happy."

"I don't give a shit. Get rid of her. Now."

Jenny rocked forward. Perrin held her down. She was strong, but he had a hundred pounds on her, all muscle. He clamped his hand over her mouth. The dog appeared beside him and whined.

The woman was still screaming in incomprehensible, broken French. The mercenary sighed, reached behind his back, and pulled out a gun. It was a new weapon, gleaming and clean, and looked nothing like the battered rifles the other men kept near.

The woman gasped, eyes widening. The mercenary aimed and pulled the trigger.

Half her head exploded.

Jenny cried out against Perrin's hand. Quiet, muffled, choked down—but the music was gone, and all the men were so silent. Sounded louder than it should have.

Perrin held his breath as backs stiffened. Some turned, scanning the forest. So did the tattooed mercenary. Gun still out. Gaze sharp.

The dog whined again, loudly, and shot through the undergrowth toward the men. Wagging its tail. Bouncing, acting incredibly excited to see them. Making a lot of noise.

Everyone relaxed. But the mercenary stared at the forest a moment longer before he put away his gun. He picked up the receiver. "It's done."

No one answered. The call, apparently, was over.

Perrin removed his hand from Jenny's mouth. Her whole body trembled, so violently he thought her teeth would start chattering. She stared at the dead woman, stared and stared, but he wasn't entirely certain she was seeing her.

He squeezed her shoulder. Someone turned the music back on though at a lower volume. The mercenary shouted orders, and the mood was somber as some men stood, ambling over to the dead Frenchwoman. One of them kicked at the dog, threw a bottle at it. Perrin heard a hard thud, the dog cried out, and he stopped listening and trying to look.

"Let's go," he whispered in Jenny's ear. No way would they get to that radio.

She shuddered, glancing at him. Eyes haunted, filled with tears. Perrin dug his fingers into her shoulder and kissed her hard. Heart aching, aching, in his throat.

"Perrin," she whispered, against his mouth. Hearing her say his name, like that—with pain and loss, and need— made him shudder, too.

He said nothing but slithered backward, drawing her with him. They moved silently, with great care, and it was a long time before they reached a distance where it was safe enough to crawl on all fours. Only when the fires were a prick in the darkness did they stand. Carefully, listening for any hint that they were not alone.

Jenny still trembled, but her jaw was set, eyes hard.

"You knew the voice on the radio," Perrin said.

"I haven't heard that man speak in six years," she replied, softly. "He's my uncle."

She didn't seem inclined to share more. Perrin wrapped his hand around hers and made her follow him on a circuitous path to the beach. He chose a spot well away from the battered encampment, afraid the cuts in their feet would be contaminated by the human waste he still scented every time the wind turned. Stars glittered overhead. Waves whispered to him. Perrin felt afraid when he entered the water, as though he would be swallowed, stolen away.

The feeling passed. He and Jenny waded in to their waists, where it was deliciously cool. He stripped off his bathing shorts and pressed them into the pack still clipped around her waist.

"Sorry," he said, but she only nodded, her gaze elsewhere. Her other hand drifted against the water's surface, and there was a weight to her movement, as though she were touching the body of some sleeping giant.

"He sent men to kill us, all those years ago," she said, voice faint. And then: "I hear singing."

Perrin stared, unsure how to respond. He heard singing, too: the waters of the sea mixing with the hum of deep earth, rising into a voice that was as old as the first rock that had formed the world. It had been a long time since he had heard that music. Lost to him, on land. Lost, with his *kra'a*.

He should not have heard it now. Just as Jenny should have been deaf to it.

Perrin pulled her close, his legs binding together in painful cracks of bone and rippling skin. He tilted them back into the water as his torn, throbbing feet expanded into the fins of a massive tail that continued to sting even after its transformation was complete. Jenny clung to his side, one leg hooked over his waist. She took a deep breath, and he sank them both down.

Dark as death beneath the waters, but Perrin could see his way well enough to the anchored yacht. He swam fast, drinking deeply from the sea, and soon they surfaced beside the hull. Jenny clung to the ladder as his tail shifted into legs. He squeezed her hand around the rung.

"Let me check," he breathed. "Stay here."

She gave him a dirty look, which made him smile. Finally. Some fire again.

Perrin climbed the ladder. His pounding heart was the loudest thing in the night. No one was on deck except the dead man he had glimpsed earlier. Bloated, distended, smelling so rotten Perrin wanted to gag. He stepped around him.

Inside, more silence. No minds, dreaming. No one hanging out, drinking a beer. Probably because the small bar he found had already been raided of its liquor.

Perrin walked through the yacht, bent over, crammed into its small spaces. He found no one but still felt uncomfortable.

He walked back on deck, and found Jenny already on board, dripping seawater and hugging herself. She stood near the dead man, staring, and made a small, throaty sound.

"Do you believe in ghosts?" Perrin asked her.

Jenny covered her mouth, swallowing hard. "Yes. You?"

"All spirits abide," he replied, and grabbed the dead man's arms, dragging him to the edge of the yacht. "I just hope this one doesn't mind what I'm about to do."

Jenny made another muffled sound—the beginning of a protest, he thought—but in the end she remained silent as he lowered the dead man overboard, as quietly, and respectfully, as he could manage. He felt her stare, though, like a brand on his neck—and when he was done, he turned to her, and said, "I'm sorry."

"Don't be," she replied, but her voice was rough.

He followed her inside the yacht. Jenny went straight to the controls. The radio had been torn out. She turned around and strode down another set of stairs. Quick, determined. Perrin tried to follow, but he was too large to move with any speed inside the yacht. He found her, finally, in the engine room.

It was a crammed, hot space. Perrin didn't follow her inside.

"It's good," she said, sounding far away. "I can get this thing started."

Perrin didn't wait. He backed out and made his way topside. He noted the warm glitter of firelight on the hill above the encampment, and heard the continuing pulsing beat of music.

He also saw movement on the beach. Four men, dragging a rubber raft behind them and carrying paddles. A cold murderous knot settled in the pit of his gut. Anger. Good sweet anger.

They would have known a tsunami was coming, because of the earthquake and receding tide. Kept their boats out in deep waters, then moored them in the lee of the seawall after the worst of the destruction. Now, they were coming out to get them. Maybe they needed something from the yacht.

Perrin ducked back inside. Jenny was just coming up the stairs, skin glistening with sea and sweat.

"Someone's coming. Get the anchor up, and the engine going. Don't wait for me."

"What do you mean, don't wait?"

"You heard me. Do it." Perrin turned away, half-expecting her to catch up and grab his hand. He wasn't disappointed. Except it wasn't his hand she grabbed, but his hair. Jenny yanked hard.

"Listen," she muttered. "I'm not leaving you. I'm not running away again, like I did on the beach—"

The beach. He remembered that slip of a human girl, standing on the hill, staring—watching him with anguish in her eyes as he was dragged back into the sea.

Perrin whirled, knocking her hand away, and pushed her hard against the wall. He towered, and she squirmed, pressing even harder against him. He was still naked, and the contact roared, making his blood run so hot, so wild, he almost lost himself in a terrible rush of frustration and lust, and love—*love*—that swelled inside him with overwhelming, drowning, force.

"You didn't run from me," he growled, filling his hands with her face and forcing her to look at him. "You didn't abandon me. There was nothing you could do. You would have died if you'd stayed."

"No," she said, but he kissed her before she could say another word, pouring everything he was into that act, gripping her around the waist and hauling her off her feet. She was hot and willing, and tasted of salty tears and something so sweet he wanted to sink, and sink, and never tear himself away.

But he did. He heard a dog barking, distant, and broke off the kiss with a groan that rose straight from his chest.

"Perrin," she breathed.

"Please," he whispered, backing away—afraid to look at her face. "Do as I ask. There's no time."

He didn't wait for her response. He ran up on deck, and dove into the water. His body was already transforming before he slipped beneath the surface, and he swam hard and fast to the anchored speedboats.

The engines. He had to disable the engines. He heard voices, distant, and peered around the hull. Saw the small raft bobbing in the water. The men were in it, but hadn't started paddling yet.

Perrin dove, propelling himself hard to the seafloor. He found a rock with sharp edges and shot back to the speedboat above him. When he broke the surface again, he heard paddles.

He hauled himself halfway into the boat and slammed the rock as hard as he could against the exposed engine. It made a terrible sound. Sparks flew. He hit it again, and again, until tubes crushed and broke loose, and the fuel line broke. He smelled gasoline and oil.

Shouts filled the night. Perrin swam to the other boat. He disabled that engine, too.

The yacht roared to life. He heard more shouts. Bullets pinged the hull. Perrin shot through the water toward that rubber raft, gaining speed. Relentless. Furious.

He slammed into the raft from underneath, striking it so hard it rose from the water and flipped. Men tumbled, splashing. Perrin did not look at their faces. He grabbed ankles and dragged them under. Deep under. He did not let go until they stopped thrashing.

He went for the others. The raft had righted itself, and one of the men had already crawled inside. Another was trying to do the same. He grabbed his legs, but the man held tight to the raft, screaming. Perrin slammed his fist into his crotch, then once more into his gut, until his grip loosened. The man let out a broken, strangled cry that choked into silence the moment Perrin dragged him underwater.

He drowned the man and didn't let himself think about it. This was life, or this was death—Jenny's life, his life—and that was all. That was all he needed to know.

Perrin surfaced one more time, but at a careful distance. He hadn't gotten a good look at the man in the raft, but he had a feeling.

He was right. Tattoos stood out in sharp relief against bronze skin, and black eyes glittered. No gun, not one he could see. Maybe it had fallen into the sea, but he doubted it.

"I know you," said the man, calm, as others shouted from shore: men running to see why shots had been fired. "You're the one who saved the woman. She must be close."

He didn't sound afraid, just interested, as though there was a chance he might still catch Jenny. The darkness in his eyes unsettled Perrin. It didn't seem entirely human.

"Why do you want her?"

"Because I'm being paid to want her. What my employers intend for Ms. Jameson is none of my business." A brittle smile touched that mouth. "But you're dead. You should know that. Those people who want her have ways. *Impossible* ways."

"Fine," Perrin said, and sank down into the sea. He listened to his blood hum, along with the vibrating roar of the yacht's engine as it motored through the water. Deeper than that was the song of the sea—and beyond, a groan. Far away, so quiet it might as well have been in his soul. The sigh of a waking beast.

It was just as easy to capsize the raft on the second try, but the tattooed man was ready. He hit the water, not with a gun, but a twelve-inch blade in his hand. Good swimmer, agile in the sea. He should not have been able to see Perrin in the darkness underwater, but those black eyes tracked his movements.

Not just human, Perrin thought, but all he could think of were witches, and there was nothing of magic in the man. Just . . . darkness.

He surged close, reaching for the man's ankles, but the mercenary seemed to know he was there, and twisted with surprising agility. He corkscrewed through the water, slashing the knife. The blade almost cut Perrin's cheek, but he spun sideways and stayed close beneath the water. Waiting for the tattooed man to breathe.

It had to happen. In that moment when the mercenary tilted his face above water to swallow air, Perrin slammed into him at full force, ramming fists into his gut. The human didn't drop the knife, but the attack slowed him long enough for Perrin to grab his wrist and break it. Fingers loosened, and the knife drifted out of sight.

The tattooed man did not give up. He grappled with his other hand, trying to push Perrin away. For a moment their gazes met, and Perrin stared into black, pitiless, empty eyes. Unafraid, even on the cusp of death. Heavy with promise.

Perrin sank, grabbing the man's ankles, and hauled him deep under. The man thrashed and fought, twisting in the water like an eel. Perrin gritted his teeth and pulled him to the ocean floor. His skin felt oily beneath his hands, burning hot, and seemed to leave a scent in the water that Perrin could taste. Like blood or ash. Corpses.

The tattooed man was dead before he reached bottom. Perrin made sure. He held the man by the throat, looking into that slack face. His eyes did not open. His body was limp. Not even a trapped bubble escaped his nostrils or mouth.

But Perrin still felt afraid.

Gut check, his old friend Tom would have said. Homeless Tom, with his thick grubby clothes and dirty backpack, and always a cigarette to smoke, even when he had nothing to eat.

Trust your gut. Check your gut.

Perrin's gut said that this wasn't over. Death wasn't enough.

He did not surface again until he reached the third speedboat, the only one that he had not yet disabled. Men were in the water again, floating inside another inflatable raft, but Perrin didn't hunt them even though they fired at the yacht. Bullets pinged, but not with the same strength. Jenny was nearly past the lip of the seawall.

He found another rock and pounded the speedboat engine until it was satisfyingly mangled. He hit it harder and longer than he needed to, burning up on the inside with a terrible pressure that started in his chest, and spread into his throat, his head. Everything felt tight enough to burst.

A short distance away, he heard a muffled whine. Perrin spun in the water, searching.

It was the dog, paddling toward him with all its strength, head barely above water. Perrin frowned at it, perplexed. He could usually see inside the minds of animals—or, at the very least, feel their surface moods—but other than a general sense of terrible need, this one was closed to him. He found that . . . unusual.

Perrin reached the dog in moments and gathered the squirming animal close. It whined and licked his jaw.

"Hold still," he muttered. "You're trouble."

The dog yipped, trying to claw from the water onto his shoulders. Perrin drifted onto his back, set the dog on his chest, and kicked hard with his tail to ghost through the sea. Wondering how the hell he was going to catch up to Jenny while trying to keep a dog from drowning.

Fortunately, he didn't have far to go. He found the yacht drifting just outside the seawall. Jenny stood on deck, a flare gun in her hands, holding it like she was ready to shoot fire up someone's ass. Her eyes were sharp and angry, her body lean, her wild red hair coming free of its braid. Beautiful. Glorious. Real.

She ran to the ladder when she saw him, but frowned as he drifted close.

"What," she began, then stopped as Perrin pushed the squirming dog into her arms. He clung to the ladder rungs as his tail shifted, tearing in two. His bones cracked and reset, skin rippling into human flesh.

He climbed onto the boat and nearly fell to his knees on the deck. A tremor raced through him. Suddenly, he did not feel quite so cold or heartless about the humans he'd drowned.

And the eyes of that tattooed man still lingered.

Claws clicked. The dog licked his face. Jenny wrapped her arms around him, warm and tight. Her lips brushed his ear.

"Rest," she said, then slipped away.

Moments later, the yacht started moving. Perrin lay down on the deck, breathless and cold, and did as she asked.

CHAPTER THIRTEEN

THERE was a first-aid kit in the main cabin, hanging from the back of the plush captain's chair. Not the usual place, but a good one. The pirates had not stolen its contents or touched the clothes Jenny found in the closet down in the sleeping quarters. The Frenchwoman's feet were smaller than hers, but socks stretched.

All the lights were off, so as not to draw attention to themselves, but her eyesight was surprisingly sharp. Or maybe the stars outside were shedding more light than usual through the broken windows. Perrin lay sprawled on the floor, beside the couch. He'd tried to sit there first, but needed to lie down, and the couch was too narrow for his frame. The dog, however, had made itself quite comfortable on the hard cushions. It thumped its tail as she approached but didn't raise its head. Jenny frowned at the animal, suspicious.

"What's all that?" Perrin looked at the oversized bucket in her hands, sloshing water, and the first-aid kit tucked under her arm.

"Playing doctor," she replied. "Your feet are a mess."

He grunted. Jenny raised her brow at him, fighting very hard to exude an air of calm competency—and not the fear, the shaken uncertainty, that was rolling through her, making her knees tremble. She wanted to stare at him, all of him, just to make certain he was all right—but, of course, he was. It was all the parts inside that were wounded.

Jenny sat beside his feet, glad to be on the floor, where she could pretend that everything was stable, solid. She looked up, quick enough to take in his scarred, battered, beautiful body—just before meeting his gaze. His eyes were ice pale, haunting. The rest of his face was as cold as his eyes should have been—too hard and grim to be called kind—but his eyes, those eyes, were all she needed to see.

What kind of man are you? Jenny wanted to ask him. *So we share dreams . . . but who's the man? Who are you now?*

"Are you ticklish?" she asked instead, slightly hoarse.

Perrin stared. "Once, I was."

Jenny swallowed hard and pulled a soaked rag from the bucket of warm water. She wrung it out, leaned in, and dabbed the soles of his right foot. The cuts bled, and despite his transformation and time in the sea, she still saw small traces of debris. He jerked away from her, and she caught his ankle, carefully as she could.

"Sorry," she muttered. He nodded roughly, even more pale as he scooted backward and pushed himself up on the couch beside the dog. Perrin was very quiet, watching her. Made her uncomfortable, but only because what she was doing felt less medicinal than intimate.

"I killed those men in the raft," he said, suddenly. "The one with the tattoos. I drowned him."

Jenny stilled. "I know."

Perrin moved his feet back, like he was going to stand. Jenny placed her hands on his knees, holding him still. Or maybe it was the fact that her palms slid a little higher than she intended, to his thighs, that made him freeze.

A tremor raced through him. Jenny forced herself to meet his gaze and found that his eyes had darkened to a rich blue, filled with a heat and hunger that thrilled her, almost as much as it frightened.

But there was loss, too, in his gaze. Grief, and that old broken loneliness she understood too well.

"I know," she whispered again, unable to look away from his eyes. "I understand."

Perrin searched her face. "I was too angry. I've hurt people before in anger. It's not . . . right."

"It's a fine line," she said, feeling as though she was walking one herself. "But those men would have hurt us."

"Would you have killed them?"

Jenny hesitated. Perrin looked away.

"Don't," she said, squeezing his knees. "Don't assume you know what I'm thinking."

He made a small sound that could have been a grim laugh or a very sad sigh. "I know what I've become. It doesn't matter what anyone thinks."

"Liar," she whispered, and settled back to continue working on his feet. He gave her a sharp look, which she ignored, squeezing antibiotic ointment onto her fingers and slathering it over his cuts. He shifted his feet. She grabbed his ankle again and held him still, a little more roughly than she needed to. He bore it in silence.

"We don't have much fuel," she told him. "We're drifting now, but we'll only have a couple hours once we start up again. We're already sitting ducks. We need a plan."

"Where are we now?"

"Two hours north of the island. Open sea."

"Open sea is good."

"You don't sound convinced."

"Two things," he said, after a moment's thought. "The first is you're right. Open sea does leave us vulnerable. I'm not sure we're done with those pirates, or the one who hired them. The man with the tattoos was not . . . quite right. He fought me in the water, and he shouldn't have been able to. He could see me. He was fast. He was not afraid."

Jenny hunched smaller. "Something about the way he held himself. His . . . eyes."

"His eyes," Perrin agreed softly. "That means something to you."

Cold settled in her bones. If she could have become a mouse, she would have. Which was stupid.

Be a tiger, she told herself. *You've got claws.*

She just didn't feel like it at the moment—especially when she thought about what she wanted to tell him. "My uncle had a wife. Her name was Beatrix. Beatrix Weave. She was never very nice, but it got worse over time. She had a strong talent for telepathy. And then, later, we discovered that she'd been making deals with . . ."

Jenny had to stop. Perrin slid his hand under her jaw but didn't make her look at him. He touched her only, just like that.

"You can tell me anything," he said, in a voice that wasn't particularly gentle but entirely straightforward.

"It'll sound ridiculous," she replied.

"Oh, no," he said dryly, and raised his brow in mock horror.

Jenny stared at him, then laughed. "You."

"Me," he said, mouth ticking into a grim smile as his other hand touched her face, ever so lightly.

Les had touched her once, like this, and Jenny had wanted to run. But Perrin's touch didn't feel oppressive, or like she was caged in. All she felt was . . . held. Safe. Warm.

"Witches," she said. "Beatrix Weave found witches. They taught her things even they didn't want to teach, but they had no choice. She could reach into their minds. From them, she learned how to summon . . . creatures."

"Creatures."

"I don't know what to call them." Jenny felt nauseous, and swallowed hard. "Demons? Bad spirits? No clue. But they gave her power. And she learned how to do other things with that power, like make people immortal."

Jenny hadn't realized she'd stopped looking at him until she felt him go very still. She tipped up her chin to search his face, wondering uneasily what she'd find.

Perrin was staring at her, but with distant eyes. Memories had taken him elsewhere. He came back to her, slowly, but with a hard glint in his gaze that made him look especially forbidding. So much so, Jenny suffered a quiet shiver of fear.

"That is very bad," he said.

"Worse than an earthquake that'll destroy the world?"

Perrin's jaw tightened. "Yes. Some doors should not be opened."

There were certain things she hadn't allowed herself to think about over the years, but hearing him say that, with such grim certainty, made her feel like a little kid hiding in the dark from monsters.

"Beatrix is dead," Jenny said. "But she taught others what to do. She *infected* others with the . . . darkness . . . that she summoned. I'm not saying that the pirate you killed was one of the infected; but if you felt something off about him, and he's working for the Consortium, it's possible something was . . . done to him. Or he could just be strange and psycho all on his own. There are plenty like that, too."

The dog whined. Jenny reached out and patted its head. "There was an unofficial truce after the family war. Everyone agreed to stay out of each other's way."

"You wouldn't have agreed to that."

"No. I wanted them dead." Jenny gave him an unapologetic smile. "Dead, burned, rotting in hell. I would never have stopped. But I'm not in charge of the family, and now I'm afraid they've waited too long."

None of the stiffness left Perrin's shoulders. "They want you. That's no truce."

"I've been out of the loop. I heard rumors that the truce was broken several years ago. My grandmother's sister, the one who left *A Priori,* lost some of her people to the Consortium, and that was the beginning of it. As for me . . . I'm nobody to them. No powers, no influence. They could have had me a long time ago."

"But they waited until now."

"The timing is strange, considering everything else that's

happened. I don't know why they want me. Leverage against my grandparents, maybe. Which would never work."

Again, the dog whined. Perrin's hand tightened against her face. "Explain."

But she was tired of talking about her family. Dead tired. And the parasite in her skull was twitching again.

I'm going to tell him, she thought. *Right now.*

"You said there were two things about the open sea," Jenny said instead, unable to squeak out even one syllable about the parasite. "What was the second?"

"It can wait," Perrin said, and Jenny found him to be a terrible liar. She liked that.

The dog jumped down from the couch and padded to the open door that led out on deck. Its tail wagged. Far away, Jenny heard the low drone of a plane. The sound faded after less than a minute, and the dog sat down, staring at the sky.

"You're only safe when you're dead," Jenny murmured. "My grandfather taught me that. He and Maurice." She shook her head, throat thick. "Supposed to make you brave, I think. But it never worked for me. We're not safe out here, and it scares me."

Something else scared her. Her big mouth. She had never told anyone so much about her family, for good reasons: shame and danger and disbelief. Who would believe her? Who could be trusted?

Jenny slid away from Perrin's touch, suffering a strange, aching hunger in her heart as she did: homesickness, maybe. But not for any home she'd ever had.

"I don't know how to make anyone feel safe," Perrin said, resting his hands on his knees. His voice was low, rough, but she was listening hard and caught the faint catch and break in his words.

Jenny didn't know how to answer him, except with the truth.

"Dreams," she told him. "Those dreams were safe. You made me feel safe there."

Feeling like a coward, she stood and walked away, past

the dog, out on deck. She kept her distance from the spot where the dead man had lain. The outline of his body was still visible, clear as day: a man-sized stain of blood and other sticky fluids that smelled like rot and death.

The boat was dark and silent, rocking gently in the waves. Clouds had cleared, and stars glittered. *Peace,* she thought. This was the peace-time of night that she had always loved. Silence and water, and her heartbeat, as though the world was made only of those three things—and starlight.

We do not suffer by accident, Jenny thought, dredging up more Jane Austen; and then a line from an old Nat King Cole song filled her head, and she hummed to herself as the parasite twitched and a raging thirst filled her, an overwhelming need that was too powerful to acknowledge except that she turned from the rail, walking around the bloody stain in the deck, toward the ladder that led down to the sea.

" '*Sometimes I wonder why I spend the lonely night, dreaming of a song,*' " she sang softly to herself, terrible pressure building in her chest, as the parasite burned hot, hot in her head. Her legs were moving and she could not stop them. All she could do was sing to herself, her voice growing more strained, desperate, her throat drying up like leather.

Jenny could not stop herself from climbing down the ladder into the dark water. Her voice broke as she clung by one hand to the rail—surrounded, cocooned.

Down. Go down, whispered that dry voice in her head.

No, Jenny told it, even as she let go and sank underwater. *I'll die.*

You will not die, replied the voice. *Death will not transform you. Just life.*

She had no choice. Her mouth opened, and the sea rushed in.

The sea tasted good, which surprised her, almost as much as it terrified. Salt water flowed down her throat like silk, filling her belly with a sweetness that made her feel full and cool, and strong.

No, part of her thought desperately. *Salt water will kill you. You will dehydrate, you will risk seizures, brain damage. Your kidneys will shut down.*

But she opened her mouth again, swallowing, inhaling—

A strong hand grabbed her braid and yanked upward.

Jenny broke the surface, choking. Perrin was there, huge and solid. He hauled her hard against him, shouting at her, his hand painfully tight around her waist. She couldn't understand a word of what he was saying. Her ears were ringing, and her heart thundered.

"—what were you thinking?" she finally heard, and buried her face against his chest, clinging to him, suffering the same tremors that raced from his body into hers. He had not changed shape—his legs bobbed against hers, and his free hand gripped the bottom ladder rung.

"I wasn't thinking," she whispered hoarsely. "Something came over me. I had to be in the water."

I had to. I was forced. There's something living in my head, and it won't let me tell you—please, please, let me tell him—

Perrin pressed his lips hard against her forehead.

"I'm sorry," he rasped. "I'm sorry this is happening to you."

"Not your fault," she mumbled. "I wish I could tell you why."

But he didn't pick up on that like she hoped he would. Perrin, trembling as badly as her, placed her hand on the ladder. "Can you climb?"

"I don't know," she said. Her teeth were beginning to chatter. *Shock,* she thought. The ocean felt warm, and so did the night air. She was still thirsty for salt water and licked the remnants off her lips before she realized what she was doing.

Fear settled like a fist in her gut. She felt faint. Perrin, watching her face, growled. Jenny tried to reassure him with a smile, but it felt more like a grimace—teeth gritted against the sudden, incredible urge to vomit.

Which she did, halfway up the ladder. All that salt water, pouring out of her in one heaving, bitter rush that left her, again, faint.

What is happening to me? What is happening to me?

Perrin held her around the waist while she vomited, holding her close so that she didn't fall back into the water. When she was done spilling her guts, he hauled her up the last few feet to the deck and pushed her on board with a hard shove. Jenny lay there, exhausted. A warm tongue licked her face, accompanied by a whiff of bad breath and dog. Perrin scooped her up into his arms.

He was talking, but Jenny could barely hear him. No more buzz, but her ears felt plugged, stuffed with cotton, and her vision darkened. A tremendous sense of pressure overwhelmed her, as though her entire body was being squeezed to death. She saw rock, and felt heat, and heard the grind of rocks shifting deep in the earth's crust.

And in that crust, a claw.

A claw. A long, coiled body. A golden eye, shifting open.

Where are my dreams? rumbled a terrible voice, and the parasite twitched like a flexed muscle.

Here, said that dry voice, soothing and gentle. *Your dreams are here.*

No, Jenny thought desperately. *I'm here. Me.*

But the earth shifted again inside her mind, a wild ripple, and she rode that pulse of released energy, tumbled and breaking, clawing inside herself for anything to hold her steady.

Until hands caught her. Strong hands, strong arms.

Jenny snapped back into the real world, thrust from that dark place. Her heart raced. She felt nauseous again. The base of her skull throbbed.

She was sitting on the floor inside the yacht, and sagged forward, gulping air. Her lungs ached.

Perrin sat behind her, a warm, solid wall of muscle. Her head leaned against his shoulder, her arms resting against his bent legs. He held her snug around the waist, his hands pressed over her stomach. Holding her upright. Just holding her. She was more grateful for that than she cared to admit.

"You scare me," he said quietly. "I think you terrify me."

"Yeah," she whispered raggedly, closing her eyes. "Did you feel that? Tell me you felt that. What I just saw in my head."

Possession, visions. She wasn't sure which one she was asking him about, but that golden eye filled her mind again, and she shivered.

Perrin's arms tightened. She thought he would say no, that he had no clue what she was talking about. Which would mean that she really was losing her mind. The parasite, wreaking delusions, turning her brain to mush.

But he did not say no.

"I felt it," Perrin said, his warm breath stirring her hair. Speaking like a man on death row, resigned and afraid. "I saw the golden eye, and felt its body shift. I shouldn't have. But neither should you. It means there was another earthquake."

Another one. Jenny wanted to ask him if he had heard the monster ask about its dreams, but she had a feeling he hadn't—and besides, when she tried to voice the question, her voice stuck.

The dog padded close, pawing at her arm. Jenny found enough energy to pat its sleek head, and it sat back, staring at her with large brown eyes that were sad, and far too intelligent. "What is down there, Perrin? What did I see inside my head? Is it the beast you and the sea witch spoke of?"

Perrin was silent a long time, reaching up to rub the back of his head. Jenny wanted to do the same, to touch the parasite. The urge made her uneasy, and afraid. Some bad instinct. Something, in her gut, beginning to brew with meaning.

"The Kraken," he whispered, finally. "We call it the Kraken."

"THERE HAVE ALWAYS BEEN THE KRAKEN," PERRIN SAID. "No one knows when they came to exist, and no one really knows what they are. But they are old. And when the seas were even vaster than they are now, they lived in the deep, and bred there, and fought."

"Big?"

"Large as mountains. Just as tough. The sea allows a weightlessness that doesn't constrain size."

"I assume there's a good reason no one's ever seen one."

"No one human," he corrected her. "The Kraken are a danger to my kind, too. Their appetites are . . . large. They eat anything, even stone, though they prefer flesh. They made the sea . . . a very dangerous place. Not much could survive there. But long ago, my people found a way to . . . quiet them. Make them sleep. Fill their heads with dreams that would make them *want* to sleep."

It sounded too strange to believe—more strange, even, than mermen—but she had seen enough oddities in her life to make the leap. "This one is waking."

"Slowly. But not slowly enough. These most recent tremors are the result of its body shifting. When it is fully awake and conscious, it will break free of its nest."

"The earthquake that you say will destroy everything."

"A Kraken sleeps deep in the heat of the earth's crust, and its waking is not gentle. It will . . . explode . . . from its nest. The shock wave from that explosion will carry unimaginable power, and the displacement of the sea as the Kraken travels . . ."

Perrin stopped and took a deep breath. "Keeping the Kraken asleep requires constant vigilance, and determination. A . . . connection . . . with the individual beast itself. Not everyone is suited to the task."

Jenny studied him, trying to steady her heartbeat, her nerves, which were screaming after hearing him talk about sea monsters exploding from the earth. "But you were."

Perrin tensed. "Imagine what I was running from when you found me on that beach."

"You were chosen."

"I was born. You either have the skill in your blood, or

you don't. There's always more than one candidate, but one is usually better than the others. I was better. I had no choice in the matter." He paused. "It's supposed to be an honor."

"Sure. You were so honored you swam screaming."

Perrin grunted. "My father was ashamed. My entire family wanted little to do with me, afterward. What I did was a disgrace. I didn't care, though. I endured my punishment. My training. I had . . . my own dreams . . . to sustain me."

"Dreams."

He shrugged. "You know."

Jenny knew. Made her glad to be sitting down. "Why were you exiled?"

"I don't want to talk about that."

"Fair enough." Jenny studied him. "Do you trust me?"

"This has nothing to do with trust."

"Does it have to do with Les? Is he the reason you were exiled?"

Perrin met her gaze with such sharpness, she flinched. "Were you close?"

"You asked me that already. Would it matter?"

"Tell me."

"We were friends. I *thought* we were friends. And no," she said coldly, rubbing her sore arms and wrists, "I never slept with him."

Perrin looked down, still tense. He rubbed a narrow white scar that covered the length of his biceps. "A'lesander was my friend, too. A long time ago. He and Pelena were my companions, when I was allowed to have any. All of us, from other clans, other seas. Outsiders."

"Why?"

"Tradition. Circumstances. Krackeni send their children away to be raised by others. It prevents inbreeding and promotes . . . good will."

"You don't sound convinced."

"It's a cold practice," he replied. "Pelena and I were sent to our foster clan for a special set of reasons having to do with the *kra'a*. Some of our family came with us, and that eased our lives. But A'lesander had a harder time, which always made things strange between us. He was part human, which I envied . . . but that was nothing to be proud of amongst the Krackeni we were living with, and he was sometimes treated poorly for it. He wanted to be more like me. Pure blood."

Perrin said *pure blood* with venom in his voice, like it was a dirty word. Jenny said, "What happened?"

"Jealousy," he whispered. "A'lesander was obsessed with becoming a candidate for the *kra'a*. It would have done him no good, but that was what he wanted. To be one step closer to having . . . power, perhaps. Acceptance. He should have known better.

When he was not chosen to become a candidate—as I knew he would not be, because those decisions are made very young—he blamed his human ancestry. Then he blamed me. We fought. He drew my blood, and that was . . ."

Perrin stopped, sighing. "You do not harm Guardians. His only defense was that he was young, no older than sixteen or seventeen of your human years. I suppose that's why he was allowed to remain in the sea after his exile."

"He didn't just stay in the sea," Jenny said. "Close to it, though. What little I know, and it was confirmed by others, is that he found jobs on oceanic science vessels, first doing grunt work and then making a name for himself finding artifacts where no one else could. He could have been famous for it, but always stayed out of the limelight. Professional exploration has been his work for the last ten years."

"I still envy him," Perrin said quietly. "Maybe I would have been as resourceful had I been allowed contact with the sea, but I have my doubts. A week ago I was working as a janitor in a Chicago Aquarium, and I was grateful for it."

"You were in Chicago," she said, numb. "Before that?"

"Indianapolis. St. Louis. Detroit. New York City. I took odd jobs, anything I could get. Most of that work involved construction, heavy lifting. My friend, the one I told you about . . . his name was Tom. He helped me get fake papers—birth certificate, a social security number. After my arrests, I suppose I would have been deported without those things."

Jenny didn't know what to say. Chicago. He had been in Chicago. New York. On land while she lived at sea.

"You're so quiet," Perrin said. "Does it bother you? The way I've lived?"

"Of course not," she replied. "I just wish . . ."

I wish I had known where you were. Maybe if I had asked for help, talked to someone in my family, trusted them enough to use those damned psychic gifts . . . I had your scale, I had something they could have used to track you . . .

No. Too late. She had made her choice.

"I'm sorry," she said. "I'm sorry we didn't find each other."

Perrin was silent a long time. "Did you ever tell anyone about that morning on the beach?"

"What was there to tell? That I found a *merman* when I was a kid, and couldn't stop him from being dragged into the ocean by his tail?" Jenny shook her head, feeling bitter. "I never breathed a word of what happened that day. To anyone."

"But the pieces have still fallen back together. You and me," he murmured, his large hands closing around her wrists, comforting and strong. His breath was warm against her hair, and if she turned her head, just so, if she let herself, if she dared—

She did. And brushed her lips against his cheek.

Just a simple touch. Hardly anything to it. But heat swelled, flowing from her throat into her stomach—making her ache in body and heart. The heartache was worse. She didn't know what she was doing here—not what was happening to her and not how she could control it. Make it safe.

Nothing is safe. Nothing. You know that. You're a big girl, and you have what you always wanted. Don't be an idiot. Grab it. Take it. Don't look back. Bear what comes. You're good at that, Jenny-girl. You're good at rolling with the punches.

Take it.

Jenny reached up and grabbed a fistful of Perrin's long hair. Silken, shimmering silver in her hands. He stilled, but when she tugged, ever so gently, he dipped his head and kissed her mouth. Soft, careful, painfully tender.

Jenny pulled away, though it hurt to do so.

"Why?" she asked him, finding it hard to breathe. "Why the dreams? Why this, now?"

His fingers drifted up her hair, to her cheek, grazing her skin and leaving a trail of heat. "Something happened that day on the beach. Something very rare. I should have realized, but I never did until now. We were bonded, Jenny."

"Bonded," she echoed.

Something lost, haunted, filled his gaze. "I don't know how it happened, I promise you that. Mind to mind—"

"A telepathic link," she interrupted. "My grandparents have one of those. Always in each other's heads."

Perrin hesitated. "You *have* lived a strange life."

Jenny poked his knee. "Tell me about this bond."

"I don't know much," he said, capturing her hand. "But what I do know is that it runs deep. It's different for each pair. And it's almost never formed between a human and *Krackeni*."

"Almost never."

"I know of only one who would admit it, and he's half-human himself. We're not supposed to mix, though it happens."

"I don't even know what's happening with us," she muttered. "I looked for you, Perrin, all my life. I was obsessed. Are you telling me it was because I didn't have a choice?"

"There's no mind control involved. There's always a choice. But the bond would have kept me in your thoughts."

Jenny begged to differ about the mind control. She was being controlled quite a lot, it seemed. But the parasite, she had to concede, had nothing to do with being a twelve-year-old girl who had sat every day on a beach, waiting for a boy to come swimming from the sea. It had nothing to do with the woman that girl had become, a woman who couldn't stare at the sea without seeing silver hair and pale eyes.

The parasite had nothing to do with dreams. Nothing to do with anything but trying to drown her and speak riddles inside her head.

Jenny sat up straighter, hoping he would look down and somehow see through her tangled matted hair to the growing lump at the base of her skull.

Look, she thought, fighting her arms that refused to move. *Look down, look, touch me there–*

"What did you think would happen if you found me?" Perrin asked suddenly, quietly. Jenny wanted to hug her knees to her chest. Like a child again, lost.

"Not this. It doesn't matter, I guess."

"It matters."

"I was a kid," she said. "A stupid kid. I imagined—"

Jenny couldn't say it. She couldn't tell him that she had imagined that he would hold her hand, like he did in those dreams, and sit with her, and just be with her. That he would be *hers*.

"So we're . . . bonded," she whispered instead, unsure what that even meant or how she felt; a little scared, a little trapped. "We're inside each other's heads. That's why we shared those dreams."

"It's more than that," he replied, with obvious reluctance. "Each bond might be different, but some elements are consistent. The longer we're together, the more . . . attuned we'll become to one another. The harder it will be for us to be apart. Until we won't be *able* to be apart."

The dog perked its ears, staring at Perrin. Jenny did the same. "What happens if we are?"

Perrin ducked his head. "What would happen if one of your grandparents died?"

Something cold slithered down her spine, and she

thought about her grandmother and grandfather, how close they were, how comfortable. How they depended on each other. It had never been a weakness, but a strength, between them. Beautiful, impossible strength.

"The other would follow," she said.

Perrin nodded, still not looking at her. Gently, carefully, he pushed away and stood. She let him, watching in silence as he walked to the door, out into the night. His absence made her cold, and she stared after him, even when he disappeared from sight, searching herself for evidence of that bond. Like it should be lit up in neon, or something.

All she felt was a hunger to be near him. That was all. An ache in her chest. She didn't feel empty, or less like herself. She was still Jenny. But Jenny wanted to be near Perrin.

She wished she knew if that was all her, or the parasite. The parasite, or something else. She didn't want to be controlled by a bond that she didn't understand. If she was going to want a man, it had to be because she really wanted him.

And don't you want him?

Simple question. Simple answer. Jenny had always wanted to be near Perrin, ever since seeing him for the first and last time on that beach.

If anything was true, it was that. She'd tried her best to live a normal life around that need, but it had always been there, in the depths of her heart. And after her carefully constructed life had fallen apart. . .

The dog pawed her thigh. She hugged the sleek, wriggling body close to her side, ignoring its wet nose against her hand.

"Good boy," she whispered absently.

Jenny went outside, swaying on weak legs. Afraid of what her reaction would be, looking at the sea. She felt nothing, though. No twitch in the parasite. No desire to drown herself.

Perrin stood at the rail, staring at the ocean. Stars glittered, tangled, wild in the sky. A breeze lifted his hair, winding it around his shoulders and throat.

Magic. Flesh and blood. She had seen him as a boy, a creature out of legend. But here, he was a man. Not a human man, but a man all the same.

She joined him. "How do *you* feel about this?"

"I'm afraid for you," he said quietly. "The sooner we separate, the safer you could be. The bond might not have had time to settle fully. But being apart . . . that has risks, too."

"I'd rather stay with you," she told him, without thinking. But it was the truth. Not a compulsion, not some strange force making her mouth move against her will.

I want to stay with you, she thought, riding on a wave of need born from some place so deep inside her she couldn't begin to describe it. If this was the bond talking, then what the hell. She wasn't like her family, who could read minds and emotions. All she had were her normal human senses—and gut instinct.

And her gut was saying, *Yes.*

Perrin gave her a haunted look. "You don't understand, Jenny. There's no *win* in this."

"I found the boy on the beach," she heard herself say, as though listening from very far away. "I call that a win. I'm still breathing," she added. "So are you. Big damn wins. Miracles, even. What more do you want?"

"You, alive," he whispered. "Long after I'm dead."

Jenny stared, wondering how one person could make her feel love and heartbreak, and anger—all at the same time.

Behind them the dog growled.

They turned. Nothing was there; but the dog stood stiffly, legs braced, staring at the sea. That low growl turned into a snarl that made her cold, and afraid.

"Get inside," Perrin said urgently. "Hurry."

"What is it?" Jenny asked him, but something hard hit her head, and she dropped, stunned. She couldn't even react when Perrin grabbed the back of her shirt and shorts and began dragging her from the rail. She tried to help him, but her feet wouldn't work. Her head throbbed.

Perrin grunted, and she landed hard on the deck again,

just inches from the open door. The dog danced around her, whining and growling. It nipped her ear, then grabbed her shirt, tugging. Jenny rolled sideways, searching for Perrin.

She found him beside her, on his stomach. He was trying to push himself up, grunting with pain. A spear quivered from his back. Slender, pale as bone.

A guttural, strangled sound left her throat, threatening to become something hysterical. Jenny clamped it down and pushed past weakness, pain. Perrin was so close, but it seemed to take forever just to grab his hand.

He turned his head, blinking at her. Dull eyes. Half-lidded. Not just with pain, she realized.

"Get out of sight," he said, words slurred, thick. "I'm the one they want."

Jenny gritted her teeth and yanked the spear from his back. Perrin cried out.

"Come on," she muttered, trying to stand. Her fingers latched on to his hair, then his wrist. "Move it."

Perrin tried to help her, but whatever poison had been in the spear was fast-acting, and there was no way she could drag a man his size. Not when she could barely stand.

Jenny was still on her knees when a large foot slammed down on Perrin's back, pushing him down. Seawater dripped from pale skin. She stared for one moment, stunned—but the spear was beside her, and she grabbed it without thinking. Jenny stabbed the sharpened point down into that foot.

She heard a roar but didn't look. Just moved, fast. Maurice—and later, the shape-shifter, Serena—had taught her that much. Never stay in one place during a fight.

But that didn't stop the panic or bad memories. A flashback hit her—gunfire, screams, a fiery pain in her belly—and then she was back again, scrabbling across the deck on all fours. Perrin was trying to stand. He met her gaze, and his eyes were clearer, stronger.

Someone grabbed her throat, fingers digging in with choking strength. Her assailant was crouched behind her, breath hot against her ear. She fought but had no leverage.

Her feet kicked uselessly against the deck. Perrin screamed her name.

The dog snarled, rushing past her in a blur of dark fur. All that hot breath puffed into a muffled shout, and the fingers loosened. Jenny twisted with all her strength, rolling on her back—

—and a knee planted itself hard on her chest, pushing out the rest of the air in her lungs.

A sharp word bit the air. The hands around her throat disappeared entirely. Jenny fought to breathe, vision blurred.

Everything was suddenly so quiet, broken only by dripping sounds.

She tilted her head, trying to see Perrin. All she found were feet, but her gaze traveled up naked bodies, male and female—stone daggers tied to forearms, long silver hair knotted with shells, bone. Braided belts clung to muscular waists. Pale eyes glittered. Jenny felt properly intimidated.

"Jenny," whispered a deep voice.

She stiffened, looking sharply at the man holding her down.

It was Les. Naked, wet. Sporting a swollen, broken nose. For some reason Jenny thought he should look different now—sinister, maybe, or with a sign on his forehead, spelling out E-V-I-L.

But he didn't, he was just as she remembered—good old Les—and that frightened her almost as much as the danger she was so obviously in.

His gaze was hard, but the corner of his mouth softened into a grim, sad smile.

"Hey," he said.

CHAPTER FOURTEEN

JENNY.

A surging roar filled Perrin's chest, as though his heart was trying to devour itself. The hole in the base of his skull throbbed, but not with pain—just heat, a terrible burning heat like fire had settled there, wild and heavy.

The poison in his blood was just as heavy, but it wasn't lethal. Even if it had been, Perrin would have kept fighting. He had lost sight of Jenny but could hear A'lesander. Rage filled him. White-hot.

One of the *Krackeni* hunters tried to kick him. He grabbed the male's foot and twisted hard. He got hit again, low in the back, but the pain was nothing. Perrin snarled, rolling sideways, grabbing up the discarded spear that Jenny had used to stab one of the hunters. The tip was poisoned with a paralytic. Perrin didn't know why it hadn't stopped him entirely, as it had the other hunter—who was sprawled in a heap, eyes open and staring.

Perrin staggered to his feet, swaying. A full pod of hunters surrounded him, three on each side, staring with their pale, unforgiving eyes. Such disdain in their faces, a terrible coldness. He didn't recognize them, but he didn't need to. A bitter taste filled his mouth. He'd had years to overcome the old hurt, but it was still there, he discovered. Sleeping behind his heart.

He saw A'lesander kneeling on Jenny's chest. Another hunter stood beside him, pale leg bleeding. The dog lay nearby, crumpled and panting.

"Get off her," Perrin snarled, wondering why the others had stopped coming at him. They stood too still, as though waiting for something.

Or someone.

"You have no power here," said a low voice, behind him.

Perrin's gut crunched into a hard ball. He turned, watching as a giant ascended the yacht ladder, dripping seawater. He wore no decoration. Carried no weapons. His hair was long and silver, and deep lines creased his face. His muscles were still taut, though, and strong. He wore his age well.

"Father," Perrin whispered, unable to put any strength in his voice.

Father. Turon O'doro. Eight years had done little to dull the sharp stab of heartbreak that traveled through Perrin when he looked into his father's eyes. He was little again, under that gaze. Just a boy. A boy, searching for some measure of compassion, anything in his father's eyes that might indicate even the faintest of small pleasures at seeing him again.

He found nothing.

But he heard Jenny breathing behind him. She made everything colder, sharper. He wasn't alone now. It wasn't just his survival that mattered.

Prison yard, Perrin told himself. *Live or die.*

"I thought you would be dead," said his father, with a particular emptiness in his voice.

Perrin hoped his expression did not change. "If you wanted to be certain, you should have taken my life yourself."

Turon's jaw tightened—and his gaze flicked past him. Perrin resisted the urge to block his view of Jenny. It would do no good and only bring more attention to her.

A frown touched his father's mouth. "Strange reward."

"But mine. As agreed," A'lesander said. Perrin whirled.

His old friend was standing, holding Jenny by the arm. She was leaning away from him, her gaze intense, flickering from A'lesander to Perrin, settling on Turon with a sharpness that he hoped his father did not notice.

But it was the possessiveness of A'lesander's grip that concerned him most.

"No," Perrin said. "*No.*"

"She was mine before you met her," A'lesander replied, switching to English. Perrin hadn't even realized they had been speaking the *Krackeni* native tongue. He'd fallen into it so naturally. "I won't let her suffer for your exile. I'll take her from here. I'll *protect* her, like I'd always planned to."

Jenny tried to twist out of his grip. "Like you protected me before? Fuck you, Les."

A terrible helplessness stole over Perrin. He felt his father watching, but this was something he could not hide. He wasn't strong enough.

Live or die.

Perrin tried to move toward her, but the hunters barred his way. He was bigger than them, but he did not fight. All he could do was stare at Jenny, watching as some awful realization crossed her face.

"Don't you dare," she whispered. "I don't know what this is, but don't you—"

"Enough," snapped Turon, his voice clicking out the melodic tones of the *Krackeni* language. "You are still under exile, A'lesander, and will be punished for your trespass into our territory. You did us a service, however, by finding Pelena's murderer. Take the human and go. What little good it will do you."

Perrin snapped around to stare at his father. "I did *not* kill Pelena."

"Show me your neck," said his father.

Perrin suppressed a growl, and yanked his hair away from his head. He turned. His father stalked close, sending a chill down his spine.

He expected roughness, but Turon was surprisingly

gentle as his thumbs traced the edges of the hole in his head. Perrin shuddered, cringed—just enough to make him hate himself, and his father, a little more than he already did.

"You lost the *kra'a*," said Turon, his voice dead, quiet.

"I lost it eight years ago," replied Perrin tightly. "A'lesander killed Pelena. He confessed it to me. Ask *him* where the *kra'a* is."

"A'lesander would not be able to hold a *kra'a*, even should he have one in his possession. He is too weak." Turon paused, not seeming to notice how A'lesander's face darkened at his words. "Pelena warned us you would return. She said your *kra'a* was calling to you. She could feel its dissatisfaction with her body."

"I didn't come here to take back my *kra'a*," Perrin told him coldly. "You're wasting your time with me. You should be searching for it. Finding some way to quiet the beast before it wakes."

"There is no quiet for the beast. Nothing for it but dreams. You remember that much." Turon hesitated. "You and your dreams."

"Don't," Perrin snapped. "You punished me. Leave it at that."

"I cannot. You are here." His father stood so still, and grim. "Temptation is an ugly thing. What did you think would happen if you killed Pelena for the *kra'a*? That your soul would be mended? That we would be forced to accept you, simply for the sake of settling the beast?"

Perrin curled his hands into fists. "I would never be so foolish. I told you, I did not come for power. I came because I felt the beast wake."

"Do not lie," whispered his father. "Your connection to the sea was severed."

Perrin swayed toward him. "I felt it. I still feel it. I hear the song of the sea, and I have witnessed the golden eye—"

Turon backhanded him. Jenny gasped, but Perrin just started laughing, cold and bitter, and furious.

"You never could see the truth," he said, spitting blood at

his father's feet. "You were never as good at divining souls as S'har or the other singers. *Never.* Even M'cal, his half-human son, was better than you at singing the souls of the living. That's why they didn't bring you on land to guard our people's secrets. They used you as nothing more than a breeder. And you took it out on me."

His father hit him again. Perrin saw it coming, but received the blow without fighting back. Nearly sent him to his knees.

"I did not kill her," he said, wiping blood from his mouth. "You see I do not have her *kra'a*."

Turon struck him in the face again, and this time Perrin did go down. He heard some commotion, A'lesander swearing, and suddenly Jenny was standing between him and his father. Back straight, breathing hard.

"Don't you touch him," she whispered.

Perrin found his feet and grabbed Jenny's arm, pulling her behind him. But Turon stared after her, frowning.

"I know your eyes," he said, in rough English. "Little girl."

Perrin swallowed hard. "A'lesander. Get her out of here."

Jenny tried to yank free. "Like hell."

"You carried a big stick," whispered his father, and Perrin snarled at him, backing Jenny up until she landed in A'lesander's arms. None of the other hunters moved. Still as statues, conserving their strength. He suspected not one of them was accustomed to the weight of gravity though their eyes tracked his every move. Ready. Waiting.

"Go with him," he told Jenny, hating himself for not being able to protect her. "Please, go."

Jenny's fingers dug into his arm. A'lesander grabbed her waist, but she did not make a sound. Just hung on to Perrin, for all she was worth.

"I love you," he breathed, prying her fingers off his arm.

Jenny slapped him with her other hand. Perrin flinched but managed to tear her off him. A'lesander hauled backward, but she continued to fight.

Perrin spun around to face his father, and got right up in his face so that Turon had to look at him, and not Jenny. Hurt, being near him. Hurt more than he could stomach.

I tried to be good, Perrin wanted to tell him. *I tried to be your son.*

Turon said, "The girl."

"Not part of this," he replied, sinking into the cold place. *Live or die. Live or die. For Jenny.*

But his father shook his head, finally looking troubled. "I was certain Pelena was mistaken."

Perrin frowned, but A'lesander swore again. He tore his gaze from Turon, just in time to watch Jenny scratch her nails across his old friend's face.

"Fuck your protection!" she screamed at him. "You murderer! You tried to kill Maurice! You killed that merwo—"

A'lesander struck her. Jenny hit the ground and didn't move.

Perrin roared, lunging at him. His father and several others caught his arms, holding him back. A'lesander stared at Jenny, then his fist. He looked stunned, utterly lost.

"Enough," his father snapped, and nodded at one of the hunters. "Give her to the sea."

Perrin froze. A'lesander's head snapped up. "No."

"You don't want her," said Turon coldly. "You told me she would keep our secrets, but I assumed it was because she cared for you. Obviously not."

Perrin did not bother arguing. He fought harder, slamming his elbows into guts, twisting and kicking, using every dirty trick he knew as two hunters grabbed Jenny under her arms. A'lesander reached out, making a small sound of protest. For a moment, Perrin thought he would fight them.

But A'lesander did not. All he did was watch, self-loathing creeping into his eyes, as Jenny was dragged to the rail. Her eyes were closed, and her head lolled. The dog, panting and still, whined.

Perrin broke free just as she was tossed over the rail. He followed, entering the water only seconds after her. He tore off his swim trunks and shifted shape, hauling Jenny to the surface. She dragged in a deep, coughing breath.

"Jenny," he said urgently, just before they were pulled under. He tried to hold on, but she was ripped out of his arms. Her eyes flew open.

More hunters appeared from the darkness below, bodies pale as daggers and armed with hooks and rope. Fists slammed into his gut, holding his arms, grappling with his tail. Every time he managed to slip free, someone else would catch him. Jenny was swept away. Hunters gripped her arms and legs, holding her underwater.

Perrin knew the moment she ran out of air. Her face twisted in a terrible grimace that was frantic and wild—and he screamed for her. He screamed. Every broken piece of his soul reaching for her heart.

Heat spread through him, that throbbing fire in the base of his skull. Old power swelled, tingling against his skin. The *Krackeni* holding him flinched in surprise, fingers loosening. Perrin broke loose, swimming from them in long, powerful strokes as he raced to reach Jenny's side. He sensed his father approaching. Faster, stronger. He had not been on land for the last eight years.

Jenny jerked, head tilting up. Her mouth opened, bubbles escaping. Perrin cried out again, desperate—

—and watched as a nimbus of blue light surrounded her head.

All the *Krackeni* froze, even Turon. Perrin faltered, as well. He knew that light. He knew it so well, but there was no way—no way at all it could be possible. Jenny was human.

And you are bonded, whispered a dry voice inside his mind, achingly familiar, and gentle. *I have known her, in dreams, as long as I have known you.*

I should not hear you, thought Perrin desperately. *You were taken from me. You are no longer in my soul.*

The voice of his *kra'a* murmured, *But she is.*

The hunters let go of Jenny, drifting away from her,

stunned. Perrin, reckless, swam straight into the human woman and hauled her away, tight in his arms. She was still alive, eyes open, clawing at her throat. Sucking down seawater. Blowing bubbles from her nose.

Breathing. She was breathing.

Perrin buried his fingers into her hair, against the base of her skull. He felt something hard and flat against her scalp—hot to the touch. The blue light intensified. Jenny shuddered against him.

Too much. He couldn't even think about it. The hole in his head ached, briefly, and for one moment he felt a terrible jealousy, a profound envy that was dark and bitter.

No, he told himself, ashamed. *No, you will not. This is not her fault.*

But how was it possible? No matter the bond, no matter the will of the *kra'a,* Jenny was human.

Wasn't she?

Not according to the sea witch, he thought. She had known all along. All her riddles. Telling him the *kra'a* was with him, that the answers were between them.

And Jenny . . . she must have known, as well. At least that something was attached to her skull. Why hadn't she said anything?

Perrin glanced over his shoulder. The hunters were following him, and he sensed movement from below. White shapes, distant. Screeching cries and clicks filled the water. Jenny stared at him with frightened eyes. The nimbus of light had faded. Bubbles poured from her nose. Still breathing.

Not that it would help her, or him. Panic clawed, bleeding fire in his belly. Perrin didn't know where to go. Not the boat. No land nearby. He was tiring. His muscles burned.

He glimpsed another flash of movement, a silver streak angling toward him from the darkness. Dolphin, he realized at the last moment.

A dolphin with glowing golden eyes.

Rik.

Perrin rolled sideways, throwing out his arm as the dolphin slid in tight beside them. He caught the dorsal fin and held on with all his strength.

Dolphins were fast. Much faster than a *Krackeni*.

But his old clan was everywhere—and they had summoned help. He glimpsed the shimmering bodies of viperous deep-sea dwellers, darting quick from the shadows in front of them; men and women shining with a faint bioluminescence, cavernous bodies mutilated and pierced with decorative bone shards. None of them would ever be able to come on land. No bones, just soft cartilage. The sun would burn their milky eyes. The only reason they could come so close to the surface now was that above it was night, and dark.

They carried nets and spears. Rik twisted, swimming hard in another direction, but the clan hunters were already well ahead of them, sharp whistling clicks vibrating through the water, translating into his mind with all the speed and ease of telepathy.

Herd them. Stop them. Kill the human first.

Jenny's fingers dug into Perrin's shoulders. He didn't see bubbles coming from her nose anymore. Her lips were clamped shut, and her gaze was wild, desperate.

He could not let go of Rik, and there was no good way to tell him to surface. No time, either. He wasn't even certain breathing for her would work.

Do something, he called out to the *kra'a*. *Save her.*

And just like that, the nimbus of light returned. Flaring blue as the sky, then deeper, shimmering from Jenny's head down to her feet like fire. Perrin remembered what that would feel like—heat and power, and the throb of a million tiny heartbeats on his skin—but all he felt now was a tingle: pins and needles, as humans would say. He held Jenny close as the light slammed outward in one single pulse.

Rik made a startled sound but did not stop swimming. Everyone else did, though. Perrin glanced back and saw bodies floating, unconscious.

He also saw his father, who was very much awake, though unmoving, his body floating straight as a silver dagger in the water. Staring at him with unfathomable eyes.

Those same eyes, even after eight years. Those same eyes, even after a lifetime of Perrin wishing he could see, just once, something warm in them. For him.

Shadows swallowed his father.

After that, they were alone.

PERRIN HAD NEVER BEEN AWARE OF THE PASSAGE OF time until his exile. Time did not exist in the world below, only the shift in tides, or the arrival of light or dark above the mirror surface. Migrations happened, and temperatures changed, and there were seasons of storms that even his people could sense—but that was not time. That was just life.

Humans were preoccupied with the cutting of lives into discrete moments, and, out of the need to survive, Perrin had learned to be equally attentive to the ticking of a clock. Even now, back in the ocean, he found himself breaking moments, trying to calculate how long they had been in the water.

But instead of time, he relied on breaths. Jenny's breaths.

Each one precious, brief interludes at the surface of the sea, holding her close while she coughed and rubbed her nose and eyes, and dragged down great lungfuls of air. She was good at holding her breath, but doing so consistently, without pause, required endurance. And she was tired. Hurt.

On her tenth breath, their tenth stop, Perrin forced her to look at him while he studied her face. Split lip, bruise forming against her left cheek. Her eye was a little swollen, too, but he thought she would still be able to see from it after all was said and done.

"I'm going to kill him," he whispered, suffering a grim rage that settled so deep in his bones that every movement felt tender, ready to explode.

Jenny closed her eyes, silent. The lack of fight in her scared him. Perrin cradled her close, kissing her brow and smoothing her hair from her face. He thought of the *kra'a* buried in the base of her skull, and it took all his strength to keep from touching it again.

The hole in his head ached.

Rik circled them tightly, golden eyes glowing. Perrin grabbed his dorsal fin, and said, "Breathe, Jenny. One deep breath and hold on to me."

She nodded, eyes still closed.

Down, down back into the sea. Perrin watched the shadows, listening to the song of the deep earth rise through the darkness into his heart, wondering if Jenny heard the song, as well.

Kra'a chosen. A human, chosen. A *kra'a* did not have to bond to just any candidate. It had a will of its own, an ability to choose the one person most compatible. Until now, that had always been a *Krackeni*. Out of necessity, availability.

But this *kra'a* had sought out Jenny. Known where she was and somehow latched itself to her.

Old memories hit him. Years of total isolation in the darkness. Years, for the Kraken and the *kra'a* to become accustomed to him. Another initiation. Old rituals.

And all he'd had, in those years alone, was Jenny. Jenny, in his dreams. Part of him. Soul bonded, he realized now. Sharing space with his *kra'a,* which had been ripped from him and given to Pelena.

She said your kra'a *was calling to you*, his father had told him. *She could feel its dissatisfaction with her body.*

That gave Perrin no comfort. Nor did it answer the question of what to do next.

Except keep you safe, he told Jenny silently, burying despair with determination.

She was small in his arms, small but strong, and the memory of her standing against his father—again, again— filled him. Filled him until even thoughts of the *kra'a* were forced to share space in his heart.

Little girl. Grown woman. Not much had changed. She still carried a big stick.

Perrin lost track of how many times Rik brought them to the surface, but he sensed it was near dawn when they arrived at a familiar, battered fishing vessel floating alone in the middle of the ocean. Golden lights burned, and a slow rock song blared, something from a James Bond movie. *For Your Eyes Only,* maybe. Perrin had seen that one at the homeless shelter. He hadn't watched much television once he found an apartment of his own.

Sajeev was on deck, arms wrapped around his waist, slow-dancing with himself. Eddie stood at the rail, watching the sea. He wasn't looking in their direction, but that changed when Rik let out a faint dolphin squeal. Eddie flinched, spinning around to run across the deck.

Jenny's arms tightened around Perrin's neck. Her eyes were bloodshot, and the bruise had deepened on her face. She watched the boat with an intensity that was all business.

"It's okay," Perrin told her, letting go of Rik when they neared the side of the fishing vessel. He took a moment to hold her with both hands, pressing his mouth against her ear. His palm touched the *kra'a,* and she shuddered. "No place is safe, Jenny, but this one is as good as any."

"Ringing endorsement," she muttered hoarsely, which were the first words he'd heard her speak in far too long.

"I trust them," he said, which surprised him because it was true. "But stay away from the crazy dancing man."

Jenny's shoulders twitched, and he kissed her cheek, burying his nose in her warmth, letting it fill him. Scent was a very different thing in the sea. Limited. Human scents, on the other hand, were rich as light—and Jenny's made him warm in places he couldn't even name, just that it was deep and secret, and his. His Jenny.

The dolphin shimmered with a golden glow that lit the water like a gasp of pure sun. Rik's body melted from dolphin into man: blue-gray skin shifting to bronze, while fins flowed into a liquid radiance that solidified into arms. Perrin did not hear bones crack, or grunts of pain. Shape-shifter magic.

Jenny watched in tense silence. Rik watched her, too, and was still eyeing her when his body settled into human. Perrin noted several deep bruises in his chest, along with a decidedly wicked-looking cut. He was certain some of those injuries were fresh, and not from their fight.

Rik tore his gaze from Jenny, settling a hard look on Perrin. For a moment, all of them were silent. Except for Sajeev, who was somewhere out of sight, crooning to himself. Perrin wasn't certain whether he should thank Rik or get ready for another fight. Jenny tensed against him.

"Hey," Eddie said, his voice low, strong. He leaned over the rail and looked pointedly at Jenny. "Ma'am, would you like to come out of the water?"

"Yes," she said quietly, and Perrin tightened his jaw, handing her up to Eddie. The young man helped her climb the short, rusty ladder, holding her against him when her knees gave out. He murmured something that made Jenny smile and laugh weakly. Perrin stifled a rush of jealousy and shifted shape with a bone-cracking jolt. Rik watched him, treading water.

"You've got problems," Rik said, and looked up at Jenny. "Not the ones I thought you did. Hope she was worth it for the hell you're going to bring down on us."

Perrin had a long reach. He didn't punch Rik, but his fingers jabbed into his chest, hard. The shape-shifter grunted, floating backward. Anger flashed in his eyes, making them burn golden.

"Leave her alone," Perrin told him, and grabbed the ladder. He paused midway up and looked down. "Thank you for coming for us."

Rik barely acknowledged him. His golden-eyed gaze was distant as he ran his hand through his wet hair.

"I didn't give you that cut," Perrin said, still hanging from the ladder.

A grim smile touched Rik's mouth. "I'm not welcome in these waters any more than you are. I embarrassed too many of my kind. The dolphin pod that found me made that clear. They were the ones who told me where to look for you."

"Your family?"

"Gone. South, maybe. I don't know." A hint of despair filled his voice, but it was replaced by a hard note of bitter resolve. "I'm not going to try to find them."

Rik glanced at him, expression unpleasant and oddly challenging. Perrin pretended not to know what bait he was supposed to take and kept his mouth shut. Held his gaze with one of his own, opening that small dark place in his heart—letting it show in his eyes. Rik looked away.

Eddie had seated Jenny in one of the lawn chairs, and produced a towel that she was using to dry her face. Her movements were sluggish, her eyes closed. The bruises on her face stood out in sharp relief against her pale skin.

"I hope the other guy looks worse," Eddie said gently, pushing a bottle of water into her hands.

"He will," Perrin rasped. Jenny sighed, and the young man gave him a speculative look. He wondered if Eddie thought he'd been the one to hit her, and the idea made him furious and sick. Partially because he had given the young man no reason to think otherwise. He'd gone after Rik with a hair-trigger temper.

And those marks on her arms *were* from his hands.

Perrin moved with extra care toward Jenny and crouched on her other side. "Jenny, this is Eddie."

"I know," she said.

Eddie blinked, settling back on his heels. "Ma'am? We've never met. I didn't tell you my name."

"Eddie," she said, meeting his gaze. "Fire-starter. Until recently you lived with your mother and grandmother in San Francisco. Started out as a car thief before Roland recruited you. Good kid, I'm told, though you had an accident that left your powers stronger and your control a bit weak. You have a nice smile. No one told me that."

Eddie stared. Jenny sipped her water and looked at Rik, who stood watching her, very still, dripping and naked.

"Rik," she said softly. "If it's any consolation, the Consortium hurt me, too."

He paled, swaying. Eddie swallowed hard. "Ma'am?"

"You're Dirk & Steele," she whispered, closing her eyes again. Sajeev hovered nearby, watching with sharp, glittering eyes. His hand rubbed the dragon tattoo on his scalp. "I've been reading files on all of you for years now. Just in case."

Eddie stood, slowly. "Who are you?"

"Family," she whispered. "My grandmother's maiden name was Dirk. She has a sister named Nancy. I think you know who *she* is."

"Shit," Rik said. Eddie said nothing, but his eyes narrowed, thoughtful. Heat rolled off his body, so much that the air shimmered around his shoulders.

Jenny reached for Perrin. Her eyes were still closed. He took her hand and stood, scooping her up into his arms. She seemed even lighter than he remembered, as though part of her had burned away.

"She needs food," he said to Eddie.

The young man nodded but didn't move. "Ma'am?"

Jenny pushed her head against Perrin's chest and made a muffled sound.

"Ma'am," Eddie said, even more softly. "I don't know who you are, but you're safe. I want you to know that. You're safe with us."

Jenny said nothing. Considering what little he knew about her family, Perrin suspected that promises of safety meant very little.

He nodded at Eddie, who gave him a solemn look in return. Rik seemed shook up, and was rubbing his arms. Not like he was cold. Just uneasy.

Perrin paused at the stairs and glanced back. "The old man?"

"Transferred him to the coast guard," Eddie said. "He'll be fine."

Jenny trembled. Perrin began to turn, but the young man reached out, stopping him.

"How much time do we have?" he asked quietly.

"If you have family in San Francisco, or on any coast . . ." Perrin said, but could not bring himself to finish.

He did not need to. Eddie nodded, pale.

Perrin carried Jenny down into the darkness.

CHAPTER FIFTEEN

THE air was cool where Perrin carried her, and smelled like engine fuel and garlic. Her feet bumped against the wall. She sensed him stooping, walking sideways, but her eyes were too tired to open.

"We're alone," he whispered. "You can stop pretending to be asleep."

"Not pretending," she murmured. "I hurt."

He was silent after that.

Silent and careful. He couldn't squeeze them both through the cabin door. Jenny would have walked, but he set her down for only a moment—her feet barely grazing the floor—before he was through and holding her again.

"The bed's right there," she told him, voice muffled against his chest. "I'll fall backward and be fine."

He grunted and set her down slow and easy, with such care she wasn't even certain she was on the bed until he pulled away—and suddenly there was a mattress beneath her and a pillow that smelled like sweat, more garlic, and hot, pickled turnips. Jenny was too exhausted to care. She could barely open her eyes to look at Perrin; but she managed, and found him standing beside the bed, looking huge and awkward, and just as tired as she felt.

Jenny tried to scoot over. "Sit down before you fall down."

Perrin's mouth twitched. "I'll break the frame."

He sat on the floor beside the cot and leaned up hard against the wall. He was big enough that she still had to look up at him even though she was lying down. A small light burned above the cot. She undid the pack clipped around her waist, and Perrin took it from her to place on the floor beside him.

"Are you okay?" she asked him.

He stared at her. "You almost died."

"I was talking about you."

"So was I," he replied, with heat. Jenny wondered if mermen had nervous breakdowns because he looked a bit like he was on the verge of some kind of break. Of course, so was she.

"I breathed underwater," she said, and speaking those words seemed to unravel a hard knot in her heart. "There's a parasite lodged to the base of my skull."

The words came out so easily. Jenny sagged against the mattress, and with some effort raised her hands and touched her sore face. "I can't believe I just said that. Every time I tried to tell you before, it wouldn't let me. I couldn't say a word. I couldn't even point."

Perrin was very quiet, his expression closed, thoughtful. His silence made her even more uneasy. She remembered all too well what had happened on that boat, in the water. She had thought of nothing else for all those hours spent traveling through the sea, holding her breath, clinging to Perrin.

"I'm a scientist," she said. "And I'm used to inexplicable things. But not this."

"Let me see it," he replied, an odd catch in his voice.

Jenny rolled over on her stomach and reached around to help him. He nudged her hand aside, gently, and set his big warm palm on her shoulder. It felt better than it should have.

"Rest," he said, his voice low, a rumble in her ear.

Jenny nodded, unable to speak. Perrin pushed aside her hair. He was careful, thorough—her hair thick, tangled, despite her braids. But she felt him still, and take a short deep breath, and a sliver of fear raced into her gut.

"Has it grown?" she murmured.

Perrin's fingers pressed lightly on either side of the parasite. "It is . . . it is just the size it should be."

His voice was raw. Jenny tried to look at him, but he held her down, with another hand on her shoulder, this one a little firmer. Her uneasiness grew.

"You going to take it out?" she asked him.

"No." Perrin's voice was even quieter, rougher. "No, I won't do that."

This time she forced his hand aside and rolled over to look at him. Perrin had pale skin—most anyone would call him albino, she thought—but he seemed even whiter than usual. Or maybe just ashen. His expression was grim and cold, but there was no hiding his eyes, and the pain in them was frightening.

"Perrin," she whispered.

"It is a *kra'a*," he said, practically breathing each word. "It should never have bonded to you."

Jenny swallowed hard. "Will it kill me?"

His hesitation was not reassuring. "I don't know."

She stared at him, helpless, filled with questions she didn't know how to ask. "What is it?"

Perrin closed his eyes. "It is the . . . larva . . . of a Kraken."

Jenny burst out laughing, then choked, feeling sick. "No."

He didn't seem disturbed by her reaction. "It's not what you think. Every thousand years, a sleeping Kraken, male or female, produces a clutch of these larvae. They do not mature. They are like . . . antennae. Linked to the Kraken's mind. A way for the beast to see the world around it and know if it is time to wake."

Jenny hugged her knees to her chest, suddenly filled with the need to be very small. "Your kind uses these . . . *kra'a* . . . to keep the Kraken down."

Perrin nodded, eyes still closed. "We destroy all but one, then bond that surviving larvae to a suitable host, as it would have bonded to any other life-form, if left on its own. When a larva is newborn, it is untrained, unfocused. Only the very strong are given the task of training an unformed *kra'a*. It requires intense mental stamina. The first three hosts usually do not live longer than a decade during that initial bonding."

Jenny frowned. Perrin said, "The one in your head is over seven hundred years old. You don't need to worry."

Creeped out was a better description for the way she felt. "It seems to have a will of its own."

"Kraken are intelligent, their larvae no less so. That *kra'a* shared the minds of twelve others before you. It is a . . . deep relationship. The *kra'a* becomes part of your soul."

Perrin looked ill when he said that—a broken quality in his voice, something broken in his eyes. Stirred her instincts in a bad way.

"This was yours," she said.

Grief twisted his face, but it smoothed into a cool hard mask. "Yes."

"It was taken from you."

"Yes."

"Maurice—the old man I was sailing with—tried to remove this thing from my head. Almost killed me. Or felt like it."

Perrin shuddered. "I had been its host for almost eight human years when my kind ripped it from me."

Fuck, she thought. *Fuck*.

The parasite twitched. Inside her head, a voice whispered, *We grieved. We grieved and did not understand. His dreams were good, strong.*

"They didn't think I would survive," he said, and again, there was a broken quality to his voice that cut her: loneliness, and despair, and a hurt that ran all the way to the soul. She heard herself in his voice. She heard her own voice, six years younger, sitting in a cemetery by a gravestone with no name.

"You did nothing wrong," she said, and didn't know if

that was the parasite talking or her. Just that she knew it was the truth—deep in the heart of her gut where all her most trusted instincts resided.

"I dreamed," he whispered. "And they tried to take my dreams."

Jenny had no idea what that meant, but the parasite twitched again, and a wild roaring heat rushed from the base of her skull down her spine. She reached out, and very gently placed her hand on top of his. Then, just as carefully, she leaned off the bed and kissed his ear, and murmured, "Breathe."

He drew in a choking laugh that sounded like a sob. And then it was a sob, strangled into a terrible silence that left him shaking so violently, Jenny was afraid for him. She wrapped her arm around his neck and pulled him close until his head rested on the cot, their cheeks pressed together, her mouth against his ear, whispering words that she forgot as soon as she said them, just that her heart was in her throat, she wanted him to feel her heart, and hear it, and know he wasn't alone.

She sensed movement at the door. Eddie. Pale, with dark hair that curled loosely over his eyes. He must have been in his early twenties, but he had an old-man gaze, something she had not noticed in the surveillance photos. He didn't look dangerous, except for his eyes. Core of steel.

Eddie looked at Perrin, his expression startled, then embarrassed. He carried power bars, and another bottle of water. He did not make a sound, but Perrin suddenly stilled.

The young man backed away, disappearing into the hall. Jenny listened for his footsteps. He was quiet, but she heard the faint scrape of sneakers against wood.

Perrin tried to pull away. She tightened her grip around his neck and slid off the cot, into his lap. He made a muffled sound of protest, but she shook her head, making herself comfortable on the floor, with him. His arms were heavy and warm, his cheeks wet.

Why did this happen? Jenny wanted to ask him. *Why me, why you?*

More questions. So many questions.

But she didn't ask them. Not yet. Instead, she listened to his heart beneath her ear and felt the rise and fall of his chest, and it dragged her under into that soft place that felt perilously close to dreams, dreams that had always been safe.

"I'm sorry," she murmured to Perrin. "I'm so sorry."

Perrin said nothing, but his fingers slid through her hair and rested warm on the parasite.

We dream again, said that quiet voice. *We dream.*

THE NEXT TIME SHE OPENED HER EYES, PERRIN WAS gone. Jenny lay on the floor. A pillow had been pushed under her head, a blanket draped over her hips. She was sweaty, her hair smelled like hot pepper—and her mouth tasted like cotton balls.

Jenny fumbled for the water bottle that had been laid beside her. She saw power bars, too. Her stomach growled, followed by a reeling ache that had her ripping one of them open, pushing it into her mouth before she realized what she was doing. Tasted dry, but good.

She washed it down with half a bottle of water, ignoring the low, throbbing ache in her face. Eating and drinking hurt. So did standing. Her entire body was sore.

The floor vibrated beneath her. She heard an engine running, a dull roar that rose and fell in a slow, chugging rhythm.

Jenny stumbled to the door. A small hand mirror had been nailed to the wall, and she caught her reflection. More like, it caught her.

Half her face was purple, though the bruising was worst around her mouth and cheek. Her eye was a little swollen, but thankfully not enough to limit her vision.

Jenny looked like someone had punched her, though. And she hated that. She hated looking like a victim. Again.

Les, how could you?

Les, I'm going to kick your ass.

Les.

Her charming friend. Her good friend. She had traveled with him for years. Laughed and cried her way around the world, with him and Maurice.

"Les," she murmured, staring into her eyes. Grateful that she still recognized the woman in the mirror. There had been a time, years ago, when she hadn't.

She remembered. Bad days. She still recalled, with perfect clarity, how she had felt then—and her current emotions were following a similar course. All she had suffered, until now, was shock and anger. Devastating shock and anger.

But until now, she hadn't let herself feel hurt. Really hurt, in the heart.

And it hurt like hell. It was like being betrayed by family, all over again.

She heard shouts. Perrin's voice. It didn't sound like they were under attack, but any anger was enough to make her uneasy. Jenny straightened her shoulders, pushed back her hair, and left the cabin for a narrow, dark hall that reminded her of some passage in a tomb. Too many shadows, and deep alcoves. She could see, though. Her vision had improved considerably over the past few days.

Breathing underwater could probably be considered an improvement, too.

And yet, she was totally unprepared for the hand that reached out from behind one of the side doors and grabbed her.

Jenny stepped back and twisted until she was flat against the wall—forcing her attacker to loosen his grip, or else risk a broken arm. He freed her, but she didn't have time to slip down the corridor toward light and freedom. A slender, wiry man flowed from the doorway, blocking her. She remembered glimpsing him last night. Fast, all muscle. Black eyes glittered, and a tattoo of a dragon covered his shaved head. He gave her a toothy grin. Jenny wondered if she should start screaming.

"I know about you," he said. "We all watch each other."

Jenny set her jaw, then forced it to relax when it ached. "Who are you?"

"Sajeev." He gave her a sly grin and smoothed his hand over his bald head. The dragon tattoo seemed to flex beneath his fingers. "Old women are powerful, yes? Powerful and deadly."

A chill touched her. "You're not *A Priori*. Are you Dirk & Steele?"

Consortium? she almost asked.

But he didn't answer. All he did was smile and sidle back into the shadows, out of sight from even her improved eyes.

Jenny fought down a shudder and tried not to run down the corridor toward the light.

Topside, she had to shield her eyes. It looked like morning, the sun only a quarter over the horizon, and blazing white in the blue sky. A sultry breeze touched her face. No land, no other boats in sight.

Perrin stood barefoot on deck, his back to her. He was dressed only in swim trunks. He wore wraparound sunglasses, and his long silver hair had been tied at the nape of his neck. Jenny glimpsed scars there, a thin trail of them leading up into his scalp. She had seen them before, in the water, but now had a terrible sense of what had caused them. His mouth was slanted into a frown, his massive arms folded over his broad chest.

Rik stood in front of him, wearing cutoff jeans. He looked angry. He wasn't as tall as Perrin, but big enough—lean, bronze. Bruised and cut. Jenny had seen his file.

The Consortium had kidnapped Rik, along with another shape-shifter and several members of Dirk & Steele—taking them to a facility in far eastern Russia. All of them had been tortured, experimented on. *A Priori* had been planning a raid of the facility, but Rik and those others had escaped by then.

Your friends killed my uncle's wife, she thought, watching Rik with satisfaction. *May Beatrix Weave burn in hell.*

Perrin's head tilted slightly, as though he knew she was behind him. Rik glanced at her. "Finally."

"Leave her out of this," Perrin said. His voice was quiet, but in a deadly sort of way that made the hairs stand on the back of her neck. Eddie, who had been leaning against the rail, pushed off and straightened.

"I don't like it any more than you do," said Rik. "But if it can be done, I don't see that we have a choice."

Jenny frowned. "What's going on here?"

"The thing on the back of your neck—" Rik began, but Perrin shook his head.

"No," he said. "I'll kill you first."

"Yeah, you would," Rik shot back. "You're good at that."

Perrin took a step toward him, and she was suddenly reminded just how big he really was. Almost seven feet of raw muscle and bone. Huge. Every inch of him pissed off.

Jenny made a small sound of protest. Eddie was suddenly at her side, a gentle hand on her elbow that disappeared as soon as she pulled away.

"Don't," he whispered to her, his gaze dark as he watched Rik and Perrin stare each other down. "I don't know what's between them, but better it gets out now."

"You sure about that?" Jenny muttered. "What was Rik talking about?"

Eddie gave her a speculative look. "Perrin should tell you. But I'll be honest, ma'am . . . I don't like the fact that you know who we are but we don't know you. I have an idea who you work for, but that doesn't make it any better."

"Talk to Roland," she replied.

"I did," he said, voice strained. "He hung up on me."

Jenny's mouth ticked up into a grim smile, and that hurt her face. "You have a phone? Radio?"

"Satellite cell," Eddie began, but Perrin moved again, swaying toward Rik with deadly grace. Rik did not retreat, but his face hardened until everything about him that was young and soft withered into anger.

"Why *are* you here?" Perrin asked him. "Why did you bother? You'd be happy to see me die."

A nasty smile flitted around Rik's mouth, but it didn't reach his eyes. "Maybe that's why I'm here."

Perrin shifted on his feet. Jenny moved, too—circling so that she could see his face better. Eddie moved with her, giving her an uncertain look, but she ignored him. She wished she could see Perrin's eyes behind the sunglasses. His jaw was rigid, shoulders tense.

"She's dead, you know," Perrin said, with deceptive gentleness. "That was never a lie. I hope . . . I hope you don't think you're going to find her."

Jenny didn't know who "she" was, but the hammer hit true. Rik's entire body hitched, as though a hook was caught between his shoulders. Grief shimmered in his eyes. Hollow, aching pain.

Then, nothing. Swallowed up. But he looked older than he should have, old and hard and tired. So did Perrin, what little she could see of his face.

The parasite twitched. Jenny's vision shimmered. She found herself looking at Rik from a different angle: taller, standing directly in front of him, the world tinted brown from sunglass lenses.

Terrible regret slammed into her—*I shouldn't have said that, I'm sorry, I'm so sorry, but it was out of my hands, done before I could stop them, and there was no fixing that, no forgiveness*—and she would have gasped from the onslaught, but she had no mouth, no body, she was nothing but a wisp riding behind someone else's eyes—

—until, suddenly, it was her eyes again, and the only mind she heard was her own.

Perrin swayed, touching his brow. So did Jenny. Eddie held her elbow, murmuring words she couldn't hear above the roar in her ears.

She had been in Perrin's head. Right there at the front of his thoughts.

Something else slid inside her mind: that dry parasitic

voice, as much a part of her as a needle jabbing into her body.

He was never like the others, it whispered. *Not like those who came before, or after, or those who surrounded us in the endless dark. We remember. We remember everything.*

You were part of us. They blamed him for that.

"Ma'am," Eddie murmured.

"I'm fine," Jenny told him, straightening. But that was a lie.

She sensed a wall inside her head. New. Strange. There was no way to describe it except that it felt like a forgotten dream: specifically, the *block* preventing the memory of a dream. Except there was no memory. Just Perrin on the other side, his presence like a battering storm howling outside a window.

And deeper, closer, the parasite: resting in the shadows, with the same sensation and weight of a nagging thought.

Perrin watched her, with a frown still touching his brow. Made her wonder if he had been in her head, too—or if he had felt her hitching a ride behind his eyes. His regret and despair continued to echo through her, but looking at him . . . He hid his feelings so well. She had experienced his emotions for only a moment, and they curled around her heart like a fist.

Jenny didn't remember moving, but suddenly she was at his side, clutching his arm, needing to show him that he wasn't alone. He flinched when she touched him, and she drew back, frowning—then set her jaw and touched him again. He gave her a long look, sunglasses making him inscrutable—but his hand was gentle when it finally wrapped around hers. Tension drained from his shoulders.

Perrin glanced at Rik. "I'm sorry. I'm sorry you were exiled for nothing more than loving her. I'm sorry she was sent away. I'm sorry she died."

Jenny was pretty certain the shape-shifter didn't give a shit. He looked tired, and his eyes were hollow. "You're still going to die. You *and* the woman."

Perrin took a step, and Rik moved forward to meet him. Jenny hauled backward on his arm—then slid between them. Hands on his chest, pushing him. Perrin stared over her head at Rik.

"Broken," Rik said, voice hard, brittle. "Maybe they'll take pity on you. See how worthless you are and just . . . throw you away like they did the first time."

Jenny whipped around to face the shape-shifter. Perrin grabbed her arms and held her still against his chest. Tension rolled through her—or maybe that was *him*. She didn't trust that all her emotions were hers alone: something heavy pressed on the edges of her mind and heart, a presence that was not the parasite.

She opened herself to it, just a little—and suffered a slam of boiling rage, frustration. Helpless regret.

"Say whatever you want," Perrin whispered. "I didn't kill Surinia. I didn't break the two of you apart."

"You found out. You *told*. What the fuck did you think would happen?"

Perrin pushed Jenny out of his way, firm but gentle. Dangerously deliberate. Eddie stepped close, shielding her. Not that distance helped. Part of her was still lost inside Perrin.

"Not that," he said softly. "I never dreamed *any* harm would come to Surinia. I was concerned. You were both so young, not even sixteen years, and she was a candidate for a *kra'a*. One of the best we had. When I saw where it was going with the two of you, I *had* to say something. For both your sakes. You didn't understand—"

Rik lunged at him. Perrin let the shape-shifter land a solid blow on his face before whipping down with his own fists, striking him hard and fast across the contusions in his chest. Rik grunted, staggering. Perrin punched him one more time, in the gut. Jenny knew he didn't use all his strength. He didn't need to. Rik was already hurting. Whatever had been done to him earlier had whipped him well and good.

Rik bent over, holding his stomach. Eyes squeezed shut,

lips pressed together, breathing hard through his nose. "I hate you. When I saw you, back in San Francisco, it was a nightmare."

"I know," Perrin said.

Rik cracked open one eye and peered at him. "You don't know what happened to me after I was sent away."

"Everyone suffers. If I learned anything from living amongst humans, it's that." Perrin looked at Jenny. "You okay?"

She nodded, flush with his concern for her. She could feel it trembling against the wall inside her mind. That, and disgrace that he had been violent in her presence. He hated himself for his temper, for how he used his fists, a curling disgust tempered with a desperate need–

—to protect you, shelter you, keep you safe—

Jenny closed her eyes, pressing a hand to her head. Warmth surrounded her, deeper and cleaner than the tropic ocean air. Perrin's deep voice rumbled, "You should lie down again."

"No time," she murmured. "Tell me what you were fighting about before I showed up."

His mind went quiet—or the wall strengthened. She lost the tickle of his presence inside her head, a loss both soothing and disquieting.

Rik straightened slowly, still holding his stomach. "I told him he should remove the *kra'a* from your head."

Perrin made an ugly sound: part fury, part disgust. "It's too dangerous. But I don't think you care about that. If she dies, you win. You think it'll punish me."

"You're an idiot. This isn't about you."

"Enough." Eddie stepped between both men, giving them a long, measuring stare that held a surprising amount of ruthlessness. Heat rolled off him in throbbing waves. Behind him, Sajeev appeared, and just as quickly slipped away.

"Enough," Eddie said again, quieter, and looked at Perrin. "The earthquakes are happening more frequently, with increasing strength. Several tsunamis have hit the region, but there was enough warning for people to reach a safe distance from the coast. According to you, though, when the big one hits . . ."

"A simple evacuation won't be enough," Perrin said.

Eddie hesitated. "I won't presume to understand what's causing this. I've seen strange things. I can do strange things. But this . . . is beyond me. Doesn't mean I don't believe it, though. And Rik . . . Rik has filled me in on what you used to be. It was your job, once, to control this thing that's waking in the sea."

Perrin's mouth twisted. "I'll have to assume you got the full truth."

Rik looked away, rubbing his knuckles—golden light spreading briefly over his hands. "It can still be stopped."

"Not for that price," Perrin whispered.

Jenny stared. "If you had the *kra'a*—"

He whipped around, blocking her from the others—forcing her to retreat until the rail pressed against her back. He leaned forward, arms braced on either side of her. Huge man. Jenny shoved her fingers into his chest. "If you can stop this—"

"Not at the expense of your life." His hand curled around hers, engulfing it completely. Muscles ticked in his face, every straining inch of him so tense he was practically shaking. *Emotions,* she remembered. Perrin hid strong emotions so well. But if he was showing this much, if his control was so frayed . . .

Jenny covered his hand with hers, wishing she could see his eyes. A terrible ache built inside her, a swell of tenderness or compassion, love—she didn't know what to call it—just that it made her voice low and thick, her knees gangly like she was that twelve-year-old girl again, seeing magic.

"We're on the beach," she whispered to him. "Just you and me."

No one else would have understood. But Perrin sucked in his breath and went very still. In that stillness, in that perfect quiet, Jenny remembered they had an audience. She didn't see Rik, but Eddie hovered within reaching distance, watching them with open concern.

Afraid for her, she realized. Afraid Perrin would hurt her.

Slowly, deliberately, she pushed away from the rail and leaned in hard against Perrin's chest, pressing her cheek against his hot skin, wrapping her arm around his waist. His breathing hitched again, then—gently, tenderly—he hugged her against him, curling around her body with heartbreaking, trembling need.

Jenny held Eddie's gaze the entire time.

He was a smart young man. Color touched his cheeks, but his gaze remained thoughtful, assessing. Finally, he gave her a single nod and backed away, out of sight.

"Jenny," Perrin said, his voice low, barely a rumble. "I refuse to lose you."

Behind him, she heard a strangled sound—not laughter, not a sob, but something gut-wrenching and frightening. Eddie murmured a low word, and Rik said, "You'll lose her. You'll lose her to the wave and what follows. You'll lose her to your people when they come to carve the *kra'a* from her head. You'll lose her when they kill you for coming back to the sea."

Rik moved into sight. Eddie had one hand clamped on his shoulder, his mouth tight with displeasure. But that didn't stop the shape-shifter, who looked Jenny dead in the eyes, and said, "You don't understand what's coming."

Jenny stared at him, and a short quiet laugh escaped her. Perrin tried to turn her away from Rik; but she twisted out of his arms and walked to the young man. Self-pity was written all over him. Defiance, too. Anger.

But she smiled at him, and some of the ugliness seemed to hiccup in his face. Rik suddenly looked at her like she might bite, and, for a moment, Jenny wanted to.

We remember him, whispered the parasite, and behind her eyes she glimpsed a golden-eyed dolphin swimming lazy circles around a merwoman with long silver hair, her sharp lovely face tilted upward toward a ray of light streaming through the water. When she laughed, it sounded like bubbles made of crystal bursting, and when she touched the dolphin with long, delicate fingers, she made it look like a dance.

Then, nothing. Jenny blinked. Rik stood before her, and the sun was shining and hot. She was not in the sea, but in a boat, and her body was human. She had to remind herself of that.

A lot of things have happened to me that I don't have a fucking clue how to understand, she wanted to tell Rik. *Take your shit and shove it. You think you're the only one who has watched someone you love die?*

But the words turned to ash on her tongue.

"You're right," she said instead. "I don't understand."

Rik stared, and that emotional hiccup happened again in his golden eyes, an involuntary twitch of anger and grief, and terrible loneliness.

The kid was so lonely. Plain as day. She knew friends surrounded him—the files on the men and women at Dirk & Steele were extensive—but there was a difference between paper and life, and the young man in front of her had been hurting so long and deep, she wondered if he would ever be able to let go of his pain.

Jenny sure as hell hadn't.

Rik tore his gaze from her and looked down at his hands. Human hands: bronze skin, strong fingers. Eddie watched him worriedly. Perrin drew near, looming over them all. Jenny felt him inside her, behind the wall. His presence was the same as some vague memory of a dream—a pressure on the edge of her mind, filled with impressions. Quiet, now. Contemplative.

"When the Kraken wakes," Rik said softly, "it's going to break the fuck out of the earth. You know what kind of wave that will make, Perrin. And then it's going to go looking for a mate. The closest nest is near Hawaii."

"There's no female there," Perrin replied, voice hollow.

"Then they'll fight. And that'll cause more destruction. The survivor will go looking for another nest. And if there's no female *there* . . ."

Jenny swallowed hard. "There's no other *kra'a*?"

"A *kra'a* is attuned only to the Kraken that it came from," Perrin said, with particular heaviness. "It's the conduit between the minds of the Guardian, and beast."

"And there's only one," she murmured. "How did Les get to your cousin? Someone that important—"

"It should have been difficult to kill her." Perrin hesitated. "It must have been planned, very carefully. She would have trusted A'lesander."

And the kra'a*? Did she trust that, too*? Jenny wondered silently, hit with strange "doubt. *Did the* kra'a *also want her dead so that it could be free?*

No, answered that dry voice inside her head. *But we did not object to the opportunity when it arrived. Pelena understood. We told her as much, before we left her body.*

Jenny closed her eyes. *You're shit. You could have saved her.*

She understood, repeated the *kra'a*. *Some things cannot be changed. Pelena was not . . . right . . . for what we needed. Her dreams were weak. And dreams can never be weak.*

I'm not any better, she told it. *Go to Perrin.*

We are already with him, it whispered. *Two is better than one.*

Jenny rubbed her eyes. Perrin said, "What is it?"

"You have to take the *kra'a* from me. You have to. There's no other choice."

The parasite twitched, but no dry voice filled her head. Perrin remained silent, as well.

Jenny drew in a deep breath. "We need to warn people, just in case this doesn't work. There's no way to evacuate everyone, but if I can reach my family—"

"Doesn't matter who you are or what connections you

have," Rik interrupted. "Millions will still die. Those waves are going to crush the coasts and go miles inland. Not just one or two miles, either. We're talking fifty, a hundred. Never mind the earthquakes. Infrastructure will break down. Disease, starvation, panic—"

"I already got the rundown," she snapped, and reached around, digging through her tangled hair until she touched the parasite. Felt like a hard flat knot in the base of her skull, smooth as bone, as tightly bound to her as if it was part of her body. And it was, she realized, feeling sick. Deeper, even. Much deeper.

She thought the parasite would stop her when she tried to dig her trembling fingers under its edges, but instead Perrin grabbed her hand. He did not speak and she could only feel a ghost of his presence against the wall inside her mind. She wanted to feel more of him, right then. She was so afraid.

Sajeev appeared from the control station, scuttling into the sunlight with a wincing squint. He reminded her of a bald, leathery, tattooed crab. Beady black eyes, included.

"Trouble," he said.

Eddie walked to the rail, joined by Rik. "Where?"

Jenny looked, as well. Perrin crossed the deck to watch the sea behind her. Not a thing in sight. The engine was still running, motoring them along a northerly route, according to the position of the sun.

Sajeev did not answer Eddie. He reached inside the bridge to tap an MP3 player taped to the wall. Queen's "Another One Bites the Dust" began blasting, so loud Jenny winced.

Swinging his skinny hips, singing to himself in a strange falsetto, Sajeev slid open a large panel in the outer wall and pulled out a sniper rifle. Bolt-action. Telescopic lens already mounted.

"Whoa," Rik said.

Sajeev ignored him, still dancing—thrusting, grinding his pelvis so vigorously, he should have dislocated his hips. Joints popped instead. Jenny vomited a little in her mouth, but she couldn't look away. She hoped the parasite was memorizing this moment for its future hosts, because *damn*.

Sajeev dirty-danced the sniper rifle to the side of the boat and dropped down on one knee. His ass twitched in time to the music as he propped the rifle on the rail. No bipod support, but there was a suppressor.

Suddenly, he didn't look very funny anymore.

When the song finished, nothing followed. Just a moment of pure dead silence, filled in seconds later with the sound of the engine spitting and rumbling, and the swell of the waves, and the wind.

Sajeev knelt perfectly still, staring through the scope. Jenny began to wonder if he was crazy.

Until he fired his weapon into the sea.

Fifty yards away, a jet of blood spurted into the air.

He pulled the trigger again. More blood, though not as much. Just enough to confirm a hit.

Sajeev leaned back, eyes narrowed, head tilted. And then he smiled.

"Better," he said.

Perrin leaned hard on the rail, staring. Without a word, he tossed his sunglasses to Jenny and leapt into the sea. She leaned over, staring. Eddie's fingers grazed the back of her shirt.

"Not jumping," she told him irritably.

"Course not, ma'am," he replied smoothly, still hovering.

Perrin did not resurface. Not right away. Two full minutes ticked by. She knew, because she kept checking Eddie's watch. His presence was quiet on the other side of the wall in her mind—quiet, except for a brief flare of fury that flashed through her like a bolt of red lightning. She almost dropped the wall to see what was in her head, but the parasite whispered, *Wait*.

"Rik," she said.

"No way I'm helping him," he replied, but Eddie gave him a sharp look, and the shape-shifter began stripping off his shorts.

He didn't need to enter the sea, though. Perrin appeared, hauling someone with him. Jenny ran to the stern, getting down on her knees and reaching.

But she pulled back when she saw who was bleeding and unconscious in Perrin's arms.

Les.

CHAPTER SIXTEEN

PERRIN wondered if being directly responsible for the end of the world was justification enough for an impromptu execution. Like in human movies. One last word, then *bang*. Dead.

He had drowned those pirates for less.

Jenny touched her bruised face and studied A'lesander like he was a wet, dirty stain on an even dirtier pair of underwear. Blood oozed from his shoulder where a bullet had ripped away a chunk of flesh. Part of his upper arm was missing, too. He still wore his water-body, iridescent blue scales turning a sickly gray. The swelling on his broken nose was slightly improved, but his nose had been set badly and was still crooked.

Perrin gave Sajeev a sharp look. "How did you know he was there?"

The old man gave him a yellow-toothed grin. "Why didn't you?"

He struggled to keep his voice even. "Is there anyone else in these waters?"

Sajeev shrugged, but that smile still played along his mouth. "You tell me."

Eddie cleared his throat, very deliberately stepping between them to kneel beside Les with a first-aid kit in hand. He opened a white packet and squeezed a liquid, granular substance over the shoulder wound. He packed it deep into the torn flesh, and it seemed to congeal, thickening on contact with the blood. He followed a similar procedure with the tear in A'lesander's arm.

"What is that?" Perrin asked.

"Clotting agent," Jenny answered for Eddie. "Military grade, for battlefield wounds. Stops bleeding, and then just . . . pulls out . . . when you finally get to a hospital."

"A'lesander isn't going to make it to a hospital," Perrin replied, ignoring Eddie's speculative glance. He was tired of the young man looking at him like that—as though he were a bomb, just ticking away.

But you are, Perrin told himself, glancing around. He saw a crowbar hooked into a nook near some fishing nets. He grabbed it, and before anyone could say a word, brought it down hard on Les's right hand. Same hand he'd used to punch Jenny in the face.

Bone crunched. Les jerked awake, screaming. Perrin slammed a foot down on his chest, holding him in place as his tail flopped wildly. He made terrible, guttural noises of pain and tried to hold his hand against his stomach. His fingers bent at strange angles.

Eddie fell back, staring—heat rolling off him in throbbing waves. Rik leaned hard against the rail, grim-faced, golden light flaring in his eyes. Jenny wore no expression at all. For a moment he wondered if he had gone too far.

But then he looked at the bruises on her face, and the shadows around her eyes—rope burns fading on her wrists—and he thought of how he'd first seen her, drowning, with A'lesander merely looking on—and then punching her—

"A'lesander," he said, just loud enough to be heard over the *Krackeni's* shuddering pants. "A'lesander. You are very desperate, or very stupid."

"You crazy fuck," he whispered, raggedly. The sounds of yet more cracking bones filled the air, and the iridescent scales on his muscular tail rippled and flexed like a waterbed. Scales receded into flesh, then split apart, folding as those long muscles tore into legs and feet. Ugly to watch, and the blood of his human ancestor made his shift more difficult than it would have been for Perrin.

"Just a little crazy," Perrin replied. "Did you lead anyone here?"

A'lesander bared his teeth in a hissing laugh. "Don't need to. Eyes everywhere."

Perrin crouched, balancing the crowbar over his thighs. Silent. Sinking into the dark place. He held A'lesander's gaze, and saw the exact moment when fear began to replace the anger.

He looked past Perrin. "Jenny."

Perrin almost grabbed his broken hand and twisted. "Don't look at her."

"Let him look," Jenny said, her voice low, cool. "My *good* friend."

A'lesander shuddered, closing his eyes. His right arm trembled violently, his broken hand hovering over his stomach.

Eddie crouched behind him. Perrin expected to see pity on his face, or righteous outrage; but the young man stared at the back of A'lesander's head with dead eyes.

"Ma'am," he said quietly. "Is this the man who hit you?"

"Yes," she told him.

Eddie nodded. When he leaned forward to help A'lesander sit up, he dug his thumb into the shoulder wound. A'lesander made a strangled sound, then clamped his mouth shut. Red-faced, quivering.

"We need to talk," he gasped, when Eddie stopped putting pressure on the wound and finally had him sitting up.

"Talk." Bitterness crept into Perrin's voice. The crowbar felt good and cold on his thighs. "You came here to *talk*."

"You were right," Jenny said. "Desperate or stupid. I say both."

Perrin's mouth ticked into a grim smile. "I left you tied up on that ship. How *did* you get free?"

"A Priori." A'lesander glanced at Jenny, then looked away like it hurt him to see her. "They came to *The Calypso Star* and let me go."

"They would have trusted him," she said with disgust. "What did you tell them, Les? That Perrin kidnapped me?"

He did not confirm or deny, which told Perrin all he needed to know. Someone else was out there who would want him dead. If they thought he had hurt Jenny, he didn't blame them.

A'lesander looked at Jenny again, but this time his gaze lingered. Perrin gritted his teeth as he watched grief and regret touch his face . . . right before slipping away into shame.

Perrin was afraid to look at Jenny. Friends . . . those two had been friends, maybe more, no matter what she said. . .

He looked. Jenny stood so still, staring down at A'lesander with her mouth set in a hard line, her unblemished cheek flushed red. The other side of her face was mottled purple, a sickly yellow. Her eyes did not match the hard bitterness of her mouth. All he saw in them was sadness, which held a strange, hypnotic power.

"You hurt me," she said, some question in her voice. *Why?* Perrin heard. *Why did you do that to me?*

Her family had betrayed her, he remembered. She had suffered violence at the hands of family. Now this.

"I didn't mean to," he began, but Eddie made a small sound of anger, and Perrin's hand snaked out, grabbing A'lesander's throat.

"Don't lie," he whispered. "I suppose your fist had a mind of its own. You already killed one friend. Are you going to tell me you didn't mean that, either?"

A'lesander's entire body tensed. Maybe there was grief, maybe there was shame inside him, and pain—but Perrin sensed burning rage when he touched the man, and he saw it when their gazes met.

"They told me what happened," he rasped. "But even they don't believe it."

"Believe what?" Perrin asked coolly.

His gaze flicked to Jenny. "That she has the *kra'a*."

Perrin tightened his fingers. "That's all you want, isn't it? That's why you're here. Like a shark for blood. You tried to kill Pelena for her *kra'a*, but it slipped away from you. Slipped away, or else refused to bond." He watched the other man's face, and his hand relaxed around his throat. "That's it, I think. You had the *kra'a*, and it refused you."

Perrin was loath to admit that his father could be right about anything, but his assessment of A'lesander had been correct—then and now. A'lesander did not have the heart to hold a *kra'a*. Not the strength, in body and spirit, to hold the dreams of a Kraken.

But the human woman does, said a quiet voice inside his mind.

Perrin's breath caught, and A'lesander's expression darkened, no doubt interpreting his stunned realization as something else entirely. "Does Jenny have it?"

Focus, Perrin thought, and dragged the other man to his feet. "She's human. How the hell could a *kra'a* have bonded to her?"

His old friend stared at him. "You always were a terrible liar."

Perrin glanced at Sajeev. "I need rope, duct tape, anything I can tie him with."

"I came to help you. And her." A'lesander twisted around to look at Jenny. "His father will rip the creature from you himself, and he won't care if you live or die."

Jenny hugged herself. If she had known how vulnerable that made her look, Perrin was certain she would have been humiliated. He wanted to wrap himself around her, too.

"And you?" she shot back. "You already tried to murder one person for it. What makes me different?"

A'lesander straightened, wincing with the effort. "You know how I feel about you. I never made that a secret."

"Bullshit," she whispered, and the hurt in her eyes killed Perrin. "You lied, Les. You lied, and you killed."

"He's no better." A'lesander tried wrenching free from

Perrin, but the effort doubled him over, breath hissing through his teeth. "Don't be fooled, just because you're obsessed with nonhumans. You don't know him. I don't know why you trust him. He's killed—"

"Stop," Jenny said.

"—he's killed," A'lesander continued, his voice gaining strength as his gaze settled on Perrin. "Maybe he'll kill you, Jenny. He killed another woman once. All she did was try to help him control his dreams—"

Perrin drove his fist into A'lesander's face. He didn't even realize he was moving until his knuckles connected. The other man grunted, going down hard on his knees—catching himself with his broken hand. The grunt turned into a scream, and he folded over his hand, panting.

Perrin stood there, breathing hard, afraid to look at Jenny. A'lesander started laughing though it was a breathless, pained sound.

"Don't tell me you actually care about her," he whispered. "You don't even know her."

"I know her," Perrin said, grim.

"You know her," echoed the other man, mockingly. "You never met her until that day on the boat. So it's some game *you're* playing, Perrin. Better game than me, and I would never have imagined that."

"Les," Jenny said, but the other man didn't seem to hear her, not in the slightest, his head bowed, his shoulders twitching with his ever-ragged breath.

"Don't know how the hell you knew to come back when you did, or how you found us. But it's done, Perrin. It's done, and maybe you're here for the *kra'a,* maybe it's for something else, but you're using her, and you'll let her die when you're done."

A'lesander finally tilted up his head, staring with bloodshot, cold eyes. "If the *kra'a* has bonded to Jenny, you'll take it from her. The chance to put your broken, *broken* heart together will be too much temptation. But it'll kill her. And I won't let you do that."

Perrin exhaled. "You won't . . . let me. Because you care . . . so much . . . about keeping her safe."

A'lesander's eye twitched. "She carries my bond. I don't have a choice but to care."

My bond.

Perrin heard a sharp intake of breath behind him, but he was still staring at A'lesander. Unsure what to say . . . or how to even wrap his mind around those words. It was impossible. Jenny was bonded to *him,* and he was bonded to *her.* He had always been hers, from that first moment they met, as children.

Jenny drew near. He did not look at her, but he felt her warmth close in on him like the sunrise. He felt her warmth on his body and beneath his skin. He felt her, for a moment, in his mind, fluttering like a butterfly, sweet inside his thoughts.

His girl on the beach. His miracle.

"No," he said to A'lesander, surprised at how calm he sounded.

"You don't know shit," he replied, as if Jenny weren't standing right there, listening. "How else do you think I've been tracking you?"

Perrin's fingers itched to hit him. "She does not . . . carry your bond."

He felt ill saying those words, the very idea of A'lesander being that close to Jenny making him feel as though something filthy was crawling around inside his soul—and hers.

Then, like magic, Jenny leaned against him—and all that discomfort faded away. She wrapped her hand around his arm. Slow, deliberate. Comfortable. Staking her claim.

A'lesander watched, and something . . . startled . . . slipped into his eyes.

"Jenny," he said. "I don't know what he's told you, but there are things you can't understand."

She made a low sound. "Les. I promise you . . . sure as hell there are things you don't understand about me. You never will. And if you try, I'll kill you."

Dead silence. A'lesander stared. Perrin wondered uneasily if perhaps he didn't truly believe he had a soul bond with Jenny.

Sajeev turned to face the sea, and it was like watching a cobra move from sleep to strike. He held the sniper rifle as though it were an extension of his arm. Everyone tensed. So did A'lesander, though that might have been pain from his wounds. Or just pissy nerves.

"More trouble," Sajeev said. Perrin didn't see anything in the water, didn't feel anything. Before his exile, he would have.

A'lesander tried to stand, grunting with the effort. His golden brown hair partially covered his eyes, and some of the color was returning to his face. "You can't kill them all."

"My father," replied Perrin.

"Not him. Others."

"Who did you lead here?"

Sajeev shot at some invisible target in the water, another and another—and then ducked as something sharp whistled through the air where his head had been.

Perrin pushed Jenny to the deck as a slender bone spear skittered toward his feet. He glanced at the engravings: a twist of narrow lines that flowed like the stingers of a jellyfish. Familiar marks, and they made him sick and angry.

Another spear flew from the water, followed by several more that came dangerously close to hitting him. One skimmed his arm, leaving a welt. He heard chattering clicks, and several shrieking wails that made the hairs rise on his neck. The boat rocked violently sideways—again, again—all of them sliding, staggering. Perrin feared they would capsize.

Rik crouched, digging his fingers into the deck. Golden light shimmered over his body, burning bright in his eyes. Eddie knelt near him, radiating waves of heat. Smoke drifted from charred holes in his shirt.

"Do something," Rik said to him. "Fry their fucking asses."

"I need to see them," Eddie snapped, but Perrin thought that might be a lie. There was a look on the young man's face that reminded him of times he'd been on the edge of doing something he knew was wrong—all that conflict and doubt, and fear. Fear that would become self-hatred later, if anything bad happened now that could have been prevented.

But the self-hatred would come anyway, from hurting others. Even the enemy.

"Eddie," Perrin said in a low, urgent voice. When the young man looked at him, he said, "There's no escaping regret when you're fighting to survive. You will *always* have to do something distasteful."

Eddie's gaze darkened. Jenny tensed beneath his hands, and A'lesander let out a bitter, rasping laugh.

"But you still condemn *me*," he said. "Oh, God, Perrin. What happened to us?"

Sanjeev loaded more bullets into his rifle, bracing his feet against a bolted-down equipment box. Perrin held Jenny tight and stared over her head at A'lesander. "What happened is that you fell in with a cult of fanatics. No wonder you killed Pelena. You *wanted* the Kraken to wake."

A'lesander hunched over his broken hand. "It's not like that. I needed something, and they had answers. Let me talk to them. They can taste my blood in the water. They know you've hurt me."

"I'm surprised they care. All they need to do is look at you to know you've got human blood in your veins."

"They need me. And they feel sorry for my . . . impurities." No mistaking the sarcasm in his voice. A'lesander backed up to the rail and looked at Jenny. "I know I've made . . . mistakes. But don't trust him. If you've got the *kra'a*, don't trust anyone."

"If you care," Jenny said tightly, "if our friendship ever meant a damn thing, you'll lead whatever is down there away from here . . . and *never* come back."

A'lesander stilled. "Jenny—"

"Get the *fuck* away from me!" she screamed at him, and for one moment Perrin felt her inside his head: raging, raging, cut with heartache.

Hurt flashed in A'lesander's eyes, then anger. "We're bonded, Jenny. You just don't realize it yet. You don't even understand what it means."

Perrin glanced at Sajeev, who had stopped firing at the water and was watching them. "Shoot him."

A grin touched his mouth. He raised his rifle, fast—but A'lesander was faster, and threw himself over the rail.

Perrin didn't follow to watch. He crouched over Jenny, shielding her from the bone-spear needles whistling onto the ship. Her small hand gripped his wrist, and he met her haunted gaze. Hit, again, with the knowledge that she had been betrayed before.

A'lesander hadn't just hurt her body. He'd made her relive the past. He'd taken friendship—trust that came so dear to Jenny—and ripped it away.

Perrin curled over her, heart in his throat, and kissed her brow. He wanted to say something to make it better, but words died in his throat.

I'm here, he wanted to tell her. *I'm here.*

"They're slowing down," Eddie said, behind them.

Perrin did not relax. He had always been outnumbered in the sea. When his kind chose to fight and kill, very little could be done to stop them. Escape was the best defense, but there were few human vessels that could travel fast enough to elude the *Krackeni*. This was not one of them.

He heard a wet slurping sound, and turned in time to see webbed, iridescent hands grip the edge of the vessel, at the stern. Enormous pale eyes appeared, blinking wildly, silver hair pressed wet against narrow skulls.

They stared at him. Then Jenny.

There and gone. The *Krackeni* disappeared so quickly, they might never have been present at all—except for the wet hand marks left on the rail.

But Perrin's heart thundered, his vision contracting to

dizzying pricks of light. He had to force himself to breathe, stunned by the fear coursing through him. He had never been afraid of his own kind before his exile. He hadn't even been afraid of his father. Wary, perhaps. But not afraid.

You are not one of them anymore, whispered a familiar, dry voice. Perrin realized he was gripping the back of Jenny's head, his palm pressed against the *kra'a*. He tried to let go, but couldn't.

They cut your heart from them, the *kra'a* continued. *You share their flesh, but not their soul.*

But you are still ours.

And you do not fear for yourself, alone.

Perrin yanked his hand away, burned—mentally and physically. His palm was hot, and red. Jenny gave him a startled look.

"I heard all that," she said.

He grunted. "Stay down."

Jenny frowned at him but kept low to the deck as they shuffled to where Rik and Eddie were crouched with Sajeev. No more spears flew from the water, and the vessel's rocking motion was subsiding.

Perrin didn't relax. There was a certain irony to the possibility that he wouldn't be able to rest easy until he returned to land. If there was any land to return to.

If the kra'a *has bonded to Jenny, you'll take it from her,* A'lesander had said.

You'll let her die when you're done.

And if he didn't take the *kra'a*, the Kraken would wake.

You would kill all but one, murmured the sea witch's memory. *And for that one, you would let the world die.*

Screwed, he thought.

"Screwed," Jenny murmured, surprising him. "So screwed."

He stared. "Are you reading my mind?"

She blinked, as though startled, and looked away from him. Rik held one of the spears in his hands and studied it with distaste. "Makes sense now, what's happening."

"Yes," Perrin said, still looking at Jenny. "We have no name for the clan that spear comes from because it's not a real clan. Just a group of individuals with a common philosophy."

"Humans suck," Rik said.

"In large numbers, anyway. Some advocate for . . . population control."

Eddie's gaze filled with shadows. "So this . . . man . . . who was just here . . . he's working with those who want to cause a natural catastrophe that will wipe out humans."

"It's more complicated than that," he replied, wishing he could be alone with Jenny, to speak to her about what had just happened with A'lesander. "The sleep of the Kraken, the waking of the beast, are living myths amongst my kind. The Kraken are not . . . monsters . . . to my people. They're not gods, either. But if there is a middle ground . . ." Perrin stopped, trying to find the right words. "Death and rebirth are part of the Kraken, and some pray for its waking as a time of profound change."

"Destruction," Eddie said.

"Remaking the world," Perrin replied. "The world, when magic walked. When men like you, who could make fire with their minds, or read minds, were more common. When shape-shifter clans were powerful and worshipped by humans as gods, or when the old winged kind, the gargoyles, ruled the mountains. A world where no one had to hide—except the bad kind, who always mask true natures."

Eddie sighed, rubbing his face. Sajeev was humming to himself, as though he hadn't heard a word. Rik turned to face the sea. Only Jenny looked at Perrin, and her gaze was unreadable.

"But it ended," she said finally. "You mentioned a war, once."

"There's always war. Some more desperate than others." Perrin's head ached, and he was suddenly aware, keenly so, of the hole in the base of his skull. "That's not the case here.

Conspiring to wake a Kraken is one of the worst crimes my kind can commit."

"Not much worse than what you did," Rik muttered. "Or so I was told by the local dolphin pod that found me."

Perrin stilled. Sajeev said, "They're gone."

A'lesander will be back, he thought, not sufficiently distracted from his desire to throttle Rik. Though he got the diversion he needed when Jenny shook her head, gaze turning inward. "Someone is watching. From a distance."

She closed her eyes and rolled her shoulders, like something cold and dirty had touched her. "That's a strange sensation."

Perrin buried a dull ache of envy. "Hosting a *kra'a* requires years of preparation and training. You're doing very well, considering."

"What would be the alternative?"

He hesitated. "That depends on the *kra'a*. Some are more . . . forceful . . . than others."

Jenny frowned. "This one is pretty spunky, let me tell you."

Perrin grunted. "So were its prior hosts."

"It's too bad Ms. Jameson can't control this . . . Kraken." Eddie peered over the side of the boat. His posture was more relaxed than his voice, which was sharp, quiet, and thoughtful.

Startled, Perrin stared at the young man, then looked at Jenny. Really looked, thinking hard about their bond, and why the *kra'a,* of all those in the sea it could have chosen, would have linked to her. A human.

"Huh," he said.

CHAPTER SEVENTEEN

SAJEEV knew of a small, uninhabited atoll located a little over three hours west of their location. Nothing but an island of coral encircling a lagoon, with little vegetation and no freshwater. But it would help prevent anyone from ambushing Perrin and Jenny while they were in the sea. Training.

As in, *Learn How to Control a Sea Monster 101*.

"You're nuts," she told Perrin, while Sajeev blasted Aerosmith over his stereo system. "Just . . . remove this thing from my head. Please. I don't want it."

"No," Perrin said.

"I don't care what Les said. He's full of shit. I know you don't want to hurt me."

They were seated on two plastic chairs. Perrin was busting out of his, one of the legs sporting a new crack that flexed wider every time he shifted. Jenny nursed a bottle of water and held the satellite cell phone in her lap. Ready to call home. Putting it off, despite how stupid that made her. Although, if Eddie had already contacted Roland Dirk, chances were good her family knew what was going on.

And, apparently, there was a helicopter full of mercenaries in the region that would be at her disposal if she needed them.

"Results matter," said Perrin, with more than a little bitterness. "I don't want to hurt you. If I remove the *kra'a*, I most certainly will. I think I might kill you."

"You lived."

"Barely. I was found naked on a beach in Singapore, bleeding from the back of my head, with my *spine* partially exposed. Disoriented. Sobbing my guts out. I couldn't speak a single human language. I didn't even know how to walk because I'd never used my human legs. Everything was bright and loud. Dirty. Heavy."

Perrin rubbed the back of his neck. "A man found me. Dragged me to a cab and took me to the Swedish embassy. I don't know why, maybe because I had the right coloring. Officials there took me in and gave me medical treatment. Sent me to Sweden, finally. I lived there for a year, just learning how to be human, before I went to the United States."

There was so much he wasn't saying. It would take a lifetime to pry out the details. Jenny wet her lips and tried to speak in a normal voice. "You could have stayed in Sweden. Why America?"

Perrin smiled to himself. "I once knew a girl who lived in that part of the world."

"Oh," she said.

"Yes," he replied.

"It's still stupid," she said, then clarified: "You can't possibly trust me with this. *I* don't trust me."

"I trust you," he told her, then, very quietly, "The *kra'a* didn't have to choose you, Jenny. It didn't choose A'lesander, after all."

"Well, he's a dick," she muttered.

Perrin's mouth twitched. "He always was, though it was more tolerable when we were children."

"This has hurt you, too," she said. "Seeing him like this. Because you friends."

"I wondered what happened to him." Perrin's gaze turned inward. "I always questioned whether there was anything I could have done to change what happened between us. But except for giving him my life . . ." He closed his eyes. "It wouldn't have made him happy. My life was hard. Like being a human monk. Isolation, discipline. But there were rewards. Power over the sea. A . . . wider awareness of the world." He shrugged, shaking his head. "You seem to be displaying some of those gifts."

Jenny swallowed, pressing a hand over her stomach— struggling to settle her nerves. "Those flulike symptoms I had. I think . . . I think the parasite was making changes to me, then. Maybe it introduced a virus. I don't know."

"I didn't make the connection," Perrin said. "I was also sick right after the initial bonding. I wasn't . . . born . . . with certain abilities, which only came to me after the *kra'a* and I were made one."

"Was it frightening? When you were bonded?"

"Was it for you?"

"I didn't even know it was there."

Perrin grunted. "I knew. There were enough outside rituals involved that I would have had to be dead not to know there was something living on the back of my head."

"How old were you?"

"The previous host died when I was . . . thirteen of your human years. I was young, either way. Very young for the responsibility. Many were concerned that I would not be strong enough to bear the isolation." He hesitated. "You and I hadn't been inside each other's dreams for long."

She tried to imagine the boy she had known, alone and shouldering the weight of keeping a sea monster asleep. Made her ill. "We met off the coast of Maine. But the Kraken nests in *these* waters?"

"I was born and trained in the part of the ocean that the humans call the Atlantic. Near . . . Greenland, I think. But I was sent here. None of the local candidates were strong enough for the *kra'a*." Perrin paused. "I never knew it was Maine."

He said that very quietly. Broke her heart a little. Perrin, lost in the world. Jenny ached at the idea. She couldn't even fathom what he had gone through, just to survive. Alone. Abandoned. Cut off from everything he had known.

Eight years ago. Jenny thought she should have felt *something*, but nothing stood out. Nothing at all. Eight years ago she had been in San Diego, exploiting family contacts in the United States Navy in order to work with, and learn from, the military's dolphin trainers. Wondering, sometimes stupidly, if any of those animals would be willing to chat with her grandfather about the existence of mermen.

You never did ask, she thought, watching Rik and Eddie play cards in the shade of the bridge. Clearly not eavesdropping.

"How did they know you would be strong enough for the *kra'a*?" she asked. "Was there a test?"

"A Kraken nests in the waters between Iceland and Greenland. Children of a certain age are presented to the local Guardian, as I was. The *kra'a* told its host what I was, and so I was selected for training. When the Guardian *here* began dying, its *kra'a* somehow knew about me. And asked for my life."

"Is that normal?"

"It happens," he said, but there was something in his voice that made her think that it wasn't common at all.

Rare, whispered the *kra'a* inside her head. *But there are times when rarity is necessary. We wanted his mind.*

Jenny winced, touching her head. Perrin said, "What is it?"

"It spoke to me," she said, and only because she was looking at him did she see the split-second devastation that filled his face. Devastation and grief, and terrible aching loss.

Then, gone.

But she felt those emotions like a slow ache inside her mind, on the other side of the wall, and wondered what would happen if she tore down the barrier between them. If she let him flood her mind. If he would feel the *kra'a* again.

"Perrin," she began, hesitantly. But before she could say more, the phone in her lap rang.

Jenny flinched, and tossed the oversized cell to Eddie. He answered quickly, was silent for several long moments, then settled that dark, old-man gaze on her. "Ma'am. It's Roland. He'd like to speak with you."

"Remind me," she said. "Is that old bastard still clairvoyant?"

"Um, yes."

She flipped the phone the middle finger. "So I guess he can see this, right now?"

Eddie wasn't standing all that close, but she very clearly heard the answering growl that came out of the phone. The young man bit back a smile. "Yes, ma'am. I believe that's the case."

Jenny smiled, though it felt crooked. "Okay. I'll talk with him."

Perrin cleared his throat. "I met Roland. His sense of humor seems limited."

"Sounds about right," she said, and frowned. "How *did* you get mixed up with this crowd?"

"A friend," he said, then Eddie was there with the phone, and Jenny took it carefully, suddenly feeling like it was a live snake.

"Hello, Roland," she said quietly.

There was a moment of long silence, filled with heavy breathing. Until, finally, she heard a gruff voice say, "You look like shit warmed over, sweetheart."

"That would be an improvement over you, I think."

"Funny," he rasped. "Been a while. I heard what happened at the old place."

"Whatever," she said tersely. "You folk keep to your side of the fence, we stay on ours, and it works out fine."

"Like hell it does. Everything changed that day. If we're going to fight the Consortium, your side has to learn to trust *us.*"

"Fuck that," she told him, not caring that it was coarse,

and he was her elder. "I'm done trusting family. And it's not like you're diving into the arms of *A Priori*."

"Guess not," he said softly. "Priorities. Expectations."

"Too many secrets," she replied, keenly aware of everyone listening. "Did you speak to my grandparents?"

"Nancy did it herself. But they already knew something was wrong. Maurice called them."

Jenny hesitated, uncomfortable. "So why *did* you want to talk to me?"

"Because I'm your uncle," he said. "And I'm sorry I can't kill my brother for what he did to you and yours."

SHE HAD TO ESCAPE, AFTER THAT. TALKING TO ROLAND had been a mistake. His voice was too familiar, too close to his brother's. She told him about the island, and hearing her uncle on the radio—but that was all she could do. She had to give the phone back to Eddie and run.

Of course, the problem with running on a boat was that a girl could only go so far. Finding a place to lick all her wounds, almost impossible.

Jenny ended up in the cabin with its weak-legged cot and garlic scents. Sitting on the edge of the sagging mattress, staring at her feet. Feeling rather small and afraid, and useless.

The *kra'a* rested in her mind with all the presence of a nagging thought, and so she closed her eyes and nagged back, just a little.

Why did you choose me?

You were needed, said the *kra'a*. *You were of us. You were of him.*

And you missed him, she replied.

We were emptier without him. Emptier without you, through him. Taken before death. Dreams torn. Dreams should never be torn.

Jenny sensed a terrible aching emptiness inside the *kra'a*—there and gone—but that glimpse of its pain made her feel strange.

I understand emptiness, she told it. *I understand.*

We know, it whispered. *We know, and we will not allow ourselves–*

—we will not—

—allow—

—we will not allow ourselves to be—

—emptied again.

"Never," Jenny breathed, pressing a fist to her stomach.

"Never," said Perrin, from the door.

She flinched and felt absurdly ashamed, as though she had been caught doing something bad. But Perrin leaned into the cabin, his body almost too wide for the door, his eyes closed as though listening to something very quiet. He wore a haunted look, and in the shadows his pale skin and silver hair made him resemble some apparition.

A warrior from the shadow lands, she thought, never mind that was the kind of thing some romantic teenager would write in her diary.

"Did you hear what the *kra'a* said to me?" she asked him.

"I heard," he said, his eyes still closed. "Right now you're thinking something warm about me."

"You can tell that?"

"Our bond," he said.

"The longer we're together," she replied. "Inside each other's heads."

"Maybe." Perrin smiled, a little sadly. "So what was your warm thought?"

Jenny studied the sharp lines of his face, marveling that he was real, that she was real, that this was not a dream. "White knight. My knight. In shining armor."

His smile gathered warmth, and he opened his eyes. "I've heard the term. But I don't understand it."

Jenny also smiled. "It comes from human medieval literature. Knight-errant. A warrior who would wander, sometimes in the service of others, sometimes on a quest. Noble. Righteous. Often performing deeds in the name of his lady."

Perrin slid into the room, closing the door behind him with a soft click. He turned the lock, too, and that gave her the same reaction as a physical touch: a sharp, intimate throb hit her low, between the legs.

It got worse the longer she watched him. He was a beautiful, unearthly man, but the attraction she felt went deeper than that. Perrin filled the cabin with heat and some subtle power that soothed the heartache and loneliness inside her—a pain that had never left her. Pushed aside, maybe. Ignored. Forgotten, at times. But ever-living, ever-present, ever-burning: some coal still carrying a spark.

"Are you my lady?" he asked.

"How many good deeds have you done lately?"

"None." Perrin knelt in front of her. "But I promise to try very hard to change that."

Jenny touched his face. He turned his cheek into her palm and kissed her wrist. She closed her eyes, drifting. Warm. Safe.

His arms were so strong, sliding around her, gathering her close against his broad, scarred chest. Jenny clung to him, burying her face in the crook of his neck. Breathing in his scent of salt and ocean. Listening to their heartbeats mingle.

"You ran up there," he murmured. "What scared you?"

"Everything," she said, pushing closer. "I remember things I don't want to remember, and it breaks my heart a little, each time."

His hands tightened. "Yes."

Jenny closed her eyes and felt the wall inside her head, Perrin warm on the other side.

Let him in, she told herself. *Let him in.*

But she was afraid of that, too. She was afraid of what he would see.

"I'm sorry," she murmured.

Perrin flinched, and she realized that his hand had been resting in her hair, against the parasite. She sensed his embarrassment at being caught touching it—as though her apology to him was some remark of pity—instead of her own remorse for being a coward.

He began to move his hand. Jenny reached back and held it in place.

"This is yours," she said.

He began to shake his head, then stopped, going very still. "When I hear its voice inside me, I feel good for a short time. But then I remember what I lost. Like you remember."

"I remember," she echoed. "I remember a boy on a beach. I always wondered why that boy didn't come back. Why he—you—came to land in the first place." Jenny pulled away, searching his eyes. "I recognized the man on the boat. The one who kept hitting you."

"My father," Perrin said.

Jenny was unsurprised. Something in their faces, the way they were together. How carefully Perrin did not strike back. "He hurt you, when you were a kid."

He still hurts you, she thought, memorizing the bruises on his face, and body. Bitterness twisted his mouth. "I had just discovered that I would be sent away as host for the *kra'a.* My family was given permission to join me, but that didn't make it easier. I had always . . . wanted to touch land. I was afraid that was my last chance."

"You were miserable when I found you."

"Terrified. Everything was so bright and heavy, and large. Like the sky. It was one thing to push my head above water to see the sky, but exposed on a beach, surrounded by nothing but air . . . I thought I would die." Perrin's lips brushed the top of her head. "Until you came."

"I never forgave myself for running away and not helping you."

"I told you. You would have died if you'd stayed. You couldn't have saved me."

"I was a stupid kid."

"No. Not like me. I never stopped being stupid."

She touched the old bullet scar in his shoulder. He tensed.

"Yes," he said quietly. "That was my fault."

The scar was large, deep. Bone had been broken. She was certain of it, given the placement. It would have taken a long time to heal.

"Who shot you?" she asked.

"A man I tried to rob." Perrin smiled, grim, at the surprise that must have been on her face. "I wish I could give you a more noble reason, but I was starving, I was a mess, and desperate. I took food from a gas station, tried to run—and the owner pulled a gun. I kept running, right at him. He was scared and shot me. I don't blame him. It was a lesson I needed to learn."

"Not to run at men with guns?"

"Or, you know, that stealing is bad."

"I was going to get to that."

He looked away, and his smile faded. "Prison followed. I almost died there. From the other inmates, the captivity, the chemicals used in cleaning. But especially from my inability to access seawater. I need to drink it to stay alive. Freshwater sustains me for only so long. There are minerals my body requires to keep functioning. So I . . . made deals . . . to have sea salt smuggled in. A poor substitute. I had to hurt people to get what I wanted. I had to be . . . frightening." His voice roughened with each word. "You don't know what I've done. I don't want you to."

"You don't frighten me."

Perrin gave her a sharp look, as though that meant something to him, as though he couldn't quite believe her.

"I mean it," she said again.

He tore his gaze from her, staring at his hands. His knuckles bore healing cuts, split skin. "I frighten myself. I feel you more and more inside my head. I know I must be inside yours. I'm afraid of what you'll see."

It was like hearing herself talk. A terrible relief stole over her, but it also stole away her voice, and she didn't know how to tell him she understood, that he was safe with her—that she hoped she was just as safe with him. She hoped it so badly.

Jenny grabbed his hand. "We all have dark places. I won't look on purpose if you don't."

Perrin regarded her in silence, his expression far more grim than his eyes, which darkened from pale ice to sky blue, and held her still and breathless. He turned his hand beneath hers and wrapped his long, strong fingers warm around her.

"You're a good person," he said, gruff.

Jenny sat back, surprised at how important those words were to her, how deep they struck. "So are you."

Perrin shrugged, as though he didn't believe her. *But thanks for trying,* he seemed to say. *Nice of you not to hurt my feelings.*

"Big strong man," she whispered. "Big strong heart. And you don't even know it."

For him, it was just the loneliness and the hardship, and the sacrifices he'd had to make to survive. He didn't see the man who held her so gently, who protected her, who took care of small dogs (*oh, the dog,* she thought; and then, *damn*), or all the infinitely small gestures, the kindnesses, that in such a short time had come to mean so much to her. It wasn't the bond, whatever that was. It wasn't the *kra'a.*

"All I know anymore is you and me," said Perrin. "Just you and me."

She nodded tightly, understanding him, suffering a fist in her heart so hard and thick with emotion, she could hardly breathe. All she could do was lean in, slow and warm, and press her lips on his mouth. Just a simple kiss, barely there; but she poured herself into it, desperate to ease the ache that had been burning inside her since that day on the beach, all those years before.

Perrin muttered something she didn't understand, but his hands were suddenly around her, his kiss deepening as she sensed something impossibly grim and hungry pass through him, followed by desperate, breathless need. Jenny pushed close, sharing that need, aching for him with a wildness that she had never felt for anyone. It scared her.

Perrin broke away from her, shuddering, his face pressed to hers. "Your hair. Take it down."

Her hands shook badly, but Jenny undid her braid. Her hair was tangled, crusty with salt and debris, but he sighed as it all came loose in a wild mess around her face. Perrin stroked it, fingers trembling. All his confidence seeming to melt away.

"I've never . . . done this before," he said, voice rough, raw. "Not with a human, and not . . . not with my own kind. I was supposed to. I was . . . given . . . females to impregnate. I always turned them away."

"I . . ." Jenny stopped. "Really?"

Perrin grimaced. "I didn't want them. I *couldn't* want them."

"Do you want me?"

He exhaled sharply. "I've wanted you since the first time I saw you. You were the only one I ever wanted. That was the problem."

Jenny didn't know what to say. All she could do was stare. Perrin rubbed his face. "I shouldn't have told you that."

"Well," she began.

"And I'm not . . . I know how it works," he interrupted. "I used to be a bouncer in a strip club."

"Strip club."

"And then there was this brothel—"

"Brothel—"

"I was there to make sure the girls didn't get hurt. They used to tease me by having sex in front of—"

"Okay," Jenny said. "I get the picture."

Perrin swallowed hard. Giant man. Merman. Looking at her like some high-school boy, awkward and uneasy. "This bothers you."

"No." Jenny shook her head, fighting the inappropriate urge to laugh. "Definitely not. I promise . . . I promise to be gentle with you."

And then she did laugh.

Perrin stared. "You think this is funny?"

She nodded, mouth clamped. Shoulders shaking. Wanting him even more. More than she had imagined ever wanting anyone. She grabbed his hands and put them on her aching breasts, and while he knelt there, frozen, she pushed his swim trunks off his hips.

He was already hard. And large. Jenny touched him, and Perrin hissed, flinching. Not away from her, but deeper into her hands.

"Jenny," he said, low and rough.

His voice dragged a hook of pleasure straight between her legs, and she pulled his head down for a deep, hard kiss. He melted against her, and she did the same, both of them clinging to each other in terrible desperation. If she let go of him, she would die. Her heart would die.

Down, down on the floor. Getting naked, fast. Jenny was rough, and he was gentle, his large hands skimming her breasts until she gripped his wrists and held him tight against her, arching into his touch with ragged gasps. Straddling him, leaning down to lick and kiss, and nip the hard lines of his body. She listened to his hoarse groans as she traveled from his throat to his erection, taking him in her mouth with a long, sucking stroke of her tongue. He trembled wildly, hands balling into fists.

"Inside you," he gasped. "Please."

Jenny didn't need to be asked twice. She crawled up his body, pushing him against her, and slid down on top of him with a slow thrust of her hips—crying out as he stretched and filled her with delicious, delirious, pleasure.

No condom. She didn't want there to be one. Reckless, stupid—but she was clean, and wanted all of him. All of him, no matter the consequences.

He grabbed her hips, thrusting upward. Jenny cried out again, planting her hands on his chest, grinding against him as he pushed into her, deep and hard. Slow at first, then fast, relentless, both of them riding each other in mindless primal pleasure.

She felt his pleasure, on the other side of the wall in her mind, and let the barrier fall.

It was almost too much. Perrin gasped, and so did she, both of them drowning in each other. Slammed with mindless joy and heartache, and a need that buried her soul, bound her soul, locked her soul against his with a click that she felt in her bones.

Her orgasm hit a moment later—violent, throbbing, rolling through her in a continuous pulse that left her breath cracking in her throat. Perrin came at the same time, rolling Jenny over on her back, thrusting so hard against her she climaxed again, hitching her legs high until her ankles crossed at the small of his back.

He shuddered into stillness, both of them gasping, sticky with sweat. The wall was up again inside her mind, but it wasn't strong enough to stop the glow of warmth that flowed between them—a floating light that fell over her like . . . like . . .

Magic, she thought.

Perrin pushed her hair from her face, peering into her eyes. Full of shadows, but there was a tenderness in his gaze, a dark hunger, that might as well have been a bullet, straight into her heart. She could not guess what was in her eyes, but she knew how she felt: dazzled, aching with the certainty she had come home.

"Are you okay?" he whispered, brushing his fingers over her lips. "Did I hurt you? I lost control in the end. If I was too rough—"

Jenny took one of his fingers into her mouth, swirling her tongue hard around it. Perrin's breath hitched, and deep inside her, where he still remained, she felt a twitch.

"You were perfect," she murmured raggedly, arching against him. "Don't ever let me go."

Perrin stared, his gaze growing even darker, and kissed her with a sweetness that stole her breath away. He began rocking, reaching down between them. She guided his hand to the right spot, and he smiled against her mouth.

Slow. Easy. Gentle. Jenny lost herself to him again, letting Perrin explore her body, speaking only to tell him *yes,* or *there,* or *please, don't stop*—and he did not stop, and he made her feel safe, with every touch, every kiss and caress. The parasite pulsed in the base of her neck, like a heartbeat. No pain. It felt . . . natural. As natural as being with him.

But something else rose inside her, too. The old hidden place inside her heart—shut away and crusty with pain.

No, she thought. *No, please. I don't want to think about it now.*

But her heart, bathed in peace and safety, was already unfolding the old hard sorrow. Or maybe that was the *kra'a.* She didn't know or care. She just wanted it to stop.

It didn't, though. Tears leaked from her eyes. Perrin stilled. "What is it?"

Jenny shook her head, fighting herself. But she couldn't hide from that sting—or the memories. She clung to him, holding on with all her strength as a terrible sob wracked her entire body.

"I did hurt you," he whispered.

Jenny shuddered. "No."

Perrin forced her to look at him. "Tell me."

She tried to stop crying, but the tears rolled down even harder. She buried her face in his neck, shaking. Not now. She didn't know why, now, she had to ruin this. But the pain wouldn't go away. Her belly ached, empty and cold.

"Jenny," he said raggedly.

"They killed my baby," she said brokenly, and it was the first time she'd said those words out loud, ever. Felt like ripping open a wound and letting it bleed.

She choked, and Perrin's hands froze against her back. "The Consortium killed my baby."

CHAPTER EIGHTEEN

THEY killed my baby.

Perrin had not let himself think about whether Jenny was married, or single. He hadn't cared, to be honest. She was giving herself to him, he was giving himself to her—and that was all that mattered. Anyone else could go to hell and stay there.

But that she had been a mother . . . that was something he had not imagined. And now that he could, now that he could see her with a baby in her arms . . .

They killed my baby.

Rage trickled into his heart. A simmering, transcendent fury that he had never experienced. Quiet, raw. Hungry for blood.

"Jenny," he said, and his voice sounded strange to him, distant and deep, and barely there.

"She had two months left to go," Jenny whispered against his throat. "She was an accident, but a good one. The father was an old friend from school, and it was just . . . it happened. I used protection, I didn't mean for it . . . but there she was. After I got over the shock, I was so happy."

"Jenny," he said again, holding her tighter. "Jenny."

She burrowed deeper into his body. "I was home. Family reunion. I knew something was wrong early on—I'd known since I was twelve—but no one would listen. And then, that day, they made their move. Men came with guns, and the fight . . . there was so much blood. I had to kill one of my cousins. I shot her in the head. I don't even remember doing it. Just that I picked up the gun and pulled the trigger, and she was dead. And when I did that, the pain started, then someone hit me—hit me so hard in the stomach—and my water broke."

Perrin trembled. He tried to calm himself into stillness, but hearing those words burned through him, and the fury curled hotter, brighter, more terrible. "You had the baby."

"A friend of the family saved me. A shape-shifter named Serena. She got me away to a place where I could hide. She tried to help, but she . . . it was too soon, and there was no hospital. No way to get help. Everyone was just trying to survive." Jenny's voice broke, and so did Perrin's heart. "She was so tiny."

He rocked her closer, holding her as tightly as he dared. Wishing desperately, furiously, that he could squeeze the pain from her. To lose a child, like that—helpless to stop it, surrounded by violence—and if that had been *his* child—

Perrin didn't let himself finish that thought. He knew what they'd done. He knew what could already be growing between them. Fool that he was, given the circumstances— but no one had ever accused him of being careful, or even remotely intelligent. All he had known beforehand—and during—and now—was that he would protect her. He would give his life for her. He would live for her, so that she would live.

Because they were bound now. They had always been bound—dream bound—but now it was different, and he'd felt something new humming inside him with that first slick thrust into her body.

"When did this happen?" he asked her, because he didn't know what to say, how to express any of the feelings burning through him.

"Six years ago," she said quietly. "More or less."

"We stopped sharing dreams when I was exiled," he said.

"I think . . . I think I would have known you were hurt if we'd still been with each other in our sleep."

Known, and fought to find her. Fought with all his strength. He would have tried at the beginning of his exile if he'd had a clue where she was.

Jenny tangled her fingers in his hair. "Not having you in my dreams . . . it made me wonder if I'd finally grown up. If it was my mind's way of telling me to . . . move on. So I tried. It wasn't easy to let go of that obsession with your memory. But it was that or never have a life."

It hurt a little, hearing her say those words. But Perrin understood. He had never expected to find her, either. And that was knowing, even, that the dreams were real.

"You never received justice," he said.

"Never," she told him quietly. "And I never went home. I got on my boat and just . . . sailed away. Looking for mysteries, again. Taking jobs writing articles for science magazines. Just . . . doing anything I could not to remember. The sea felt safe. The sea always felt safe."

"The sea is anything but," Perrin replied, more harshly than he intended. "If I could change things—"

"I know," she said. "I miss her, and I didn't even know her."

"What was her name?"

"I didn't have one yet. I liked Harriett, for some reason. Everyone told me that was awful. And there was Lucy, and Chloe, and Bridget. I wanted to get it just right, but nothing ever stuck. So on the gravestone, all I had inscribed was: MY BABY. No date. Nothing else. I didn't know what to say. It hurt too much."

Perrin buried his lips against her hair. "You would have been a good mother."

"I would have been a mess," she muttered. "But I would have loved her."

You did love her, he wanted to say, but silence seemed safer. Nothing he said could make this better. He understood now why she hadn't wanted to talk about what the

Consortium had done, and he was glad—desperately so—
that he hadn't pushed.

Jenny tried to pull away. Perrin held her close.

"We don't have time," she said, voice muffled with tears.

"If we don't have time now, we never will," he replied.

She hesitated, then relaxed again in his arms, very slowly.
Warm and small, and strong. His girl. His woman.

He was not alone anymore.

Perrin pressed his lips against her brow, listening to her
breathing steady. She wasn't asleep, but she was resting, her
presence warm inside his mind.

Are you angry with us? whispered the *kra'a,* also in his
thoughts.

No, he told it, wanting to say more, but unable to do anything but throw his emotions at that too-familiar presence
that skimmed now along the bond between him and Jenny.
The bond felt like a rope around his heart. Physical, throbbing. Hot.

For a moment, he thought about the Frenchwoman who
had died on the island, and the dead man on the boat, her
husband. Perrin wondered what it had been like for them to
be torn apart from each other.

Chilled him. Made him nauseous. Afraid. He felt the surrounding sea, soft and vast, buoying the ship as though it sat
upon a curved palm; but all that did was make him feel like
they were trapped inside a coffin. Or a hand about to close,
and crush.

Perrin closed his eyes and forced himself to take deep,
steadying breaths. His body still ached from lovemaking—
"lovemaking," what a word—and it didn't take much for
him to want to be inside Jenny again. Covering her with his
body, sheltering her, holding her safe and full while those
green eyes stared into his with that half-lidded pleasure and
need—and that trust he craved so badly, he didn't know how
he had survived this long without her.

He could survive another eight years on land, twenty,
fifty, a hundred—if she was there with him.

All because of one moment on a beach, sixteen years ago.

The only other bonded pair Perrin had ever known was so old, their bodies had practically floated through the sea as shriveled husks. He had been very young. All he remembered was that they were always holding hands. And they died together, one last breath ending another.

Maybe it would make a difference that Jenny was human.

Maybe she would survive his death.

If they kill me, make sure she lives, he told the *kra'a. Promise me.*

We promise you, all of us, replied the *kra'a. All of us, together.*

Which was not the comforting answer Perrin wanted.

NO ONE SAID A WORD WHEN PERRIN AND JENNY ventured back on deck. The sky was bright with sun, but after a moment spent blinking hard, his vision adjusted. His eyes were getting better in the light.

Eddie and Rik stood inside the bridge with Sajeev, staring out the window at the distant rise of the atoll. Eddie glanced at Jenny, stared a moment too long—as if he could see the grief she was hiding so well—and then looked away, rubbing his jaw.

A yacht was anchored three hundred yards west. Perrin was no expert, but it looked large and expensive, with many windows and a sleek white hull.

"Pleasure cruiser," Jenny said thoughtfully, her voice still raw from her tears—though she held herself together with a calm that Perrin admired. "Large enough to require a crew."

"Your ship is the same size," he remarked.

"The Calypso Star was designed to be handled by only one or two well-trained people." Jenny quirked her mouth. "I see a lot of skin over there."

Sajeev grinned and tapped the digital player taped to the wall. His finger scrolled down, then clicked. Marvin Gaye's "Let's Get It On" began blaring over the stereos. Eddie frowned at him and turned off the music.

The fishing boat drifted closer to the yacht. Everyone but Sajeev ventured from the bridge to stand on deck. Perrin glimpsed crisp white uniforms, and a lot of bikinis. In fact, most of the passengers seemed to be young women, who were lounging on lawn chairs, holding drinks, and laughing. Pleasure cruise, indeed.

Some of the crew watched their boat with concern. He wouldn't have been surprised to see guns, but none appeared.

"Well," Jenny said. "This is awkward."

Perrin frowned. "Go or stay?"

One of the women on the vessel seemed to get a good look at Rik and waved. Her swimsuit was barely there, and she was tanned, long-legged, and lean as a cat. Her white teeth practically sparkled.

"I'm torn," he replied, waving back. "Very torn."

"Rik," Eddie said.

"If it's the end of the world, and they're some of the survivors?" Rik held out his hands, smiling—though it didn't reach his eyes. "Come on, man. I suddenly feel like being a hero."

Perrin wasn't fooled. Shape-shifters mated for life. And Rik, young as he had been all those years ago, had loved Surinia enough to claim her as his—if not in body, then in soul. A pretty face wouldn't be enough to heal that wound, but there was nothing wrong with pretending.

"The atoll is over a mile wide," Eddie said. "If we anchor on the other side, no one should be able to see anything strange."

"I'm more worried about luring trouble here," Jenny said, but even as she spoke, the yacht's anchor began to crank up, and the engines purred to life.

"I think we made them nervous," Perrin said mildly, as the girl who had been waving to Rik screamed good-bye at him, then bounced back to her friends with a loud, delighted laugh.

Sajeev turned the music back on. This time, no one

stopped him. Perrin glanced at Jenny and found her rubbing the back of her neck.

Her knees suddenly buckled. He caught her as a tremor poured through her body, from head to foot—deepening into a violent quaking shiver that made her teeth chatter.

"What—" Rik began, just as Jenny's entire body bent backward, rigid, seizing. Horrifying sounds tore from her throat.

Her muscles relaxed just as Perrin began to lay her down, but the pain didn't seem to ease. She cried out, a deep throaty sound that was part scream, part groan, and that rose from so deep inside her he imagined it was the sound of her soul.

He saw, inside his head, a shimmer of darkness. A vision of terrible golden eyes straining to open, buried in the fire burning below the earth's crust. Listening for dreams that would not come.

Close, whispered the *kra'a. We are still close. The dreams will come. Dreams always come.*

Perrin shuddered. And then the pain hit him, too.

He went blind. Lost the ability to breathe. Fingers dug into the base of his skull, but his hands were firmly around Jenny, and it was only memory, terrible memory, though the pain was real and the same. Taking an ax to his skull would have been kinder, faster, than the prying, the sensation of someone trying to pull out his spine—along with a sudden liquid heat that felt like acid pouring into that old gaping scar.

When it stopped, it was sudden—and felt like death. Or maybe heroin. The relief was bliss, sinking into his veins, pooling in all the parts of him that were still and quiet. He'd taken the drug only twice but had been frightened of how good it made him feel, how bereft of thought and any instinct to survive. He felt the same now.

Except for Jenny. Fear for her crashed him down.

Perrin tried to open his eyes, but it was impossible, at first. Nothing worked right. He felt Jenny beside him, his hand around her arm. Her skin was soft, cool. He heard the faint hiss of her breathing and wanted to press his ear against her heart.

If he could even move.

"Perrin," Jenny murmured.

"Here," he whispered, relieved beyond measure to hear her speak.

Eddie crouched, pale. "What just happened?"

Jenny shuddered. Perrin said, "Earthquake."

Not the entire truth, but close enough. He was certain there had been an earthquake, just as he was certain that he did not want to explain the vision of a waking, increasingly restless, Kraken.

Rik held a water bottle to Jenny's mouth, and helped her drink. Her color improved, but the faint, reassuring smile she gave him was deeply shaken.

"We're running out of time," she said.

Less than fifteen minutes later, Perrin and Jenny were in the sea.

The fishing boat was anchored less than twenty feet away. The atoll was another twenty feet behind them. If Perrin stood on his toes, he could keep his head above the surface. Jenny alternated between holding his shoulders and treading water. Every inch of him wanted to transform into his water-body, but he forced himself to stay human.

Jenny's face was pale and bruised, but her eyes remained intent. Focused. Perrin thought of everything they had shared, what she had told him, and a desperate love clawed up his throat, along with an equally desperate desire to protect her.

Perrin could not help himself. He kissed her, long and slow, wishing he was in a time and place where he could bury his body inside hers, and take her—in the sea, on the beach of the atoll—and watch her body, straining and naked beneath his, in sunlight.

He got hard. Jenny sighed against his mouth and deliberately swiped her hand over him. It took all his strength not to groan in pleasure, or do something even more embarrassing. Like fuck her in front of the men standing on the boat.

Jenny said, "I think I heard that."

Perrin cleared his throat. "When this is over—"

He stopped, unable to finish that sentence. When this was over, he might be dead. Both of them, dead. But if he wasn't . . . if they weren't. . .

Jenny grazed her fingers over his mouth, her eyes dark with understanding. "Tell me what to do."

Perrin captured her hand, kissing her palm. Unable to keep from noticing the tremor that raced through her. He wanted to pretend it was because of his touch, but the longer he looked at her, the more he sensed a wildness. Like some small part of her was ready to bolt.

"When I was first chosen to be a candidate," he said carefully, "I was forced to learn a series of meditations in an effort to prepare me for having another mind residing within mine. We don't have time for that, and besides, it seems that you've merged quite well already."

"I think the . . . bond . . . between us helped," she replied, and again, he sensed her trepidation in his mind. "The *kra'a* already knew me."

Such dreams, whispered that dry voice, and Jenny closed her eyes.

Perrin said, "I heard it speak."

"Good," she mumbled. "That should help."

"The key," he went on, uneasy, "is in your mind, what you feed the *kra'a*. A Kraken must be soothed, and that can't happen with violent thoughts. Its dreams must be quiet and gentle. You must lull the beast."

"We're being watched," she said.

"Ignore it," he replied, wondering if it was A'lesander or that strange cult that had gathered. This place wasn't safe—but then, in the sea, there was no such thing as safety.

They had to be in the water for this. At least no one would be able to ambush them from below or behind. Just to the sides and from under the fishing boat, where Sajeev and his uncanny senses—and impossible aim—stood guard with his sniper rifle.

"Dreams," he continued. "The Kraken sleeps because of dreams."

Jenny began shivering. "Peaceful dreams. Okay."

Perrin frowned, gripping her arms, then her face. He reached around to touch the *kra'a*, and was slammed with an overwhelming wave of uncertainty and fear.

I can't do this, he heard Jenny think.

"You can," he told her.

"Just take the damn thing," she snapped, trying to pull away from him. Perrin refused to let go and drew her tight against his chest, nearly losing his footing and sinking them both.

"We talked about this," he said urgently. "The *kra'a* doesn't makes mistakes when it chooses a host. It picked *you*. You, Jenny. Never mind the link between us. It wanted *you*. It rejected A'lesander when he tried to steal it, just as it has rejected many others over the last seven hundred years. But it sees in you the strength that's required. And so do I."

Jenny dragged in a deep breath. "I think you're wrong."

"And I think you don't have a choice." Perrin focused on the *kra'a*, which wasn't in his mind, though he felt it close, in hers. *Can't you help her?*

Open your mind, it replied. *Show her what she needs to understand.*

Open his mind. Open himself so she could see all the ugliness inside him.

If Jenny was disgusted afterward, if she hated him, the bond would not dissolve. She was stuck with him. Neither would be able to venture far without being pulled back to the other's side. Cage or bliss. A bond like theirs did not require love, though it usually led to such. Or for others, he had been told, a need so profound that it masked as love.

Perrin knew better, with her. No masks for what he felt. He had loved Jenny before he even realized what love was, or need.

He had taken the punishment for that. Would do so again, in a heartbeat.

Perrin heard a splash behind them. Rik surfaced a moment later, golden light streaming from his eyes. His jaw was set, earlier smiles gone. Cold now, faintly mocking— perhaps to hide a split-second glint of uneasiness.

"I'll watch the waters," he said, and without another word, sank below the surface. Golden light shimmered beneath, and seconds later a dolphin appeared, sleek and blue-gray. Rik dove again out of sight.

Jenny didn't seem to notice. Her eyes were closed.

"You can trust me," she said to him, quiet. "I won't judge."

She had heard the *kra'a,* realized Perrin—and felt like a fool for forgetting that she would. He was not a Guardian any longer. He was not a host. Just an exile with a hole in his head and a bond that allowed him to share a part of what he had lost.

Not just a part, said the *kra'a. We are together.*

Together, he replied, and inside his head he heard Jenny whisper, *You lost nothing.*

"Jenny," he said.

"I'll show you mine, if you show me yours," she said, floating close against his body, burying her face in his throat as though she couldn't stand the sunlight. "I don't know what to do and we don't have time. Words won't be enough."

Perrin hesitated. Jenny said, "Please."

Please, no, he remembered saying once, eight years ago. *Please, no.*

His throat burned, and so did the base of his skull. His chest felt hollow. *Live or die,* he told himself. *Live in the past, or live now.*

Live, whispered the *kra'a.*

You're not alone, said Jenny, her presence spreading through his mind, filling the dark places, drawing him close and warm. *You will never be alone again.*

Perrin closed his eyes and drew in a deep, shuddering breath.

"Come in," he said.

And the world turned upside down.

—

PERRIN LOST HIS BODY. HE LOST HIS MIND. MERGING with another was overwhelming—in the same way that being hit in the ribs with a baseball bat tended to hurt, just a little.

He found himself, though, all the disparate pieces of his soul sliding into place, stitching together like a human quilt of patchwork memories. He was surprised it looked like a quilt until he realized that the symbol was important to Jenny. He didn't know how, just that it was.

He felt her with him, her own patchwork wrapped around her like a shield. He sensed her uneasiness—that he would see too much and not want her.

Minds were never meant to be this close, she said, inside him.

Perrin surveyed the patchwork of his life, shimmering dark blue, with silver stitches that pulsed as though filled with strange blood, or maybe just the sea. *Both of us have been alone for too long. We're used to our own company.*

And then he folded her into a memory.

Perrin found himself back in his body, only he was much smaller, and the world was dark. Fifteen in human years, resting on the seafloor, drifting in any direction the current pushed him. Not much current where he was, which was sandwiched between rocks. Crabs scuttled. Fish brushed against him. In the distance, he heard whale song.

He was barely conscious. Sinking into dreams.

Look, Perrin said, feeling Jenny draw close. *These are the dreams a Kraken needs.*

Dreams of the sea, songs of the sea. Music flowed through him, a natural harmony born from the slow rumble of the earth, and the hush of deep waters, and the hum of minds all around him: fish, distant *Krackeni,* migrating whales, and, somewhere, dolphins. Notes and shards, drawn into him, filtered through the *kra'a* into the Kraken, which he felt beneath him, sleeping so still and warm.

Perrin's younger self slipped deeper into dreams, and the music faded.

Until there was nothing but a silver beach, and silver waves, and a girl sitting beside him, with her hands held tightly in his.

"Hello," she said, in the dream, and her voice was a younger, softer version of the spirit-woman who pressed close against his side. Even here, he could not see the face of the girl. But he felt her. He felt her as though she was inside his soul.

Just as she was now.

Oh, Jenny breathed. *Oh, my.*

And the boy he had been said, "I missed you."

Perrin pulled Jenny away from the memory, but she went reluctantly. As did he. It was so real here, like this.

Dreams, he told her. *The* kra'a *gave the Kraken those dreams of us on the beach. I didn't realize it, at first. And when I did, there seemed to be no harm. The beast slept.*

All it needs is dreams? It seems too easy.

It's not easy.

Will I need to sleep?

No, he told her. *You just need to . . . be.*

Perrin tried to show her more, though it was hard to know which memories would be helpful. He had forgotten certain things, encounters with Pelena, who had journeyed with his family into these waters to train as a candidate; and A'lesander, who would tag along with her, and tease him. Sometimes cruelly, he realized now—though at the time, it had seemed like nothing.

I was naïve, he said.

You were so young, Jenny replied. *You thought you were safe.*

Perrin felt the *kra'a* hovering on the edges of their minds.

Show her, it said. *Show her why you were stolen from me.*

No, he said.

Show her, insisted the *kra'a.*

Perrin resisted, with all his strength. The *kra'a* overpowered him.

And he found himself in the old nightmare.

Flashes only. He saw again that powerful, wild-haired *Krackeni* tutor, who trained the candidates, venturing down to him with her breasts bared.

Her voice, haranguing him for not doing his duty to produce children who might carry singer blood, or bodies suitable to host a *kra'a.*

Her hands, reaching out to touch his *kra'a,* determined to read his mind and discover his reluctance.

She found you, Perrin whispered, feeling Jenny crowd close, watching his memories. *She found us. I did not know we were bonded, but she must have realized that, too.*

Perrin, Jenny said, but her voice choked into silence, and he found himself dragged down into his old body, reliving how that *Krackeni* tutor fled in disgust and panic, only to return with others.

Ambushing him. Surrounding him. Holding him. Paralyzing him with poison so they could reach into his mind.

Vile. Impure. How did this happen? When was he with the humans? We must speak with his father, someone will be punished, could the kra'a *have been in error? No, yes, it does not matter, just the Kraken, the Kraken has been tainted, and we must not tell the others, we must not breathe a word, no one ever has to know a human was in the mind of the beast, inside the* kra'a, *inside him—and there, there it is, do you see—just snip it, cut the thread, cut her out, cut her out, cut her out now before he realizes what–*

But Perrin had realized what they were doing. And the rage that filled him in his memories was rich and cold, and ugly. Because this was all he had. *She* was all he had. And here *they* were, violating the mind of a Guardian, trying to alter his dreams—which was against the laws of their people. Laws that meant nothing, it seemed.

He remembered the nimbus of blue light. He remembered the poison burning away and regaining his ability to move. He remembered power surging from his mind into the mind of the one about to make that final cut. A cut that would have stolen away the girl on the beach. A cut that would have killed his heart and destroyed the dream bond burning in his soul.

He remembered destroying the *Krackeni* tutor's mind, with a thought. He remembered reaching up, unthinking, grabbing that slender neck, and crushing it with his bare hands.

He remembered feeling nothing afterward. No remorse. Nothing but the relief of a man who had survived attempted murder.

Perrin tore himself away, but sank into another memory that was almost worse.

The past bloomed like fire inside his head, pain like fire—hooks buried in his body, restraining him, dragging him to a slab of natural stone on the seafloor. He felt the stone beneath his brow and hands holding him down. He heard his father singing, and, when he screamed, no one tried to help him.

Then, the blade. Digging into his head around the *kra'a*. White fire exploded in his vision, beyond agony. His soul was being torn in half. His soul was being destroyed. Every dig of the blade, severing him.

Perrin knew he was going to die. At the last moment, he reached out—clinging to the dream, the reason he was being destroyed: the girl with the red hair.

And the memory faded.

Faded, leaving nothing in its place but pain.

Perrin drifted in darkness. Aching. Heartsore. Alone.

And then, he was not alone. Jenny's presence surrounded him, the *kra'a* bound around them both. Both of them strong and warm.

You were exiled because of me, Jenny whispered, and the sadness in her voice forced him to find his strength again. *You killed to save . . . us.*

I killed. So did the kra'a.

Righteous blow, said the *kra'a. For not listening to the voice, and the dream. For presuming to know the heart of the Kraken.*

Perrin hesitated, having never heard the *kra'a* speak of that death. There had been no time to discuss what happened. The judgment against him had been almost instantaneous following the murder.

He had never considered, not in eight years, that the *kra'a* had cared.

But that was anger he heard in its dry voice.

I was desperate, he told Jenny. *She was so close to taking you from me. One moment more, and she would have broken us. I could not let that happen. I would not let them. I would have preferred death. I loved you.*

Perrin, she said, but her presence stuttered, like a flame going out—

—and cold ripped through him, tearing him from Jenny—

—into the sea.

He had been standing, earlier, but now he was below the surface, breathing hard through his gills. Legs, bound together with scales that shimmered in the half-light. His heart thundered. For a moment he did not know if this was memory or reality, but he sensed movement on his left and saw a dolphin drifting on its side in the water, bleeding heavily from a gash in its stomach.

He did not see Jenny.

Perrin reached Rik in moments and yanked several small spears from his side. The shape-shifter grunted, but his golden eyes were dull. The paralytic had been used.

He cast around a wild look and saw the fishing vessel. No sign of Eddie and Sajeev, though there were other bodies drifting in the water. Perrin swam hard to them, heart in his throat.

But it was *Krackeni* he found. Dead. Charred, as though they had burned to death.

"Jenny!" Perrin roared, but no one answered. He dove

deep, searching, but saw no sign of her in the water. So he hunted for her inside himself, pursuing the presence that he had grown so accustomed to feeling—that warmth, that flutter of another soul pressing on the edges of his mind. He felt the bond between them, roped around his heart, and tugged hard.

Jenny did not respond, but a dry voice whispered, *Hurry.*

Keep her safe, he told the *kra'a,* sensing that it was still close. South, perhaps. Yes, south.

Perrin almost left. But he saw Rik still drifting, now upside down, unable to right himself to breathe.

Gritting his teeth, Perrin grabbed the shape-shifter by the tail and pulled him to the fishing vessel. He had to regain his human legs in order to haul him on board, and was not as gentle as he could have been when he pushed the dolphin across the deck. Rik would live, but it might be hours before he could move again.

Eddie sprawled nearby, and so did Sajeev. Perrin checked their pulses. Thready, but alive. Also paralyzed. The young man's clothes had partially burned off his body, and beneath him was a large ring of ash that had been part of the deck.

He noticed something else, then.

Another boat was drifting less than one hundred yards away. It had cut its engines early, he thought. Sidling in, quiet as the waves. He had been too distracted to notice.

The vessel was small, but narrow—shaped like a dagger in the water. Men stood on board, dressed in black. Armed with guns. A very familiar dog sat between their legs. It jumped up and started barking when it saw Perrin.

A woman stood with them. Tall, lithe, with short red hair and a black patch over her right eye. Even from this distance, he could tell that her good eye was the color of gold, and shimmering with a light that trailed down her strong hard face.

She aimed a handgun at him.

And fired.

CHAPTER NINETEEN

JENNY was paralyzed. And if she hadn't miraculously developed the ability to breathe—badly—underwater, she would have been very dead.

As it was, by the time she was ripped from Perrin's mind, she was already being dragged beneath the sea, caught in a net that cut into her skin and crunched her into a ball.

Each breath felt as though it might be her last. Whatever changes had been made to her physiology, she was still human. Her chest ached, there didn't seem to be enough air in her lungs to feel comfortable—not that she was complaining—and her nostrils and throat stung. So did her eyes, but the paralytic prevented her from closing them. Her pulse rate should have dropped, given the water depth and pressure, but instead it felt like drums were pounding beneath her ribs. Unfortunately, she was caught in a net under the sea, being towed by three mermaids—and there wasn't much she could do to tell herself to calm the hell down.

If Jenny hadn't already been an experienced free diver, the physiological and psychological effects of the water pressure alone would have made the experience unbearable. She had learned from the best, though—an old Japanese woman who had trained to be an *Ama* in the forties, back when the women wore only loincloths on their free dives.

At eighty years old, Chiyoko had still been able to dive

one hundred feet on one breath—and linger there, looking for pearl oysters, seaweed, lobsters, and whatever else caught her fancy. Two weeks after moving in with her teacher, Chiyoko had forbidden Jenny to eat anything she didn't catch on the seafloor. Fortunately, the seafloor, for a beginner, was at a considerably shallower depth.

Jenny had ulterior motives for asking Chiyoko to train her. The old woman had seen a merman once, back in her twenties.

She described him as long and lean, with dark hair tied at the nape of his neck. His scales had shimmered blue in the underlight, the same color as his eyes; and he had been alien and handsome, intrigued—so the old woman had claimed, with a smirk—by her nudity.

"Intrigued" being a euphemism for hot, wild, ocean sex. Which Chiyoko had described, later, in enthusiastic detail.

Chiyoko was rumored to have a daughter with blue eyes, and an uncanny ability to free dive—but she'd had a family of her own and lived in Canada. Jenny had never gotten around to making the trip to introduce herself.

She would do that if she got out of this. Back to Perrin.

Jenny could feel him inside her mind, his presence fluttering cold and frantic on the other side of the wall. Alive. When she tried to reach him, though, he slipped away, elusive. Not on purpose. It was though something prevented her from touching him.

That scared Jenny. She might never have had anyone living in her mind before, but now that he was there, part of her, she could not imagine existing any other way.

We have to escape, she told the *kra'a*. *Is there anything you can do?*

You are paralyzed, it whispered. *Wait.*

Right. Wait. Genius plan.

So Jenny focused on breathing. She pretended she was not in the sea, and that the *Krackeni* who had captured her did not occasionally snarl, and beat the sides of the net with vicious strikes of their spears. She felt the blows and endured them.

The women were spindly and pale, their arms a little too long, their joints a little too sharp. Their breasts were small and tight, the rest of their bodies all muscle, with flowing silver hair and enormous eyes that seemed polished from ice. Scales covered their forearms, and their hands, each finger tipped with long black claws. Shells dangled from their wrists, and around their waists. Their tails were long, shining with silver scales that caught the dim light from the sky above the sea, and glowed.

Alien. Beautiful. Terrifying. Moving with a predatory grace that hurt to watch. Not that Jenny was capable of looking away.

They resembled Perrin's cousin, but while Pelena might have been able to pass as human on land, these *Krackeni* were too different, in too many subtle ways, to look anything but wrong if one saw them walking down a street.

Assuming they could even shift shape. There was so much Jenny didn't understand. She had been naïve to imagine that it would be simple. Life was never simple.

The mermaids slowed. Jenny could not move, but inside she braced herself, searching the waters ahead for any sign of what was coming.

Such as a great white shark.

Jenny stared, heart thudding in her throat as the shark swam close. It was huge, and the mermaids glanced at each other. One of them made a sharp clicking sound, then reached back, jabbed her hand through the net, and raked her claws down Jenny's arm and leg. Hurt like hell.

And there was a lot of blood.

The mermaids smiled, baring rows of sharp teeth, and pushed Jenny's netted body toward the oncoming shark.

It was well over twenty feet long, old and battered. How old, she couldn't say, but great whites had been known to live up to one hundred years. She didn't think this one was that ancient; he was scarred from so many dolphin attacks, his hide looked like a scratching post for some underwater cat.

For the first time, Jenny was glad to have been given the paralytic. Sharks could sense electromagnetic fields generated by movement. Remaining still wouldn't save her—even her heartbeat emitted a faint electrical pulse—but it was something. Great whites were naturally curious, highly intelligent, and surprisingly social. Ambush hunters. Stalking prey like serial killers.

It would probably come from below, though hunting techniques varied by prey. She was in a ball. Just a ball of flesh in a net.

Facts. More facts, she told herself, trying not to succumb to terror. And then the shark passed so close it bumped her, and she looked into its cold black eye, and thought, *Oh, my God.*

The parasite twitched. Jenny felt a pulse of energy, a throb that traveled from the base of her skull into her eyes. Her vision shifted, everything around her turning a deeper blue. A tingle rode over her skin.

The great white made another pass, skimming beneath her. Jenny couldn't see it, but it bumped her again—

—and she sensed its presence in her mind, like a shadow.

She couldn't explain it. Just that it was there, suddenly, and the *kra'a* whispered, *We are born from the Kraken, and there is nothing we cannot touch in the sea.*

The calm confidence in that voice steadied Jenny enough that she allowed herself to taste the shark's mind. She sensed hunger and curiosity, and a peripheral awareness of the mermaids—who were best avoided.

The shark was also aware of the *kra'a.*

Go, whispered Jenny, touching its mind. She almost told it to attack the mermaids, but she had no doubt they would wound the shark, or kill it, and the creature didn't deserve that.

Go, she said again. *Get out of here.*

The shark assented, though not before making one more pass. Still curious. It had not felt the energy of a *kra'a* in a long time.

Jenny sensed a flurry of movement beneath her—and found her net was suddenly yanked backward with incredible force. She bounced inside it, and glimpsed a broad chest, and long strong arms. For a moment, she thought it was Perrin—and then the net shifted again, and she saw Les looking back at her, broken nose and all. His body was a mess of wounds, and his broken hand had been bound close to his body.

He looked pissed and stared past her at the shark, which was rumbling through her mind with a hint of proprietary concern. Great whites sometimes lived in clans, like wolf packs, she remembered. And this one considered a *kra'a* to be part of every clan, with special protections.

No, she told it. *You'll be hurt.*

The great white swam lazily in a wide circle around Les and her. Les made a sharp, piercing sound, and waved angrily at one of the mermaids. She bared her teeth at him and did not approach.

Les dragged the net away again, and finally the great white turned and swam from them. Jenny watched it go with some regret—and, despite her circumstances, a sharp thrill. Her mind suddenly felt so . . . large. Everything around her, burning with light.

And deeper, deeper, another fire.

In the earth, a terrible, sleeping fire.

A fire with a golden eye opening to stare at her.

Claws moved, and the earth buckled. Jenny saw it, felt it, all that lava oozing free just beneath the crust, covering those claws with delicious warmth.

Another claw moved, and this time broke the seafloor. This crack traveled through her like a lightning bolt slamming into her soul.

No, Jenny said, reaching instinctively for the mind behind that staring golden eye. *No, don't.*

The darkness is immense, and we are alone, rumbled the beast, its voice rolling over her until Jenny felt as though she hardly knew herself. *We are alone.*

No, Jenny said, again, but it was so hard to speak, to re-member who she was. *We're here.*

Dreams, said the *kra'a. Feed it dreams.*

But she still didn't know *how.* All she could think to do was sing inside her mind. Her favorite song, the song she had sung to Perrin when he was a boy. She was too upset to remember the words, but the melody was true.

The Kraken stopped moving. Listening.

But it did not sleep. She knew that, deep inside, like knowing her own heartbeat. The Kraken was there, waiting . . . waiting for something more than a temporary respite.

You must go to it, said the *kra'a. You must go now, so that it knows you, and the bond is made.*

Jenny tensed. *What bond?*

But the Kraken stirred again, and though Jenny could not see it, except in her mind—and though what parts she saw were only glimpses of the whole—she felt the immensity of the beast as though she stood at a great height with the world beneath her, with the Kraken as that world.

And Jenny supposed, too, all of that was true. She was floating, flying, at the top of the sky of another world, on the edge between dark and light.

Les appeared, staring at her bleeding arm and leg. Her cheek ached when she saw his dark, furious gaze. He tore the net away, struggling with using only one hand.

The mermaids swam close, making sharp cries that rolled over Jenny's skin. Inside her head, she heard words.

. . . *easier to let her die that way. . .*

. . . *the* kra'a *would have come free. . .*

. . . *now you will need to dig it out. . .*

Les stabbed something sharp against her throat. Fear lanced through her, but almost immediately her fingers twitched, and she could move her lips. He pricked her again, in her stomach, then in each leg. Her mobility returned, leaving her to twitch uncontrollably. The mermaids swam circles around them, watching him with their teeth bared. Fast, sleek, turning on a dime to streak above and below in movements that skimmed her hair and feet. Close enough to let her know without a doubt that if they chose to, they could kill her.

Jenny wondered why they hadn't instead of using a shark to do their dirty work.

Because killing the host of a kra'a *is considered worse than murder,* Perrin's voice said suddenly in her mind. *It is like slapping the hand of a god. Unless,* he added, *you're me.*

At the first sound of his voice, Jenny flinched, kicking out like a crazy little puppet. Les gave her hard look, and she hoped he mistook her wild grin as a grimace. The ocean's surface shone like a white mirror overhead, reminding her of the wall inside her head, which flared with its own white light as Perrin's presence settled hard and strong on the other side. No longer elusive. When she cracked the wall, he was right there, waiting for her.

You, she whispered, shivering with relief and terrible joy. *I wondered when you would catch up to my mind.*

Warmth flared, like a smile, and she sensed an equal amount of relief.

Show me what's happened.

Jenny showed him, conscious of Les frowning at her. She looked at him once, then dropped her gaze, afraid of the wildness she saw in him. Afraid, too, that he would see more in her than he should.

The Kraken is waking, she told him.

I'm coming, Perrin said. *I'm close.*

Les pulled her to the surface. Jenny broke through into the light, and her first deep breath made her vomit water. Her lungs hurt like tiny knives were cutting them from the inside out.

"Jenny," he said, holding her close with his good arm. She didn't fight him. Her limbs weren't functioning well enough yet to tread water. Her head lolled, despite her best efforts, and she couldn't stop him when he reached into her hair and touched the *kra'a*.

His breath hitched. "It's true."

Jenny coughed. "Get off me."

"How?" he breathed, ignoring her, his eyes haunted. "How did you do it?"

"I didn't *do* anything. I was in the water. It attached itself."

"I don't believe you. It doesn't make sense." He squeezed her shoulder, his hand too close to her neck for comfort. "Why you?"

Jenny stared at him, ignoring his question, searching his bruised, shadowed eyes for something of the man she'd known. Goofy, charming. Treasure hunter. Man whom all the girls loved.

She stared too long. Les broke a little, and looked away.

"Hey," she said.

"Don't look at me like that," he whispered. "Don't."

She kept staring, a strange calm stealing over her, taking away her anger and most of her hurt. It was so surreal, floating in the sea with him, like this. So much had changed. More than she would have wanted to imagine.

"I thought you were my friend," she said.

"I was," he said. "I am."

"My face hurts."

His jaw tightened. "I didn't put those marks on your arms."

Jenny almost laughed, and gave him a bitter, grim smile. "I can tell you're so sorry."

"You can't trust him."

It's different, she wanted to say, and she believed that. Some might call her a fool, but Perrin had been caught in a dream. He had not lashed out in anger. He had not used his fist to shut her up.

"Why *were* you exiled from your people?" she asked him, already knowing the answer, but wanting to needle him. "Maybe you punched another woman in the face?"

"Stop."

"Poor baby," she whispered. "Did you always know you were going to betray us?"

His hand slipped away from her shoulder. "No, I was happy with you and Maurice. I was more myself with the two of you than I'd been in a long time."

"Then why?"

His face twisted with hunger and distaste. "I need the *kra'a*. I let that . . . cult . . . think what they wanted about me, that I could control the *kra'a*, that I had learned things on land that confirmed their worst beliefs about humans. I promised anything, everything, to get me close to Pelena."

You're sick. All this time I never imagined. How many midnight swims did you take, how did you arrange so much without my knowing?

"You want power," Jenny said.

Les shook his head, something terrible moving through his eyes as he reached for her again. Jenny tried to swim away, but he caught her easily and dug his fingers into her hair against the *kra'a*.

"I just want to live," he whispered. "You don't know what it's like for my kind to live on land. We're sensitive to chemicals, disease. The common flu could kill us. I've gotten nosebleeds from just breathing the scent of bleach. I might have more tolerance to some things because my grandmother was human, but I'm not immune."

"Les," she said.

"I'm dying," he told her.

Jenny tried to process those words. "No."

"I have brain cancer." His voice dropped so low she could barely hear him. "Cancer in my colon. In my stomach. Probably other places I don't want to think about, given that it's started getting hard to piss. It's all in the beginning stages."

Jenny stared, wondering if Perrin was ill, too. "Why didn't you tell someone?"

He shook his head. "You don't understand."

"I understand how selfish you are. You think the *kra'a* will heal you. So you kill someone for it when all you had to do was ask for help. *A Priori* could have given you the very best medical care."

"And tell them what I am? Even *you* don't trust your family." Les rubbed his face, looking haggard and weary. "I won't be their guinea pig. Not for them, or the Consortium. The *kra'a* is the only way I won't die. It keeps its hosts healthy. Though it looks as though it did . . . more for you."

"Of course," she said, with calculating coldness. "It didn't want *you*, after all. Did you think you would force it?"

Anger crept into his eyes. "You don't know anything."

"I know what it does," she told him, deliberately filling her voice with contempt. "*I* know how important it is. Even if it did bond and heal you, what were you going to do? Return the damn thing? Put the Kraken back to sleep?"

"Shut up," he said.

"Shut up or you'll hit me," she replied with a sneer. "Poor Les. Poor little Les, who's dying like every other fucking person on this planet. But instead of dealing with it, you decide to take out everyone with you. Jesus, you *are* a bastard. What were you *thinking*, Les?"

He grabbed her throat, squeezing. His face was stricken, but pale, his eyes lost in anger and fear, and remorse. "I was thinking I want to live."

Jenny snarled at him, no longer pretending to be furious. Les planted his mouth over hers—kissed her so hard their teeth scraped. He tasted wet and sloppy, and when she tried to wrench her head away, he held her in place, forcing his tongue into her mouth. Jenny bit down.

Les jerked back, swearing. Blood dribbled from his mouth. Jenny tasted it and spat. His eyes glittered, with fury or hurt. She still wasn't certain which when he turned away, breathing hard, staring at the sea.

"You think you understand the world," whispered Les. "You and your crazy family. But it's so much bigger than you realize, and there's so much *wrong* with it, too. Don't you ever think about what it would be like to just . . . start over?"

"Start over with your own life," she told him, hating her

voice for trembling. "Don't make that choice for everyone else."

Les caught her hand, squeezing too hard. "I know what the Consortium did to you. I know how they view the world. I know their methods. What they've done is beyond forgiveness. But they *are* right about one thing. There is something coming, Jenny. If it's not the Kraken, it will be something else that ends the world we know. It's only a matter of time."

Jenny wrenched her hand away, but he made it clear that it was only because he let her. Her wrist ached, and so did her fingers.

"Coward," she whispered, heart breaking for all those memories that would be forever tainted. "You and the Consortium. All of you, cowards. You get all your prophecies and precogs, and glimpses of a bad future, and you want to help it along, or hurt people because you think it'll put you in a better position to survive. You think the world has to change? Fine, grow a pair and change it. You want to survive what you *think* is coming? Or just survive to the end of the month?" Jenny gave him a look of pure disdain. "You're not going to survive *shit* by turning on your friends. Go to hell, Les. Go to fucking hell."

Les had been silent, pale, his eyes dead as he listened to her. She couldn't imagine his thoughts, and didn't want to. Jenny treaded water in front of him, feeling the *kra'a* burn against her skull while Perrin burned on the other side of his wall, that wall that she had cracked open the moment Les had brought her to the surface. Perrin had heard, seen, everything—assuming she understood how all this worked.

And he was close now. She had stalled almost long enough.

"I'm sorry you feel that way," Les finally said, a little too quiet. "Because there's something between us." He grabbed her hair, forcing her to look at him. "A bond. A. Very. Real. Bond." He spat out the words with a clenched jaw.

"Not between us," she told him, through her own gritted teeth.

"It happens sometimes," he went on. "But it's rare. Special. Something every *Krackeni* desires, to find that one soul—"

"Stop."

"—that is yours alone, in all the world." Les leaned in, staring into her eyes. "There doesn't have to be love, Jenny, but it makes it easier."

She shivered. "I'm not yours. There's no bond."

"I feel it!" he hissed. "I felt the echo of it the first time I met you, but I thought it was just my imagination. Just before everything went to hell, though, it . . . flared. I could see it in you. And if you're not bonded to me—"

"It's Perrin," she told him, unable to bear listening to another word of what he was saying. "Perrin is mine. I'm his. That's *our* bond you felt."

Les stared. "No."

Tears bit her eyes. "You want to know what I was searching for all these years? What drove me? It was *him*. Always him. I found him when I was a child, and that was it. I've known Perrin all my life and I love him. I love him, Les, more than anything."

He shoved her away, and the look in his eyes was stunned, brokenhearted. "Not him. Anyone but him, Jenny."

Because he has always had what you wanted, she thought. *Oh, God. Les.*

"I always made it clear I felt nothing for you, except friendship," she whispered.

Les dragged in a deep breath, and reached out again to grab her arm. His fingers squeezed too tightly, but she didn't make a sound.

"I suppose you think . . . Perrin . . . can give you something I can't," he said, hoarse. "You just don't know him, Jenny. Or maybe you do. Maybe you like a little pain."

Those tears rolled down her cheeks, but not because he was hurting her body. Just her heart. Les was gone. Her friend was dead.

"I'll miss you," she whispered.

Les frowned. "What?"

Jenny head-butted him. He was not expecting it, and she had good aim. His broken nose crunched. She tried to dart away, but he grabbed her, swearing ugly words as fresh blood streamed down his face.

Jenny was certain he would hit her. The rage in his eyes was terrifying. But just as quickly it turned into disbelief, a terrible hurt that reminded her too much of the Les she had known, the man she had believed him to be. Good, vulnerable, cocky Les. Les, who had been her friend.

Les, who spun her around. His good hand disappeared— and then reappeared, holding a knife. He was so fast, Jenny didn't have time to fight before he dug the blade into the meat of her neck, so hard he pushed her underwater. Jenny screamed, the sea flooding her mouth, choking her. Les pulled her deep under the surface. Jenny glimpsed the mermaids watching, teeth bared in excitement.

The *kra'a* screamed with her. Power pulsed, like a shotgun being pumped. Jenny slammed her elbow into Les's gut. Again and again, trying to twist away. Les stopped trying to pry out the *kra'a* just long enough to punch her side, and then her ribs, making her double over. The knife flashed back to her skull, digging in harder.

Enough, whispered the *kra'a.*

A pulse of blue light roared over Jenny's body, slamming from her in a shock wave that sent Les spinning into the mermaids with crushing force. Blood streamed from their noses as they drifted against each other, stunned and twitching.

Jenny went blind, clawing at her throat. She tried kicking, but was too weak to reach the surface.

Perrin, she called out, widening the crack in the wall between them. A rush of images surrounded her, along with the sensation of extended arms, neck and shoulders hunched, her large, muscular body undulating as her hips were forced up, tail driving down in a propulsive, distance-eating beat—

I'm coming, he said, and she snapped back into her own body.

Something very large bumped her legs, and her mind reached out instinctively. She wanted Perrin, but it was the great white shark that filled her thoughts: cool, restrained, and filled with strange purpose.

No time, whispered the *kra'a,* and Jenny's hand moved of its own accord, reaching out. When the shark made another pass beneath her, her fingers closed around its fin, and she was pulled into swift, graceful flight.

Stop, Jenny told the *kra'a,* afraid. *Stop controlling me.*

We know your heart. You would do this anyway.

Doesn't matter. This is my body.

Our body. One flesh. One spirit. Three minds.

Three minds? asked Jenny.

Me. You. It, Perrin said, breaking in. *Where are you taking her?*

Below, whispered the *kra'a. To the Kraken.*

IT MIGHT HAVE BEEN AROUND CHRISTMAS, OR MAYBE the New Year, but while some folks were eating turkey and fighting with family over the remote control, Jenny had climbed into a submersible, alone, to dive almost three miles below the ocean's surface.

Lost, sinking, drifting. Listening to the walls groan as the ocean tried to crush her little metal bubble. VHF radio turned off. No lights except the pinprick glow of dials.

Peaceful. Safe. No one around who could hurt her. Nature might take her life, but that was okay. Wouldn't be personal. Not malicious, or vindictive, or cruel. In nature, life and death happened. It just happened, and you couldn't always stop it.

Sometimes, you didn't want to stop it.

Jenny knew there was magic in the sea. It was not the only reason she loved the sea, but it added one more element of wonder to an unseen world that was already awe-inspiring. The sea was life. More life than could be dreamed.

But dreams, apparently, were the cornerstone of all that life.

And she was the chosen dreamer.

SHARKS COULD DIVE TO A DEPTH OF SIX THOUSAND FEET. A little over a mile. For humans without protection from pressure and cold, one thousand feet was the limit. And even that was too much.

She didn't know how deep they had gone, but it was already difficult enough to breathe. Each rush of salt water into her body made her feel as though she was on the edge of drowning.

The cold was terrible. The pressure, crushing.

You are going to kill me, Jenny told the *kra'a. I'm only human, no matter what changes you've made.*

Wait, it whispered. *Wait.*

Perrin's warmth filled her mind. *Bring her back.*

Wait, whispered the *kra'a,* again.

And the shark continued its descent.

Jenny tried opening her eyes, but the pressure was too much. She journeyed, blind, helpless to do anything but grip the fin in her hand, suffering the weight of the sea and what was facing her below, the immensity of which continued to grow inside her mind.

The Kraken opened its golden eye.

You, whispered a low voice. *You, of the song.*

Each word fell into her. Each word a blow. Each word drowning her identity. Jenny struggled with all her strength to remember herself. For a moment, she didn't even recall her name.

Jenny, said a low voice. *You are Jenny.*

She clung to that name, and the voice, which sank into her as warm and strong as the rumble of the Kraken inside her head. Anchoring her. Rooting her so that she did not rip away. A masculine presence, filling her mind, holding the hand of her spirit. It was the most freeing, transcendent, sensation she had ever experienced—joined and strengthened, and made one—as though her soul was capable of miracles. Bigger than the heart of the beast waking beneath her in the darkness, staring at her with its golden eye.

Strong hands slid around her waist.

Who? she asked.

Perrin, he said. *I am Perrin.*

Jenny remembered, in flashes. A beach. A boy. Silver light and silver scales, and the silver waves of the sea. She remembered a man with pale eyes, and the hands that held her now, she remembered, too. She reached, fumbling, her movements slow and painful and cold, and touched a muscular arm that wrapped around her, drawing her close and tight against a hard chest and a broad tail that undulated against her legs.

The shark continued to pull Jenny down, but she hardly noticed. Her fingers were tight as iron clamps around its fin, and that was the only part of her physical self that still felt strong. Her body had moved beyond discomfort, past pain and cold. Dying, a little more with each passing second.

But inside, she was safe and warm, and didn't care.

I care, whispered Perrin, holding her even closer, warming her skin. *I care, Jenny.*

We're being watched, she thought at him, numb. *I feel eyes.*

Ignore them.

She ignored the gathering *Krackeni,* because the Kraken chose that moment to lift its head from where it was buried beneath thousands of years of rock and sediment. Sluggish. Still partially asleep. But slipping into a deeper awareness.

She felt it all her in her mind, part of her observing from within the Kraken itself, and another part seemingly gifted with magic eyes that were able to see the seafloor buckle and heave upward. The shock wave that rippled from that movement spun the shark sideways. Jenny lost her grip on its fin and rolled with Perrin, who held her tight against him.

The Kraken moved again. Claws. Tail.

Speak to it, said Perrin urgently. *We're close enough now.*

Speak, whispered the *kra'a. Dream.*

I don't know how, she told them, her mind flirting with a very pressing need to fall unconscious. All that was left of her was her mind, it seemed. She could not feel her body anymore.

Then feel mine, Perrin told her, and his soul gathered her beneath his skin.

She could see again, suddenly—the outlines of massive rocks, where she glimpsed movement: flowing silver hair and narrow muscular bodies that darted amongst fish, fleeing into shadows; and huge, pale eyes that stared at her in passing.

She saw herself, in Perrin's arms. Small and still, pale as a corpse. Bubbles trickled from her nostrils, but so few she was surprised her brain had enough oxygen to keep functioning. Maybe it wasn't. Maybe she was hallucinating all of this. Seeing herself was frightening.

Fear, rumbled the Kraken. *Fear tastes like prey.*

No, Jenny said instantly, forgetting for one brief second that she was speaking to a sea monster. *Fear of death is a fear of losing what you love, and not experiencing more. Fear, at the loss of never knowing something else, or having the chance to be something else.*

The Kraken stirred. *I have slept too long. I feel the weight of time.*

No, Perrin soothed, mentally reaching over Jenny's shoulder. *No time has passed since you entered your slumber. You still have many lives yet to experience.*

Many lives. Jenny suddenly understood.

The Kraken had to *want* to sleep. Its dreams had to be better than life. Its dreams had to make it forget itself. And live, as something else.

So many dreams, Jenny told it. *Good dreams.*

Dreams are not the same as life, said the Kraken, breaking more earth. The shock wave spun them into a pile of rocks. Searing pain lanced down Perrin's side, and Jenny felt it.

Then let us live for you, she said, fighting not to be buried in that pain. *We can live what you never will.*

And Jenny reached for the first thing that came to mind, and pushed it at the Kraken.

It was a simple memory. Perrin, kneeling in front of her, speaking of knights and shining armor—and the rush of warmth that had filled her as she watched him: the overwhelming, heart-in-her-throat ache of safety and love, chasing away a lifetime of loneliness. Emotions that bloomed again, inside her. Raw and shining.

Jenny pushed those memories upon the Kraken with a deep, wild satisfaction—and all the force two souls could muster. Because Perrin was behind her, feeding her his strength and compounding it with a rush of love so powerful she would have choked had she still been in her body.

And, for one moment following that, Perrin lay exposed to her—his whole life, his darkest thoughts—everything spread out before the eyes of her heart.

And she looked with her heart. Even as she felt him looking at her.

Jenny heard a deep rumbling sigh inside her head—the thunder of a mental voice so powerful it should have killed her.

She sent the Kraken another memory, of Perrin holding her after they had made love, before she started crying and remembering her baby. She sent the Kraken her memory of seeing Perrin shape-shift after leaving *The Calypso Star*—the magic of it, the awe she had felt–

—and she sent it, too, the memory of her joy after she had learned that she was pregnant—

—the secret hope that she might have another child—

—the secret desire to live a long life with the man inside her mind—

—the secret and terrible joy—

—of being loved—

—loved so deeply—

—and having her—

—deepest dream—

—come true—

Every good thing in her heart and memories, she fed to the Kraken. Relentless in her outpouring, flooding the beast, until she heard another thunderous sigh that was nonetheless soft and full of pleasure.

Dream, said the Kraken. *Dream your life. That is a life I wish to dream.*

Sleep, then, Jenny told it gently, as Perrin said the same words, even softer. *Sleep, and we will give you dreams to live on.*

Sleep to live, rumbled the Kraken, and closed its golden eye. *For a little while longer.*

Sleep, Jenny whispered, and hummed to it the old song from the beach, feeling a strange tenderness for the immense beast settling deeper into the seafloor. *Sleep.*

Dream, murmured the Kraken, and its presence faded from her mind. Jenny hung there, waiting for more, for something to go wrong. A rush of admiration and love rolled over her mind.

You did it, Perrin said. *You did it.*

He settles into sleep, said the *kra'a*. *We will dream him a life no other Kraken has ever known.*

Good, Jenny told them, but couldn't even think another word. The rush was gone. She felt her real body, suddenly, tugging her back. She tried to hold on to Perrin, but slipped away—slamming into human flesh that felt like a corpse. Her thoughts slowed. She could not move. Or breathe.

Perrin swam with her toward the surface. Her chest hurt. Everything was numb. Heart, mostly not beating. Decompression sickness was a serious danger. If she survived the ascent, it would be a miracle.

Jenny forgot that anyone wanted them dead.

And by the time it mattered, she mostly was.

CHAPTER TWENTY

Three times Jenny's heart almost stopped beating. Three times he almost died with her. Perrin swam for the surface, knowing the ascent might kill her as much as anything but seeing no alternative.

You changed her enough to breathe underwater, he said to the *kra'a,* wishing it were a person so he could throttle it. *Make another miracle. Keep her alive.*

But the *kra'a* was silent. All it did was tear down the wall between his mind and Jenny's. Her spirit flowed over him, but it was quiet, and he fed it with all his strength.

Live, he begged her, desperate. *Live.*

Perrin was so deep in Jenny's mind, he didn't realize they were surrounded until a blunt object hit him hard against the back of his head. He twisted in the water, still wrapped around Jenny's body and spirit, and found himself facing a pod of *Krackeni* hunters, swimming silently around him in a large circle. Sleek, strong, their pale gazes hard.

His father hovered in the water, watching him.

In his eight years on land, Perrin had spoken of his father only once—with Tom, on an early-winter morning after they left the homeless shelter to walk to a construction site that was rumored to need strong bodies.

Perrin had a strong body. Tom went along to keep him

company before heading out into the city for a day of pan-handling.

The subject came up because Tom happened to see a newspaper and remembered that his father, a "righteous dude," would have been eighty that day had he still been alive, and Tom, much as he missed him, was sort of glad he wasn't because the world had gotten ugly and dirty, and his only son was living on the streets instead of being the up-standing taxpayer all good folk were supposed to be.

Tom had asked Perrin about his father, and Perrin said, "We had an . . . uneasy relationship."

Now, it was just deadly.

Perrin studied his father's pale eyes. There was nothing there to find: no anger, no remorse.

There were many things he wanted to say to his father. Instead, he continued swimming toward the surface. If they wanted him dead, it wouldn't matter whether it was below or above.

Moments later, his father caught up. He said nothing. Simply swam with him, less than an arm's length away. Jenny was so still.

Perrin broke the surface, holding Jenny high out of the waves. He expected her to cough, vomit seawater—but she didn't react to the air.

She wasn't breathing.

You, Perrin snapped at the *kra'a,* and floated Jenny on her back, trying to hold them steady as the waves swelled. He pinched her nose shut, tried to tilt up her neck, and as the waves sent them spinning, he planted his mouth over hers and breathed for her.

Jenny, he called out to her. *Jenny.*

Jenny, breathe. Jenny, breathe.

Don't leave me. Don't. Please.

Please.

Each breath. Each breath he reached for her, inside. Each breath, begging, dying with her. He would die without her. He knew it. All his years surviving, and if he lost her, it wouldn't be a day before his heart gave out. Whatever bond they shared bound them too tightly for anything less.

He realized, then, that his father was helping hold her body. So carefully not looking at Perrin.

Jenny twitched. Her back arched, and her eyes flew open. Bloodshot, blood red, through and through. A tangle of broken veins covered her cheeks, and her lips were peeling and raw. Her bruises were wicked. She floundered in the water, coughing, vomiting, scrabbling against Perrin's chest and shoulders as her body rebelled. It was the most painful thing he had ever witnessed, but all he wanted to do was laugh with relief, and weep.

"Shhh," he whispered, tears burning his eyes—holding her as she trembled and tried to breathe. The sounds she made, forcing air into her lungs, were horrible. Blood appeared at the corner of her mouth. Her nose began to bleed, too.

Perrin held her as close as he dared and risked a look at his father. Turon floated near, his gaze unreadable. No others were with him, but Perrin could feel his kind amassed below, watching, waiting. No doubt wondering what it meant that a *kra'a* had chosen a human woman, who had then settled a waking Kraken. No *Krackeni,* Perrin was certain, would have been able to accomplish what she had done, in so little time, and with such ease.

I wasn't alone, she said in his mind. *You were with me. We did it together. It was the two of us and what we've shared that made the difference.*

Perrin kissed her brow, drowning in the pained warmth flooding him through their bond. He looked at his father again and rode on her love, letting it fill him until he felt transcendent, beyond all the old pain and bitterness. He could not be bitter, given the blessing in his arms. Not then, maybe not ever.

But there was still the possibility of battle.

"I won't let you hurt her," Perrin said. "Don't even think of it."

"Bold," whispered his father.

"No. When I first returned from exile, I would have let you take my life. I would have let you do as you must and not fought. But not anymore." Perrin looked his father dead in the eyes, letting eight years of exile rise in his gaze— eight years, being forged into a different man, a survivor, a fighter, uncompromising and cold. "*She* is my life now. And I *will* live for her. I will protect her from you—all of *them*— who remain so small in their hearts."

"Small in our hearts," echoed Turon, with a great deal of thoughtfulness. His gaze flicked down to Jenny. "I felt her quiet the Kraken. We all did, in different ways."

Perrin watched him warily. "The *kra'a* chose her. She might still die for it."

"She might," agreed his father. "There are many who were frightened by that display of power, who believe the *kra'a* should be taken from her."

Jenny coughed until she shuddered. "You people are good at that sort of thing."

Turon tilted his head. Perrin said, "The *kra'a* will defend her."

"And will it defend you, my son?" he replied, with deadly softness.

"Yes," Jenny rasped. "Go to hell."

Perrin kissed the top of her head, never looking away from his father. "Do it now if you're going to try. Finish it if you can. Otherwise, get away from us."

Turon frowned. "There was always something . . . wild . . . about you. I was not the only one who noticed. And when you killed Frilia . . ."

His father paused. Perrin sensed a strange vulnerability inside him but did not allow himself to hope. A good thing, because when Turon met his gaze again, anything vulnerable was gone, and in its place was a cold remoteness that was far more familiar than affection.

"Guardians have lost their minds in the past. It is the isolation, the pressure of dreamtime. The *kra'a,* and the presence of the Kraken, too much to bear. And with the power a *kra'a* gives a Guardian, there can be no . . . hesitation . . . if there is a possibility that all is not well within."

"I don't forgive you," Perrin said. "If you had listened to me—"

"I would do it again," replied Turon, though he did not sound entirely sure of himself. "What you did, both the murder and the dreams you fed the Kraken . . ."

Turon did not finish. Perrin whispered, "I would have told you then, as I'll tell you now . . . all I gave the Kraken were dreams of someone I loved. And that was something no one . . . no one had the right to try to take from me."

Jenny stilled against him. Perrin held her close, though there was nothing closer than the space they shared, side by side, in their minds.

Turon looked at Jenny again but spoke to Perrin. "Pelena had many visions while you were gone. She claimed that a human woman would bear the burden of the *kra'a,* and that we must not harm her when that happened. No one, of course, believed her."

His father drifted backward. "Take the girl and go. We will not remove the *kra'a.* Not unless she proves herself . . . too weak . . . to bear the burden. As for you . . ." Again, he hesitated, and Perrin wondered if he would ever find common waters with his father, or if this was it. Always an exile.

"You are bonded to the woman," said his father. "I look at you both and know it. I hear it in your voices. If I take your life, I will be taking hers." He looked at Jenny. "I should have killed you when I had the chance, all those years ago. It would have saved my son . . . so much."

"You're the one who's hurt him," Jenny replied.

Turon frowned. Perrin said, "I didn't kill Pelena."

"Perhaps not," replied his father, tearing his gaze from Jenny. "But she is dead."

He sank below the waves and was gone.

"I think your father likes me," Jenny croaked, before being wracked with coughs all over again. "Jesus, I hurt."

"Don't talk," Perrin murmured, trying not to shiver. Whether it was adrenaline or nerves, or just relief, his entire body trembled as he lay back in the water, holding Jenny against his chest.

She laid her hand over his heart, and inside his mind whispered, *Perrin?*

We're alive, he said tersely.

You thought you would die, she said. *You thought your father would kill you.*

Yes. Perrin just hadn't realized how afraid he was, until then. It wasn't death that scared him—just the possibility that his father would be the one to pass judgment and take his life. He had come close once before. Looked Perrin in the eye and condemned him to exile, which was the same as death.

But here Perrin was, still alive. Holding his dreams in his arms.

I'm afraid to breathe, he told Jenny. *Is this real?*

She didn't answer him. Unconscious. Perrin held her close, swimming carefully, slowly. No land. No sign of help. He was certain there must be other *Krackeni* watching, but he did not expect any of them to offer their help. His kind were slow to change and accept new things. Perrin doubted that he and Jenny would ever be welcome. Tolerated, perhaps, out of necessity—which meant that vigilance would always be required, just in case any of the *Krackeni* took it upon themselves to challenge the *kra'a*'s choice in Jenny. Not to mention there were other, practical concerns, that needed to be addressed.

Enough. One thing at a time.

Like getting Jenny to safety.

I found my answers, thought Perrin, focusing on the sea witch and her island. Filling his heart with need. He didn't trust the crone, but surrounding them was nothing but open sea, and Jenny needed help.

No island appeared, though. No magic swell of lush mountain and mist.

Nothing, except a golden streak of light in the ocean.

Perrin couldn't hide his relief when Rik drew near; but he said nothing, just nodded at the circling dolphin, who melted and shifted until a young human man took its place, treading water.

"Jenny," Rik said, studying her with genuine concern.

"She's alive. Is anyone following you?"

"I don't know. I was searching for you, then . . . here you were. As if you came out of nowhere."

Sea witch, thought Perrin, and hugged Jenny a little closer. Her mind was cool and dark, drifting close to dreams. Heartbeat steady. He pressed his lips against her brow, closed his eyes, and said, "Thank you for coming, Rik."

When Rik said nothing, Perrin opened his eyes and found the shape-shifter staring at him with a strange sort of resignation.

"You love her," said Rik quietly. "I wish I could say I hate you for it, but I can't. I wanted to. I wanted to punish you both. But I can't do it anymore."

Perrin looked away, at the far-off horizon that was empty and silver with the sea. Alive. He was alive, but just as easily he could have been dead, Jenny dead, the Kraken awake, the world already shifting into a new age.

Rik had lost his miracle.

"Razor's edge," Perrin said, to himself and Rik. "It's so easy to fall."

Rik closed his eyes, which still didn't hide his pain. "They say the *kra'a* is part of your soul. How did you cope after it was cut from you?"

"You know how I coped. The same way you did."

"One moment at a time," Rik murmured, disappearing briefly under the water. When he resurfaced, he rubbed his face and said, "I wanted to die after I lost Surinia, but I didn't have the guts to take my life. And then the Consortium captured me. They . . . did things to me, for a long time, and I realized that I wanted to live. But that felt wrong, too, like I was . . . betraying her somehow."

Perrin shook his head, holding Jenny closer. "Never."

"Never," Rik whispered. "I wish I could love again."

"I think—" he began, and then choked as the *kra'a* reached through his link with Jenny and yanked hard on his heart. Wild, wordless warning.

Moments later, someone stabbed Perrin in the lower back.

Bad aim saved him. The tip of the blade skittered off Perrin's hipbone, but the cut was still deep, shocking. He twisted, thrusting Jenny toward Rik, just as the blade slashed across the back of his tail. Perrin dove, gritting his teeth, his blood spreading through the water.

He was not surprised to find A'lesander.

He was surprised, however, to find desperate grief in his old friend's eyes, and a self-loathing so thick and heavy, Perrin could almost taste it.

A'lesander held an old relic of a blade, probably taken from a shipwreck. Long, curved, rusted almost to rotting— but still sharp.

The two *Krackeni* men stared at each other, swimming in slow circles, deeper, deeper, away from the light; and Perrin felt all his rage disappear, and all his bitterness, and inside his mind Jenny was warm and quiet, warm and with him, warm and in his soul.

You fool, he said to A'lesander, speaking in the old sea tongue, full of echoing clicks and vibrating whistles that translated into his mind, like telepathy. *You had her friend-ship, and you threw it away. You threw Pelena away. You threw a life away that was yours.*

A'lesander closed his eyes. *I know what I did.*

He attacked Perrin. It was not hard to take the knife. A'lesander only had one good hand, and a quick blow to his broken nose was all it took to disarm him. Perrin knew his old friend had not intended to win.

Perrin held the knife and stared at A'lesander. All around them drifted pale ghosts, other *Krackeni,* gathering to watch the end.

Do it, said A'lesander.

Do it. Cold blood. Perrin searched for the rage he should have felt, for all those crimes A'lesander had committed. He found his anger, that righteous charge, but it felt as tired as he did.

Perrin dropped the knife, watching it drift and spin out of sight into the darkness. *I know you are dying. I will not make it easier.*

A'lesander's face twisted with grief, and he looked up. Perrin followed his gaze and saw Jenny and Rik, far above them, floating along the surface. He tensed, afraid that A'lesander would charge them—but in the end, all he did was charge Perrin.

He never reached him. An immense flash of silver surged from the shadows, and a voice sang out. One note, terrible with power. A'lesander crumpled around himself, with such violence it was as though he was nothing but a puppet—strings cut. He did not move again, except to sink into the abyss. His eyes were open. Empty. Lifeless.

Perrin tore his gaze away and stared at his father.

No words. Nothing had ever been easy between them. His father gave Perrin a sharp nod and turned from him. Whispers rose from the watching *Krackeni.*

Justice . . . injustice . . . what will come . . . from human dreams . . .

Perrin gave his father one last look, then swam upward, toward the light, toward his dream.

SOON AFTER, A SHIP CAME. *THE CALYPSO STAR.*

In its wake, some distance away, was Sajeev's fishing vessel and a speedboat filled with those black-clad, hard-faced mercenaries. Perrin imagined he heard a helicopter in the distance.

Eddie stood aboard *The Calypso Star*, and with him was the red-haired shape-shifter who had fired a warning shot at Perrin. She had, after that initial bullet, introduced herself as Serena McGillis, a name Perrin recognized. Jenny's friend, who had tried to save her baby.

Sharing that, he thought, was one of the reasons he had been allowed to leave the old fishing vessel, alive. That and the fact that Eddie had vouched for him once he'd regained consciousness. It seemed those two knew each other. Enough to maintain a polite distance.

Serena and Eddie helped pull Jenny onto the boat. She had been slipping in and out of consciousness. The woman looked hard at her face, something dangerous moving through her single golden eye: pupil little more than a slit, caught between human and cat.

"Come with me," she said. Perrin carried Jenny into the boat, down the narrow stairs, into her cabin. The bed had been remade, and a slender man was sorting through medical equipment stacked on the small desk. He hardly looked at Perrin. Once he saw Jenny, his focus was only on her.

Perrin was pushed aside, crowded into a corner, ignoring his own wounds as he watched the man and Serena strip off Jenny's clothes with careful efficiency. An IV was placed in her arm. Hot packs stacked around her body. Heart and lungs listened to, questions asked. Jenny remained quiet the entire time though Perrin knew she was awake.

It feels like a dream, she said, as her eyelid was peeled back, and examined with a bright light that Perrin knew would have made her wince had she not been so unnaturally exhausted. *I'm not dying, am I?*

No, said the *kra'a,* before Perrin could give his reassurance. *We are healing you even now, though it will take time.*

We have time, Perrin told her, and found himself confronted with the profound truth of those words. *We have all the time in the world.*

The corner of Jenny's mouth cracked into a faint smile.

EPILOGUE

IN the end, the excuse everyone used was that someone needed to bring the dog to Maine.

The dog from the island. No ordinary dog, something Jenny had long suspected, though she'd kept those thoughts to herself—and Perrin—until Serena confirmed the truth some months later.

Her grandfather had a talent with animals. He could possess them, piggyback—take flight inside the head of an eagle, live blind as a mole, sleep warm in the body of a rattlesnake—or, in one case, take over the mind of a particular dog, on a particular island, to help his granddaughter—whom he'd never had much difficulty locating with his mind, no matter where she hid herself in the world.

That last bit of information was something even Jenny hadn't known.

It was spring when she and Perrin brought the dog to the old home in Maine. They stopped first at the graveyard. Jenny laid flowers at the headstone of her unnamed child, and Perrin sat for a time with his hand on the grave, eyes closed and his head bowed.

Jenny did not hear his thoughts. His warmth, though, flowed through the wall between them. His compassion. His startling love for the baby girl he would never meet. She took that warmth and love, and wrapped it around her grief, which still felt new even after so many years.

Ten minutes away from the old home, Jenny said, "I don't know if I can do this."

"Nothing is going to happen," Perrin said.

Nothing, whispered the *kra'a. We are with you.*

"I'm scared," she told them, gripping the car wheel until her knuckles turned white. Perrin shifted the dog in his lap, and reached out to cover her hand. He filled up his side of the car, and the wind from the rolled-down window whipped his silver hair over his shoulder.

They had been in the United States for almost two months. It was their first trip away from the Kraken nesting ground, where they had made a home on a little tropical island, inside an abandoned fisherman's home that they had renovated with their own two hands—and some help from Eddie and Rik, and Serena. Maurice had supervised.

One room. Rudimentary plumbing. Electricity generated from solar panels. *The Calypso Star,* moored several hundred feet off-shore. It was all they needed.

But then a letter had come. Delivered by e-mail.

Jenny,

Rest easy, sweetheart. We don't want you anymore. Don't worry about why we needed you in the first place. Our . . . sources . . . now say you're more valuable alive.

For the time being.

But you're still family. Remember that.

Give my regards to the merman.

Your uncle,
Richard

And Perrin, after reading that, had said, "It's time to go home, Jenny."

He was right, of course. But she stalled, anyway.

Paris first, where Perrin and Jenny visited Notre Dame and walked over bridges, and drank coffee at little cafes where old women gossiped with poodles in their laps. Then, to London, which they fled after only a day, when Perrin found the air hard to breathe, and his skin developed a rash. On to New York City, where Perrin took Jenny to the homeless shelter where he had lived, and showed her the sky rises he had helped build, and the streets he had walked while pretending to be a human man, alone in the human world.

From New York to Chicago, though Perrin lingered outside the Shedd Aquarium for thirty minutes before Jenny could get him to go inside. They did not stay long. The *kra'a* was disturbed by the creatures within their cages, and the dolphins wept inside Jenny's mind when they saw her, and Perrin.

Chicago to the Grand Canyon, then upward to Seattle—from there to Vancouver where Jenny introduced herself to Chiyoko's daughter, who was not entirely human, after all—and then another long drive across the Rockies through Montana, into Wyoming and Yellowstone National Park where Perrin saw his first wild bear, into South Dakota and the Badlands, and onward, and onward, everything new, everywhere they went, as though sunlight was rubbing a shine on the world.

Jenny wondered how she had lived her life before—blind, maybe. Blind, deaf, and dumb. She couldn't explain the change within herself, but she knew Perrin felt it, too, inside his own heart. Especially him. She had seen in his dreams what he'd suffered for those eight years on land. Some good moments, but never time or money to simply *be*, and to find those places off the beaten path, lost, exploring a world that few of his people would ever understand.

Dreams for the Kraken. Dreams they sent through the *kra'a* every night and morning, their combined strength allowing them to leave their new island home near the nesting ground while maintaining the link to the sleeping beast.

A risk. If anything happened to them . . .

It is worth the risk, the *kra'a* had said. *For dreams.*

And now, here they were. Home. Finally.

The old house was in better shape then Jenny remembered. It looked nothing like the sagging gray place of her nightmares. Never had, actually—but for so long that was how she had remembered it, that seeing the fresh white paint and green roof, and the gingerbread trim along the eaves—sent a strange shock through her. The house perched on the grassy hill, facing the sea, and the chimes hanging from the porch whistled and sang.

Her grandparents waited on the steps. Maurice was with them. Jenny sat in the car, staring.

"You love them," Perrin said quietly, opening his door and letting the dog out. "Don't blame them for the loss of your baby."

"It could happen again," she whispered, watching the dog run ahead to the house and straight to her grandfather. "When I come here, that's all I can think of. The Consortium might have given up on me for now, but that won't last. This family . . ."

Perrin dismantled the wall between their minds, and his warmth rolled through her, slow and easy, bringing with it a sense of complete and utter peace. Tears bit her eyes, and she closed them, savoring the miracle.

"There are many miracles," he told her, gently. "We'll be fine."

Jenny took a deep breath and nodded. "Okay. Okay, you're right."

Perrin kissed her cheek, his mouth lingering until she turned her head and brushed her lips over his. Sweet, gentle, making her ache to press close against him, hidden from the world. She missed their island, suddenly, with a sharpness that stole her breath away. "Jenny," Perrin said.

"I do love them," she told him. "I do."

NEAR SUNSET, PERRIN AND JENNY ESCAPED FROM THE big house on the hill and made their way down the twisty trail to the beach. It was windy and the temperature had dropped. Jenny felt fat in her big coat, but Perrin rarely felt the cold and wore nothing more than a silver cashmere sweater and jeans.

The sun was white behind a thin layer of clouds, and the water glittered as though scattered with diamonds and starlight. Jenny gripped Perrin's hand, and they walked slowly and carefully through the sand, over driftwood and stone, until they came to the spot.

"I'm sure this is it. I came here every day, every summer, for years." Jenny clutched his arm, pressing her cheek against him. When he said nothing, when he remained so still, she glanced at his face and found his jaw tight, his eyes hard and heavy as he stared at that patch of sand.

Slowly, with infinite care, Perrin knelt and drew Jenny down beside him. They sat together, side by side, holding each other's hands, staring at the sea, and the sky and water was silver and full of light, and it was the dream. Only this time, when Jenny turned to look at Perrin, she could see his face, his eyes, and when she wanted to kiss him, he met her halfway, hungry and hard, and hot.

Her heart was so full. The *kra'a* hummed inside their minds. And when Perrin unzipped her coat, and pushed up her sweater to expose her round stomach to the ocean air, she leaned back on her elbows and laughed.

"This is where you began," he told their baby. "Once upon a time."

"There was a girl who loved a boy from the sea," said Jenny, smiling. "And they found each other in dreams."